HINDS' FEET ON H

and

MOUNTAINS OF SPICES

The Lord God is my strength, and he will
make my feet like hinds' feet, and he will
make me to walk upon mine high places.
Hab 3:19

Make haste, my beloved, and be thou like
to a roe or to a young hart upon the
mountains of spices.
Song 8:14

CHRISTIAN CLASSICS FOR A NEW GENERATION

Two Timeless Books in One

Hinds' Feet
on
High Places

HANNAH HURNARD

KINGSWAY PUBLICATIONS
EASTBOURNE

Cover design: PinnacleCreative.co.uk
Front cover photo © Perception I Dreamstime.com

ISBN 978 1 84291 388 8

Published by
KINGSWAY COMMUNICATIONS LTD
26–28 Lottbridge Drove, Eastbourne, BN23 6NT, UK
books@kingsway.co.uk

Printed in Great Britain

FOREWORD TO THE ALLEGORY

ONE morning during the Daily Bible Reading on our Mission Compound in Palestine, our little Arab nurse read from Daily Light a quotation from the Song of Songs, 'The voice of my Beloved! behold, He cometh leaping upon the mountains, skipping upon the hills' (Song of Solomon 2:8). When asked what the verse meant, she looked up with a happy smile of understanding and said, 'It means there are no obstacles which our Saviour's love cannot overcome, and that to Him, mountains of difficulty are as easy as an asphalt road!'

From the garden at the back of the Mission house at the foot of Mount Gerizim we could often watch the gazelles bounding up the mountain-side, leaping from rock to rock with extraordinary grace and agility. Their motion was one of the most beautiful examples of exultant and apparently effortless ease in surmounting obstacles which I have ever seen.

How deeply we who love the Lord of Love and desire to follow Him long for the power to surmount all the difficulties and tests and conflicts in life in the same exultant and triumphant way. To learn the secret of 'victorious living' has been the heart's desire of those who love the Lord, in every generation. We feel we would 'give anything' if only we could, in actual experience, live on the 'High Places' of Love and Victory here on this earth and during this life; able always to react to evil, tribulation, sorrow, pain, and every wrong thing in such a way that they would be overcome and transformed into something to the praise and glory of God for ever. As Christians we know, in theory at least, that in the life of a Child of God there are no 'Second Causes', that even the most unjust and cruel things, as well as all seemingly pointless and undeserved sufferings, have been *permitted* by God as a glorious opportunity for us to RE-ACT to them in such a way that our Lord and Saviour is able to produce in us, little by little, His own lovely character.

The Song of Songs expresses the desire implanted in every human heart, to be re-united with God Himself, and to know perfect and unbroken union with Him. He has made us for Himself, and our hearts can never know rest and perfect satisfaction until they find it in Him. It is God's will that some of His children should learn this deep union with Himself through the perfect flowering of natural human love in marriage. For others it is equally His will that the same perfect union should be learnt through the experience of learning to lay down completely this natural and instinctive desire for marriage and parenthood, and accept the circumstances of life which deny them this experience. This instinct for love, so firmly implanted in the human heart, is the supreme way by which we learn to desire and love God Himself above all else. But the 'High Places' of victory and union with Christ cannot be reached by any mental 'reckoning of Self to be dead to sin', or by seeking to devise some way or 'discipline' by which the Will can be 'crucified'. The only way is by learning to accept, day by day, the actual conditions and tests permitted by

God, by a continually repeated laying down of our own will and acceptance of His as it is presented to us in the form of the people with whom we have to live and work, and in the things which happen to us. Every acceptance of His will becomes an altar of sacrifice, and every such surrender and abandonment of ourselves to His will is a means of furthering us on the way to the High Places to which He desires to bring every child of His while they are still living on earth.

The lessons of accepting and triumphing over evil, of becoming 'acquainted with grief' and pain, and, ultimately, of finding them transformed into something incomparably precious; of learning through constant glad surrender to know the Lord of Love Himself in a new way and to experience unbroken union with Him—these are the lessons of the allegory in this book. The 'High Places' and the 'hinds' feet' do not refer to heavenly places after death, but are meant to be the glorious experience of God's children here and now—if they will follow the path He chooses for them.

Perhaps the Lord will use it to speak comfort to some of His loved ones who are finding themselves forced to keep company with Sorrow and Suffering, or who 'walk in darkness and have no light' or feel themselves 'tossed with tempest and not comforted'. It may help them to understand a new meaning in what is happening, for the experiences through which they are passing are all part of the wonderful process by which the Lord is making real in their lives the same experience which made David and Habakkuk cry out exultantly, 'The Lord God maketh my feet like hinds' feet, and setteth me upon mine High Places' (Psa. 18:33 and Hab. 3:19).

CONTENTS

PART TWO
'Joy cometh in the morning'

PART ONE

'WEEPING MAY ENDURE FOR A NIGHT'

(Psalm 30:5)

'O thou afflicted, tossed with tempest, and not
comforted,
Behold, I will lay thy stones with fair colours,
   And lay thy foundations with sapphires,
And I will make thy windows of agates,
   And thy gates of carbuncles,
And all thy borders of pleasant stones.'

(Isa. 54:11, 12)

CHAPTER I

THE INVITATION TO THE HIGH PLACES

THIS is the story of how Much-Afraid escaped from her Fearing relatives and went with the Shepherd to the High Places where 'perfect love casteth out fear'.

For several years Much-Afraid had been in the service of the Chief Shepherd, whose great flocks were pastured down in the Valley of Humiliation. She lived with her friends and fellow-workers Mercy and Peace in a tranquil little white cottage in the village of Much-Trembling. She loved her work and desired intensely to please the Chief Shepherd, but happy as she was in most ways, she was conscious of several things which hindered her in her work and caused her much secret distress and shame.

In the first place she was a cripple, with feet so crooked that they often caused her to limp and stumble as she went about her work. She had also the very unsightly blemish of a crooked mouth which greatly disfigured both expression and speech and was sadly conscious that these ugly blemishes must be a cause of astonishment and offence to many who knew that she was in the service of the great Shepherd. Most earnestly she longed to be completely delivered from these shortcomings and to be made beautiful, gracious, and strong as were so many of the Shepherd's other workers, and above all to be made like the Chief Shepherd Himself. But she feared that there could be no deliverance from these two crippling disfigurements and that they must continue to mar her service always.

There was, however, another and even greater trouble in her life. She was a member of the Family of Fearings, and her relatives were scattered all over the valley, so that she could never really escape from them. An orphan, she had been brought up in the home of her aunt, poor Mrs. Dismal Forebodings, with her two cousins Gloomy and Spiteful and their brother Craven Fear, a great bully who habitually tormented and persecuted her in a really dreadful way.

Like most of the other families who lived in the Valley of Humiliation, all the Fearings hated the Chief Shepherd and tried to boycott His servants, and naturally it was a great offence to them that one of their own family should have entered His service. Consequently they did all they could both by threats and persuasions to get her out of His employment, and one dreadful day they laid before her the family dictum that she must immediately marry her cousin Craven Fear and settle down respectably amongst her own people. If she refused to do this of her own free will, they threatened to use force and compel her. Poor Much-Afraid was, of course, overwhelmed with horror at the mere idea, but her relatives always terrified her, and she had never learnt to resist or ignore their threats, so she simply sat cowering before them, repeating again and again that nothing would induce her to marry Craven Fear, but quite unable to escape from their presence.

The unhappy interview therefore lasted a long time, and when finally they did leave her for a little, it was already early evening. With a surge of relief, Much-Afraid remembered that the Chief Shepherd would then be leading His flocks to their accustomed watering-place beside a lovely cascade and pool on the outskirts of the village. To this place she was in the habit of going very early every morning to meet Him and learn His wishes and commands for the day, and again in the evenings to give her report on the day's work. It was now time to meet Him there beside the pool, and she felt sure He would help her and not permit her relatives to kidnap her and force her to leave His service for the dreadful slavery of marriage with Craven Fear.

Still shaking with fear and without pausing to wash the tears from her face, Much-Afraid shut the door of the cottage and started off for the cascade and the pool.

The quiet evening light was filling the Valley of Humiliation with a golden glow as she left the village and started to cross the fields. Beyond the river, the mountains which bounded the eastern side of the Valley like towering ramparts were already tinged with pink, and their deep gorges were filled with lovely and mysterious shadows. Through the quiet and peace of this tranquil evening, poor, terrified Much-Afraid came to the pool where the Shepherd was waiting for her, and told Him of her dreadful plight.

'What shall I do?' she cried as she ended the recital. 'How can I escape? They can't really force me to marry my cousin Craven, can they? Oh!' cried she, overwhelmed again at the very thought of such a prospect, 'it is dreadful enough to be Much-Afraid, but to think of having to be Mrs. Craven Fear for the rest of my life and never able to escape from the torment of it is more than I can bear.'

'Don't be afraid,' said the Shepherd gently. 'You are in My service, and if you will trust Me they will not be able to force you against your will into any family alliance. But you ought never to have let your Fearing relatives into your cottage, because they are enemies of the King who has taken you into His employment.'

'I know, oh, I know,' cried Much-Afraid, 'but whenever I meet any of my relatives I seem to lose all my strength and simply cannot resist them, no matter how I strive. As long as I live in the Valley I cannot escape meeting them. They are everywhere and now that they are determined to get me into their power again I shall never dare venture outside my cottage alone for fear of being kidnapped.'

As she spoke she lifted her eyes and looked across the Valley and the river to the lovely sunset-lighted peaks of the mountains, then cried out in desperate longing, 'Oh, if only I could escape from this Valley of Humiliation altogether and go to the High Places, completely out of reach of all the Fearings and my other relatives!'

No sooner were these words uttered when to her complete astonishment the Shepherd answered, 'I have waited a long time to hear you make that suggestion, Much-Afraid. It would indeed be best for you to leave the Valley for the High Places, and I will very willingly take you there Myself. The lower slopes of those mountains on the other side of the river are the border-land of My Father's Kingdom, the Realm of Love. No Fears of any kind are able to live there because 'perfect LOVE casteth out fear and everything that torments'.

Much-Afraid stared at Him in amazement. 'Go to the High Places,' she exclaimed, 'and live there? Oh, if only I could! For months past the longing has never left me. I think of it day and night, but it is not possible. I could never get there. I am too lame.' She looked down at her malformed feet as she spoke, and her eyes again filled with tears of despair and self-pity. 'The mountains are so steep and dangerous. I have been told that only the hinds and the deer can move on them safely.'

'It is quite true that the way up to the High Places is both difficult and dangerous,' said the Shepherd. 'It has to be, so that nothing which is an enemy of Love can make the ascent and invade the Kingdom. Nothing blemished or in any way imperfect is allowed there, and the inhabitants of the High Places do need "hinds' feet". I have them Myself,' He added with a smile, 'and like a young hart or a roebuck I can go leaping on the mountains and skipping on the hills with the greatest ease and pleasure. But, Much-Afraid, I could make yours like hinds' feet also, and set you upon the High Places. You could serve Me then much more fully and be out of reach of all your enemies. I am delighted to hear that you have been longing to go there, for, as I said before, I have been waiting for you to make that suggestion. Then,' he added, with another smile, 'you would never have to meet Craven Fear again.'

Much-Afraid stared at Him in bewilderment. 'Make my feet like hinds' feet,' she repeated. 'How is that possible? And what would the inhabitants of the Kingdom of Love say to the presence of a wretched little cripple with an ugly face and a twisted mouth, if nothing blemished and imperfect may dwell there?'

'It is true,' said the Shepherd, 'that you would have to be changed before you could live on the High Places, but if you are willing to go with Me, I promise to help you develop hinds' feet. Up there on the mountains, as you get near the real High Places, the air is fresh and invigorating. It strengthens the whole body and there are streams with wonderful healing properties, so that those who bathe in them find all their blemishes and disfigurements washed away. But there is another thing I must tell you. Not only would I have to make your feet like hinds' feet, but you would have to receive another name, for it would be as impossible for a Much-Afraid to enter the Kingdom of Love as for any other member of the Fearing family. Are you willing to be changed completely, Much-Afraid, and to be made like the new name which you will receive if you become a citizen in the Kingdom of Love?'

She nodded her head and then said very earnestly, 'Yes, I am.'

Again He smiled, but added gravely, 'There is still one thing more, the most important of all. No one is allowed to dwell in the Kingdom of Love unless they have the flower of Love already blooming in their hearts. Has Love been planted in your heart, Much-Afraid?'

As the Shepherd said this He looked at her very steadily and she realised that His eyes were searching into the very depths of her heart and knew all that was there far better than she did herself. She did not answer for a long time, because she was not sure what to say, but she looked rather flinchingly into the eyes which were gazing at her so penetratingly and became aware that they had the power of reflecting what they looked upon.

She could thus really see her own heart as He saw it, so after a long pause she answered, 'I think that what is growing there is a great longing to experience the joy of natural, human love and to learn to love supremely one person who will love me in return. But perhaps that desire, natural and right as it seems, is not the Love of which You are speaking?' She paused and then added honestly and almost tremblingly, 'I see the longing to be loved and admired growing in my heart, Shepherd, but I don't think I see the kind of Love that You are talking about, at least, nothing like the love which I see in You.'

'Then will you let Me plant the seed of true Love there now?' asked the Shepherd. 'It will take you some time to develop hinds' feet and to climb to the High Places, and if I put the seed in your heart now it will be ready to bloom by the time you get there.'

Much-Afraid shrank back. 'I am afraid,' she said. 'I have been told that if you really love someone you give that loved one the power to hurt and pain you in a way nothing else can.'

'That is true,' agreed the Shepherd. 'To love does mean to put your SELF into the power of the loved one and to become very vulnerable to pain, and you are very MUCH-AFRAID of pain, are you not?'

She nodded miserably and then said shamefacedly, 'Yes, VERY much afraid of it.'

'But it is so happy to love,' said the Shepherd quietly. 'It is happy to love even if you are not loved in return. There is pain too, certainly, but Love does not think that very significant.'

Much-Afraid thought suddenly that He had the most patient eyes she had ever seen. At the same time there was something in them that hurt her to the heart, though she could not have said why, but she still shrank back in fear and said (bringing the words out very quickly because somehow she was ashamed to say them), 'I would never dare to love unless I were sure of being loved in return. If I let You plant the seed of Love in my heart will You give me the promise that I shall be loved in return? I couldn't bear it otherwise.'

The smile He turned on her then was the gentlest and kindest she had ever seen, yet once again, and for the same indefinable reason as before, it cut her to the quick. 'Yes,' He said, without hesitation. 'I promise you, Much-Afraid, that when the plant of Love is ready to bloom in your heart and when you are ready to change your name, then you will be loved in return.'

A thrill of joy went through her from head to foot. It seemed too wonderful to be believed, but the Shepherd Himself was making the promise, and of one thing she was quite sure, He could not lie. 'Please plant Love in my heart now,' she said faintly. Poor little soul, she was still Much-Afraid even when promised the greatest thing in the world.

The Shepherd put His hand in His bosom, drew something forth, and laid it in the palm of His hand. Then He held His hand out towards Much-Afraid. 'Here is the seed of Love,' He said.

She bent forward to look, then gave a startled little cry and drew back. There was indeed a seed lying in the palm of His hand, but it was shaped exactly like a long, sharply-pointed thorn. Much-Afraid had often noticed that the Shepherd's hands were scarred and wounded, but now she saw that the scar in the palm of the hand held out to her was the exact shape and size of the seed of Love lying beside it.

'The seed looks very sharp,' she said shrinkingly. 'Won't it hurt if You put it into my heart?'

He answered gently, 'It is so sharp that it slips in very quickly. But, Much-Afraid, I have already warned you that Love and Pain go together, for a time at least. If you would know Love, you must know pain too.'

Much-Afraid looked at the thorn and shrank from it. Then she looked at the Shepherd's face and repeated His words to herself.

'When the seed of Love in your heart is ready to bloom, you will be loved in return,' and a strange new courage entered into her. She suddenly stepped forward, bared her heart, and said, 'Please plant the seed here in my heart.'

His face lit up with a glad smile and He said with a note of joy in His voice, 'Now you will be able to go with Me to the High Places and be a citizen in the Kingdom of My Father.'

Then He pressed the thorn into her heart. It was true, just as He had said, it did cause a piercing pain, but it slipped in quickly and then, suddenly, a sweetness she had never felt or imagined before tingled through her. It was bitter-sweet, but the sweetness was the stronger. She thought of the Shepherd's words, 'It is so happy to love,' and her pale, sallow cheeks suddenly glowed pink and her eyes shone. For a moment Much-Afraid did not look afraid at all. The twisted mouth had relaxed into a happy curve, and the shining eyes and pink cheeks made her almost beautiful.

'Thank You, thank You,' she cried, and knelt at the Shepherd's feet. 'How good You are. How patient You are. There is no one in the whole world as good and kind as You. I will go with You to the mountains. I will trust You to make my feet like hinds' feet, and to set me, even me, upon the High Places.'

'I am more glad even than you,' said the Shepherd, 'and now you really act as though you were going to change your name already. But there is one thing more I must tell you. I shall take you to the foot of the mountains Myself, so that there will be no danger from your enemies. After that, two special companions I have chosen will guide and help you on all the steep and difficult places while your feet are still lame and while you can only limp and go slowly. You will not see Me all the time, Much-Afraid, for as I told you I shall be leaping on the mountains and skipping on the hills, and you will not at first be able to accompany Me or keep up with Me. That will come later. However, you must remember that as soon as you reach the slopes of the mountains there is a wonderful system of communication from end to end of the Kingdom of Love, and I shall be able to hear you whenever you speak to Me. Whenever you call for help I promise to come to you at once. At the foot of the mountains My two servants whom I have chosen to be your guides will be waiting for you. Remember, I have chosen them Myself with great care, as the two who are most able to help you and assist you in developing hinds' feet. You will accept them with joy and allow them to be your helpers, will you not?'

'Oh, yes,' she answered at once, smiling at Him happily. 'Of course I am quite certain that You know best and that whatever You choose is right.' Then she added joyfully, 'I feel as though I shall never be afraid again.'

He looked very kindly at the little shepherdess who had just received the seed of Love into her heart and was preparing to go with Him to the High Places, but also with full understanding. He knew her through and through, in all the intricate labyrinth of her lonely heart, better far than she knew herself. No one understood better than He, that growing into the likeness of a new name is a long process, but He did not say this. He looked with a certain tender pity and compassion at the glowing cheeks and shining eyes which had so suddenly transformed the appearance of plain little Much-Afraid.

Then He said, 'Now you may go home and make your preparations for leaving. You are not to take anything with you, only leave everything in order. Do not tell anyone about it, for a journey to the High Places needs to be a secret matter. I cannot now give you the exact time when we are to start for the mountains, but it will be soon, and you must be ready to follow Me whenever I come to the cottage and call. I will give you a secret sign. I shall sing one of the Shepherd's songs as I pass the cottage, and it will contain a special message for you. When you hear it, come at once and follow Me to the trysting-place.' Then, as the sun had already gone down in a blaze of red and gold, and the eastern mountains were now veiled in misty mauve and grey, and the shadows were lengthening, He turned and led His flock away towards the sheepfolds.

Much-Afraid turned her face homewards, her heart full of happiness and excitement, and still feeling as though she would never be frightened again. As she started back across the fields she sang to herself one of the songs from an old book of songs which the shepherds often used. Never before had it seemed to her so sweet, so applicable.

'The Song of Songs', the loveliest song,
        The song of Love the King,
No joy on earth compares with His,
        But seems a broken thing.
His Name as ointment is poured forth,
        And all His lovers sing.

Draw me—I will run after Thee,
        Thou art my heart's one choice,
Oh, bring me to Thy royal house,
        To dwell there and rejoice.
There in Thy presence, O my King,
        To feast and hear Thy voice.

Look not upon me with contempt.
        Though soiled and marred I be,

The King found me—an outcast thing—
And set His love on me.
I shall be perfected by Love,
Made fair as day to see.

(Cant. 1:1–6)

She walked singing across the first field and was half-way over the next when suddenly she saw Craven Fear himself coming towards her. Poor Much-Afraid: for a little while she had completely forgotten the existence of her dreadful relatives, and now here was the most dreaded and detested of them all slouching towards her. Her heart filled with a terrible panic. She looked right and left, but there was no hiding-place anywhere, and besides it was all too obvious that he was actually coming to meet her, for as soon as he saw her he quickened his pace and in a moment or two was right beside her.

With a horror that sickened her very heart she heard him say, 'Well, here you are at last, little Cousin Much-Afraid. So we are to be married, eh, what do you think of that?' and he pinched her, presumably in a playful manner, but viciously enough to make her gasp and bite her lips to keep back a cry of pain.

She shrank away from him and shook with terror and loathing. Unfortunately this was the worst thing she could have done, for it was always her obvious fear which encouraged him to continue tormenting her. If only she could have ignored him, he soon would have tired of teasing and of her company and would have wandered off to look for other prey. In all her life, however, Much-Afraid had never been able to ignore Fear. Now it was absolutely beyond her power to conceal the dread which she felt.

Her white face and terrified eyes immediately had the effect of stimulating Craven's desire to bait her. Here she was, alone and completely in his power. He caught hold of her, and poor Much-Afraid uttered one frenzied cry of terror and pain. At that moment Craven Fear loosed his grasp and cringed away. The Shepherd had approached them unperceived and was standing beside them. One look at His stern face and flashing eyes and at the stout shepherd's cudgel grasped in His strong, uplifted hand was more than enough for the bully. Craven Fear slunk away like a whipped cur, actually running from the village instead of towards it, not knowing where he was going, urged by one instinct alone, to find a place of safety.

Much-Afraid burst into tears. Of course she ought to have known that Craven was a coward and that if only she had lifted her voice and called for the Shepherd, he would have fled at once. Now her dress was torn and disordered, and her arms bruised by the bully's grip, yet that was the least part of her distress. She was overwhelmed with shame that she had so quickly acted like her old name and nature, which she had hoped was beginning to be changed already. It seemed so impossible to ignore the Fearings, still less to resist them. She did not dare look at the Shepherd, but had she done so she would have seen with what compassion He was regarding her. She did not yet realise that the Prince of Love is 'of very tender compassions to them that are afraid'. She supposed that, like everybody else, He was despising her for her silly fears, so she muttered a shamed 'thank you'. Then, still without looking at Him, she limped painfully towards the village, weeping bitterly as she went and saying over and over again to herself, 'What is the use of even thinking of going to the High Places. I could never reach them, for the least little thing is enough to turn me back.'

However, when at last she reached the security of the cottage she began to feel better, and by the time she had drunk a cup of tea and taken her evening meal she had so far recovered that she was able to remind herself of all that had happened there beside the cascade and the pool. Suddenly she remembered, with a thrill of wonder and delight, that the seed of Love had been planted in her heart. As she thought of it, the same almost intolerable sweetness stole over her, the bitter-sweet, indefinable but wholly delightful ecstasy of a new happiness. 'It is happy to love,' said little Much-Afraid to herself and then she repeated: 'It is happy to love.' After putting the cottage in order for the night, because she was utterly tired out with all the conflicting emotions of that strange day, she went to bed. Lying there before falling asleep, she sang over and over again to herself another of the lovely songs from the old song book.

O Thou Whom my soul loveth,
 Tell me where Thou dost feed,
And where Thy flocks at noonday
 To rest and browse dost lead.
  For why should I
  By others be,
  And not by Thee?

O fairest among women,
 Dost thou indeed not know?
Then lead thy little flocklet
 The way that My flocks go;
  And be to Me,
  As I to thee,
  Sweet company.

(Cant. 1:7, 8)

Then she fell into a heavy, dreamless sleep.

CHAPTER II

THE FEARING INVASION

MUCH-AFRAID woke early the next morning and all her fears were gone. Her first thought was, 'Probably some time today I am to start for the High Places with the Shepherd.' This so excited her that she could hardly eat her breakfast, and as she began making arrangements for her departure, she could not help singing.

It seemed to her that ever since the seed of Love had been planted in her heart, songs of joy were welling up in her innermost being. And the songs which best expressed this new happiness and thankfulness were from the old book which the shepherds so loved to use as they worked among the flocks and led them to the pastures. As she carried out the simple arrangements the Shepherd had told her to make, she sang another of these songs:

> Now when the King at table sits,
> My spikenard smelleth sweet,
> And myrrh and camphire from my store

I pour upon His feet.
My thankful love must be displayed,
He loved and wooed a beggar maid.

Ye daughters of Jerusalem,
    I'm black to look upon
As goatskin tents; but also as
    The tent of Solomon.
Without, I bear the marks of sin,
But Love's adorning is within.

Despise me not that I am black,
    The sun hath burned my face,
My mother's children hated me,
    And drove me from my place.
In their vineyards I toiled and wept.
But mine own vineyard have not kept.

I am not fair save to the King,
    Though fair my royal dress,
His kingly grace is lavished on
    My need and worthlessness.
My blemishes He will not see
But loves the beauty that shall be.

(Cant. 1:12–15, 5, 6)

From time to time as she went about her work her heart
fluttered, half with excitement, half with dread of the unknown,
but whenever she remembered the thorn in her heart, she tingled
from head to foot with the same mysterious sweetness. Love was
for her, too, even for her, crippled little Much-Afraid. When she

reached the High Places she was to lose her humiliating disfigurements and be made beautiful, and when the plant in her heart was ready to bloom she was to be loved in return. Even as she thought of this, doubt mingled with the sweetness. Surely it could not possibly be true; just a beautiful dream, but not reality.

'Oh, I am afraid it won't ever happen,' she would say to herself, and then, when she thought of the Shepherd, her heart quickened again and she would run to the door or window to see if He were coming to call her.

The morning wore on and still He had not come, but just after mid-day something else came, an invasion by her terrible relatives. All of a sudden, before she realised what was happening, they were upon her. There was a trampling of feet and a clamour of voices and then she was surrounded by a whole army of aunts and uncles and cousins. Craven, however, was not with them. The family, hearing of his reception the evening before, and realising that she shrank from him with peculiar dread and terror, had decided that it would not be wise to take him with them.

They were determined to overrule Much-Afraid's objections to the marriage, and if possible get her out of the cottage and into one of their own dwelling-places. Their plan was to make a bold attack while she would be alone in the cottage and the Shepherd far away with His flocks, so they hoped she would be at their mercy. She could not be forcibly abducted in broad daylight; there were too many of the Shepherd's servants in the village who would instantly come to her assistance. However, they knew Much-Afraid's timidity and weakness and they believed that, if there were enough of them present, they could cow her into consenting to go with them to the Mansion of old Lord Fearing. Then they would have her in their power.

The old lord himself was actually with them, assuring her in a fatherly tone of voice that they had come with the kindest and friendliest intentions. He understood that she had some objections to the proposed marriage, and he wanted to have the opportunity of quietly talking them over with her, to see if he could set them at rest. It seemed to him that it was a suitable and attractive match in every way and that there must be some extraordinary misconception in her mind which a little understanding talk together would set right. If not, he assured her kindly, he would not permit her to be married against her will.

When he had finished, a babel of other Fearing voices broke in, reasoning with her and making all sorts of suggestions. The fact was, they told her, that she had cut herself off from her relatives for so long, it was now quite apparent that she had all kinds of strange notions about their feelings and intentions towards her. It was really only right that she should now spend a little time with them and thus give them the opportunity of proving that she had misjudged and misunderstood them. Craven might not be just as handsome and pleasing in appearance as a prince in a fairy-tale, and it was true that he had, unfortunately, rather a rough manner, but that was because he had known nothing of the softening and refining influences of marriage. Certainly the responsibilities and joys of married life would quickly alter this, and would indeed effect a transformation in him. It was to be her delightful privilege to assist as principal mover in bringing about this reformation which they all so eagerly wished to see.

The whole gang talked on and on, while poor Much-Afraid sat cowering in their midst, almost too dazed to know what they were saying and suggesting. Just as they had hoped, they were gradually bringing her to a state of bewilderment and incoherent fear. It looked as though they soon would be able to persuade her that it was her duty to attempt the impossible task of trying to convert Craven Fear into something less objectionable than he really was. Suddenly there came an interruption from without.

The Fearings had carefully closed the door when they entered the cottage and even contrived to bolt it, so that Much-Afraid could not escape. Now came the distant sound of a man's voice raised in song, singing one of the songs from the old book which Much-Afraid knew and loved so well. Then the singer Himself came in view, slowly passing along the lane. It was the Chief Shepherd, already leading His flock to the watering-place. The words floated in through the open window, accompanied by the soft bleating of the sheep and the scuffling of many little dusty feet as they pattered after Him.

It seemed as though all other sounds were hushed to stillness on that quiet summer afternoon as the Shepherd sang while passing the cottage. Inside, the clamour of voices had ceased instantly and was succeeded by a silence which could be felt. This is what He sang:

> The Voice of my Belovèd!
>   Through all my heart it thrills,
> He leaps upon the mountains,
>   And skips upon the hills.
>
> For like a roe or young hart,
>   So swift and strong is He,
> He looketh through my window,
>   And beckoneth unto me.
>
> 'Rise up, My love, My fair one,
>   And come away with Me,

Gone are the snows of winter,
   The rains no more we see.

'The flowers are appearing,
   The little birds all sing,
The turtle dove is calling,
   Through all the land 'tis spring.

'The shoots are on the grapevines,
   The figs are on the tree,
Arise, My love, My fair one,
   And come away with Me.'

Why is My dove still hiding?
   When all things else rejoice,
Oh, let Me see thee, fair one,
   Oh, let Me hear thy voice.

(Cant. 2:8–14)

As she sat listening in the cottage, Much-Afraid knew with a pang of agonising pain that the Shepherd was calling her to go with Him to the mountains. This was the secret signal He had promised, and He had said that she must be ready to leave instantly, the moment she heard it. Now here she was, locked inside her own cottage, beleaguered by her terrible Fears and unable to respond in any way to His call, or even to give any sign of her need. There was one moment indeed, when the song first started and everyone was startled into silence that she might have called to Him to come and help her. She did not realise that the Fearings were holding their breath lest she did call, and had she done so, they would have fled helter-skelter through the door.

However, she was too stunned with fear to seize the opportunity, and then it was too late.

The next moment she felt Coward's heavy hand laid tightly over her mouth, then other hands gripped her firmly and held her in the chair. So the Shepherd slowly passed the cottage, 'showing Himself at the window,' and singing the signal song, but receiving no response of any kind.

When He had passed and the words of the song and the bleating of the sheep had died away in the distance, it was found that Much-Afraid had fainted. Her cousin Coward's gagging hands had half-choked her. Her relatives would dearly have liked to seize this opportunity and carry her off while she was unconscious, but as this was the hour when everybody was returning from work it was too dangerous. The Fearings decided therefore that they would remain in the cottage until darkness fell, then gag Much-Afraid and carry her off unperceived. When this plan had been decided upon, they laid her upon the bed to recover as best she might, while some of the aunts and cousins went out into the kitchen to see what provisions for refreshing themselves might be plundered. The men sat smoking in the sitting-room, and Gloomy was left to guard the half-conscious victim in the bedroom.

Gradually Much-Afraid regained her senses, and as she realised her position she nearly fainted again with horror. She dared not cry out for help, for all her neighbours would be away at their work; but were they? No, it was later than she had thought, for suddenly she heard the voice of Mrs. Valiant, her neighbour in the cottage next door. At the sound, Much-Afraid braced herself for one last desperate bid for escape.

Gloomy was quite unprepared for such a move, and before she realised what was happening, Much-Afraid sprang from the bed and shouted through the window as loudly as her fear permitted, 'Valiant! Valiant! Come and help me. Come quickly. Help!'

At the sound of her first cry, Mrs. Valiant looked across the garden and caught a glimpse of Much-Afraid's white, terrified face at the window and of her hand beckoning entreatingly. The next moment the face was jerked away from view and a curtain suddenly drawn across the window. That was enough for Mrs. Valiant, whose name described her exactly. She hurried straight across to her neighbour's cottage and tried the door, but finding it locked, she looked in through a window and saw the room full of Much-Afraid's relatives.

Mrs. Valiant was not the sort of person to be the least intimidated by what she called 'a pack of idle Fears'. Thrusting her face right in through the window, she cried in a threatening voice, 'Out of this house you go, this minute, every one of you. If you have not left in three seconds, I shall call the Chief Shepherd. This cottage belongs to Him, and won't you catch it if He finds you here.'

The effect of her words was magical. The door was unbolted and thrown open and the Fearings poured out pell-mell, tumbling over one another in their haste to get away. Mrs. Valiant smiled grimly as she watched their ignominious flight. When the last one had scuttled away she went into the cottage to Much-Afraid, who seemed quite overcome with fear and distress. Little by little she learnt the story of those hours of torment and the plan to kidnap the poor victim after darkness fell.

Mrs. Valiant hardly knew herself what it was to feel fear, and had just routed the whole gang of Fearings single-handed. She felt much inclined to adopt a bracing attitude and to chide the silly girl for not standing up to her relatives at once, boldly repulsing them before they got her into their clutches. But as she looked at the white face and terrified eyes and saw the quaking body of poor Much-Afraid, she checked herself. 'What is the use of saying it? She can't act upon it, poor thing; she is one of them herself and has got Fearing in the blood, and when the enemy is within you it's a poor look-out. I think no one but the Shepherd Himself can really help her,' she reflected.

So instead of an admonition, she patted the trembling girl and said with all the kindness of her motherly heart, 'Now, my dear, while you are getting over your fright, I'll just pop into the kitchen and make a good cup of tea for both of us and you'll feel better at once. My! If they haven't been in here and put the kettle on for us,' she added, as she opened the kitchen door and found the cloth already on the table and the preparations for the plundered meal which the unwanted visitors had so hastily abandoned.

'What a pack of harpies,' she muttered angrily to herself, then smiled complacently as she remembered how they had fled before her.

By the time they had drunk their tea and Mrs. Valiant had energetically cleared away the last traces of the unwelcome invaders, Much-Afraid had nearly recovered her composure. Darkness had long since fallen, and now it was much too late for her to go to the pool to keep tryst with the Shepherd and explain why she had not responded to His call. She would have to wait for the morning light. So at Mrs. Valiant's suggestion, as she was feeling utterly exhausted, she went straight to bed. Her neighbour saw her safely tucked up, and kissed her warmly and reassuringly. Indeed, she offered to sleep in the cottage herself that night, but Much-Afraid, knowing that she had a family waiting for her at home, refused the kind offer. However, before leaving, Mrs. Valiant placed a bell beside her bed and assured her that if anything alarmed her in the night she had only to ring the bell and the whole Valiant family would be over instantly to assist her. Then she went away and Much-Afraid was left alone in the cottage.

CHAPTER III

THE FLIGHT IN THE NIGHT

FOR hours poor Much-Afraid lay sleepless on her bed, too bruised in mind and body to rest in one position, but tossing and turning wearily from side to side until long after midnight. Somewhere at the back of her mind was a dreadful uneasiness, as though there was something she ought to remember, but was unable to do so. When at last she fell asleep this thought still haunted her.

She woke suddenly an hour or two later, her mind intensely alert, conscious of an agonising pain such as she had never known before. The thorn in her heart was throbbing and aching in a manner she could scarcely bear. It was as though the pain was hammering out something which at first she was still too confused to be able to understand. Then, all of a sudden, in a terrible flash, it became clear to her, and she found herself whispering over and over again, 'The Shepherd came and called me as He promised, but I didn't go to Him or give any answer. Supposing He thought that I had changed my mind and didn't want to go with Him. Supposing He has gone and left me behind! Gone without me! Yes, left me behind!'

The shock of this thought was awful. This was the thing she had forgotten. He would not be able to understand why she had not gone out to Him as He had told her. He had urged her to be ready to go with Him *the instant that He called*, that there must be no delay, that He Himself had to go to the mountains on urgent business. She had not been able to go even to the trysting-place as usual that evening. Of course He would think that she was afraid. Perhaps He was gone already and alone. Much-Afraid turned icy cold and her teeth chattered, but it was the pain in her heart which was the most awful part of her distress. It seemed to suffocate her as she lay there in bed. She sat up, shivering with cold and with the horror of the thought. She could not bear it if He had gone and left her behind.

On the table beside her bed lay the old song book. Glancing down at it in the light of the lamp, she saw it was open at the page whereon was written a song about another shepherdess. She, just like herself, had failed to respond to the call of love and then found, too late, that Love had gone away. It had always seemed to her such a sad song that she could hardly read it, but now as she read the words again in the dark loneliness of the night, it seemed as though it was the cry of her own forlorn and terrified heart,

> By night on my bed I sought Him,
> > He Whom my soul loveth so.
> I sought—but I could not find Him,
> > And now I will rise and go—
>
> Out in the streets of the city,
> > And out on the broad highway;
> For He Whom my soul so loveth,
> > Hath left me and gone away.

The page in the little song book ended there, and she did not turn the leaf. Suddenly she could bear the uncertainty no longer. She must see for herself at once if He really had gone away and left her behind. She slipped out of bed, dressed herself as quickly as her shaking fingers would permit, and then unlocked the cottage door. She, too, would go out into the street and the broad highway and would see if she could find Him, would see if He had gone and left her behind, or—oh, if only it were possible—if He had waited to give her another chance.

Opening the door, she went out into the darkness. A hundred Craven Fears lurking in the lonely street could not have deterred her at that moment, for the pain in her heart swallowed up fear and everything else and drove her forth. So in the dark hours, just before the dawn, Much-Afraid started off to look for the Shepherd.

She could not go quickly because of her lameness, but limped along the village streets towards the open fields and the sheepfolds. As she went she whispered to herself, 'O Shepherd, when You said that Love and pain go together, how truly You spoke.' Had she but known or even dimly sensed what it would be like, would she, could she, possibly have consented to let Him put the thorn in her heart? It was too late now: it was there. Love was there and pain, too, and she *must* find the Shepherd. At last, limping and breathless, she came to the sheepfolds, still and silent in the dim starlight. One or two under-shepherds were there, keeping watch over the flocks through the night, and when they heard footsteps approaching they rose up from the ground and went to meet the intruder.

'Who are you?' they challenged her in the darkness, then stared in amazement as their lanterns flashed on the white face and frightened eyes of Much-Afraid.

'Is the Chief Shepherd here?' she gasped as she leant against the wall of the sheepfold, panting and trying to recover her breath.

'No,' said the watchman, staring at her curiously. 'He left the flocks in our charge this night and gave His orders. He said that He had to make a journey to the mountains, as He often does, and did not say when He would be back.'

Much-Afraid could not speak. She moaned and pressed her hands to her heart, feeling as though it would break. What could she do now? He was gone. He *had* thought that she did not want to go and had not waited for her. Then, aching with despair, as she leant tremblingly against the wall of the fold, she remembered the Shepherd's face and the loving kindness of the look with which He had invited her to accompany Him to the mountains. It came into her mind that He who understood her so well, who knew all about her fears and had compassion on her, would not leave until He was quite sure that she really meant to refuse to go with Him. She lifted her eyes, looked across the Valley towards the eastern mountains and the High Places. A faint streak of light was appearing in the east, and she knew that soon the sun would rise. Suddenly she remembered the last verse of the sad song which she had read, the last verse on the page which she had not waited to turn over. It came whispering into her mind just as a little bird began to sing in one of the bushes beside her.

And then—in the dawn I saw Him,
He Whom my heart loveth so.
I found Him, held Him and told Him
I never could let Him go.

(Cant. 3:1–5)

Much-Afraid ceased trembling and said to herself, 'I will go to the trysting-place, and see if He is waiting for me there.' With scarcely a word to the watchmen she turned and hurried southwards, over the field where Craven Fear had met her towards the sheep pool. Almost forgetting that she was lame, she sped towards the distant trees which fringed the pool. Just as the sky turned red above the mountains, the joyous, babbling sound of cascading water reached her ears, and as she hurried forward Much-Afraid suddenly found a cascade of song pouring forth from her own heart. He *was* there, standing by the pool, looking towards her with the light of the sunrise shining on His face. As Much-Afraid stumbled towards Him, He stepped quickly to her side and she fell at His feet sobbing, 'O my Lord, take me with You as You said. Don't leave me behind.'

'I knew you would come,' He said gently, 'but, Much-Afraid, why were you not at the trysting-place last evening? Did you not hear Me when I passed your cottage and called? I wanted to tell you to be ready to start with Me this morning at sunrise.' As He spoke the sun rose fully over the peaks of the mountains and bathed them both in a lovely golden light.

'I am here,' said Much-Afraid, still kneeling at His feet, 'and I will go with You *anywhere.*'

Then the Shepherd took her by the hand and they started for the mountains.

CHAPTER IV

THE START FOR THE HIGH PLACES

IT was early morning of a beautiful day. The valley lay as though still asleep. The only sounds were the joyful laughter of the running streams and the gay little songs of the birds. The dew sparkled on the grass and the wild flowers glowed like little jewels. Especially lovely were the wild anemones, purple, pink, and scarlet, which dotted the pastures everywhere, thrusting their beautiful little faces up through the straggling thorns. Sometimes the Shepherd and Much-Afraid walked over patches of thousands of tiny little pink or mauve blossoms, each minutely small and yet all together forming a brilliant carpet, far richer than any seen in a king's palace.

Once the Shepherd stooped and touched the flowerlets gently with His fingers, then said to Much-Afraid with a smile, 'Humble yourself, and you will find that Love is spreading a carpet of flowers beneath your feet.'

Much-Afraid looked at Him earnestly. 'I have often wondered about the wild flowers,' she said. 'It does seem strange that such unnumbered multitudes should bloom in the wild places of the earth where perhaps nobody ever sees them and the goats and the cattle can walk over them and crush them to death. They have so much beauty and sweetness to give and no one on whom to lavish it, nor who will even appreciate it.'

The look the Shepherd turned on her was very beautiful. 'Nothing My Father and I have made is ever wasted,' He said quietly, 'and the little wild flowers have a wonderful lesson to teach. They offer themselves so sweetly and confidently and willingly, even if it seems that there is no one to appreciate them. Just as though they sang a joyous little song to themselves, that it is so happy to love, even though one is not loved in return.'

'I must tell you a great truth, Much-Afraid, which only the few understand. All the fairest beauties in the human soul, its greatest victories, and its most splendid achievements are always those which no one else knows anything about, or can only dimly guess at. Every inner response of the human heart to Love and every conquest over self-love is a new flower on the tree of Love. Many a quiet, ordinary, and hidden life, unknown to the world, is a veritable garden in which Love's flowers and fruits have come to such perfection that it is a place of delight where the King of Love Himself walks and rejoices with His friends. Some of My servants have indeed won great visible victories and are rightly loved and reverenced by other men, but always their greatest victories are like the wild flowers, those which no one knows about. Learn this lesson now, down here in the valley, Much-Afraid, and when you get to the steep places of the mountains it will comfort you.'

Then He added 'Come, the birds are all singing so joyously, let us join them too, and the flowers shall suggest the theme of our song.' So, as they walked down the Valley towards the river, they sang together another of the old songs in the Shepherd's book, singing the parts in turn.

> I am the rose of Sharon,
>   A wild anemone.
> As lily 'mong the thorn trees
>   So is My love to Me.
>
> An apple tree 'mong wild trees,
>   My Love is in my sight,
> I sit down in His shadow,
>   His fruit is my delight.
>
> He brought me to His palace,
>   And to the banquet hall,
> To share with me His greatness,
>   I, who am least of all.
>
> Oh, give me help and comfort,
>   For I am sick with shame,
> Unfit to be His consort,
>   Unfit to bear His Name.
>
> I charge you, O ye daughters,
>   Ye roes among the trees,
> Stir not my sleeping loved one,
>   To love me e'er He please.

(Cant. 2:1–4, 7)

Just as they finished singing this song they came to a place where a rushing stream poured itself across the path they were following and went cascading down the other side. It was running so swiftly and singing so loudly that it seemed to fill the valley around them with its laughing voice.

As the Shepherd lifted Much-Afraid across the slippery, wet stones she said to Him, "I do wish I knew what it is that all running water sings. Sometimes in the silence of the night I lie in bed and listen to the voice of the little stream which runs past our cottage garden. It sounds so happy and so eager, and as though it were repeating to itself over and over again some very lovely, secret message. I think all running water seems to be singing the same song, either loud and clear or soft and low. I do wish I knew what the waters were saying. It is quite different to the voice of the sea and of salt waters, but I never can understand it. It is in an unknown tongue. Tell me, Shepherd, do YOU know what all the waters sing as they hurry on their way?"

The Shepherd smiled again, and they stood silently for a few moments by the little torrent, which seemed to shout even more loudly and exultantly as though it knew they had paused to listen. Suddenly, as Much-Afraid stood beside the Shepherd, it seemed as though her ears and her understanding were open, and bit by bit the water-language became clear. It is, of course, impossible to write it in water-language, but this is the best I can do to translate it. Of course, it is a very poor effort, for though a water song perhaps may be set to music, words are quite a different matter. But it went something like this:

THE WATER SONG

Come, oh come! let us away—
Lower, lower every day,
Oh, what joy it is to race

Down to find the lowest place.
This the dearest law we know—
'It is happy to go low.'
  Sweetest urge and sweetest will,
  'Let us go down lower still.'

Hear the summons night and day,
Calling us to come away.
From the heights we leap and flow
To the valleys down below.
Always answering to the call,
To the lowest place of all.
  Sweetest urge and sweetest pain,
  To go low and rise again.

'That is very puzzling,' said Much-Afraid, after she had listened for a little and found that this was the refrain, repeated over and over again, though with a thousand variations of little trills and murmurs and bubbles and splashing sighs. ' "Let us go down lower still", the water seems to be singing so gladly, because it is hurrying to go down to the lowest place, and yet You are calling me to the Highest Places. What does it mean?'

'The High Places,' answered the Shepherd, 'are the *starting places* for the journey down to the lowest place in the world. When you have hinds' feet and can go "leaping on the mountains and skipping on the hills", you will be able, as I am, to run down from the heights in gladdest self-giving and then go up to the mountains again. You will be able to mount to the High Places swifter than eagles, for it is only up on the High Places of Love that anyone can receive the power to pour themselves down in an utter abandonment of self-giving.'

This saying seemed very mysterious and strange, but now that her ears had been opened to understand the water song, she heard it repeated over and over again by all the little streams which crossed their pathway or ran beside it. It seemed, too, that the wild flowers were also singing the same sort of song, only in yet another language, a colour language, which like the water tongue, could only be understood by the heart and not by the mind. They seemed to have a little chorus, all their own, which thousands upon thousands of them were singing in different colour notes.

> This is the law by which we live—
> It is so sweet to give and give.

After that it seemed to Much-Afraid that all the little birds were chirping and trilling and lilting a tiny theme song also, with unnumbered variations, but still with one chorus breaking in all the time.

> This is the joy of all winged life above
> Happy it is to be able to love.

'I never knew before,' said Much-Afraid suddenly, 'that the Valley is such a beautiful place and so full of song.'

The Shepherd laughed and answered, 'Only Love can really understand the music and the beauty and the joy which was planted in the heart of all created things. Have you forgotten that two days ago I planted the seed of Love in your heart? Already it has begun to make you hear and see things which you did not notice before. As Love grows in you, Much-Afraid, you will come to understand many things which you never dreamed of before. You will develop the gift of understanding many "unknown tongues" and you will learn to speak Love's own language too, but first you must learn to spell out the alphabet of Love and to develop hinds' feet. Both these things you will learn on the journey to the High Places, and now here we are at the river, and over on the other side the foothills of the mountains begin. There we shall find your two guides waiting for you.'

It was strange and wonderful indeed, thought Much-Afraid, that they had reached the river so quickly and were already approaching the mountains. Upheld by the Shepherd's hand and supported by His strength, she had really forgotten her lameness and had been unconscious of either tiredness or weakness. Oh, if only He would take her the whole way to the mountain places, instead of giving her over to the care of other guides.

When she thought of this, she said to Him imploringly, 'Will you not take me all the way? When I am with You I am strong and I am sure no one else but You can get me up to the High Places.'

He looked at her most kindly, but answered quietly, 'Much-Afraid, I could do what you wish. I could carry you all the way up to the High Places Myself, instead of leaving you to climb there. But if I did, you would never be able to develop hinds' feet, and become My companion and go where I go. If you will climb to the heights this once with the companions I have chosen for you, even though it may seem a very long and in some places a very difficult journey, I promise you that you will develop hinds' feet.

'Afterwards you will be able to go with me, "leaping on the mountains" and be able to make the ascent and the descent in the twinkling of an eye. Moreover, if I carry you up to the High Places now, with only a tiny seed of Love in your heart, you will not be able to live in the Kingdom of Love. You will have to stay outside on places not so high, still within reach of your enemies. Some of them, you know, can visit the lower parts of the mountain. I have no doubt that you will meet them as you make the ascent. That is why I have most carefully chosen for you two of the very best and strongest guides. I assure you, however, that never for a moment shall I be beyond your reach or call for help, even when you cannot see Me. It is just as though I shall be present with you all the time, even though invisible. And you have My faithful promise that this journey which you are now to make will be the means of developing your hinds' feet.'

'You *will* give me a new name when I get to the top?' quavered poor Much-Afraid, who all of a sudden seemed to have become deaf to the music around her and to be full of fears and forbodings again.

'Yes, certainly. When the flower of Love is ready to bloom in your heart, you will be loved in return and will receive a new name,' replied the Shepherd.

Much-Afraid paused on the bridge and looked back over the way they had come. The Valley looked very green and peaceful, while the mountains to whose foot they had come towered above them like gigantic and threatening ramparts. Far away in the distance she could see the trees growing around the village of Much-Trembling, and with a sudden pang she pictured the Shepherd's helpers going about their happy work, the flocks wandering over the pastures and the peaceful little white cottage in which she had lived.

As these scenes rose before her, tears began to prick in her eyes and the thorn pricked in her heart, but almost at once she turned to the Shepherd and said thankfully, 'I *will* trust You and do whatever You want.'

Then, as she looked up in His face, He smiled most sweetly and said something He had never said before 'You have one real beauty, Much-Afraid, you have such trustful eyes. Trust is one of the most beautiful things in the world. When I look at the trust in your eyes I find you more beautiful to look upon than many a lovely queen.'

In a very short time they were over the bridge and had come to the foot of the mountains, where the path began the ascent of the lower slopes. Here great boulders were scattered all around, and suddenly Much-Afraid saw the figures of two veiled women seated on one of the rocks at the side of the path. As the Shepherd and she came up to that place, the two rose and bowed silently to Him.

'Here are the two guides which I promised,' said the Shepherd quietly. 'From now on until you are over the steep and difficult places, they will be your companions and helpers.'

Much-Afraid looked at them fearfully. Certainly they were tall and appeared to be very strong, but why were they veiled? For what reason did they hide their faces? The longer and closer she looked at them, the more she began to dread them. They were so silent, so strong, and so mysterious. Why did they not speak? Why give her no friendly word of greeting?

'Who are they?' she whispered to the Shepherd. 'Will you tell me their names, and why don't they speak to me? Are they dumb?'

'No, they are not dumb,' said the Shepherd very quietly, 'but they speak a new language, Much-Afraid, a dialect of the mountains which you have not yet learnt. But as you travel with them, little by little, you will learn to understand their words. They are good teachers; indeed, I have few better. As for their names, I will tell you them in your own language, and later you will learn what they are called in their own tongue. This,' said He, motioning towards the first of the silent figures, 'is named Sorrow. And the other is her twin sister, Suffering.'

Poor Much-Afraid! Her cheeks blanched and she began to tremble from head to foot. She felt so like fainting that she clung to the Shepherd for support.

'I can't go with them,' she gasped. 'I can't! I can't! O my Lord Shepherd, why do You do this to me? How can I travel in their company? It is more than I can bear. You tell me that the mountain way itself is so steep and difficult that I cannot climb it alone. Then why, oh why, must You make Sorrow and Suffering my companions? Couldn't You have given Joy and Peace to go with me, to strengthen me and encourage me and help me on the difficult way? I never thought You would do this to me!' and she burst into tears.

A strange look passed over the Shepherd's face as He listened to this outburst, then, looking at the veiled figures as He spoke, He answered very gently, 'Joy and Peace. Are those the companions you would choose for yourself? You remember your promise, to accept the helpers that I would give, because you believed that I would choose the very best possible guides for you. Will you still trust Me, Much-Afraid? Will you go with them, or do you wish to turn back to the Valley, and to all your Fearing relatives, to Craven Fear himself?'

Much-Afraid shuddered. The choice seemed terrible. Fear she knew only too well, but Sorrow and Suffering had always seemed to her the two most terrifying things which she could encounter. How could she go with them and abandon herself to their power and control? It was impossible. Then she looked at the Shepherd and suddenly knew she could not doubt Him, could not possibly turn back from following Him; that if she were unfit and unable to love anyone else in the world, yet in her trembling, miserable little heart, she *did* love Him. Even if He asked the impossible, she could not refuse.

She looked at Him piteously, then said, 'Do I wish to turn back? O Shepherd, to whom should I go? In all the world I have no one but You. Help me to follow You, even though it seems impossible. Help me to trust You as much as I long to love You.'

As He heard these words the Shepherd suddenly lifted His head and laughed—a laugh full of exultation and triumph and delight. It echoed round the rocky walls of the little canyon in which they stood until for a moment or two it seemed as though the whole mountain range was laughing with Him. The echoes bounded higher and higher, leaping from rock to rock, and from crag to crag, up to the highest summits, until it seemed as though the last faint echoes of it were running into heaven itself.

When the last note had faded into silence, His voice said very softly, 'Thou art all fair, My love; there is no spot in thee' (Cant. 4:7). Then He added, 'Fear not, Much-Afraid, only believe. I promise that you shall not be put to shame. Go with Sorrow and Suffering, and if you cannot welcome them now, when you come to the difficult places where you cannot manage alone, put your hands in theirs confidently and they will take you exactly where I want you to go.'

Much-Afraid stood quite still, looking up into His face, which now had such a happy, exultant look, the look of One who above all things else delights in saving and delivering. In her heart the words of a hymn, written by another of the Shepherd's followers, began to run through her mind and she started to sing softly and sweetly:

> Let Sorrow do its work, send grief or pain;
> Sweet are Thy messengers, sweet their refrain.
> If they but work in me, more love O Christ to Thee,
> More love to Thee, more love to Thee.

'Others have gone this way before me,' she thought, 'and they could even sing about it afterwards. Will He who is so strong and gentle be less faithful and gracious to me, weak and cowardly though I am, when it is so obvious that the thing He delights in most of all is to deliver His followers from all their fears and to take them to the High Places?' With this came the thought that the sooner she went with these new guides, the sooner she would reach those glorious High Places.

She stepped forward, looking at the two veiled figures, and said with a courage which she had never felt before, 'I will go with you. Please lead the way,' for even then she could not bring herself to put out her hands to grasp theirs.

The Shepherd laughed again and then said clearly, 'My Peace I leave with you. My Joy be fulfilled in you. Remember that I pledge Myself to bring you to the High Places at the top of these mountains and that you shall not be put to shame and now "till the day break and the shadows flee away, I will be like a roe or a young hart on the mountains" ' (Cant. 2:17).

Then before Much-Afraid could realise what was happening, He had leapt on to a great rock at the side of the path and from there to another and to yet another, swifter almost than her eyes could follow His movements. He was leaping up the mountains, springing from height to height, going on before them until in a moment or two He was lost to sight. When they could see Him no longer, Much-Afraid and her two new companions began to ascend the foothills. It would have been a curious sight, had there been anyone to watch, as Much-Afraid started on her journey, limping towards the High Places, shrinking as far as possible from the two veiled figures beside her, pretending not to see their proffered hands. But there was no one there to see, for if there is one thing more certain than another, it is that the development of hinds' feet is a secret process, demanding that there should be *no onlookers.*

CHAPTER V

THE ENCOUNTER WITH PRIDE

FROM the very beginning the way up the mountains proved to be steeper than anything Much-Afraid had supposed herself capable of tackling, and it was not very long before she was forced to seek the help of her companions. Each time she shrinkingly took hold of the hand of either Sorrow or Suffering a pang went through her, but once their hands were grasped she found they had amazing strength, and seemed able to pull and even lift her upwards and over places which she would have considered utterly impossible to reach. Indeed, without their aid they *would* have been impossible, even for a strong and sure-footed person.

It was not very long, too, before she began to realise how much she needed their help in another way, for it was not only the steepness of the climb and her own lameness and weakness which made the journey difficult. To her surprise and distress she found there were enemies to meet on the way who would certainly have succeeded in making her turn back had she been alone. To explain this we must now go back to the Valley of Humiliation and see what was happening there. Great was the wrath and consternation of the whole Fearing clan when it was discovered that Much-Afraid had made her escape from the Valley and had actually gone off to the mountains in the company of the Shepherd they so much hated. So long as she had been just ugly, crippled, and miserable little Much-Afraid, her relatives had cared nothing about her. Now they found it quite intolerable that of them all she alone should be singled out in this way and be taken to live on the High Places. Perhaps she would be given service in the palace of the great King Himself.

Who was Much-Afraid that this should happen to her while the rest of the family drudged away in the Valley of Humiliation? It was not that they wanted to go to the mountains themselves, far be it, but it was intolerable that Much-Afraid should do so. So it happened that instead of being a little nobody in the eyes of her relatives, Much-Afraid had suddenly become the central figure in their interest and thought. Not only was her own immediate circle of Fearing relatives concerned about the matter but all her more distant connections as well. Indeed, the whole population of the Valley, apart from the King's own servants, were angered by her departure, and determined that by some means she *must* be brought back and the hated Shepherd be robbed of His success in filching her from them.

A great consultation went on between all the more influential relatives, and ways and means discussed by which she could be captured most effectively and be brought back to the Valley as a permanent slave. Finally, it was agreed that someone must be sent after her as quickly as possible in order to force her to return. But they could not conceal from themselves that force might prove impossible, as apparently she had put herself under the protection of the Great Shepherd. Some means, then, would have to be found to beguile her into leaving Him of her own free will. How could this be accomplished?

In the end it was unanimously decided to send a distant connection of the family named Pride. The choice fell on him for several reasons. First, he was not only very strong and powerful but was also a handsome young man, and, when he chose, could be extremely attractive. It was emphasised that if other means proved unsuccessful he was to feel no scruples against exerting all his powers of fascination in order to coax Much-Afraid away from the Shepherd. Besides, it was a well-known fact that the young man was by nature far too proud to admit defeat or lack of success in any undertaking, and that there would be no giving up on his part until he accomplished his purpose. As everybody knew, to confess defeat and return without Much-Afraid would be the last thing possible to Pride, so when he consented to undertake the task it was felt that the matter was as good as settled.

Much-Afraid and her two companions therefore had only been a few days upon their journey and had made but slow though steady progress, when one morning, on turning a corner of the rocky pathway, Pride was seen striding towards them. She was certainly surprised and discomforted at this unexpected apparition, but not unduly alarmed. This cousin had always so disdained and ignored her very existence that at first it never occurred to her that he would even speak to her, but expected to see him pass by in the same haughty manner as usual.

Pride himself, who had been skulking and spying for several hours before he showed himself, was on his part delighted to find that though Much-Afraid seemed to be travelling in the care of two strong companions, yet the Shepherd Himself apparently was not with her. He approached her therefore quite confidently but

with a most unusual affability of manner, and to Much-Afraid's
great surprise stopped when they met, and greeted her.

'Well, Cousin Much-Afraid, here you are at last. I have had
such ado to catch up with you.'

'How do you do, Cousin Pride?' said that poor little simpleton.
Much-Afraid, of course, ought to have known better than to greet,
much less to stop and talk with one of her own relatives from the
Valley. But it is rather pleasant, after being snubbed and ignored
for years suddenly to be greeted as an equal. Besides this, her
curiosity was awakened. Of course, had it been that awful and
detestable Craven, nothing would have induced her to stop and
speak with him.

'Much-Afraid,' said Pride seriously, actually taking her hand in
a kindly and friendly manner (it so happened that at that place the
path was not quite so steep and she had freed her hands from those
of both Sorrow and Suffering). 'I have made this journey on purpose to try to help you. I do beg you to allow me to do so and to
listen very attentively and seriously. My dear cousin, you must give
up this extraordinary journey and come back with me to the Valley. You don't realise the true position in which you have put yourself, nor the dreadful future before you. The one who has
persuaded you to start on this improper journey' (Pride could not
bring himself even to mention the Shepherd by name) 'is well
known to have seduced other helpless victims in this same way.
Do you know what will happen to you, Much-Afraid, if you persist in going forward? All those fair promises He has made, about
bringing you into His Kingdom and making you live happily ever
afterwards, will prove false. When He gets you up to the wild, desolate parts of the mountains He will abandon you altogether, and
you will be put to lasting shame.'

Much-Afraid tried to pull her hand away, for now she began to understand the meaning of his presence there and his bitter hatred of the Shepherd, but as she struggled to free her hand, he only grasped it tighter. She had to learn that once Pride is listened to, struggle as one may, it is the hardest thing in the world to throw him off. She hated the things that he said, but with her hand grasped in his they had the power to sound horribly plausible and true. Did she not often find herself in her heart of hearts thrusting back the same idea and possibility which Pride was suggesting to her? Even if the Shepherd did not abandon her (and *that* she could not believe), might it not be that He who did allow Sorrow and Suffering to be her companions, would also allow her (for her soul's good, of course) to be put to shame before all her relatives and connections? Was she not almost certainly exposing herself to ridicule? Who could know what the Shepherd might allow her to go through (for her ultimate good, perhaps, but quite unbearable to contemplate). It is a terrible thing to let Pride take one by the hand, Much-Afraid suddenly discovered; his suggestions are so frightfully strong, and through the contact of touch he can press them home with almost irresistible force.

'Come back, Much-Afraid,' he urged vehemently. 'Give it up before it is too late. In your heart of hearts you know that what I am saying is true and that you WILL be put to shame before everybody. Give it up while there is still time. Is a merely fictitious promise of living on the High Places worth the cost you are asked to pay for it? What is it that you seek there in that mythological Kingdom above?'

Entirely against her will, and simply because he seemed to have her at his mercy, Much-Afraid let the words be dragged out of her. 'I am seeking the Kingdom of Love,' she said faintly.

'I thought as much,' sneered Pride. 'Seeking your heart's desire, eh? And now, Much-Afraid, have a little pride, ask yourself honestly, are you not so ugly and deformed that nobody even in the Valley really loves you? That is the brutal truth. Then how much less will you be welcome in the Kingdom of Love, where they say nothing but unblemished beauty and perfection is admitted? Can you really expect to find what you are seeking? No, I tell you again that you feel this yourself and you know it. Then be honest at least and give it up. Turn back with me before it is too late.'

Poor Much-Afraid! The urge to turn back seemed almost irresistible, but at that moment when she stood held in the clutch of Pride, feeling as though every word he spoke was the hideous truth, she had an inner vision of the face of the Shepherd. She remembered the look with which He had promised her, 'I pledge Myself to bring you there, and that you shall not be put to shame.' Then it was as though she heard Him again, repeating softly, as though looking at some radiant vision in the distance:

> Behold, thou art fair, My love; thou hast dove's eyes.
> Thou art all fair, My love; there is no spot in thee.

Before Pride could realise what was happening, Much-Afraid uttered a desperate cry for help and was calling up the mountain, 'Come to me, Shepherd! Come quickly! Make no tarrying, O my Lord.'

There was a sound of loose, rattling stones and of a prodigious leap, and the next moment the Shepherd was on the path beside them, His face terrible to look at, His Shepherd's staff raised high above His head. Only one blow fell, and then Pride dropped the hand he had been grasping so tightly and made off down the path and round the corner, slipping and stumbling on the stones as he went, and was out of sight in a moment.

'Much-Afraid,' said the Shepherd, in a tone of gentle but firm rebuke, 'why did you let Pride come up to you and take your hand? If you had been holding the hands of your two helpers this could never have happened.'

For the first time, Much-Afraid of her own free will held out both hands to her two companions, and they grasped her strongly, but never before had their hold upon her been so full of pain, so bitter with sorrow. She learnt in this way the first important lesson of her journey upward, that if one stops to parley with Pride and listens to his poisonous suggestions and, above all, if he is allowed to lay his grasp upon any part of one, Sorrow becomes unspeakably more unbearable afterwards and anguish of heart has bitterness added to it. Moreover, for a while she limped more painfully than ever she had since leaving the Valley. Pride had trodden on her feet at the moment she called for help and left them more lame and sore than ever.

CHAPTER VI

THE DETOUR THROUGH THE DESERT

AFTER meeting Pride, Much-Afraid and her companions went on their way, but she was obliged to hobble painfully and could go but slowly. However, she accepted the assistance of her two guides with far greater willingness than before, and gradually the effects of the encounter wore off and she was able to make better progress. Then one day the path turned a corner, and to her amazement and consternation she saw a great plain spread out beneath them. As far as the eye could see there seemed to be nothing but desert, an endless expanse of sand dunes, with not a tree in sight. The only objects breaking the monotony of the desert were strange, towering pyramids, rising above the sand dunes, hoary with age and grimly desolate. To the horror of Much-Afraid her two guides prepared to take the steep path downwards.

She stopped dead and said to them, 'We *mustn't* go down there. The Shepherd has called me to the High Places. We must find some path which goes up, but certainly not down there.' But they made signs to her that she was to follow them down the steep pathway to the desert below.

Much-Afraid looked to left and right, but though it seemed incredible, there was no way possible by which they could continue to climb upward. The hill they were on ended abruptly at this precipice, and the rocky cliffs towered above them in every direction straight as walls with no possible foothold.

'I can't go down there,' panted Much-Afraid, sick with shock and fear. 'He can never mean that—never! He called me up to the High Places, and this is an absolute contradiction of all that He promised.' She then lifted up her voice and called desperately, 'Shepherd, come to me. Oh, I need You. Come and help me.'

In a moment He was there, standing beside her.

'Shepherd,' she said despairingly, 'I can't understand this. The guides You gave me say that we must go down there into that desert, turning right away from the High Places altogether. You don't mean that, do You? You can't contradict Yourself. Tell them we are not to go there, and show us another way. *Make a way* for us, Shepherd, as You promised.'

He looked at her and answered very gently, 'That *is* the path, Much-Afraid, and you *are* to go down there.'

'Oh, no,' she cried. 'You can't mean it. You said if I would trust You, You would bring me to the High Places, and that path leads right away from them. It contradicts all that You promised.'

'No,' said the Shepherd, 'it is not contradiction, *only postponement for the best to become possible.*'

Much-Afraid felt as though He had stabbed her to the heart. 'You mean,' she said incredulously, 'You really mean that I am to follow that path down and down into that wilderness and then over that desert, away from the mountains indefinitely? Why' (and there was a sob of anguish in her voice) 'it may be months, even years, before that path leads back to the mountains again. O Shepherd, do You mean it is indefinite postponement?'

He bowed His head silently, and Much-Afraid sank on her knees at His feet, almost overwhelmed. He was leading her away from her heart's desire altogether, and gave no promise at all as to when He would bring her back. As she looked out over what seemed an endless desert, the only path she could see led farther and farther away from the High Places, and it was all desert.

Then He answered very quietly, 'Much-Afraid, do you love Me enough to accept the postponement and the apparent contradiction of the promise, and to go down there with Me into the desert?'

She was still crouching at His feet, sobbing as if her heart would break, but now she looked up through her tears, caught His hand in hers, and said tremblingly, 'I *do* love You, You know that I love you. Oh, forgive me because I can't help my tears. I *will* go down with You into the wilderness, right away from the promise, if You really wish it. Even if You cannot tell me why it has to be, I *will* go with You, for You know I *do* love You, and You have the right to choose for me anything that You please.'

It was very early morning, and high above them, hanging in the sky over the silent expanse of desert, was a young crescent moon and the morning star shining like a brilliant jewel close beside it. There Much-Afraid built her first altar on the mountains, a little pile of broken rocks, and then, with the Shepherd standing close beside her, she laid down on the altar her trembling, rebelling will. A little spurt of flame came from somewhere, and in an instant nothing but a heap of ashes was lying on the altar. That is to say, she thought at first there were only ashes, but the Shepherd told her to look closer, and there among the ashes she saw a little stone of some kind, a dark-coloured, com-mon-looking pebble.

'Pick it up and take it with you,' said the Shepherd gently, 'as a memorial of this altar which you built, and all that it stands for.'

Much-Afraid took the stone out of the ashes, scarcely looking at it and feeling that to her life's end she would never need a reminder of that altar, for how could she ever forget it or the anguish of that first surrender, but she dropped the pebble into a little purse or bag which the Shepherd gave her and put it away carefully. Then they began the descent into the desert, and at the first step Much-Afraid felt a thrill of the sweetest joy and comfort surge through her, for she found that the Shepherd Himself was going down with them. She would not have Sorrow and Suffering as her only companions, but He was there too. As she started down the path He began a song which Much-Afraid had not heard before, and it sounded so sweet and comforting that her pain began to melt away. It was as though the song suggested to her a part at least of the reason for this strange postponement of all her hopes. This is the song He sang,

THE CLOSED GARDEN

A garden closed art thou, My love,
    Where none thy fruits can taste,
A spring shut up, a fountain sealed,
    An orchard run to waste.

Awake, north wind! and come, thou south!
    Blow on My garden fair,
That all the spices may flow out
    As perfume on the air.

(Cant. 4:12–16)

They reached the desert surprisingly quickly, because, although the path was very steep indeed, Much-Afraid was leaning on the Shepherd, and did not feel her weakness at all. By the evening of that same day they were down on the pale sand dunes and walking towards some huts built in the shadow of one of the great pyramids, where they were to rest that night. At sunset, when the sky burned fiery red over the western rim of the desert, the Shepherd led Much-Afraid away from the huts, to the foot of the pyramid.

'Much-Afraid,' He said, 'all My servants on their way to the High Places have had to make this detour through the desert. It is called "The furnace of Egypt, and an horror of great darkness" (Gen. 15:12, 17). Here they have learnt many things which otherwise they would have known nothing about. Abraham was the first of My servants to come this way, and this pyramid was hoary with age when *he* first looked upon it. Then came Joseph, with tears and anguish of heart, and looked upon it too and learnt the lesson of the furnace of fire. Since that time an endless succession of My people have come this way. They came to learn the secret of royalty, and now you are here, Much-Afraid. You, too, are in the line of succession. It is a great privilege, and if you will, you also may learn the lesson of the furnace and of the great darkness just as surely as did those before you. Those who come down to the furnace go on their way afterwards as royal men and women, princes and princesses of the Royal line.'

Much-Afraid looked up at the towering pyramid, now shadowy and black against the sunset sky, and desolate as it looked in the waste of desert, yet it seemed to her to be one of the most majestic objects she had ever seen. Then all of a sudden the desert was full of people, an endless procession of them. There was Abraham himself and Sarah his wife, those first lonely exiles in a strange land; there was Joseph, the betrayed and wounded brother who had been sold into slavery, who when he wept for his father's tent, saw only the alien pyramid. Then one after another she saw a great host which no man could number stretching across the desert in an endless line. The last one in the line held out a hand which she took, and there she was in the great chain herself. Words came to her ears also, and she heard them quite plainly.

'Fear not, Much-Afraid, to go down into Egypt; for I will there make of *thee* a great nation; *I will go down with thee* into Egypt; *and I will also surely bring thee up again*' (Gen. 46:3).

After this they went back to the huts to rest that night. In the morning the Shepherd called Much-Afraid again and led her away, but this time He opened a little door in the wall of the pyramid and took her inside. There was a passage which led to the centre, and from there a spiral staircase went up to the floors above. But the Shepherd opened another door leading out of the central chamber on the ground floor and they entered a very large room which looked like a granary. There were great piles of grain everywhere except in the middle. There on the open space men were threshing the different kinds of grain in many different ways and then grinding them to powder, some coarse and some finer. At one side were women sitting on the ground with hollow smooth stones before them, grinding the very best of the wheat into the finest possible powder.

Watching them for a while, Much-Afraid saw how the grains were first beaten and bruised until they crumbled to pieces, but still the grinding and beating process continued, until at last the powder was fine enough to be used for baking the best wheaten bread.

'See,' said the Shepherd gently, 'how various are the methods used for grinding the different varieties of grain, according to their special use and purpose.' Then He quoted, 'The fitches are not threshed with a threshing instrument, neither is a cart wheel turned about upon the cummin; but the fitches are beaten out with a staff, and the cummin with a rod. Bread corn is bruised, but no one crushes it for ever; neither is it broken with the wheel of a cart nor bruised with horsemen driving over it' (Isa. 28:27, 28).

As Much-Afraid watched the women pounding the bread corn with their heavy stones she noticed how long the process took before the fine white powder was finished and ready for use. Then she heard the Shepherd saying, 'I bring My people into Egypt that they, too, may be threshed and ground into the finest powder and may become bread corn for the use of others. But remember, though bread corn *is* bruised, no one threshes it for ever; only until the bruised and broken grain is ready for its highest use. This also cometh forth from the Lord of Hosts, which is wonderful in counsel and excellent in working' (v. 29).

After this the Shepherd took her back to the central chamber and they ascended the spiral staircase, twisting up and up into the darkness above. There, on the next floor, they came to another and smaller room, in the centre of which stood a great wheel, flat, like a table. Beside it stood a potter who wrought a work on the wheel. As he spun the wheel he fashioned his clay into many beautiful shapes and objects. The material was cut and kneaded and shaped as he saw fit, but always the clay lay still upon the wheel, submitting to his every touch, perfectly unresisting.

As they watched, the Shepherd said, 'In Egypt, too, I fashion My fairest and finest vessels and bring forth instruments for My work, according as I see fit' (Jer. 18). Then He smiled and added,

'Cannot I do with you, Much-Afraid, as this potter? Behold, as the clay is in the hand of the potter so are you in My hand' (Jer. 18:6).

Last of all He took her up the stairway to the highest floor. There they found a room with a furnace in which gold was being smelted and refined of all its dross. Also in the furnace were rough pieces of stone and rock containing crystals. These were put in the great heat of the oven and left for a time. On being taken out, behold, they were glorious jewels, flashing as though they had received the fire into their very hearts. As Much-Afraid stood beside the Shepherd, looking shrinkingly into the fire, He said the loveliest thing of all.

'O thou afflicted, tossed with tempest, and not comforted, behold, I will lay *thy* stones with fair colours, and lay thy foundations with sapphires. And I will make thy windows of agates, and thy gates of carbuncles, and all thy borders of pleasant stones' (Isa. 54:11). Then He added, 'My rarest and choicest jewels and my finest gold are those who have been refined in the furnace of Egypt,' and He sang one verse of a little song:

> I'll turn my hands upon thy heart,
>> And purge away thy dross,
> I will refine thee in My fire,
>> Remake thee at My cross.

They stayed at the huts in the desert for several days, and Much-Afraid learnt many things which she had never heard before.

One thing, however, made a special impression upon her. In all that great desert there was not a single green thing growing, neither tree nor flower nor plant, save here and there a patch of straggly grey cacti. On the last morning she was walking near the tents and huts of the desert dwellers, when in a lonely corner behind a wall she came upon a little golden-yellow flower, growing all alone. An old pipe was connected with a water tank. In the pipe was one tiny hole through which came an occasional drop of water. Where the drops fell one by one, there grew the little golden flower, though where the seed had come from, Much-Afraid could not imagine, for there were no birds anywhere and no other growing things. She stooped over the lonely, lovely little golden face, lifted up so hopefully and so bravely to the feeble drip, and cried out softly, 'What is your name, little flower, for I never saw one like you before.'

The tiny plant answered at once in a tone as golden as itself, 'Behold me! My name is Acceptance-with-Joy.'

Much-Afraid thought of the things which she had seen in the pyramid: the threshing-floor and the whirring wheel and the fiery furnace. Somehow the answer of the little golden flower which grew all alone in the waste of the desert stole into her heart and echoed there faintly but sweetly, filling her with comfort. She said to herself, 'He has brought me here when I did not want to come for His own purpose. I, too, will look up into His face and say, "Behold me! I am Thy little handmaiden Acceptance-with-Joy." ' Then she stooped down and picked up a pebble which was lying in the sand beside the flower and put it in the purse with the first altar stone.

CHAPTER VII

ON THE SHORES OF LONELINESS

AFTER that they walked together through the burning desert sands, then one day, quite unexpectedly, a path crossed the main track which they were following. 'This,' said the Shepherd quietly, 'is the path which you are now to follow.' So they turned westward with the High Places right behind their backs and came in a little while to the end of the desert. They found themselves on the shore of a great sea.

'It is now time for Me to leave you, Much-Afraid,' He said, 'and to return to the mountains.' Remember, even though you seem to be farther away than ever from the High Places and from Me, there is really no distance at all separating us. I can cross the desert sands as swiftly as I can leap from the High Places to the valleys, and whenever you call for Me, I shall come. This is the word I now leave with you. Believe it and practise it with joy. MY SHEEP HEAR MY VOICE, AND THEY FOLLOW ME.

'Whenever you are willing to obey Me, Much-Afraid, and to follow the path of My choice, you will always be able to hear and recognise My voice, and when you hear it you must always obey.

Remember also that *it is always safe to obey My voice*, even if it seems to call you to paths which look impossible or even crazy.' On saying this He blessed her and went from them, leaping and bounding over the desert towards the High Places, which were now actually right behind her.

Much-Afraid and her two companions walked along the shores of the great sea for many days, and at first it seemed to her that up till then she had never known real loneliness. The green valley where all her friends and she had lived was far away behind her. Even the mountains were out of sight, and there seemed to be nothing in the whole wide world but the endless sandy desert on one side and the endless sea moaning drearily on the other. Nothing grew there, neither tree nor shrub nor even grass, but the shores were scattered with broken driftwood and with great tangled masses of brown and shrivelled seaweed. Nothing lived in the whole region save the sea-gulls wheeling and crying overhead and the crabs scuttling across the sand into their burrows. At intervals, too, an icy wind came shrilling across the billows, stabbing sharp as a knife.

In those days Much-Afraid never let go the hands of her two companions, and it was amazing how swiftly they helped her along. Stranger still, perhaps, was the way in which Much-Afraid walked, swifter and more upright than ever before, and with scarcely a limp, for something had happened in the wilderness which had left a mark upon her for the rest of her life. It was an inner and secret mark, and no one would have noticed any difference outwardly, but all the same, a deep inner change had taken place which indicated a new stage in her life. She had been down into Egypt and had looked upon the grinding-stones, the wheel, and the furnace, and knew that they symbolised an experience which she herself must pass through. Somehow, incredible as it was, she, Much-Afraid, had been enabled to accept that knowledge and to acquiesce in it, and she knew within herself that with that acceptance a gulf had opened between herself and her past life, even between her past self; a gulf which could never again be closed. She could look back across it to the green valley between the mountains and see herself there with the Shepherd's workers, feeding her little flock, cringing before her relatives and going to the pool morning and evening to keep tryst with the Shepherd. But it was like looking at somebody else altogether, and she said to herself, '*I was that woman, but am not that woman now.*'

She did not understand how it happened, but what the Shepherd had said had come to pass in herself, for those who go down into the furnace of Egypt and find there the flower of Acceptance come up changed and with the stamp of royalty upon them. It is true that Much-Afraid did not feel at all royal, and certainly did not as yet look it. Nevertheless, she had been stamped with the mark, and would never be the same again. Therefore, though she went with Sorrow and Suffering day after day along the shores of the great sea of Loneliness, she did not go cringingly or complainingly. Indeed, gradually an impossible thing seemed to be happening. A new kind of joy was springing up in her heart, and she began to find herself noticing beauties in the landscape of which until then she had been quite unconscious. Her heart often thrilled with an inner ecstasy when she caught sight of the sun shining on the wings of the wheeling sea-gulls, making them gleam as dazzlingly white as the snow on the peaks of the far-off High Places. Even their wild, mournful cries and the moanings of the water stirred in her a sorrow which was strangely beautiful. She had the feeling that somehow, in the very far-off places, perhaps even in far-off ages, there would be a meaning found to all sorrow and an answer too fair and wonderful to be as yet understood.

Often, too, she found herself laughing aloud as she watched the antics of the funny little scuttling crabs. When the sun shone brightly, as it did at times, even the grey, dreary sea was transformed into a thing of surpassing beauty, with the light gleaming on the curving green breakers and the foaming spray and the horizon blue as a midnight sky. When the sun thus shone on the wild wastes of waters it seemed as though all their sorrows had been swallowed up in joy, and then she would whisper to herself, 'When He hath tried me I shall come forth as gold. Weeping may endure for a night, but joy cometh in the morning.'

One day they came to a place on the shore where were high cliffs and great rocks scattered all about. In this place they were to rest for a time, and while there Much-Afraid wandered off by herself. After climbing the cliff she found herself looking down into a lonely little cove completely enclosed on three sides by the cliffs and with nothing in it but drift-wood and stranded seaweed. The chief impression it made upon her was its emptiness. It seemed to lie there like an empty heart, watching and longing for the far-off tide which had receded to such a distance that it could never again return.

When, however, drawn by an urge to revisit the lonely cove, Much-Afraid went back to the same spot some hours later, all was changed. The waves were now rushing forward with the strength of a high tide urging them onwards. Looking over the edge of the cliff, she saw that the cove which had been so empty was now filled to the brim. Great waves, roaring and laughing together, were pouring themselves through the narrow inlet, and were leaping against the sides, irresistibly taking possession of every empty niche and crevice.

On seeing this transformation, she knelt down on the edge of the cliff and built her third altar. 'O my Lord,' she cried, 'I thank Thee for leading me here. Behold me, here I am, empty as was this little cove, but waiting Thy time to be filled to the brim with the flood-tide of Love.' Then she picked up a little piece of quartz and crystal which was lying on the rocky cliff and dropped it beside the other memorial stones in the little bag which she carried with her.

It was only a short time after the building of that new altar that her enemies were all upon her again. Far away in the Valley of Humiliation, her relatives had been awaiting the return of Pride with his victim, but as time passed and he did not return and Much-Afraid did not reappear it became obvious that he must have been unsuccessful in his undertaking and was too proud to admit it. They decided that reinforcements must be sent as soon as possible, before Much-Afraid could reach the really High Places and be altogether beyond their reach.

Spies were sent out, who met Pride and brought back word that Much-Afraid was nowhere on the mountains but was far away on the shores of the Sea of Loneliness. She was going in quite a different direction from the mountains altogether. This was unexpectedly delightful and encouraging news, and quickly suggested to them the best reinforcements to be sent to the help of Pride. There was complete unanimity in deciding that Resentment, Bitterness, and Self-Pity should hurry off at once to assist in bringing back Much-Afraid to her eagerly-awaiting relatives.

Off they went to the shores of Loneliness, and Much-Afraid now had to endure a time of really dreadful assaults. It is true that her enemies soon discovered that this was not the same Much-Afraid with whom they had to deal. They could never get within close reach, because she kept so near to Sorrow and Suffering and accepted their assistance so much more willingly than before. However, they kept appearing before her, shouting out their horrid suggestions and mocking her until it really seemed that wherever she went one or another popped up (there were so many hiding-places for them among the rocks) and hurled their darts at her.

'I told you so,' Pride would shout viciously. 'Where are you now, you little fool? Up on the High Places? Not much! Do you know that everyone in the Valley of Humiliation knows about this and is laughing at you? Seeking your heart's desire, eh, and left abandoned by Him (just as I warned you) on the Shores of Lone-liness. Why didn't you listen to me, you little fool?'

Then Resentment would raise his head over another rock. He was extremely ugly to look at, but his was a horribly fascinating ugliness. Sometimes Much-Afraid could hardly turn her eyes away when he stared at her boldly and shouted, 'You know, Much-Afraid, you act like a blind idiot. Who is this Shepherd you fol-low? What sort of a person is He to demand everything you have and take everything you offer and give nothing in return but suf-fering and sorrow and ridicule and shame? Why do you *let* Him treat you like this? Stand up for yourself and demand that he fulfil His promise and take you at once to the High Places. If not, tell Him that you feel absolved from all necessity to follow Him any longer.'

Bitterness would then break in with his sneering voice, 'The more you yield to Him, the more He will demand from you. He is cruel to you, and takes advantage of your devotion. All He has demanded from you so far is nothing to what He will demand if you persist in following Him. He lets His followers, yes, even women and children, go to concentration camps and torture chambers and hideous deaths of all kinds. Could you bear that, you little puling? Then you'd better pull out and leave Him before He demands the uttermost sacrifice of all. Sooner or later He'll put you on a cross of some sort and abandon you to it.'

Self-Pity would chime in next, and in some dreadful way he was almost worse than any of the others. He talked so softly and in such a pitying tone that Much-Afraid would feel weak all over. 'Poor little Much-Afraid,' he would whisper. 'It *is* too bad, you know. You really are so devoted, and you have refused Him nothing, absolutely nothing; yet this is the cruel way in which He treats you. Can you really believe when He acts towards you like this that He loves you and has your real good at heart? How can that be possible? You have every right to feel sorry for yourself. Even if you are perfectly willing to suffer for His sake, at least other people ought to know about it and pity you instead of misunderstanding and ridiculing as they do. It really seems as though the one you follow takes delight in making you suffer and leaving you to be misunderstood, for every time you yield to him he thinks up some new way of wounding and bruising you.'

That last remark of Self-Pity's was a mistake, because the word 'bruising' suddenly reminded Much-Afraid of what the Shepherd had said when they stood together on the threshing-floor in the Pyramid. *'Bread corn is bruised'*, He had said, 'but no one threshes it for ever, only till it is ready to be made bread for others. This also cometh forth from the Lord of Hosts who is wonderful in counsel and excellent in working' (Isa. 28:28, 29). When she thought of this, to Self-Pity's dismayed astonishment, Much-Afraid actually picked up a piece of rock and hurled it at him, and as he said afterwards to the other three in an aggrieved tone of voice, 'If I hadn't ducked and bolted like a hare it could have laid me out altogether, the little vixen!'

But it is exhausting to be assaulted day after day with suggestions like these, and while Sorrow and Suffering were holding her
hands, naturally Much-Afraid could not cover her ears, so her enemies were really able to give her a dreadful time. At last, things
came to a crisis. One day when her companions actually seemed to
be sleeping for a little while, Much-Afraid unwarily wandered off
alone. Not this time to her favourite spot looking down into the
little cove, but in a new direction, and she came to a place where
the cliffs jutted out into the sea, forming a very narrow peninsula,
which ended in a sheer precipice. When she reached the end of this
promontory she stood looking out over the endless expanse of sea,
and suddenly found to her horror all four of her enemies
approaching and closing in on her. That already she was becoming
a different person was then quite apparent, for instead of nearly
fainting with fright at their approach, although she did look very
pale and frightened, she actually seized a stone in each hand and,
putting her back against a great rock, prepared to resist them to the
limit of her strength. Fortunately the place was too narrow for all
four to approach together, but Pride put himself in front of the
others and stepped towards her holding a strong cudgel.

'You can put down those stones, Much-Afraid,' said he savagely.
'There are four of us here, and we mean to do as we please with
you now that you are in our power. You shall not only listen to us
but shall go with us.'

Much-Afraid lifted her face towards the seemingly empty sky,
and with all her strength called out, 'Come to my deliverance and
make no tarrying, O my Lord.'

To the horror of the four ruffians, there was the Shepherd Himself, leaping towards them along the narrow promontory more terrible than a great mountain stag with thrusting horns. Resentment,

Bitterness, and Self-Pity managed to hurl themselves flat on the ground and edge away as He bounded towards the place where Pride was just seizing hold of Much-Afraid. Catching him by the shoulders, the Shepherd spun him around, lifted him in the air, where he uttered a loud, despairing shriek, and then dropped him over the edge of the cliff into the sea.

'O Shepherd,' gasped Much-Afraid, shaking with relief and hope, 'thank you. Do you think Pride is really dead at last?'

'No,' said the Shepherd, 'it is most unlikely.' He glanced over the cliff as He spoke, and caught sight of Pride swimming like a fish towards the shore, and added, 'There he goes, but he has had a fall today which he will not forget, and I fancy he will limp for some time to come. As for the other three, they have made off into some hiding-place, and are not likely to trouble you again in the same way now that they realise that I am within call.'

'Shepherd,' asked Much-Afraid earnestly, 'tell me why I nearly got into Pride's clutches again, and why Resentment, Bitterness, and Self-Pity have been able to pester me for so long in this dreadful way. I did not call You before, because they never dared to come close to me or to make a real attack, but they have been lurking around all the time and making their horrible suggestions, and I couldn't get away from them. Why was it?'

'I think,' said the Shepherd gently, 'that lately the way seemed a little easier and the sun shone, and you came to a place where you could rest. You forgot for a while that you were my little handmaiden Acceptance-with-Joy and were beginning to tell yourself it really was time that I led you back to the mountains and up to the High Places. When you wear the weed of impatience in your heart instead of the flower Acceptance-with-Joy, you will always find your enemies get an advantage over you.'

Much-Afraid blushed. She knew how right He was in His diagnosis. It *had* been easier to accept the hard path and to be patient when the sea was grey and dull than now when the sun shone and everything else around looked bright and happy and satisfied. She put her hand in the Shepherd's and said sorrowfully, 'You are quite right. I *have* been thinking that You are allowing me to follow this path too long and that You were forgetting Your promise.' Then she added, looking steadfastly into His face, 'But I do tell You now with all my heart that You are my Shepherd whose voice I love to hear and obey, and that it is my joy to follow You. You choose, my Lord, and I will obey.'

The Shepherd stooped down and picked up a stone which was lying beside her feet and said smilingly, 'Put this in your bag with the other stones as a memorial of this day when for the first time you saw Pride toppled over before you, and of your promise that you will wait patiently until I give you your heart's desire.'

CHAPTER VIII

ON THE OLD SEA WALL

A FEW days had passed after the victory over Pride, and Much-Afraid and her companions were continuing their journey along the shore of the great sea. One morning the path unexpectedly turned inland again and they found themselves facing back over the desert in the direction of the mountains, although, of course, they were too far away to be visible. With a thrill of indescribable joy Much-Afraid saw that at last the path did actually run straight towards the east and that it would lead them back to the High Places. She dropped the hands of her two guides in order to clap her own, and gave a little skip of joy. No matter how great the distance between them and the mountains, now at last they were to go in the right direction. All three started back across the desert, but Much-Afraid could not wait for her guides, and actually ran on ahead as though she had never been lame at all.

Suddenly the path took another turn at right angles and went straight before her as far as she could see, not towards the mountains at all, but southwards again to where far ahead the desert seemed to end in some sort of hill country. Much-Afraid stood quite still, dumb with dismay and shock. Then she began to tremble all over. It could not be possible, no, it couldn't, that yet again the Shepherd was saying 'No', and turning her right away from the High Places. 'Hope deferred maketh the heart sick,' said the wise man of long ago, and how truly he spoke! Now she had been skipping and running so excitedly along the path towards the mountains that she had left Sorrow and Suffering quite behind, and while they were catching up with her she was standing quite alone at the place where the path turned away from the mountains.

Up from behind a sand dune close beside her rose the form of her enemy Bitterness. He did not come any nearer, having learnt a little more prudence, and was not going to make her call for the Shepherd if he could avoid it, but simply stood and looked at her and laughed and laughed again, the bitterest sound that Much-Afraid had heard in all her life. Then he said, as venomously as a viper, 'Why don't you laugh too, you little fool? You knew this would happen.' There he stood, uttering these awful bursts of laughter until it seemed that the whole desert was filled with the echoes of his mockery. Sorrow and her sister came up to Much-Afraid and stood by her side quite silently, and for a little while everything was swallowed up in pain and 'an horror of great darkness'. A sudden swirling wind shrieked over the desert and raised a storm of dust and sand which blinded them.

In the silence which succeeded the storm Much-Afraid heard her voice, low and trembling, but quite distinct, saying, 'My Lord, what dost Thou want to say to me? Speak—for Thy servant heareth.'

Next moment the Shepherd was standing beside her. 'Be of good cheer,' He said, 'it is I, be not afraid. Build Me another altar and lay down your whole will as a burnt offering.'

Obediently Much-Afraid raised a little heap of sand and loose stones, which was all that she could find in the desert and again laid down her will and said with tears (for Sorrow had stepped forward and knelt beside her), 'I delight to do Thy will, O my God.'

From somewhere, though they could not see the source, there came a spurt of flame which consumed the offering and left a little heap of ashes on the altar. Then came the Shepherd's voice. 'This further delay is not unto death, but for the glory of God; that the Son of God may be glorified.'

Another gust of wind sprang up and whirled the ashes away in every direction, and the only thing remaining on the altar was a rough, ordinary-looking stone which Much-Afraid picked up and put into the bag with the others. Then she rose to her feet, turned her face away from the mountains, and they all started southwards. The Shepherd went with them for a little way so that Resentment and Self-Pity, who were hiding close at hand awaiting an opportunity to attack, lay flat behind the sand dunes and were not seen at that time at all.

Presently they reached a place where the sea, which they had left behind when they turned inland, came sweeping into the desert, forming a great estuary. A strong tide was surging into it, filling it completely with swiftly-flowing waters. However, a stone causeway with many arches had been built across the estuary, and an earthen ramp led up to it. The Shepherd led Much-Afraid to the foot of the ramp and told her to follow this path across the sea. Once more He repeated with great emphasis the words which He had spoken beside the altar, then departed.

Much-Afraid, followed by her two companions, scrambled up the ramp and found themselves on top of the old sea wall. From the height on which they now stood they could look back over the

desert. On one side was the sea, and on the other, so blurred with
distance that they could not be sure if they really saw it, was a haze
which might be part of the mountains, or was it only wishful
thinking? Then, looking ahead they saw that the causeway would
indeed bring them across the estuary into a different kind of country altogether, a well-wooded land of hills and valleys with cottages
and farmsteads among orchards and fields. The sun was shining
brilliantly, and up there on the wall they could feel the full force of
the great wind which was urging and lashing the rushing waves to
flow swifter and swifter. It reminded Much-Afraid of a pack of
hounds, urged on by the huntsmen, following one another, leaping and surging and roaring beneath the causeway and then
flowing forward far inland, brimming the shores of the estuary.
Somehow the roar of the wind and the surge of the waters seemed
to get into her blood and course through her being like a glorious
wine of life. The wind whipped her cheeks and tore at her hair and
clothes and nearly toppled her over, but she stood there, shouting
at the top of her voice, though the wind seized the sound of it and
carried it off, drowned in a deafening roar of its own. What Much-
Afraid was shouting up there on the old sea wall, was this:

> 'And now shall mine head be lifted up above mine enemies
> round about; therefore I will sing praises unto the Lord; yea I
> will offer the sacrifice of joy and will praise the Name of the
> Lord.'

> (Psa. 27:6)

As she sang she thought to herself, 'It must be really dreadful to
be the Shepherd's enemies. Always, always to find themselves frus-
trated. Always, always to have their prey snatched away. How simply maddening it must be to see even the silliest little weaklings set

up out of reach on the High Places and made to triumph over all their enemies. It must be unbearable.' While still on the causeway she picked up another stone as the Shepherd had taught her, this time as a memorial of His victory in making her triumph over her enemies, and dropped it into the little bag of treasured memories. So they made their way across the causeway and down the ramp on the other side and immediately found themselves in a wood.

The change in scene after their long journey through the desert was wonderful. A long-deferred spring was just loosening everything from the grip of winter, and all the trees were bursting into fairest green and the buds were swelling. In between the trees were glades of bluebells and wild anemones, and violets and primroses grew in clumps along the mossy banks. Birds sang and called to one another and rustled about, busily absorbed in nestbuilding.

Much-Afraid told herself that never before had she realised what the awakening from the death of winter was like. Perhaps it had needed the desert wastes to open her eyes to all this beauty, but she walked through the wood, almost forgetting for a little that Sorrow and her sister also walked with her. Everywhere she looked it seemed that the unfurling green on the trees and the nesting birds and the leaping squirrels and the blossoming flowers were all saying the same thing, greeting one another in their own special language with a sort of ecstasy and calling cheerfully, 'You see, the winter has gone at last. The delay was not unto death but for the glory of God. Never was there a fairer spring than this.' At the same time Much-Afraid herself was conscious of a wonderful stirring in her own heart, as though something were springing up and breaking into new life there too. The feeling was so sweet, yet so mixed with pain that she hardly knew which predominated.

She thought of the seed of Love which the Shepherd had planted in her heart, and, half-afraid and half-eager, she looked to see if it had really taken root and was springing up. She saw a mass of leaves, and at the end of the stem a little swelling which might almost prove to be a bud.

As Much-Afraid looked at it another stab went through her heart, for she remembered the words of the Shepherd that when the plant of Love was ready to bloom she would be loved in return and would receive a new name up there on the High Places. But here she was, still far away from them, indeed farther than ever before, and with apparently no possibility of going there for a long time to come. How could the Shepherd's promise prove true? When she thought of that her tears fell again. You may think that Much-Afraid was altogether too much given to shedding tears, but remember that she had Sorrow for a companion and teacher. There is this to be added, that her tears were all in secret, for no one but her enemies knew about this strange journey on which she had set out. The heart knoweth its own sorrow and there are times when, like David, it is comforting to think that our tears are put in a bottle and not one of them forgotten by the One who leads us in paths of sorrow. But she did not weep for long, for almost at once she caught sight of something else, a gleam of gold. Looking closer, what should she see but an exact replica of the little golden flower which she had found growing near the pyramid in the desert. Somehow it had been transplanted and was actually growing in her own heart. Much-Afraid gave a cry of delight, and the tiny golden thing nodded and said in its little golden voice, 'Behold me, here I am, growing in your heart, "Acceptance-with-Joy".'

Much-Afraid smiled and answered, 'Why, yes, of course. I was forgetting,' and she knelt down there in the wood, put a pile of stones together and laid sticks on them. As you have noticed, altars are built of whatever materials lie close at hand at the time. Then she hesitated. What should she lay on the altar this time? She looked at the tiny swelling on the plant of Love which might be a bud and again might not, then she leant forward, placed her heart on the altar and said, 'Behold me, here I am; Thy little hand-maiden Acceptance-with-Joy and all that is in my heart is Thine.'

This time, though there came a flame of fire and burnt up the sticks, the bud was still on the stem of the plant. Perhaps, thought Much-Afraid, because it was too small to offer. But nevertheless something lovely had happened. It was as though a spark from the flame had entered her heart and was still glowing there, warm and radiant. On the altar among the ashes was yet another stone for her to pick up and put with the rest, so now there were six stones of remembrance lying in the bag she carried. Going on their way, in a very short time they came to the edge of the wood and she uttered a cry of joy, for who should be standing there, waiting to meet them, but the Shepherd Himself. She ran towards Him as though she had wings on her feet.

'Oh, welcome, welcome, a thousand times welcome!' cried Much-Afraid, tingling with joy from head to foot. "I am afraid there is nothing much in the garden of my heart as yet, Shepherd, but all that there is, is Yours to do with as You please."

'I have come to bring you a message,' said the Shepherd. 'You are to be ready, Much-Afraid, for something new. This is the message, "Now shalt thou see what I will do" ' (Ex. 6:1).

The colour leapt into her cheeks, and a shock of joy went through her, for she remembered the plant in her heart and the promise that when it was ready to bloom she would be up on the High Places and ready to enter the Kingdom of Love.

'O Shepherd,' she exclaimed, almost breathless with the thought. 'Do you mean that I am really to go to the High Places at last? Really—at last?'

She thought He nodded, but He did not answer at once, but stood looking at her with an expression she did not quite understand.

'Do you mean it?' she repeated, catching His hand and looking up at Him with almost incredulous joy. 'Do You mean You soon will be taking me to the High Places?'

This time He answered, 'Yes,' and added with a strange smile, 'now shalt thou see what I will do.'

CHAPTER IX

THE GREAT PRECIPICE INJURY

AFTER that, for a little while Much-Afraid had a song in her heart as she walked among the fields and orchards and the low hills of the country to which they had come. It hardly seemed to matter now that Sorrow and Suffering were still with her because of the hope leaping up in her heart, that soon they would cease to be her companions altogether, for when she came to the mountains again and they had helped her up to the High Places she would need them no longer. Neither did it matter that the path they followed still led southwards, twisting among the hills and leading through quiet valleys, because she had the Shepherd's own promise that soon it would lead her back to the eastern mountains and to the place of her heart's desire. After a time the path began sloping upwards towards the summits of the hills.

One day they suddenly reached the top of the highest of the hills and just as the sun rose found themselves on a great plateau. They looked eastward towards the golden sunrise, and Much-Afraid burst into a cry of joy and thankfulness. There, at no great distance, on the farther side of the plateau, were the mountains, quite distinct and rising like a great wall, crowned with ramparts and towers and pinnacles, all of which were glowing rose-red and gold in the sunrise. Never, thought she, had she seen anything so beautiful. As the sun rose higher and the glow faded from the sky, she saw that the highest peaks were covered with snow, so white and glittering that her eyes were dazzled with their glory. She was looking at the High Places themselves. Best of all, the path they were following here turned eastward and led directly towards the mountains.

Much-Afraid fell on her knees on the hill-top, bowed her head and worshipped. It seemed to her at that moment that all the pain and the postponement, all the sorrows and trials of the long journey she had made, were as nothing compared to the glory which shone before her. It seemed to her, too, that even her companions were smiling with her. When she had worshipped and rejoiced she rose to her feet and all three started to cross the plateau. It was amazing how quickly they went, for the path was flat and comparatively smooth, and before they could have believed it possible they found themselves approaching the mountains and were amongst the slopes and boulders at their very foot.

As they approached, Much-Afraid could not help being struck by the steepness of these slopes, and the nearer they drew, the more like impassable walls the mountains appeared to become. But she told herself that when she was right up to them they would find a valley or gorge, or a pass up which they could proceed, and that she certainly would not mind how steep the way was if only it led upwards. In the late afternoon they did come to the top of the lower slopes and to the very foot of the mountains. The path they were following led them right up to the foot of an impassable precipice and there stopped dead.

Much-Afraid stood still and stared. The more she looked, the more stunned she felt. Then she began to tremble and shake all over, for the whole mountain range before her, as far as she could see to left and right, rose up in unbroken walls of rock so high that it made her giddy when she put her head back and tried to look up to the top. The cliffs completely blocked the way before her, yet the path ran right up to them, then stopped. There was no sign of a track in any other direction, and there was no way at all by which the over-hanging, terrifying wall of cliff could be ascended. *They would have to turn back.*

Just as this overwhelming realisation came to her, Suffering caught her hand and pointed to the rocky walls. A hart, followed by a hind, had appeared from among the jumbled rocks around them and were now actually beginning to ascend the precipice. As the three stood watching, Much-Afraid turned dizzy and faint, for she saw that the hart, which was leading the way, was following what appeared to be a narrow and intensely steep track which went zig-zagging across the face of the cliff. In some parts it was only a narrow ledge, in others there appeared to be rough steps, but in certain places she saw that the track apparently broke right off. Then the hart would leap across the gap and go springing upward, always closely followed by the hind, who set her feet exactly where his had been, and leaped after him, as lightly, as sure-footed, and apparently unafraid as it was possible for any creature to be. So the two of them leaped and sprang with perfect grace and assurance up the face of the precipice and disappeared from sight over the top.

Much-Afraid covered her face with her hands and sank down on a rock with a horror and dread in her heart such as she had never felt before. Then she felt her two companions take her hands in theirs and heard them say, 'Do not be afraid, Much-Afraid, this is not a dead end after all, and we shall not have to turn back. There is a way up the face of the precipice. The hart and the hind have shown it to us quite plainly. We shall be able to follow it too and make the ascent.'

'Oh, no! No!' almost shrieked Much-Afraid. 'That path is utterly impossible. The deer may be able to manage it, but no human being could. I could never get up there. I would fall headlong and be broken in pieces on those awful rocks.' She burst into hysterical sobbing. 'It's an impossibility, an absolute impossibility. I cannot get to the High Places that way, and so can never get there at all.'

Her two guides tried to say something more, but she put her hands over her ears and broke into another clamour of terrified sobs. There was the Shepherd's Much-Afraid, sitting at the foot of the precipice, wringing her hands and shaking with terror, sobbing over and over again, 'I can't do it; I can't. I shall never get to the High Places.' Nothing less like royalty could be imagined, but far worse was to follow.

As she crouched on the ground, completely exhausted, they heard a crunching sound and a rattling of loose stones, then a voice close beside her.

'Ha, ha! My dear little cousin, we meet again at last! How do you find yourself now, Much-Afraid, in this delightfully pleasant situation?'

She opened her eyes in fresh terror and found herself looking right into the hideous face of Craven Fear himself.

'I thought somehow,' he went on with a look of the most horrible gloating. 'Yes, I really thought that we would come together again at last. Did you really believe, you poor little fool, that you could escape from me altogether? No, no, Much-Afraid, you are one of the Fearings, and you can't evade the truth, and what is more, you trembling little idiot, you belong to me. I have come to take you back safely and make sure that you don't wander off again.'

'I won't go with you,' gasped Much-Afraid, too shocked by this awful apparition to have her wits about her. 'I absolutely refuse to go with you.'

'Well, you can take your choice,' sneered Craven. 'Take a look at the precipice before you, my dear cousin. Won't you feel lovely up there! Just look where I'm pointing, Much-Afraid. See there, half-way up, where that dizzy little ledge breaks right off and you have to jump across the chasm on to that bit of rock. Just picture yourself jumping that, Much-Afraid, and finding yourself hanging over space, clutching a bit of slippery rock which you can't hold on to another minute. Just imagine those ugly, knife-like rocks at the foot of the precipice, waiting to receive and mangle you to pieces as your strength gives out, and you plunge down on them. Doesn't it give you a lovely feeling, Much-Afraid? Just take time to picture it. That's only one of many such broken places on the track, and the higher you go, you dear little fool, the farther you will have to fall. Well, take your choice. Either you MUST go up there, where you know that you can't, but will end in a mangled heap at the bottom, or you must come back and live with me and be my little slave ever afterwards.' And the rocks and cliffs seemed to echo again with his gloating laughter.

'Much-Afraid,' said the two guides, stooping over her and shaking her by the shoulder gently but firmly. 'Much-Afraid, you know where your help lies. Call for help.'

She clung to them and sobbed again. 'I am afraid to call,' she gasped. 'I am so afraid that if I call Him, He will tell me that I MUST go that way, that dreadful, dreadful way, and I can't. It's impossible. I can't face it. Oh, what shall I do? Whatever shall I do?'

Sorrow bent over her and said very gently but urgently, 'You *must* call for him, Much-Afraid. Call at once.'

'If I call Him,' shuddered Much-Afraid through chattering teeth, 'He will tell me to build an altar, and I can't. This time I can't.'

Craven Fear laughed triumphantly and took a step towards her, but her two companions put themselves between him and his victim. Then Suffering looked at Sorrow, who nodded back. In answer to the nod Suffering took a small but very sharp knife which hung at her girdle, and, bending over the crouching figure, pricked her. Much-Afraid cried out in anguish, and then, in utter despair at finding herself helpless in the presence of all three, did that which she ought to have done the moment the path brought them to the foot of the precipice. Though now she felt too ashamed to do it, she did so because she was forced by her extremity. She cried out, 'O Lord I am oppressed, undertake for me. My fears have taken hold upon me, and I am ashamed to look up.'

'Why, Much-Afraid.' It was the Shepherd's voice close beside her. 'What is the matter? Be of good cheer, it is I, be not afraid.'

He sounded so cheery and full of strength, and, moreover, without a hint of reproach, that Much-Afraid felt as though a strong and exhilarating cordial had been poured into her heart and that a stream of courage and strength was flowing into her from His presence. She sat up and looked at Him and saw that He was smiling, almost laughing at her. The shame in her eyes met no answering reproach in His, and suddenly she found words echoing in her heart which other trembling souls had spoken. 'My Lord is of very tender compassion to them that are afraid.' As she looked, thankfulness welled up in her heart and the icy hand of fear which had clutched her broke and melted away and joy burst into bloom. A little song ran through her mind like a trickling stream.

My Belovèd is the chiefest
Of ten thousand anywhere
He is altogether lovely
He is altogether fair,
My Belovèd is so gentle
And is strong beyond compare.

'Much-Afraid,' said the Shepherd again, 'tell Me, what is the matter. Why were you so fearful?'

'It is the way You have chosen for me to go,' she whispered. 'It looks so dreadful, Shepherd, so impossible. I turn giddy and faint whenever I look at it. The roes and hinds can go there, but they are not limping, crippled, or cowardly like me.'

'But, Much-Afraid, what did I promise you in the Valley of Humiliation?' asked the Shepherd with a smile.

Much-Afraid looked startled, and the blood rushed into her cheeks and ebbed again, leaving them as white as before. 'You said,' she began and broke off and then began again. 'O Shepherd, You said You would make my feet like hinds' feet and set me upon mine High Places.'

'Well,' He answered cheerily, 'the only way to develop hinds' feet is to go by the paths which the hinds use—like this one.'

Much-Afraid trembled and looked at Him shamefacedly. 'I don't think—I want—hinds' feet, if it means I have to go on a path like that,' she said slowly and painfully.

The Shepherd was a very surprising person. Instead of looking either disappointed or disapproving, He actually laughed again.

'Oh, yes you do,' He said cheerfully. 'I know you better than you know yourself, Much-Afraid. You want it very much indeed, and I promise you these hinds' feet. Indeed, I have brought you on purpose to this back side of the desert, where the mountains are particularly steep and where there are no paths but the tracks of the deer and of the mountain goats for you to follow, that the promise may be fulfilled. What did I say to you the last time that we met?'

'You said, "Now shalt thou see what I will do",' she answered, and then, looking at Him reproachfully, added, 'But I never dreamt you would do anything like this! Lead me to an impassable precipice up which nothing can go but deer and goats, when I'm no more like a deer or a goat than is a jellyfish. It's too—it's too——' She fumbled for words, and then burst out laughing. 'Why, it's too preposterously absurd! It's crazy! Whatever will You do next?'

The Shepherd laughed too. 'I love doing preposterous things,' He replied. 'Why, I don't know anything more exhilerating and delightful than turning weakness into strength, and fear into faith, and that which has been marred into perfection. If there is one thing more than another which I should enjoy doing at this moment it is turning a jellyfish into a mountain goat. That is My special work,' He added with the light of a great joy on His face. 'Transforming things—to take Much-Afraid, for instance, and to transform her into——' He broke off and then went on laughingly. 'Well, we shall see later on what she finds herself transformed into.'

It was a really extraordinary scene. In the place where just a little while before all had been fear and despair were the Shepherd and Much-Afraid, sitting on the rocks at the foot of the impassable precipice, laughing together as though at the greatest joke in the world.

'Come now, little jellyfish,' said the Shepherd, 'do you believe that I can change you into a mountain goat and get you to the top of the precipice?'

'Yes,' replied Much-Afraid.

'Will you let Me do it?'

'Yes,' she answered, 'if You want to do such a crazy and preposterous thing, why certainly You may.'

'Do you believe that I will let you be put to shame on the way up?'

Much-Afraid looked at Him and then said something that she had never been willing to say before. 'I don't think I mind so very much if You do; only have Your will and way in me, Shepherd. Nothing else matters.'

As she spoke, something lovely happened. A double rainbow appeared above the precipice, arching it completely, so that the zigzag path up which the roe and the doe had gone was framed in the glowing colours. It was such a beautiful and extraordinary sight that Much-Afraid gasped with wonder and delight, but there was something else about it which was almost more wonderful. She saw that Sorrow and Suffering, who had drawn aside while the Shepherd spoke to her, were standing one at either side of the path, and where the ends of the rainbow touched the earth, one touched Suffering and the other Sorrow. In the shining glory of the rainbow colours, the two veiled figures were so transfigured with beauty that Much-Afraid could only look at them for a moment before being dazzled. Then she did that which only a short time before had seemed utterly impossible. She knelt down at the foot of the precipice and built an altar and laid on it her will, her dread, and her shrinking, and when the fire had fallen she found amongst the ashes a larger and rougher-looking stone than any of the others, sharp-edged and dark in colour, but otherwise quite ordinary-look-ing. This she put in her purse and then rose to her feet and waited for the Shepherd to show her what to do. In her heart she was hop-ing that He would accompany her up the dreadful ascent as He had gone with her down into the desert, but this He did not do.

Instead, He led her to the foot of the precipice and said, 'Now, Much-Afraid, you have really come at last to the foot of the High Places, and a new stage of the journey is to begin. There are new lessons for you to learn. I must tell you that this precipice to which the path has led you is at the foot of Mount Injury. The whole mountain range stretches a long way beyond this in either direc-tion, and everywhere it is as steep or even steeper than here. There are even more terrible precipices on the sides of Mount Reviling and Mount Hate and Mount Persecution and others besides, but nowhere is it possible to find a way up to the High Places and into the Kingdom of Love, without surmounting at least one of them. This is the one which I have chosen for *you* to ascend.

'On the way here you have been learning the lesson of accept-ance-with-joy, which is the first letter in the alphabet of Love. Now you must learn the B of the alphabet of Love. You have come to the foot of Mount Injury, and I hope and expect that on the way up the precipice you will discover what is this next letter of the alphabet, and that you will learn and practise it as you have the A of Love. Remember that though you must now meet Injury and surmount it, *there is nothing* on the way up this terrible-looking precipice nor indeed anything that you may meet above and beyond it that can do you the slightest harm or hurt if you will learn and steadfastly practise the second lesson in the Ascent of Love.'

When He had said this He put His hands upon her with special solemnity and gentleness and blessed her. Then He called her companions, who immediately stepped forward. Next He took a rope from a crevice in the wall of rock, and with His own hands roped together the three who were to ascend the precipice, Sorrow was in front and Suffering behind, with Much-Afraid in the middle, so that the two who were so strong and sure-footed went before and after. In this way, even if Much-Afraid slipped and fell, they would be able to hold her up and support her by the rope. Lastly, He put His hand to His side and brought out a little bottle of cordial which He gave to Much-Afraid, telling her to drink a little at once and to make use of it if ever she felt giddy or faint on the way up. The label on the bottle read, 'Spirit of Grace and Comfort', and when Much-Afraid had taken a drop or two she felt so revived and strengthened that she was ready to begin the ascent without any feeling of faint-ness, although there was still a sensation of dread in her heart.

By this time the evening was well advanced, but being summer there were yet two or three hours before it would begin to be dark, and the Shepherd charged them to start at once for, said He, 'Although you cannot possibly reach the top before nightfall, there is a cave farther up the cliff which you cannot see from here, and there you can rest and spend the night in perfect safety. If you stay down here at the foot of the precipice your enemies will most cer-tainly steal upon you and seek to do you harm. However, they will not follow you up this track, and while you are going up you will be beyond their reach. Though I doubt not,' He added warningly, 'that you will meet them again when you have reached the top.'

With that He smiled encouragingly upon them, and immedi-ately Sorrow put her foot upon the first step of the narrow little track which zig-zagged up the face of the cliff. Much-Afraid fol-lowed next, and then Suffering, and in a moment or two they were beginning the ascent.

CHAPTER X

THE ASCENT OF THE PRECIPICE INJURY

ONCE on the track, Much-Afraid discovered to her surprise and deep thankfulness that it was not nearly so appalling in actual fact as it had seemed in anticipation. Steep, difficult, and slippery it certainly was, and also painfully narrow, but the feeling of being securely roped to her strong companions was very reassuring. Also, the cordial of the Spirit of Grace and Comfort which she had just drunk kept her from feeling giddy and faint when she looked over the edge, the thing she had most dreaded. Moreover, for the first half-hour of their ascent the rainbow still shone above them, and though the Shepherd had disappeared from view Much-Afraid had a lovely sense that He was still close beside them.

She did not look down unless obliged to do so, but once quite soon after they had started she had to wait in a little niche in the rock at one of the difficult places while Sorrow felt her way forward and Suffering waited in the rear. Just then, she looked down, and felt very thankful indeed that the Shepherd had charged them to start the ascent that evening and not spend the night down below. Sitting on the rocks below were all five of her enemies, gazing up at them and grimacing with fury and spite. Indeed, as she looked she was startled to see Self-Pity (who always looked less ugly and dangerous than his companions) stoop down and pick up a sharp stone which he flung at her with all his might. Fortunately they were already practically out of reach of stone-throwing, but the jagged piece did hit the cliff just below her, and Much-Afraid was greatly relieved when she felt Sorrow pull gently on the rope to tell her that she now could move forward. She remembered the Shepherd's warning that she was likely to meet these enemies again when the precipice was surmounted, though how they would get up on to the Mount Injury she did not know; only that there must be some other way which they could use.

So the three of them climbed higher and higher while the shadows thrown by the cliffs lengthened over the plain below and the sun went down in a blaze of glory beyond the desert and the great sea. From the height which they had now reached they could plainly see the western sea, along the shores of which they had travelled for so long. The track they followed wound up and ever upwards, back and forth across the face of the cliff, and though it was crumbling and even broken in some places, Much-Afraid was tremendously relieved to find that nowhere at all was it too difficult, not even at the spot half-way up the cliff which Craven Fear had so particularly pointed out to her. On arriving there just as darkness fell, she found that though the path had indeed broken right away, a plank had been laid across the gap and a rope placed through iron rings in the rock face to form a hand-rail to which she could cling as she walked across the narrow bridge. The hart and the hind, of course, had disdained such unnecessary assistance and had leaped across the chasm, making it look as though there was nothing there. However, even with the hand-rail to steady her, Much-Afraid was very careful to close her imagination altogether to the picture which Craven Fear had painted. From bitter experience she knew that pictures thrown on the screen of her imagination could seem much more unnerving and terrible than the actual facts.

When the plank was crossed in safety they discovered themselves to be in an exceedingly narrow gorge quite invisible from below. Directly facing them was the very resting-place which the Shepherd had spoken of, a little cave where they were to pass the night. With a sense of great relief and thankfulness she went inside and looked round. Its situation was such that though she could not look down into the dizzy depths beneath, it was possible to look right out over the plateau and the desert to the far-off sea. The moon had just risen and was shedding a pure silver light over everything, and the first stars appeared like faint flickers in the darkening sky. In the cave itself flat rocks had been placed to form rude seats and a table, and on the ground at one side were piled sheepskins on which they could rest.

Not far from the cave entrance a tiny waterfall trickled down the cliff, and they went to it in turn and refreshed themselves. Then Sorrow and Suffering produced two packages of bread and dried fruits and nuts which the Shepherd had given them at the foot of the ascent. With these they gladly satisfied their hunger, and then, overcome by weariness, they laid themselves down in the cave and fell into dreamless slumber.

Much-Afraid woke with the first light of the dawn, and getting up, walked to the entrance of the cave. In the cold light of early morning she could not help telling herself that a scene of utter desolation lay before her. As far as the eye could see was nothing but empty plain and sea, with towering cliffs above her and jagged rocks below. The pleasant wooded country which they had left was out of sight, and in all the vast area upon which she looked she saw not a single tree and scarcely a stunted bush. 'How desolate,' thought Much-Afraid, 'and those rocks beneath look very cruel indeed, as if they are waiting to injure and destroy anything which falls upon them. It seems as though nothing can grow anywhere in all this barren waste.'

Just then she looked up at the cliffs above her head and started with surprise and delight. In a tiny crevice of the rock, where a few drops from the trickling waterfall could occasionally sprinkle it, was a single plant. It had just two or three leaves, and one fragile stem, almost hair-like in its slenderness, grew out at right-angles to the wall. On the stem was one flower, blood red in colour, which glowed like a lamp or flame of fire in the early rays of the sun.

Much-Afraid stared at it for some moments, noticing the wall which completely imprisoned it, the minute aperture through which it had forced its way to the light, and the barren loneliness of its surroundings. Its roots were clamped around by sheer rock, its leaves scarcely able to press outside the prison house, yet it had insisted on bursting into bloom, and was holding its little face open to the sun and burning like a flame of joy. As she looked up at it Much-Afraid asked, as she had in the desert, 'What is your name, little flower, for indeed I never saw another like you.'

At that moment the sun touched the blood-red petals so that they shone more vividly than ever, and a little whisper rustled from the leaves.

'My name is "Bearing-the-Cost", but some call me "Forgiveness".'

Then Much-Afraid recalled the words of the Shepherd, 'On the way up the precipice you will discover the next letter in the alphabet of Love. Begin to practise it at once.'

She gazed at the little flower and said again, 'Why call you that?'

Once more a little whispering laugh passed through the leaves, and she thought she heard them say, 'I was separated from all my companions, exiled from home, carried here and imprisoned in this rock. It was not my choice, but the work of others who, when they had dropped me here, went away and left me to bear the results of what they had done. I have borne and have not fainted; I have not ceased to love, and Love helped me push through the crack in the rock until I could look right out on to my Love the sun Himself. See now! There is nothing whatever between my Love and my heart, nothing around to distract me from Him. He shines upon me and makes me to rejoice, and has ATONED to me for all that was taken from me and done against me. There is no flower in all the world more blessed or more satisfied than I, for I look up to Him as a weaned child and say, "Whom have I in heaven but Thee, and there is none upon earth that I desire but Thee".'

Much-Afraid looked at the glowing flame above her head, and a longing which was almost envy leaped into her heart. She knew what she must do. Kneeling on the narrow path beneath the imprisoned flower, she said, 'O my Lord, behold me—I am Thy little handmaiden Bearing-the-Cost.'

At that moment a fragment of the rock which imprisoned the roots of the flower above her loosened and fell at her feet. She picked it up and put it very gently with the other seven stones in her purse, then returned to the cave. Sorrow and Suffering were waiting for her with a further supply of bread and raisins and nuts, and after they had given thanks and had eaten, they roped themselves together again and continued up the precipice. After a little they came to a place which was very steep and slippery. Suddenly

Much-Afraid had her first fall and cut herself quite badly on the pieces of jagged rock which had tripped her. It was a good thing she was so securely roped, for a great terror came upon her and she became so giddy and faint that had she not been tied she might have slipped over the edge of the path and been dashed to pieces on the rocks below. As this thought struck her she was so overcome with panic and trembling that all she could do was to crouch against the wall of rock and cry out to her companions that she was fainting and was in terror of falling. Immediately Sorrow, who was in front, tightened the rope, then Suffering came up to her, put her arms around her and said urgently, 'Drink some of the cordial which the Shepherd gave you.'

Much-Afraid was so faint and frightened that she could only lie in the arms of Suffering and gasp, 'I don't know where the bottle is—I can't move even to fumble for it.'

Then Suffering herself put her hand into the bosom of the fainting girl, drew out the bottle, and poured a few drops between her lips. After a few moments the colour returned to Much-Afraid's cheeks, and the faintness began to pass off, but still she could not move. She took more of the Spirit of Grace and Comfort and began to feel strengthened. Then Sorrow, who had come back to the place where she was crouching, gently shortened the rope so that Much-Afraid could take her hand and again they started to climb. In the fall, however, Much-Afraid had cut both knees so severely that she could only limp forward very painfully, moaning continually and halting constantly. Her companions were very patient, but progress was so slow that finally it became necessary to make greater speed, or they would not reach the top of the precipice before nightfall, and there was no other cave where they could rest.

At last Suffering stooped over her and asked, 'Much-Afraid, what were you doing when you left the cave this morning and went off by yourself?'

Much-Afraid gave her a startled look, then said with a painful flush, 'I was looking at a flower which I had not seen before, growing in the rock by the waterfall.'

'What flower was that?' persisted Suffering very gently.

'It was the flower of Bearing-the-Cost,' replied Much-Afraid in a very low voice, 'but some call it Forgiveness.' For a few moments she was silent, remembering the altar she had built and realising that she was not practising this new and difficult letter of the alphabet of Love. Then said she, 'I wonder if it would help my knees if we put a few drops of the cordial on them.'

'Let us try,' said Sorrow and Suffering both together. 'It is an excellent suggestion.'

As they dropped a little of the cordial on both knees, almost at once the bleeding ceased, and the worst of the smart and pain died away. Her legs remained very stiff and she was still obliged to limp quite badly, but they did go forward at a much better pace. By late afternoon they were right at the top of the awful ascent, and found themselves in a forest of young pine-trees with moss and whortle-berries growing on the banks beside the path, and the precipice which had looked so impassable actually behind them. They sat down on one of the mossy banks in the wood to rest, then heard a voice singing quite close at hand.

> Thou art all fair, My dearest love,
> There is no spot in thee.
> Come with Me to the heights above,
> Yet fairer visions see.
> Up to the mount of Myrrh and thence

Across the hills of Frankincense,
To where the dawn's clear innocence
  Bids all the shadows flee.

Come with Me, O My fairest dear,
  With Me to Lebanon,
Look from the peaks of grim Shenir,
  Amana and Hermon.
The lions have their dens up there—
The leopards prowl the glens up there,
But from the top the view is clear
  Of land yet to be won.

                              (Cant. 4:7, 8)

There, coming towards them through a clearing in the trees, was the Shepherd Himself.

CHAPTER XI

IN THE FORESTS OF DANGER
AND TRIBULATION

WITH what joy they welcomed the Shepherd as He sat down in
their midst, and after cheerfully congratulating them on having
surmounted the precipice, He laid His hands gently on the
wounds which Much-Afraid had received when she fell, and
immediately they were healed. Then He began to speak to them
about the way which lay ahead.

'You have now to go through the forests which clothe the sides
of these mountains almost up to the snowline. The way will be
steep, but you will come to resting-places here and there. These are
the Forests of Danger and Tribulation, and often the pine-trees
grow so tall and so closely together that the path may seem quite
dark. Storms are very frequent up here on these slopes, but keep
pressing forward, for remember that nothing can do you any real
harm while you are following the path of My will.'

It did seem strange that even after safely surmounting so many
difficulties and steep places, including the 'impassable precipice'
just below them, Much-Afraid should remain so like her name. But

so it was! No sooner did the Shepherd pronounce the words 'danger and tribulation' than she began to shake and tremble all over again.

'The Forests of Danger and Tribulation!' she repeated with a piteous quaver in her voice. 'O Shepherd, wherever will You lead me next?'

'To the next stage on the way to the High Places,' He answered promptly, smiling at her as nicely as possible.

'I wonder if You will ever be able to get me there!' groaned poor foolish little Much-Afraid. 'I wonder You continue to bother with me and don't give up the job altogether. It looks as though I never shall have anything but lame feet, and that even You won't be able to make them like hinds' feet.' She looked disconsolately at her feet as she spoke. Certainly at that moment they did look even more crooked than ever.

'I am not a man that I should lie,' said the Shepherd gravely. 'Look at Me, Much-Afraid. Do you believe that I will deceive you? Have I said, and shall I not do it? Or have I spoken, and shall I not make it good?'

Much-Afraid trembled a little, partly at the tone of His voice and partly because she was still Much-Afraid by nature and was already trying to picture what the Forests of Danger and Tribulation would be like. That always had a disastrous effect upon her, but she answered penitently, 'No—I know that You are not a man who would lie to me; I know that You will make good what You have said.'

'Then,' said the Shepherd, speaking very gently again, 'I AM going to lead you through danger and tribulation, Much-Afraid, but you need not be the least bit afraid, for I shall be with you. Even if I lead you through the Valley of the Shadow itself you need not fear, for My rod and My staff will comfort you.' Then

He added, 'Thou shalt not be afraid for the terror by night; nor for the arrow that flieth by day; nor for the pestilence that walketh in darkness; nor for the destruction that wasteth at noonday. Though a thousand fall at thy side, and ten thousand at thy right hand, they shall not come nigh thee. . . . For I will cover thee with My feathers, and under My wings shalt thou trust' (Psa. 91:4–6). The gentleness of His voice as He said these things was indescribable.

Then Much-Afraid knelt at His feet and built yet another altar and said, 'Yea, though I walk through the Valley of the Shadow of Death, I will fear no evil: for Thou art with me.' Then, because she found that even as she spoke her teeth were chattering with fright and her hands had gone quite clammy, she looked up into His face and added, 'For Thou art not a man that thou shouldest lie, nor the Son of man that Thou shouldest repent. Hast Thou said, and shalt Thou not do it? And hast Thou spoken and shalt Thou not make it good?'

Then the Shepherd smiled more comfortingly than ever before, laid both hands on her head and said, 'Be strong, yea be strong and fear not.' Then He continued, 'Much-Afraid, don't ever allow yourself to begin trying to picture what it will be like. Believe me, when you get to the places which you dread you will find that they are as different as possible from what you have imagined, just as was the case when you were actually ascending the precipice. I must warn you that I see your enemies lurking amongst the trees ahead, and if you ever let Craven Fear begin painting a picture on the screen of your imagination, you will walk with fear and trembling and agony, where no fear is.' When He had said this, He picked up another stone from the place where she was kneeling, and gave it to her to put with the other memorial stones. Then He went His way, and Much-Afraid and her companions started on the path which led up through the forests.

Almost as soon as they had reached the trees they saw the face of mean, sickly Self-Pity, looking out from behind one of the trunks. He gabbled ever so quickly before he dodged back into hiding: 'I say, Much-Afraid, this really is a bit too thick. I mean, whatever will He do next, forcing a poor little lame, frightened creature like yourself to go through dangers which only brave, strong men ought to be expected to face. Really, your Shepherd is almost more of a bully than Craven Fear himself.'

Hardly had he stopped before Resentment put his head out and said crossly, 'There's absolutely no reason for it either, because there's another perfectly good path which skirts the forest altogether and brings you right up to the snowline without going anywhere near these unnecessary dangers. Everybody else goes that way, so why shouldn't you? Tell Him you WON'T go this way, Much-Afraid, and insist on being taken by the usual path. This way is for martyrs only, and you, my dear, don't fit into the picture at all.'

Then Craven Fear leered at her for a moment and said contemptuously, 'So you think you're going to become a little heroine, do you? and go singing through the Forest of Danger! What will you bet, Much-Afraid, that you won't end up shrieking and screaming like a maniac, maimed for the rest of your life?'

Bitterness was next to speak, and sneered from behind another tree, 'He would do this. It's just as I told you. After you have dutifully gone through one terrifying experience He's always got something still worse lying ahead of you.'

Then Pride (who was still limping badly and seemed extra venomous as a result) said, 'You know, He won't be able to rest content until He has put you to complete shame, because that's the way He produces that precious humility He's so crazy about. He'll humble you to the dust, Much-Afraid, and leave you a grovelling idiot in front of everyone.'

Much-Afraid and her companions walked on without answering and without taking any notice, but as before, Much-Afraid discovered that she limped more painfully whenever she heard what they said. It was really terribly perplexing to know what to do. If she listened, she limped, and if she put her fingers in her ears, she couldn't accept the hands of her two guides, which meant that she stumbled and slipped. So they stopped for a moment or two and discussed the matter, and then Suffering opened the little First Aid kit hanging at her girdle, took out some cotton-wool and firmly plugged the ears of Much-Afraid. Although this was uncomfortable, it did seem to have the desired effect, at least temporarily, for when the five skulkers saw that they could not make her hear them they soon tired of bawling at her and left her alone until another opportunity should occur for badgering her again.

At first the forest did not really seem too dreadful. Perhaps it was that up there on the mountains the air was so fresh and strong that it made those who breathed it fresh and strong too. Also, the sun was still shining, and Much-Afraid began to feel a sensation which was completely new to her, a thrill of excitement and, incredible as it seemed, of almost pleasurable adventure. Here she was, lame Much-Afraid, actually walking through the Forest of Danger and not really minding. This lasted for quite a time until huge black clouds gradually rolled over the sky, and the sun went in. In the distance thunder rolled and the woods became dark and very still. Suddenly a bolt of lightning scorched across the sky, and somewhere ahead of them was a rending crash as a great forest tree fell to the earth, then another and another. Then the storm in all its fury was bursting around them, thunder rolling, lightning sizzling and crackling in every direction until the whole forest seemed to be groaning and shaking and falling about them.

The strangest thing was that though Much-Afraid felt a shuddering thrill go through her at every crash she was not really afraid. That is, she felt neither panic nor desire to run, nor even real dread, for she kept repeating to herself, 'Though a thousand shall fall at thy side and ten thousand at thy right hand, it shall not come nigh thee. . . . For I will cover thee with My feathers, and under My wings shalt thou trust.' So throughout the whole storm she was filled with a strange and wonderful peace such as she had never felt before, and walked between her two companions saying to herself, 'I shall not die, but live and declare the works of the Lord.'

At last the storm began to rumble off into the distance, the crashes died down, and there was a quiet lull. The three women stopped to wring the water out of their clothes and hair and try to tidy themselves. While doing this, Craven Fear appeared near them again and yelled at the top of his voice, 'I say, Much-Afraid, the storm has only gone round the mountains for a short time. Already it is beginning to approach again and will be worse than before. Make a bolt back down the path as quickly as you can and get away from these dangerous trees before it starts again or you will be killed. There is just time for you to make good your escape.'

'Look here,' exclaimed Much-Afraid most unexpectedly, water still dripping from her hair and her sodden skirts clinging like wet rags around her legs, 'I can't stand that fellow shouting at me any longer. Please help me—both of you,' and setting the example, she stooped down, picked up a stone and flung it straight at Craven Fear.

Her two companions actually laughed for the very first time and started hurling a barrage of stones among the trees where the five were lurking. In a moment or two none of their enemies were visible. Then, just ahead of them, through the trees, they saw a log hut which seemed to offer a promise of shelter and protection from the storm, which certainly was again drawing nearer. Hurrying towards the cabin, they found that it stood in a clearing well away from the trees, and when they tried the door latch, to their joy it opened and they thankfully slipped inside. With great presence of mind, Suffering immediately closed the door and bolted it behind them, and none too soon!

Next minute their enemies were banging on the door and shouting, 'Hi! I say—open the door and let us in. The storm is starting again. You can't be so inhuman as to shut us outside and leave us to our fate.'

Much-Afraid went to the door and shouted through the keyhole the advice they had offered her, 'Make a bolt down the path as quickly as you can and get away from these dangerous trees, or you will be killed. You have just time to make good your escape before the storm starts again.'

There was a sound of muttered curses outside, then of hurrying feet fading away into the distance, and it seemed as though this time the advice was being acted upon. Back rolled the storm, fiercer and more terrible than before, but they were safely sheltered in the hut out of range of the crashing trees, and their shelter proved perfectly weatherproof, for not a drop came through the roof.

They found in the room a supply of firewood stacked beside a small kitchen-range with a kettle and some saucepans on it. While Suffering busied herself lighting the fire, Sorrow held the kettle under a spout outside the window and filled it with rain-water. Much-Afraid went to a cupboard on the wall to see if it would yield any treasure. Sure enough, there was crockery on the shelves and a supply of tinned foods, as well as a big tin of unleavened biscuits. So in a very little time, while the storm still furiously raged and rattled outside, there they were, sitting around a crackling fire, warming themselves and drying their sopping garments while they drank comforting hot cocoa and satisfied their hunger. Though the uproar of the tempest without was almost deafening and the hut shuddered and shook in every blast, yet inside was nothing but peace and thanksgiving and cheerful contentment. Much-Afraid found herself thinking with astonished awe that it was really the happiest and the most peaceful experience during the whole of her journey up till that time. As they lay down on the mattresses which they discovered piled in another part of the hut, she repeated again to herself very softly: 'He *has* covered me with His feathers, and under His wings I do trust.'

The storm continued with great violence for two or three days, but while it lasted the three travellers rested quietly in the shelter of the hut, going outside only during the brief lulls to gather wood. This they dried in the oven to replenish the stock they were using, so that others, following on behind, might not be left without fuel. There seemed to be a good store of tinned foods and unleavened biscuits and they supposed that some of the Shepherd's servants must visit the hut from time to time with a new supply.

During those quiet days in the midst of the raging tempest Much-Afraid came to know her two companions in a new way and also to understand more of the mountain dialect which they spoke. In some strange way she began to feel that they were becoming real friends, and not just attendants whom the Shepherd had commanded to go with her as guides and helpers. She found, too, that now she was accepting their companionship in this way she seemed more alive than ever before to beauty and delight in the world around her. It seemed as though her senses had been quickened in some extraordinary way, enabling her to enjoy every little detail of her life; so that although her companions actually were Sorrow and Suffering, she often felt an almost inexplicable joy and pleasure at the same time. This would happen when she looked at the bright, crackling flames in the log fire, or listened to the sound of lashing rain overhead emphasising the safety and peace within the hut, or when she saw through the window the tossing trees waving their arms against a background of scurrying clouds or lightning-rent sky. Or again, very early before daybreak, when she saw the morning-star shining serenely through a rift in the clouds or heard the clear, jubilant note of a bird during a lull in the storm. All these things seemed to be speaking to her in the mountain dialect, and to her growing astonishment, she found it an incredibly beautiful language, so that sometimes her eyes filled with tears of pure joy and her heart seemed so full of ecstasy that she could hardly bear it.

One morning when the storm was rattling and raging through the forest louder than ever, she noticed Sorrow sitting by the fire singing quietly to herself, the words, of course, being in the mountain dialect, which Much-Afraid was learning to understand. This is the best translation that I can give, but you will realise that the original was much more beautiful and full of forest sounds and music.

How lovely and how nimble are thy feet,
   O prince's daughter!
They flash and sparkle and can run more fleet
   Than running water.
On all the mountains there is no gazelle,
   No roe or hind,
Can overtake thee nor can leap as well—
   But lag behind.

(Cant. 7:1)

'Why, Sorrow,' exclaimed Much-Afraid, 'I didn't know that you could sing, nor even that you knew any songs.'

Sorrow answered quietly, 'Neither did I, but on the way up here through the forest I found the words and tune coming into my head just as I am singing them now.'

'I like it,' said Much-Afraid. 'It makes me think of the time when I shall have hinds' feet myself, and so it is comforting and the tune is so nice and springy. It makes me want to jump.' She laughed at the thought of her crooked feet being able to jump, then coaxed, 'Teach me the song—please do.'

So Sorrow sang it over several times until Much-Afraid knew it perfectly and went about the hut humming it to herself, trying to picture what it would be like to be a gazelle leaping on the mountains, and able to jump from crag to crag, just as the Shepherd did. When the day came for her to receive her hinds' feet, she would be able to follow Him wherever He went. The picture was so lovely she could hardly wait for it to come true.

CHAPTER XII

IN THE MIST

A⊤ last the storm gradually died down, the clamour on the mountains ceased, and it was time to resume the journey. However, the weather had broken completely, and though the storm itself was over, thick mist and cloud remained, shrouding everything on the heights. When they started the mist was so thick that they could see only the trees on either side of the narrow path, and even they looked ghostly and unreal. The rest of the forest was simply swallowed up and entirely lost to sight, veiled in a cold and clammy white curtain. The ground was dreadfully muddy and slippery, and although the path did not climb nearly so steeply as before, after some hours Much-Afraid found to her amazement that she was missing the rolling thunder of the storm and even the sickening crash of the trees as the lightning splintered them. She began to realise that, cowardly though she was, there was something in her which responded with a surge of excitement to the tests and difficulties of the way better than to easier and duller circumstances. It was true that fear sent a dreadful shuddering thrill through her, but nevertheless it was a thrill, and she found herself realising with astonishment that even the dizzy precipice had been more to her liking than this dreary plodding on and on through the bewildering mist. In some way the dangers of the storm had stimulated her; now there was nothing but tameness, just a trudge, trudge forward, day after day, able to see nothing except the white, clinging mist which hung about the mountains without a gleam of sunshine breaking through.

At last she burst out impatiently, 'Will this dull, dreary mist never lift, I wonder?' And would you believe it! a voice she knew all too well immediately answered from beyond the trees.

'No it won't,' replied Resentment. 'Moreover, you might just as well know now that this is going to continue for no one knows how long. Higher up the mountains the mist hangs thicker and thicker still. That's all you can expect for the rest of the journey.'

Much-Afraid pretended not to hear, but the voice went on again almost at once.

'Have you noticed, Much-Afraid, that the path which you are following isn't going *up* the mountain at all, but is almost level? You've missed the upward way, and you are just going round and round the mountain in circles.'

Much-Afraid had not exactly noticed this fact, but now she could not help realising that it was true. They were *not* climbing at all, but simply moving along the mountain-side with constant ups and downs, and the downs seemed to be getting more frequent. Could it be possible that they were really gradually descending the mountain instead of going up? In the bewildering mist one simply could not see anything, and she found she had lost all sense of direction. On asking her companions what they thought about it they answered rather shortly (because, of course, she ought not to have listened to any suggestion from Resentment) that they were on the path which the Shepherd had pointed out, and would certainly not allow anyone to persuade them to leave it.

'But,' persisted Much-Afraid petulantly, 'don't you think that we may have missed the way in this mist? The Shepherd said the path led upwards, and as you see, this one doesn't. It runs along the side of the mountain. There may easily have been a more direct way up which we didn't notice in the mist.'

Their only answer was that they knew better than to listen to any suggestion made by Resentment.

At that the voice of Bitterness broke in quite clearly, 'You might at least be willing to go back a little way and look, instead of insisting in going on and on along what may prove to be a wrong path leading you round in circles.'

Sorrow and Suffering took absolutely no notice, but unfortunately Much-Afraid did, and said with still greater petulance, 'I think you ought to consider the suggestion. Perhaps it would be better to go back a little way and see if we have missed the right path. Really, it is no use going on and on in circles, getting nowhere.'

To this they replied, 'Well, if we are going round in circles, we shall eventually arrive back where we went wrong, and if we keep our eyes open we shall be able to see the path we missed—always provided that it does exist and is not just a bit of imagination on the part of Bitterness.'

'You poor little thing,' came the whisper of Self-Pity through the mist. 'It is too bad that you have been put in the charge of such obstinate mule-like creatures. Just think of the time you are wasting, getting nowhere at all. Trudge, trudge, day after day, nothing to show for it, and you ought to be getting up on to the High Places.'

So they went on, whispering and talking at her through the clinging mist, which shrouded everything and made it all seem so ghostly and dreary. Of course, she ought not to have listened to them, but the mist was so bewildering and the path so unspeakably tame that she found something in her heart responding to them almost against her will. Suffering doggedly led the way, and Sorrow just as doggedly was her rearguard, so that there was no possibility of turning back, but Much-Afraid found herself limping and slipping and stumbling far more often and badly than at any other stage of the journey. It made her very disagreeable and difficult to deal with. It is true that after every stumble her conscience smote her and she apologised sorrowfully and abjectly to her companions, but that did not prevent her slipping again almost directly afterwards. Altogether it was a miserable time, and the mist, instead of clearing, seemed to get thicker and colder and drearier than ever.

At last, one afternoon, when the only word which at all describes her progress is to say that she was slithering along the path, all muddy and wet and bedraggled from constant slips, she decided to sing. It has not been mentioned before, but Much-Afraid did not possess the gift of a sweet voice any more than a pretty face. It is true that she was fond of singing, and that if the Shepherd sang with her she could keep in tune and manage quite nicely, but if she tried alone the results were by no means so good. However, the mist was so thick and clammy that she was nearly stifled, and she felt she must do something to try to cheer herself and to drown the ghostly voices which kept whispering to her through the trees. It was not pleasant to think of her relatives now having the opportunity to entertain themselves at the expense of her very unmelodious voice, but she decided to risk their ribald comments. 'If I sing quite loudly,' she told herself, 'I shall not be able to hear what they say.' The only song which she could think of at the moment was the one which Sorrow had taught her in the hut, and though it seemed singularly inappropriate she lifted up her voice and sang quaveringly:

> How lovely and how nimble are thy feet,
>   O prince's daughter!
> They flash and sparkle and can run more fleet
>   Than running water.
> On all the mountains there is no gazelle,
>   No roe or hind,
> Can overtake thee nor can leap as well—
>   But lag behind.

(Cant. 7:1)

There was perfect silence as she sang. The loud, sneering voices of her enemies had died away altogether. 'It is a good idea,' said Much-Afraid to herself jubilantly, 'I wish I had thought of it before. It is a much better way to avoid hearing what they are saying than putting cotton-wool in my ears, and I believe, yes, I really do believe, there is a little rift in the mist ahead. How lovely, I shall sing the verse again.' And she did so.

'Why, Much-Afraid,' said a cheery voice close beside her, 'I have not heard that song before. Where did you learn it?'

There, striding towards her with a particularly pleased smile on His face, was the Shepherd Himself. It is just impossible to describe in words the joy of Much-Afraid when she saw Him really coming towards them on that dreary mountain path, where everything had been swallowed up for so long in the horrible mist and everything one touched had been so cold and clammy. Now with His coming the mist was rapidly clearing away and a real gleam of sunshine—the first they had seen for days—broke through at last.

'O Shepherd,' she gasped, and caught hold of His hand and could say no more. It really had seemed as though she would never see Him again.

'Tell me,' He repeated cheerily as He smiled at them all, 'where did you learn that song, Much-Afraid?'

'Sorrow taught it to me,' she replied. 'I didn't think that she knew any songs, Shepherd, but she said the words and the music came to her as we were climbing up through the forest. I asked her to teach it to me because—I know I am a goose, but it makes me think of the time when You will have made my feet like hinds' feet and I won't ever have to slither along again,' and she looked shamefacedly at her bedraggled and muddy condition.

'I am glad you sing it,' said the Shepherd more pleasantly than ever. 'I think it is a particularly nice song. Indeed,' he added smiling, 'I think I will add another verse to it Myself,' and at once He began to sing these words to the same tune:

> Thy joints and thighs are like a supple band
>> On which are met
> Fair jewels which a cunning master hand
>> Hath fitly set.
> In all the palace, search where'er you please,
>> In every place
> There's none that walks with such a queenly ease,
>> Nor with such grace.

(Cant. 7:1)

'O Shepherd,' exclaimed Much-Afraid, 'where did you find that verse to fit in so nicely to the tune which Sorrow taught me?'

Again he smiled at her in the nicest possible way and answered, 'The words came to Me just now as I followed you along the path.'

Poor Much-Afraid, who knew that she had been slipping and stumbling in the most dreadful way, indeed worse than at any other time, flushed painfully all over her face. She said nothing, only looked at Him almost reproachfully.

'Much-Afraid,' said He very gently in answer to that look, 'don't you know by now that I never think of you as you are now but as you will be when I have brought you to the Kingdom of Love and washed you from all the stains and defilements of the journey? If I come along behind you and notice that you are finding the way especially difficult, and are suffering from slips and falls, it only makes me think of what you will be like when you are with Me leaping and skipping on the High Places. Wouldn't you like to learn and sing My verse just as much as the one which Sorrow taught you?'

'Yes,' said Much-Afraid thankfully, and taking His hand again, 'Certainly I will learn it and sing about the cunning master hand which takes such pains with me.'

By this time the mist had actually melted right away and the sun, shining brilliantly, was making the dripping trees and grass sparkle with joy and brightness. All three thankfully accepted the suggestion of the Shepherd that they should sit down for a short time and rest and rejoice in the sunshine. Sorrow and Suffering withdrew a little, as they always did when the Shepherd was present, leaving Him to talk with Much-Afraid alone. She told Him all the dismal tale of their long wanderings in the mist, the way Resentment, Bitterness, and Self-Pity had been bothering her and her fear that perhaps, after all, they had wandered from the path and lost their way.

'Did you really think that I would let you stray from the right path to the High Places without doing anything to warn you or to prevent it?' asked the Shepherd quietly.

She looked at Him sorrowfully and said with a sigh, 'When Resentment and the others are shouting at me I am almost ready to believe anything, no matter how preposterous.'

'You had better become a singer,' said He, smiling. 'Then you won't hear what they say to you. Ask Sorrow and Suffering if they have any more songs which they can teach you. Do you find them good guides, Much-Afraid?'

She looked at Him earnestly and nodded her head. 'Yes, *very* good. I never could have believed it possible, Shepherd, but in a way I have come to love them. When first I saw them they looked so terrifyingly strong and stern, and I was sure that they would be rough with me and just drag me along without caring how I felt. How I dreaded it, but they have dealt with me very, very kindly indeed. I think they must have learnt to be so gentle and patient with me by seeing Your gentleness. I never could have managed without them,' she went on gratefully, 'and the queer thing is I have a feeling that they really like helping an ugly little cripple like me in this way. They do truly want to get me up to the High Places, not just because it is the commandment which You have given them, but also because they want a horrid coward like myself to get there and be changed. You know, Shepherd, it makes a great difference in my feelings towards them not to look upon them any longer with dread, but as friends who want to help me. I know it seems ridiculous, but sometimes I get the feeling that they really love me and want to go with me of their own free will.'

As she finished speaking she looked up in His face and was surprised to see that He actually looked as though He were trying not to laugh. He said nothing for a moment or two, but turned slightly so that He could look round at the two guides. Much-Afraid looked too. They were sitting apart in the background and were unaware that they were being watched. They sat close to one another and were looking away up to the mountains towards the High Places. Their veils had been thrown back, although she still could not see their faces because their backs were towards the Shepherd and herself. She was struck by the fact that they seemed even taller and stronger than when she had first seen them waiting for her at the foot of the mountains. There was something almost indescribably majestic about them at that moment, a sort of radiant eagerness expressed in their attitude. They were talking quickly to one another, but their voices were so low that she could not catch what they were saying. Was it possible—yes it was! They were actually laughing! That they were talking about something which thrilled them with eagerness and expectation, she felt quite sure.

The Shepherd watched them for a few moments without speaking, then He turned back to Much-Afraid. His eyes were laughing at her, but He said quite gravely, 'Yes, I really believe you are right, Much-Afraid. They do look to me as though they really enjoy their task, and perhaps even feel a little affection for the one they serve.' Then He really did laugh out aloud.

Sorrow and Suffering dropped the veils back over their faces and looked round to see what was happening, but the Shepherd had something more to say before He sped them farther on the journey.

The laughter died out on His face, and very seriously He asked, 'Do you love Me enough to be able to trust Me completely, Much-Afraid?'

She looked at Him in the usual startled fashion so natural to her whenever she sensed that He was preparing her for a new test, then faltered: 'You know that I DO love You, Shepherd, as much as my cold little heart is capable. You know that I love You and that

I long to trust You as much as I love You, that I long both to love and trust You still more.'

'Would you be willing to trust Me,' He asked, 'even if everything in the wide world seemed to say that I was deceiving you—indeed, that I had deceived you all along?'

She looked at Him in perplexed amazement. 'Why, yes,' she said, 'I'm sure I would, because one thing I KNOW to be true, it is impossible that You should tell a lie. It is impossible that You should deceive me. I know that I am often very frightened at the things which You ask me to do,' she added shamefacedly and apologetically, 'but I could never doubt You in that way. It's myself I am afraid of, never of You, and though everyone in the world should tell me that You had deceived me, I should know it was impossible. O Shepherd,' she implored, 'don't tell me that You think I really doubt You, even when I am most afraid and cowardly and despicably weak. You know—you KNOW I trust You. In the end I know I shall be able to say Thy gentleness hath made me great.'

He said nothing for a little, only looked down very tenderly, almost pitifully at the figure now crouching at His feet. Then, after a time, He said very quietly, 'Much-Afraid, supposing I really did deceive you? What then?'

It was then her turn to be quite silent, trying to grasp this impossible thing He was suggesting and to think what her answer would be. What then? Would it be that she could never trust, never love Him again? Would she have to be alive in a world where there was no Shepherd, only a mirage and a broken lovely dream? To know that she had been deceived by One she was certain could not deceive? To lose Him?

Suddenly she burst into a passion of weeping, then after a little while looked straight up into His face and said, 'My Lord—if You

CAN deceive me, You may. It can make no difference. I MUST love You as long as I continue to exist. I cannot live without loving You.'

He laid His hands on her head, then with a touch more tender and gentle than anything she had ever felt before, repeated as though to Himself, 'If I CAN, I MAY deceive her.' Then without another word He turned and went away.

Much-Afraid picked up a little icy-cold pebble which was lying on the ground where He had stood, put it in her bag, then tremblingly rejoined Sorrow and Suffering, and they continued their journey.

CHAPTER XIII

IN THE VALLEY OF LOSS

THE mist had cleared from the mountains and the sun was shining, and as a consequence the way seemed much more pleasant and easy than it had for a very long time. The path still led them along the side of the mountain rather than upwards, but one day, on turning a corner, they found themselves looking down into a deep valley. To their surprise, their path actually plunged straight down the mountain-side towards it, exactly as at the beginning of the journey when Much-Afraid had been led down into Egypt. All three halted and looked first at one another, then down into the valley and across to the other side. There the ascent was as steep and even higher than the Precipice of Injury and they saw that to go down and then ascend again would not only require an immense amount of strength and effort, but also take a VERY LONG TIME.

Much-Afraid stood and stared, and at that moment experienced the sharpest and keenest test which she had yet encountered on the journey. Was she to be turned aside once again, but in an even more terrible way than ever before? By now they had ascended far higher than ever before. Indeed, if only the path they were following would begin to ascend, they could not doubt that they would soon be at the snowline and approaching the real High Places, where no enemies could follow and where the healing streams flowed. Now instead of that the path was leading them down into a valley as low as the Valley of Humiliation itself. All the height which they had gained after their long and toil-some journey must now be lost and THEY WOULD HAVE TO BEGIN ALL OVER AGAIN, just as though they had never made a start so long ago and endured so many difficulties and tests.

As she looked down into the depths of the valley the heart of Much-Afraid went numb. For the first time on the journey she actually asked herself if her relatives had not been right after all and if she ought not to have attempted to follow the Shepherd. How could one follow a person who asked so much, who demanded such impossible things, who took away everything? If she went down there, as far as getting to the High Places was concerned she must lose everything she had gained on the journey so far. She would be no nearer receiving the promise than when she started out from the Valley of Humiliation. For one black, awful moment Much-Afraid really considered the possibility of following the Shepherd no longer, of turning back. She need not go on. There was absolutely no compulsion about it. She had been following this strange path with her two companions as guides simply because it was the Shepherd's choice for her. It was not the way which she naturally wanted to go. Now she could make her own choice. Her sorrow and suffering could be ended at once, and she could plan her life in the way she liked best, WITHOUT THE SHEPHERD.

During that awful moment or two it seemed to Much-Afraid that she was actually looking into an abyss of horror, into an

existence in which there was no Shepherd to follow or to trust or
to love—no Shepherd at all, nothing but her own horrible self.
Ever after, it seemed that she had looked straight down into Hell.
At the end of that moment Much-Afraid shrieked—there is no
other word for it.

'Shepherd,' she shrieked, 'Shepherd! Shepherd! Help me!
Where are You? Don't leave me!' Next instant she was clinging to
Him, trembling from head to foot and sobbing over and over
again, 'You may do anything, Shepherd. You may ask anything—
only DON'T LET ME TURN BACK. O My Lord, don't let me leave you.
Entreat me not to leave Thee, nor to return from following after
Thee.' Then as she continued to cling to Him she sobbed out, 'If
You can deceive me, My Lord, about the promise and the hinds'
feet and the new name or anything else, You may, indeed You may;
only don't let me leave You. Don't let anything turn me back. This
path looked so wrong I could hardly believe it was the right one,'
and she sobbed bitterly.

He lifted her up, supported her by His arm, and with His own
hand wiped the tears from her cheeks, then said in His strong,
cheery voice, 'There is no question of your turning back, Much-
Afraid. No one, not even your own shrinking heart, can pluck you
out of My hand. Don't you remember what I told you before?
"This delay is not unto death but for the glory of God." You
haven't forgotten already the lesson you have been learning, have
you? It is no less true now that "what I do thou knowest not now,
but thou shalt know hereafter". My sheep hear My voice, and they
follow Me. It is perfectly safe for you to go on in this way even
though it looks so wrong, and now I give you another promise:
Thine ears shall hear a word behind thee saying "This is the way,
walk ye in it," when ye turn to the right hand or to the left.'

He paused a moment, and she still leant against Him, speechless with thankfulness and relief at His Presence. Then He went on. 'Will you bear this too, Much-Afraid? Will you suffer yourself TO LOSE or to be deprived of all that you have gained on this journey to the High Places? Will you go down this path of forgiveness into the Valley of Loss, just because it is the way that I have chosen for you? Will you still trust and still love Me?'

She was still clinging to Him, and now repeated with all her heart the words of another woman tested long ago. 'Entreat me not to leave Thee, or to return from following after Thee: for whither Thou goest I will go; Thy people shall be my people and Thy God my God.' She paused and faltered a moment, then went on almost in a whisper, 'And where thou DIEST, WILL I DIE, AND THERE WILL I BE BURIED. The Lord do so to me, and more also, if ought but death part Thee and me' (Ruth 1:16, 17).

So another altar was built at the top of the descent into the Valley of Loss and another stone added to those in the bag she still carried in her bosom. After that they began the downward journey, and as they went she heard her two guides singing softly:

> O whither is thy Belovèd gone,
>> Thou fairest among women?
> Where dost thou think He has turned aside?
>> That we may seek Him with thee.

The Shepherd Himself sang the next verse:

> He is gone down into His garden,
>> To the beds of spices sweet,
> For He feedeth among the lilies,
>> 'Tis there we are wont to meet.

Then Much-Afraid herself sang the last two verses, and her heart was so full of joy that even her unmelodious voice seemed changed and sounded as sweet as the others.

> So I went down into the garden
> The valley of buds and fruits,
> To see if the pomegranates budded,
> To look at the vinestock shoots.

> And my soul in a burst of rapture,
> Or ever I was aware,
> Sped swifter than chariot horses,
> For lo! He was waiting there.

(Cant. 6:1–3)

Considering how steep it was, the descent down into the valley seemed surprisingly easy, but perhaps that was because Much-Afraid desired with her whole will to make it in a way that would satisfy and please the Shepherd. The awful glimpse down into the abyss of an existence without Him had so staggered and appalled her heart that she felt she could never be quite the same again. However, it had opened her eyes to the fact that right down in the depths of her own heart she really had but one passionate desire, not for the things which the Shepherd had promised, but for Himself. All she wanted was to be allowed to follow Him for ever. Other desires might clamour strongly and fiercely nearer the surface of her nature, but she knew now that down in the core of her own being she was so shaped that nothing could fit, fill, or satisfy her heart but He Himself. 'Nothing else really matters,' she said to herself, 'only to love Him and to do what He tells me. I don't quite know why it should be so, but it is. All the time it is suffering to love and sorrow to love, but it is lovely to love Him in spite of this, and if I should cease to do so, I should cease to exist.' So, as has been said, they reached the valley very quickly.

The next surprising thing was that though the valley did seem at first a little like a prison after the strong bracing air of the mountains, it turned out to be a wonderfully beautiful and peaceful place, very green and with flowers covering the fields and the banks of the river which flowed quietly through it. Strangely enough, down there in the Valley of Loss, Much-Afraid felt more rested, more peaceful, and more content than anywhere else on the journey. It seemed, too, that her two companions also underwent a strange transformation. They still held her hands, but there was neither suffering nor sorrow in the touch. It was as though they walked close beside her and went hand in hand simply for friendship's sake and for the joy of being together. Also, they sang continually, sometimes in a language quite different from the one which she had learnt from them, but when she asked the meaning of the words they only smiled and shook their heads. This is one of the many songs which all three sang down in the Valley of Loss, and it was another from the collection in the old song-book which Much-Afraid so loved.

> I am my Love's and He is mine,
>   And this is His desire,
> That with His beauty I may shine
>   In radiant attire.
> And this will be—when all of me
>   Is pruned and purged with fire.
>
> Come, my Belovèd, let us go
>   Forth to the waiting field;

And where Thy choicest fruit trees grow,
    Thy pruning knife now wield
That at Thy will and through Thy skill
    Their richest store may yield.

And spices give a sweet perfume,
    And vines show tender shoots,
And all my trees burst forth in bloom,
    Fair buds from bitter roots.
There will not I my love deny,
    But yield Thee pleasant fruits.

(Cant. 7:10–13)

It is true that when Much-Afraid looked at the mountains on the other side of the valley she wondered how they would ever manage to ascend them, but she found herself content to wait restfully and to wander in the valley as long as the Shepherd chose. One thing in particular comforted her; after the hardness and slipperiness of the way on the mountains, where she had stumbled and limped so painfully, she found that in those quiet green fields she could actually walk without stumbling, and could not feel her wounds and scars and stiffness at all. All this seemed a little strange because, of course, she really was in the Valley of Loss. Also, apparently, she was farther from the High Places than ever before. She asked the Shepherd about it one day, for the loveliest part of all was that He often walked with them down there, saying with a beautiful smile that it was one of His favourite haunts.

In answer to her question, He said, 'I am glad that you are learning to appreciate the valley too, but I think it was the altar which you built at the top, Much-Afraid, which has made it so easy for you.'

This also rather puzzled her, for she said, 'But I have noticed that after the other altars which You told me to build, the way has generally seemed harder and more testing than before.'

Again He smiled, but only remarked quietly that the important thing about altars was that they made possibilities of apparent impossibilities, and that it was nice that on this occasion it had brought her peace and not a great struggle. She noticed that He looked at her keenly and rather strangely as He spoke, and though there was a beautiful gentleness in the look, there was also something else which she had seen before, but still did not understand. She thought it held a mixture of two things, not exactly pity—no, that was the wrong word, but a look of wonderful compassion together with UNFLINCHING DETERMINATION. When she realised that, she thought of some words which one of the Shepherd's servants had spoken down in the Valley of Humiliation before ever the Shepherd had called her to the High Places. He had said, 'Love is beautiful, but it is also terrible—terrible in its determination to allow nothing blemished or unworthy to remain in the beloved.'

When she remembered this, Much-Afraid thought with a little shiver in her heart, 'He will never be content until He makes me what He is determined that I ought to be,' and because she was still Much-Afraid and not yet ready to change her name, she added with a pang of fear, 'I wonder what He plans to do next, and if it will hurt very much indeed?'

CHAPTER XIV

THE PLACE OF ANOINTING

As it happened, the next thing which the Shepherd had planned was very beautiful indeed. Not long after this conversation the path finished its winding way through the valley and led them to the foot of the mountains on the other side to a place where they rose up like a wall, far higher and steeper than the Precipice of Injury. However, when Much-Afraid and her two companions reached this place they found the Shepherd waiting for them beside a little hut, and lo! just where the cliffs were steepest and highest was an overhead cable suspended between that spot and the summit far above. On this cable hung chairs, in which two could sit side by side and be swung right up to the top without any effort on their part at all. It is true that at first the very sight of these frail-looking aerial chairs swinging along so high above the ground made Much-Afraid feel giddy and panicky. She felt she could never voluntarily place herself in one of them and be swung up that frightful-looking precipice, with only a little footrest and nothing to prevent her casting herself out of the chair if the urge should come upon her. However, that passed almost at once, for the Shepherd smiled and said, 'Come, Much-Afraid, we will seat ourselves in the first two chairs, and Sorrow and Suffering will follow in the next. All you have to do is to trust yourself to the chair and be carried in perfect safety up to the place to which I wish to take you and without any struggling and striving on your part.'

Much-Afraid stepped into one of the seats, and the Shepherd sat beside her while the two companions occupied the next pair. In a minute they were moving smoothly and steadily towards the High Places which had looked so impossibly out of reach, supported entirely from above, and with nothing to do but rest and enjoy the marvellous view. Though the chairs swung a little in places, they felt no giddiness at all, but went upwards and still upwards until the valley below looked like a little green carpet and the gleaming white peaks of the Kingdom of Love towered around and above them. Soon they were far above the place to which they had climbed on the mountains opposite, and still they swung along.

When at last they stepped out of the aerial chairs they were in a place more beautiful than anything Much-Afraid had seen before, for though these were not the real High Places of the Kingdom of Love, they had reached the border-land. All around were Alps with grassy meadows almost smothered in flowers. Little streams gurgled and splashed between banks of kingcups, while buttercups and cowslips, violets and pink primulæ carpeted the ground. Clumps of delicate purple soldanella grew in vivid clusters, and all over the fields, glowing bright as gems, were gentians, more blue than the sky at midday, looking like jewels on a royal robe. Above were peaks of pure white snow which towered up into a cloudless sky like a roof of sapphire and turquoise. The sun shone so brilliantly it almost seemed that one could see the flowers pushing their way up through the earth and unfolding themselves to receive the glory of its rays. Cow-bells and goat-bells sounded in every direction, and a multitude of bird notes filled the air, but above the rest was one voice louder and more dominant than them all, and which seemed to fill the whole region. It was the voice of a mighty waterfall, leaping down another great cliff which towered above them, and whose rushing waters sprang from the snows in the High Places themselves. It was so unspeakably lovely that neither Much-Afraid nor her companions could utter a word, but stood, drawing deep breaths and filling their lungs with the spicy, pine-scented mountain air.

As they wandered forward, they stooped down at every other step, gently touching the jewel-like flowers or dabbling their fingers in the splashing brooks. Sometimes they just stood still amidst the profusion of shining beauty around them and laughed aloud with pure joy. The Shepherd led them across meadows where the warm, scented grass grew nearly waist high, towards the mighty waterfall. At the foot of the cliffs they found themselves standing in cool shadows with a light spray sometimes splashing their faces, and there the Shepherd bade them stand and look up. There stood Much-Afraid, a tiny figure at the foot of the mighty cliffs, looking up at the great, never-ending rush of waters as they cast themselves down from the High Places. She thought that never before had she seen anything so majestic or so terrifyingly lovely. The height of the rocky lip, over which the waters cast themselves to be dashed in pieces on the rocks below, almost terrified her. At the foot of the fall, the thunderous voice of the waters seemed almost deafening, but it seemed also to be filled with meaning, grand and awesome, beautiful beyond expression.

As she listened, Much-Afraid realised that she was hearing the full majestic harmonies, the whole orchestra as it were, playing the original of the theme song which all the little streamlets had sung far below in the Valley of Humiliation. Now it was uttered by thousands upon thousands of voices, but with grander harmonies than anything heard down in the valleys, yet still the same song.

> From the heights we leap and go
> To the valleys down below,
> Always answering to the call,
> To the lowest place of all.

'Much-Afraid,' said the Shepherd's voice in her ear, 'what do you think of this fall of great waters in their abandonment of self-giving?'

She trembled a little as she answered. 'I think they are beautiful and terrible beyond anything which I ever saw before.'

'Why terrible?' He asked.

'It is the leap which they have to make, the awful height from which they must cast themselves down to the depths beneath, there to be broken on the rocks. I can hardly bear to watch it.'

'Look closer,' He said again. 'Let your eye follow just one part of the water from the moment when it leaps over the edge until it reaches the bottom.'

Much-Afraid did so, and then almost gasped with wonder. Once over the edge, the waters were like winged things, alive with joy, so utterly abandoned to the ecstasy of giving themselves that she could almost have supposed that she was looking at a host of angels floating down on rainbow wings, singing with rapture as they went.

She gazed and gazed, then said, 'It looks as though they think it is the loveliest movement in all the world, as though to cast oneself down is to abandon oneself to ecstasy and joy indescribable.'

'Yes,' answered the Shepherd in a voice vibrant with joy and thanksgiving, 'I am glad that you have noticed that, Much-Afraid. These are the Falls of Love, flowing from the High Places in the Kingdom above. You will meet with them again. Tell Me, does the joy of the waters seem to end when they break on the rocks below?'

Again Much-Afraid looked where He pointed, and noticed that the lower the water fell, the lighter it seemed to grow, as though it really were lighting down on wings. On reaching the rocks below, all the waters flowed together in a glorious host, forming an exuberant, rushing torrent which swirled triumphantly around and over the rocks. Laughing and shouting at the top of their voices, they hurried still lower and lower, down through the meadows to the next precipice and the next glorious crisis of their self-giving. From there they would again cast themselves down to the valleys far below. Far from suffering from the rocks, it seemed as though every obstacle in the bed of the torrent was looked upon as another object to be overcome and another lovely opportunity to find a way over or around it. Everywhere was the sound of water, laughing, exulting, shouting in jubilation.

'At first sight perhaps the leap does look terrible,' said the Shepherd, 'but as you can see, the water itself finds no terror in it, no moment of hesitation or shrinking, only joy unspeakable, and full of glory, because it is the movement natural to it. Self-giving is its life. It has only one desire, to go down and down and give itself with no reserve or holding back of any kind. You can see that as it obeys that glorious urge the obstacles which look so terrifying are perfectly harmless, and indeed only add to the joy and glory of the movement.' When He had said this, He led them back to the sunny fields, and gently told them that for the next few days they were to rest themselves there in preparation for the last part of their journey.

On hearing these words, 'the last part of the journey,' Much-Afraid felt almost as though she would sink to the ground with happiness. Moreover, the Shepherd Himself remained there with them the whole time. Not for a single hour was He apart from them, but walked and talked with them. He taught them many things about the Kingdom to which they were going, and it was as though grace flowed from His lips and sweet ointments and spices were diffused wherever He went. How thankfully Much-Afraid would have stayed there for the rest of her life; she would have cared no more about reaching the High Places, had it not been that she still walked on crooked feet, still had a twisted mouth, still had a fearing heart.

It was not, however, that the sun always shone, even there on that border-land of the High Places. There were days of mist when all the gleaming peaks were completely blotted out by a curtain of cloud, so that if one had never seen them it would have been impossible to be sure that they really existed and were round about, quite close at hand, towering high above the mist and clouds into the clear blue sky above. Every now and again, however, there would be a rent in the veil of mist, and then, as though framed in an open window, would appear a dazzling whiteness. For a moment one of the vanished peaks would gleam through the rent, as if to say, 'Be of good courage, we are all here, even though you cannot see us.' Then the mist would swirl together again and the window in heaven would close.

On one such occasion the Shepherd said to Much-Afraid, 'When you continue your journey there may be much mist and cloud. Perhaps it may even seem as though everything you have seen here of the High Places was just a dream, or the work of your own imagination. But you have seen REALITY, and the mist which seems to swallow it up is the illusion. Believe steadfastly in what you have seen. Even if the way up to the High Places appears to be obscured and you are led to doubt whether you are following the right path, remember the promise, "Thine ears shall hear a word behind thee, saying, This is the way, walk ye in it, when ye turn to the right hand and when ye turn to the left." Always go forward along the path of obedience as far as you know it until I intervene, even if it seems to be leading you where you fear I could never mean you to go. Remember, Much-Afraid, what you have seen before the mist blotted it out. Never doubt that the High Places ARE there, towering up above you, and be quite sure that whatever happens I mean to bring you up there exactly as I have promised.' As He finished speaking another rent appeared in the curtain of mist, and one of the peaks of the High Places framed in blue sky shone down on them.

Before the curtain closed again Much-Afraid stooped down and picked a few of the gentians growing near her feet as a reminder of what she had seen, for, said she to herself, 'These actually grew on the lower slopes of the High Places and are an earnest that though the peaks may again become invisible they are there all the time.'

On the last day they stayed there the Shepherd did a very wonderful thing. He took Much-Afraid apart by herself and carried her right up to the summit of one of the High Places—in the Kingdom of Love itself. He took her to a high peak, dazzlingly white, uplifted like a great throne with numberless other peaks grouped round about. Up there on the mountain-top He was transfigured before her, and she knew Him then to be what she had dimly sensed all along—the King of Love Himself, King of the whole Realm of Love. He was clothed in a white garment glistening in its purity, but over it He wore a robe of purple and blue and scarlet studded with gold and precious gems. On His head He wore the crown royal, but as Much-Afraid bowed herself and knelt at His feet to worship, the face that looked down upon her was that of the Shepherd whom she had loved and followed from the very low places up to the heights. His eyes were still full of gentleness and tenderness but also of strength and power and authority.

Putting out His hand, without a word He lifted her up and led her to a place where on the topmost pinnacle of all they could look right out on the whole realm around them. Standing there beside Him and so happy as to be scarcely conscious of herself at all, Much-Afraid looked out over the Kingdom of Love. Far, far below were the valleys and the plains and the great sea and the desert. She even thought she could recognise the Valley of Humiliation itself, where she had lived so long and had first learnt to know the Shepherd, but that seemed so long ago it was like remembering another existence altogether. All around her, in every direction, were the snowy peaks of the High Places. She could see that the bases of all these mountains were extremely precipitous and that higher up they were all clothed with forests, then the green slopes of the higher alps and then the snow. Wherever she looked, the slopes at that season of the year were covered with pure white flowers through whose half-transparent petals the sun shone, turning them to burning whiteness. In the heart of each flower was a crown of pure gold. These white-robed hosts scented the slopes of the High Places with a perfume sweeter than any she had ever breathed before. All had their faces and golden crowns turned down the mountains as if looking at the valleys, multitudes upon multitudes of them, which no man could number, like 'a great cloud of witnesses', all stooping forward to watch what was going on in the world below. Wherever the King and His companion walked, these white-robed flowers bowed beneath their feet and rose again, buoyant and unsullied, but exuding a perfume richer and sweeter than before.

On the utmost pinnacle to which He led her was an altar of pure gold, flashing in the sun with such splendour that she could not look at it but had to turn her eyes away at once, though she did perceive that a fire burned on it and a cloud of smoke perfumed with incense rose from it.

Then the King told her to kneel and with a pair of golden tongs brought a piece of burning coal from off the altar. Touching her with it He said, 'Lo! this hath touched thy lips; and thine iniquity is taken away, and thy sin purged' (Isa. 6:7).

It seemed to her that a burning flame of fire too beautiful and too terrible to bear went through her whole being, and Much-Afraid lost consciousness and remembered no more.

When she recovered she found that the Shepherd was carrying her in His arms and they were back on the lower slopes of the border-land. The royal robes and the crown were gone, but something of the expression on His face remained, the look of utmost authority and power. Above them towered the peaks, while everything below was shrouded in cloud and mist. When He found that she was sufficiently recovered, the Shepherd took her by the hand, and they walked together down into the white mist and through a little wood where the trees were scarcely visible and there was no sound but of drops of water splashing on to the ground. When in the middle of the wood a bird burst into song. They could not see

it for the mist, but high and clear and indescribably sweet the bird
sang and called the same series of little notes over and over again.
They seemed to form a phrase constantly repeated, always with a
higher chirrup at the end which sounded just like a little chuckling laugh. It seemed to Much-Afraid that this was the song the
bird was singing:

> He's gotten the victory, Hurrah!
> He's gotten the victory, Hurrah!

The wood rang with the jubilant notes, and they both stood still
among the dripping trees to listen.

'Much-Afraid,' the Shepherd said, 'you have had a glimpse of
the Kingdom into which I am going to bring you. Tomorrow you
and your companions start on the last part of your journey which
will bring you thither.' Then with wonderful tenderness He spoke
words which seemed too glorious to be true. 'Thou hast a little
strength and hast kept My word, and hast not denied My name.
. . . Behold I will make thine enemies to come and worship before
thy feet, and to know that I have loved thee. Behold, I come
quickly: HOLD FAST THAT WHICH THOU HAST, THAT NO MAN TAKE
THY CROWN, and she that over-cometh will I make a pillar in the
temple of My God, and she shall go no more out: and I will write
upon her the name of My God . . . I will write upon her My new
name' (Rev. 3:8–12).

It was then that Much-Afraid took courage to ask Him something which she had never dared ask before. With her hand held
in His she said, 'My Lord, may I ask one thing? Is the time at last
soon coming when You will fulfil the promise that You gave me?'

He said very gently, yet with great joy, 'Yes—the time is not
long now. Dare to begin to be happy. If you will go forward in the

way before you, you will SOON RECEIVE THE PROMISE, and I will give you your heart's desire. It is not long now, Much-Afraid.'

So they stood in the mist-filled wood, she trembling with hope and unable to say a word, worshipping and wondering if she had seen a vision, or if this thing had really happened. Upon His face was a look which she would not have understood even if she had seen it, but she was too dazed with happiness even to look at Him. High over the dripping trees the little bird still sang his jubilant song, 'He's gotten the victory,' and then in a burst of trills and chuckles, 'Hurrah! Hurrah! Hurrah!'

A little later they were down in the meadows where Sorrow and her sister were waiting for their return. It was time to go forward on the journey, but after the Shepherd had blessed them and was turning to go His way again, Suffering and Sorrow suddenly knelt before Him and asked softly, 'Lord, what place is this where we have been resting and refreshing ourselves during these past days?'

He answered very quietly, 'This is the place to which I bring My beloved, that they may be anointed in readiness for their burial.'

Much-Afraid did not hear these words, for she was walking a little ahead, repeating over and over again, 'He said, "Dare to begin to be happy, for the time is not long now, and I will give you your heart's desire." '

CHAPTER XV

THE FLOODS

THE path they now followed did not go straight up to the heights but sloped gently up the mountain-side. The mist still shrouded everything, and indeed grew a little thicker. All three walked in silence, occupied with different thoughts. Much-Afraid was thinking of the promise the Shepherd so recently had given her, 'Behold, I come quickly . . . and will give thee thy heart's desire.' Suffering and Sorrow perhaps were thinking of the answer they had received to the question asked of Him at parting. Whether or not this was so there was no indication, for they walked in complete silence, though the help they gave their lame companion was, had she noticed it, even more gentle and untiring than before.

Towards evening they came to another log cabin standing at the side of the path with the Shepherd's secret mark inscribed upon the door, so they knew that they were to rest there for the night. Once inside they noticed that someone must have been there quite recently, for a fire was burning brightly on the hearth and a kettle of water was singing on the hob. The table, too, was laid for three, and a supply of bread and fruit upon it. Evidently their

arrival had been expected and these kindly preparations made, but
of the one who had thus gone in the way before them there was no
sign. They washed themselves and then sat down at the table, gave
thanks, and ate of the prepared meal. Then, being weary, they lay
down to rest and immediately fell asleep.

How long she had slept Much-Afraid could not tell, but she
woke suddenly while it was still quite dark. Her companions
slumbered peacefully beside her, but she knew that someone had
called her. She waited in silence, then a Voice said:

'Much-Afraid.'

'Behold me, here I am, my Lord,' she answered.

'Much-Afraid,' said the Voice, 'take now the PROMISE you
received when I called you to follow Me to the High Places, and
take the natural longing for human love which you found already
growing in your heart when I planted My own love there and go
up into the mountains to the place that I shall show you. Offer
them there as a Burnt Offering unto Me.'

There was a long silence before Much-Afraid's trembling voice
spoke through the darkness.

'My Lord—am I understanding You aright?'

'Yes,' answered the Voice. 'Come now to the entrance of the hut
and I will show you where you are to go.'

Without waking the two beside her, she rose silently, opened
the door of the hut, and stepped outside. Everything was still
shrouded in mist, and the mountains were completely invisible,
swallowed up in darkness and cloud. As she looked, the mist
parted in one place and a little window appeared through which
the moon and one star shone brightly. Just below them was a
white peak, glimmering palely. At its foot was the rocky ledge over
which the great waterfall leaped and rushed down to the slopes

below. Only the lip of rock over which it poured itself was visible, all below being shrouded in the mist.

Then came the Voice, 'That is the appointed place.'

Much-Afraid looked, and replied, 'Yes, Lord. Behold me—I am Thy handmaiden, I will do according to Thy word.'

She did not lie down again, but stood at the door of the hut waiting for daybreak. It seemed to her that the voice of the fall now filled the whole night and was thundering through her trembling heart, reverberating and shouting through every part and repeating again and again, 'TAKE NOW THE PROMISE THAT I GAVE YOU, AND THE NATURAL HUMAN LOVE IN YOUR HEART, AND OFFER THEM FOR A BURNT OFFERING.'

With the first glimmer of dawn she bent over her sleeping companions and said, 'We must start at once. I have received commandment to go up to the place where the great fall pours itself over the precipice.'

They rose immediately, and after hurriedly eating a meal to strengthen themselves, they started on their way. The path led straight up the mountain-side towards the thunderous voice of the fall, though everything was still shrouded in mist and cloud and the fall itself remained invisible.

As the hours passed they continued to climb, though the path was now steeper than ever before. In the distance thunder began to roll and flashes of lightning rent the veil of mist. Suddenly, higher up on the path, they heard the sound of running feet, slipping and scraping on the rocks and stones. They stopped and pressed themselves closely to one side of the narrow path to allow the runners to pass, then out of the ghostly mist appeared first Fear, then Bitterness, followed by Resentment, Pride, and Self-Pity.

They were running as though for their lives, and as they reached the three women they shouted, 'Back! Turn back at once! The avalanches are falling ahead, and the whole mountain-side is shaking as though it will fall too. Run for your lives!'

Without waiting for an answer, they clattered roughly past and fled down the mountain-side.

'What are we to do?' asked Suffering and Sorrow, apparently at a loss for the very first time. 'Shall we turn back to the hut and wait until the avalanches and the storm are over?'

'No,' said Much-Afraid in a low, steady voice, speaking for the first time since she had called them to rise and follow her. 'No, we must not turn back. I have received a commandment to go up to the place where the great fall pours over the rock.'

Then the Voice spoke close at hand. 'There is a place prepared for you here beside the path. Wait there until the storm is over.'

In the rocky wall beside them was a little cave so low that it could be entered only if they stooped right down, and with just enough room for them to crouch inside. Side by side, they sat huddled together, then all of a sudden the storm burst over them in frightful fury. The mountains reverberated with thunder and with the sound of falling rocks and great avalanches. The lightning flashed incessantly and ran along the ground in sizzling flames. Then the rains descended and the floods came, and the winds blew and beat upon the mountains until everything around them seemed to be shivering and quaking and falling. Flood waters rushed down the steep cliffs and a torrent poured over the rocks which projected over the cave so that the whole entrance was closed with a waterfall, but not a single drop fell inside the cave where the three sat together on the ground.

After they had been there for some time and the storm, far from abating, seemed to be increasing in strength, Much-Afraid silently put her hand in her bosom and drew out the leather bag which she always carried. Emptying the little heap of stones and pebbles into her lap, she looked at them. They were the memorial stones from all the altars which she had built along the way, from the time that she stood beside the Shepherd at the pool and allowed Him to plant the thorn in her heart and all along the journey until that moment of crouching in a narrow cave upon which the whole mountain seemed to be ready to topple. Nothing was left to her but a command to offer up the promise on which she had staked her all, on the strength of which she had started on the journey.

She looked at the little pile in her lap and asked herself dully, 'Shall I throw them away? Were they not all worthless promises which He gave me on the way here?' Then with icy fingers she picked up the first stone and repeated the first words that He had spoken to her beside the pool. 'I will make thy feet like hinds' feet and set thee upon thine High Places' (Hab. 3:19). She held the stone in her hand for a long time, then said slowly, 'I have not received hinds' feet, but I am on higher places than ever I imagined possible, and if I die up here, what does it matter? I will not throw it away.' She put the stone back in the bag, picked up the next and repeated, 'What I do thou knowest not now; but thou *shalt* know hereafter' (John 13:7); and she gave a little sob and said, 'Half at least of that is true, and who knows whether the other half is true or not—but I will not throw it away.'

Picking up the third stone, she quoted, 'This is not unto death, but for the glory of God' (John 11:4). 'Not unto death,' she repeated, 'even though He says, "Offer the Promise as a Burnt Offering"?' but she dropped the stone back into the bag and took the fourth. 'Bread corn IS bruised . . . but no one crushes it for ever' (Isa. 28:28). 'I cannot part with that,' she said, replaced it in the bag, and took the fifth. 'Cannot I do with you as the Potter? saith the Lord' (Jer. 18:6). 'Yes,' said she, and put it back into the bag.

Taking the sixth, she repeated, 'O thou afflicted, tossed with tempest, and not comforted, behold, I will lay thy stones with fair colours . . .' (Isa. 54:11), then could go no farther but wept bitterly. 'How could I part with that?' she asked herself, and she put it in the bag with the others, and took the seventh. 'My sheep hear My voice, and they follow Me' (John 10:27). 'Shall I not throw this one away?' she asked herself. 'Have I really heard His voice, or have I been deceiving myself all the time?' Then as she thought of His face when He gave her that promise she replaced it in the bag, saying 'I will keep it. How can I let it go?' and took the eighth. 'Now shalt thou see what I will do' (Ex. 6:1). Remembering the precipice which had seemed so terribly impossible and how He had brought her to the top, she put the stone with the others and took the ninth. 'God is not a man, that He should lie . . . hath He said, and shall He not do it? or hath He spoken, and shall He not make it good?' (Num. 23:19).

For a very long time she sat trembling with *that* stone in her hand, but in the end she said, 'I have already given the only answer possible when I told Him, "If Thou CANST, Thou mayest deceive me." ' Then she dropped the icy-cold little pebble into the bag and took the tenth. 'Thine ears shall hear a word behind thee, saying "This is the way, walk ye in it, when ye turn to the right hand, and when ye turn to the left" ' (Isa. 30:21). At that she shuddered, but after a while added, 'Thou hast a little strength, and *hast not denied My name . . . Hold that fast which thou hast, that no man take thy crown'* (Rev. 3:8, 11). Returning the tenth stone to the bag, after a long pause she picked up an ugly little stone lying on the floor of the cave and dropped it in beside the other ten, saying, 'Though He slay me, YET WILL I TRUST IN HIM' (Job 13:15). Tying up the bag again, she said, 'Though everything in the world should tell me that they are worthless—yet I cannot part with them,' and put the bag back again in her bosom.

Sorrow and her sister had been sitting silently beside her watching intently as she went over the little heap of stones in her lap. Both gave a strange laugh, as though of relief and thankfulness, and said together, 'The rain descended, and the floods came, and the winds blew, and beat upon that house; AND IT FELL NOT: FOR IT WAS FOUNDED UPON A ROCK' (Matt. 7:25).

By this time, the rain had ceased, the cataract was no longer pouring over the rocks, and only a light mist remained. The rolling of the thunder and the roar of the avalanches were fading away into the distance, and as they looked out of the cave, up from the depths beneath came through the wreaths of mist the clear, jubilant notes of a bird. It might have been brother to that which sang in the dripping woods at the foot of the High Places:

> He's gotten the victory. Hurrah!
> He's gotten the victory. Hurrah!

As the pure clear notes came floating up to them the icy coldness in the heart of Much-Afraid broke, then melted away. She pressed her hands convulsively against the little bag of stones as though it contained priceless treasure which she had thought lost, and said to her companions, 'The storm is over. Now we can go on our way.'

From that place on, it was VERY steep going, for the path now went straight up the mountain-side, so straight and steep that often

Much-Afraid could hardly do more than crawl forward on hands and knees. All along she had hoped that the higher she went and the nearer she got to the High Places, the stronger she would become and the less she would stumble, but it was quite otherwise. The higher they went, the more conscious she was that her strength was leaving her, and the weaker she grew, the more she stumbled. She could not help dimly realising that this was not the case with her companions. The higher they went, the more vigorous and strong they seemed to become, and this was good, because often they had almost to carry Much-Afraid, for she seemed utterly spent and exhausted. Because of this they made very slow progress indeed.

On the second day they came to a place where a little hollow in the mountain-side formed a tiny plateau. Here a spring bubbled out of the cliff and trickled across the hollow and down the side of the mountain in a little waterfall. As they paused to rest, the Voice said to Much-Afraid, 'Drink of the brook at the side of the way and be strengthened.'

Stooping down at the spring where it bubbled up from between the rocks, she filled her mouth with the water, but as soon as she had swallowed it she found it so burning and bitter that her stomach rejected it altogether and she was unable to retain it. She knelt by the spring, gasping for a moment, and then said very quietly and softly through the silence, 'My Lord, it is not that I *will* not, but that I CANNOT drink of this cup.'

'There is a tree growing beside this spring of Marah,' answered the Voice. 'Break off a piece of branch, and when you have cast it into the waters they will be sweetened.'

Much-Afraid looked on the other side of the spring and saw a little stunted thorn-tree with but one branch growing on either side of the splintered trunk, like the arms of a cross. They were covered all over with long, sharp spines. Suffering stepped forward, broke off a piece of the thorn-tree, and brought it to Much-Afraid, who took it from her hand and cast it into the water. On doing this she stooped her head again to drink. This time she found that the stinging, burning bitterness was gone, and though the water was not sweet, she could drink it easily. She drank thirstily and found that it must have contained curative properties, for almost at once she was wonderfully refreshed and strengthened. Then she picked up her twelfth and last stone there beside the water of Marah and put it into her bag.

After they had rested a little while she was able to resume the journey, and for a time was so much stronger that although the way was even steeper than before, she was not nearly so faint and exhausted. This greatly comforted her, for by that time she had only one desire in her heart, to reach the place appointed and fulfil the command which had been given her before her strength ebbed away altogether. On the third day 'they lifted up their eyes and saw the place afar off', the great rock cliff and the waterfall, and continuing up the rocky path, at midday they came through the shrouding mist to the place which had been appointed.

CHAPTER XVI

THE GRAVE ON THE MOUNTAINS

THE path led forward to the edge of a yawning chasm, then stopped dead. This grave-like gorge yawned before them in each direction as far as they could see, completely cutting off all further progress. It was so filled with cloud and mist that they could not see how deep it was, nor could they see across to the other side, but spread before them like a great gaping grave, waiting to swallow them up. For a moment Much-Afraid wondered whether this could be the place, after all, but as they halted on the edge of the canyon, they could plainly hear the sound of mighty, swirling waters, and she realised that they must be standing somewhere near the lip of the great fall and that this was indeed the place appointed.

Looking at her companions, she asked quietly, 'What must we do now? Can we jump across to the other side?'

'No,' they said, 'it would be impossible.'

'What, then, are we to do?' she asked.

'We must leap down into the canyon,' was the answer.

'Of course,' said Much-Afraid at once. 'I did not realise at first, but that is the thing to do.'

Then for the last time on that journey (though she did not know it at the time) she held out her hands to her two companions that they might help her. By this time she was so weak and exhausted that instead of taking her hands, they came close up to her and put their hands beneath her arms so that she leant with her full weight against them. Thus with Suffering and Sorrow supporting her, Much-Afraid cast herself down into the yawning grave.

The place into which they had thrown themselves was deep, and had she been alone she must have been badly hurt by the fall. However, her companions were so strong that the jump did not seem to harm them at all, and they bore her so easily between them and broke the fall so gently that she was no more than bruised and shaken. Then, because the canyon was so filled with mist and cloud that nothing was visible, they began to feel their way slowly forward and saw, looming up before them, a flat, oblong rock. On reaching it, they found it to be some kind of stone altar with the indistinct figure of someone standing behind it.

'This is the place,' said Much-Afraid quietly. 'This is where I am to make my offering.' She went up to the altar and knelt down. 'My Lord,' she said softly through the mist. 'Will You come to me now and help me to make my burnt offering as You have commanded me?'

But for the first time on all that journey there seemed to be no answer—no answer at all—and the Shepherd did not come.

She knelt there quite alone in the cold, clammy mist, beside the desolate altar in this valley of shadow, and into her mind came the words which Bitterness had flung at her long before when she walked on the shores of Loneliness: 'Sooner or later, when He gets you up on the wild places of the mountains He will put you on some sort of a cross AND ABANDON YOU TO IT.' It seemed that in a way Bitterness had been right, thought Much-Afraid to herself, only he had been too ignorant to know and she too foolish at that time to understand that in all the world only one thing really mattered, to do the will of the One she followed and loved, no matter what it involved or cost. Strangely enough, as she knelt there by the altar, seemingly abandoned at that last tremendous crisis, there was no sign or sound of the presence of her enemies. The grave up on the mountains is at the very edge of the High Places and beyond the reach of Pride and Bitterness and Resentment and Self-Pity, yes, and of Fear too, as though she were in another world altogether, for they can never cast themselves down into that grave. She knelt there feeling neither despair nor hope. She knew now without a shadow of doubt that there would be no Angel to call from heaven to say that the sacrifice need not be made, and this knowledge caused her neither dread nor shrinking. She felt nothing but a great stillness in which *only one desire remained*, to do that which He had told her, simply because He had asked it of her. The cold, dull desolation which had filled her heart in the cave was gone completely; one flame burned there steadily, the flame of concentrated desire to do His will. Everything else had died down and fallen into ashes.

After she had waited for a little and still He had not come, she put out her hand and with one final effort of failing strength grasped the natural human love and desire growing in her heart and struggled to tear them out. At the first touch it was as though anguish pierced through her every nerve and fibre, and she knew with a pang almost of despair that the roots had wound and twined and thrust themselves into every part of her being. Though she put forth all her remaining strength in the most desperate effort to wrench them out, not a single rootlet stirred. For the first time she felt something akin to fear and panic. She was NOT ABLE to do this thing which He had asked of her. Having reached the altar at last, she was powerless to obey. Turning to those who had been her guides and helpers all the way up the mountains, she asked for their help, and for them to do what she could not for herself, to tear the plant out of her heart. For the first time Suffering and Sorrow shook their heads.

'We have done all that we can for you,' they answered, 'but this we cannot do.'

At that the indistinct figure behind the altar stepped forward and said quietly, 'I am the priest of this altar—I will take it out of your heart if you wish.'

Much-Afraid turned towards him instantly. 'Oh, thank you,' she said. 'I beg you to do so.'

He came and stood beside her, His form indistinct and blurred by the mist, and then she continued entreatingly, 'I am a very great coward. I am afraid that the pain may cause me to try to resist you. Will you bind me to the altar in some way so that I cannot move? I would not like to be found struggling while the will of my Lord is done.'

There was complete silence in the cloud-filled canyon for a moment or two, then the priest answered, 'It is well said. I will bind you to the altar.' Then he bound her hand and foot.

When he had finished, Much-Afraid lifted her face towards the High Places which were quite invisible and spoke quietly through the mist. 'My Lord, behold me—here I am, in the place Thou didst send me to—doing the thing Thou didst tell me to do, for where Thou diest, will I die, and there will I be buried: the Lord do so to me, and more also, if ought but death part Thee and me' (Ruth 1:17).

Still there was silence, a silence as of the grave, for indeed she was in the grave of her own hopes and still without the promised hinds' feet, still outside the High Places with even the promise to be laid down on the altar. This was the place to which the long, heart-breaking journey had led her. Yet just once more before she laid it down on the altar, Much-Afraid repeated the glorious promise which had been the cause of her starting for the High Places. 'The Lord God is my strength, and He WILL make my feet like hinds' feet, and He WILL make me to walk upon mine High Places. TO THE CHIEF SINGER ON MY STRINGED INSTRUMENTS' (Hab. 3:19).

The priest put forth a hand of steel, right into her heart. There was a sound of rending and tearing, and the human love, with all its myriad rootlets and fibres, came forth.

He held it for a moment and then said, 'Yes, it was ripe for removal, the time had come. There is not a rootlet torn or missing.'

When he had said this he cast it down on the altar and spread his hands above it. There came a flash of fire which seemed to rend the altar; after that, nothing but ashes remained, either of the love itself, which had been so deeply planted in her heart, or of the suffering and sorrow which had been her companions on that long, strange journey. A sense of utter, overwhelming rest and peace engulfed Much-Afraid. At last, the offering had been made and there was nothing left to be done. When the priest had unbound her she leant forward over the ashes on the altar and said with complete thanksgiving, 'It is finished.'

Then, utterly exhausted, she fell asleep.

PART TWO

'JOY COMETH IN THE MORNING'

(Psalm 30:5)

CHAPTER XVII

THE HEALING STREAMS

WHEN at last Much-Afraid awoke the sun was high in the sky, and she looked out through the mouth of the cave in which she found herself lying. Everything was shimmering in a blaze of radiant sunshine which burnished every object with glory. She lay still a little longer, collecting her thoughts and trying to understand where she was. The rocky cave into which the sunbeams were pouring was warm and quiet and drenched with the sweet perfume of spikenard, frankincense, and myrrh. This perfume she gradually realised was emanating from the wrappings which covered her. She gently pushed back the folds, sat up, and looked about her. Then the memory of all that had happened returned to her. She and her two companions had come to a cloud-filled canyon high up on the mountains and to an altar of sacrifice, and the priest had wrenched out of her heart her flower of human love and burnt it on the altar. On remembering that, she glanced down at her breast and saw it was covered with a cloth soaked in the spices whose perfume stole out and filled the cave with sweetness. She pushed the cloth aside a little curiously and was astonished to find no trace of a wound—not even a scar, nor was there any hint of pain or aching or stiffness anywhere in her body.

Rising quietly, she went outside, then stood still and looked about her. The canyon, which had been so shrouded in mist that nothing had been distinguishable, now shimmered in the golden sunlight. Soft, verdant grass grew everywhere, starred with gentians and other little jewel-like flowers of every variety. There were banks of sweet-smelling thyme, moss, and myrtle along the sides of the rocky walls, and everything sparkled with dew. In the centre of the canyon, at a little distance from the cave, was the long stone altar to which she had been bound, but in the sunlight she saw that the flowers and mosses grew all about it and clothed its sides with verdure. Little birds hopped about here and there, scattering the dewdrops off the grasses and chirping merrily as they preened their plumage. One was perched on the altar itself, its little throat throbbing as it trilled forth a song of joy, but the most beautiful and wonderful thing of all was that out from under the rock altar there gushed a great 'river of water, clear as crystal'. It then flowed in a series of cascades and through rock pools right through the canyon till it came to a broad lip of rock, over which it poured with a noise of shouting and tumultuous gladness. She was at the very source of the great fall and knew now that it flowed from under the altar to which the priest had bound her.

For some time she stood looking about her, her heart leaping and thrilling with a growing joy which was beyond her understanding and a peace indescribably sweet which seemed to enfold her. She was quite alone in the canyon. There were no signs of her companions Sorrow and Suffering nor of the priest of the altar. The only things which breathed and moved in the canyon beside herself were the cheerful little chirping birds and the insects and butterflies flitting amongst the flowers. High overhead was a cloudless sky, against which the peaks of the High Places shone dazzlingly white.

The first thing she did, after she had taken in her surroundings, was to step towards the river which gushed out from under the altar. It drew her irresistibly. She stooped down when she got to the bank and dabbled her fingers in the crystal water. It was icy cold, but it sent a shock of ecstasy tingling through her body, and without further delay she put off the white-linen robe she was wearing and stepped into one of the rocky pools. Never had she experienced anything so delicious and exhilarating. It was like immersing herself in a stream of bubbling life. When at last she again stepped out of the pool she was immediately dry and tingling from head to foot with a sense of perfect well-being.

As she stood on the mossy bank by the pool she happened to glance down and noticed for the first time that her feet were no longer the crooked, ugly things which they always had been, but were 'straight feet', perfectly formed, shining white against the soft green grass. Then she remembered the healing streams of which the Shepherd had spoken, which gushed out of the ground on the High Places. Stepping straight back into the pool with a shock of sweetest pleasure and putting her head beneath the clear waters, she splashed them about her face. Then she found a little pool among the rocks, still and clear as a mirror. Kneeling down, she looked into its unruffled surface and saw her face quite clearly. It was true, the ugly, twisted mouth had vanished and the face she saw reflected back by the water was as relaxed and perfect as the face of a little child.

After that she began to wander about the canyon and noticed wild strawberries and whortleberries and other small berries growing on the banks. She found a handful of these as refreshing and sustaining a meal as ever she had eaten. Then she came to the lip of the rock cliff over which the river cast itself, and stood a long time watching the water as it leaped over the edge with the noise of its tumultuous joy drowning every other sound. She saw how the sun glorified the crystal waters as they went swirling downwards and far below she saw the green alps where the Shepherd had led her and where they had stood at the foot of this same fall. She felt completely encompassed by peace, and a great inner quietness and contentment drowned every feeling of curiosity, loneliness and anticipation. She did not think about the future at all. It was enough to be there in that quiet canyon, hidden away high up in the mountains with the river of life flowing beside her, and to rest and recover herself after the long journey. After a little she lay down on a mossy bank and slept, and when she woke again, bathed herself in the river. So the long, quiet day passed like a sweet dream while she rested and bathed and refreshed herself at intervals with the berries and then slept again.

When at last the shadows lengthened and the sun sank in the west and the snow peaks glowed glorious in rose and flame colour she went back into the cave, laid herself down amongst the spice-perfumed coverings and slept as deeply and dreamlessly as she had the first night when the priest laid her there to rest.

CHAPTER XVIII

THE HINDS' FEET

On the third day while it was still almost dark she woke suddenly, and sprang to her feet with a shock of joy tingling through her. She had not heard her name called, had not even been conscious of a voice, yet she knew that she HAD been called. Some mysterious, poignantly sweet summons had reached her, a summons which she knew instinctively she had been awaiting ever since she woke up for the first time in the cave. She stepped outside into the fragrant summer night. The morning star hung low in the sky, and in the east the first glimmer of dawn appeared. From somewhere close at hand a solitary bird uttered one clear, sweet note and a light breeze stirred over the grasses. Otherwise there was no sound save the voice of the great waterfall.

Then it came again—tingling through her—a call ringing down from some high place above. Standing there in the pale dawn, she looked eagerly around. Every nerve in her body surged with desire to respond to the call, and she felt her feet and legs tingling with an almost irresistible urge to go bounding up the mountains, but where was the way out of the canyon? The walls seemed to rise smooth and almost perpendicular on all sides, except at the end which was blocked by the waterfall. Then, as she stood, straining every nerve to find a possible means of exit, up from a nearby mossy bank sprang a mountain hart with the hind close behind him, just as she had seen them at the foot of the great Precipice Injury. As she watched, the hart sprang on to the altar of rock, and from there with a great leap he reached a projecting ledge on the wall on the farther side of the ravine. Then, closely followed by the hind, he began springing up the great wall of the canyon.

Much-Afraid did not hesitate one instant. In a moment she was on the rock altar herself, the next, with a flying leap, she, too, reached the ledge on the wall. Then, using the same footholds as the hart and the hind, leaping and springing in a perfect ecstasy of delight, she followed them up the cliff, the hooves of the deer ringing on the rocks before her like little silver hammers. In a moment or two all three were at the top of the canyon, and she was leaping up the mountain-side towards the peak above, from which the summons had come. The rosy light in the east brightened, the snow on the summits of the mountains caught the glow and flushed like fire, and as she skipped and jumped from rock to rock excitedly the first sunbeams streamed over the mountain-top. HE WAS THERE—standing on the peak—just as she had known He would be, strong and grand and glorious in the beauty of the sunrise, holding out both hands and calling to her with a great laugh, '*You*—with the hinds' feet—jump over here.'

She gave one last flying spring, caught His hands and landed beside Him on the topmost peak of the mountain. Around them in every direction towered other and greater ranges of snow mountains, whose summits soared into the sky higher than her sight could follow them. He was crowned, and dressed in royal robes just as she had seen Him once before when He had carried her up to the High Places, and had touched her with the live coal from off the golden Altar of Love. Then His face had been stern in its majesty and gravity, now it was alight with a glory of joy which excelled anything which she had ever imagined.

'At last,' He said, as she knelt speechless at His feet, 'at last you are here and the "night of weeping is over and joy comes to you in the morning".' Then, lifting her up, He continued, 'This is the time when you are to receive the fulfilment of the promises. Never am I to call you Much-Afraid again.' At that He laughed again and said, 'I will write upon her a new name, the NAME OF HER GOD. The Lord God is a sun and shield: the Lord will give GRACE AND GLORY: no good thing will He withhold from them that walk upright' (Psa. 84:11). 'This is your new name,' He declared. 'From henceforth you are GRACE AND GLORY.'

Still she could not speak, but stood silent with joy and thanksgiving and awe and wonder.

Then He went on, 'Now for the flower of Love and for the promise that when it blooms you will be loved in return.'

Grace and Glory spoke for the first time. 'My Lord and King,' she said softly, 'there is no flower of Love to bloom in my heart. It was burnt to ashes on the altar at Thy command.'

'No flower of Love?' He repeated, and laughed again so gently and joyfully that she could hardly bear it. 'That is strange, Grace and Glory. How, then, did you get here? You are right on the High Places, in the Kingdom of Love itself. Open your heart and let us see what is there.'

At His word she laid bare her heart, and out came the sweetest perfume she had ever breathed and filled all the air around them with its fragrance. There in her heart was a plant whose shape and form could not be seen because it was covered all over with pure white, almost transparent blooms, from which the fragrance poured forth.

Grace and Glory gave a little gasp of wonder and thankfulness. 'How did it get there, my Lord and King?' she exclaimed.

'Why, I planted it there Myself,' was His laughing answer. 'Surely you remember, down there by the sheep pool in the Valley of Humiliation, on the day that you promised to go with Me to the High Places. It is the flower from the thornshaped seed.'

'Then, my Lord, what was the plant which the priest tore out of my heart when I was bound to the altar?'

'Do you remember, Grace and Glory, when you looked into your heart beside the pool, and found that My kind of love was not there at all—only the plant of Longing-to-beloved?'

She nodded wonderingly.

'That was the natural human love which I tore out from your heart when the time was ripe and it was loose enough to be uprooted altogether so that the real Love could grow there alone, and fill your whole heart.'

'YOU tore it out!' she repeated slowly and wonderingly, and then, 'O my Lord and King, were YOU the priest? Were YOU there all the time, when I thought You had forsaken me?'

He bowed His head and she took His hands in hers, the scarred hands which had sown the thorn-shaped seed in her heart, and the hands with the grasp of steel which had torn out that love which had been the cause of all her pain, and kissed them while tears of joy fell on them.

'And now for the promise,' said He, 'that when Love flowers in your heart you shall be loved again.' Taking her hand in His, He said, 'Behold I have set MY LOVE upon thee and thou art MINE . . .

yea, I have loved thee with an everlasting love: therefore with lovingkindness have I drawn thee' (Jer. 31:3). After that He said, 'Give Me the bag of stones of remembrance that you have gathered on your journey, Grace and Glory.'

She took it out and passed it to Him and then He bade her hold out her hands. On doing so, He opened the little purse and emptied the contents into her hands. Then she gasped again with bewilderment and delight, for instead of the common, ugly stones she had gathered from the altars along the way, there fell into her hands a heap of glorious, sparkling jewels, very precious and very beautiful. As she stood there, half-dazzled by the glory of the flashing gems, she saw in His hand a circlet of pure gold.

'O thou who wast afflicted, tossed with tempest and not comforted,' He said, 'behold I lay thy stones with fair colours.'

First He picked out of her hand one of the biggest and most beautiful of the stones—a sapphire, shining like the pavement of heaven and set it in the centre of the golden circlet. Then, taking a fiery, blood-red ruby, He set it on one side of the sapphire and an emerald on the other. After that He took the other stones—twelve in all—and arranged them on the circlet, then set it upon her head. At that moment Grace and Glory remembered the cave in which she had sheltered from the floods, and how nearly she had succumbed to the temptation to discard as worthless those stones which now shone with glory and splendour in the crown upon her head. She remembered, too, the words which had sounded in her ears and had restrained her, 'Hold fast that thou hast, that no man take thy crown.' Supposing she had thrown them away, had discarded her trust in His promises, had gone back on her surrenders to His will. There could have been no jewels now to His praise and glory, and no crown for her to wear. She marvelled at the grace and love and tenderness and patience which had led and trained and guarded and kept poor faltering Much-Afraid, which had not allowed her to turn back, and which now changed all her trials into glory. Then she heard Him speaking again and this time the smile on His face was almost more joyful than before.

'Hearken, O daughter, and consider, and incline thine ear; forget also thine own people, and thy father's house; so shall the King greatly desire thy beauty: for He is thy Lord; and worship thou Him. . . . The King's daughter is all glorious within. She shall be brought unto the King in clothing of wrought gold, in raiment of needlework. The virgins, HER COMPANIONS THAT FOLLOW HER, shall be brought unto Thee. With gladness and rejoicing shall they be brought: they shall enter into the King's palace' (Psa. 45:10–15). Then He added, 'Now you are to live with Me here on the High Places, to go where I go, and to share My work in the valley below, it is fitting, Grace and Glory, that you should have companions and handmaidens, and I will bring them to you now.'

At that Grace and Glory regarded Him earnestly, and there were almost tears in her eyes, for she remembered Suffering and Sorrow, the faithful companions whom He had given her before. It had been through their help and gentleness and patience she had been able to ascend the mountains to the High Places. All the time she had been with her Lord and King, receiving her new name, and being crowned with joy and glory, she had been thinking of them and wishing—yes, actually wishing and longing that they were there too, for why should she receive everything? They had endured the same journey, had supported and helped her, had been through the same trials and besetments of the enemy. Now she was here and they were not. She opened her mouth to make her first request, to beg her Lord to let her keep the companions

He had chosen in the beginning and who had brought her to the glory of the High Places. Before she could speak, however, He said with the same specially lovely smile, 'Here are the handmaidens, Grace and Glory, whom I have chosen to be with you henceforth and for ever.'

Two radiant, shining figures stepped forward, the morning sunshine glittering on their snowy garments, making them dazzling to look at. They were taller and stronger than Grace and Glory, but it was the beauty of their faces and the love shining in their eyes which caught at her heart and made her almost tremble with joy and admiration. They came towards her, their faces shining with mirth and gladness, but they said not a word.

'Who are you?' asked Grace and Glory softly. 'Will you tell me your names?'

Instead of answering they looked at one another and smiled, then held out their hands as though to take hers in their own. At that familiar gesture, Grace and Glory knew them and cried out with a joy which was almost more than she could bear.

'Why! You are Suffering and Sorrow. Oh, welcome, welcome! I was longing to find you again.'

They shook their heads. 'Oh, no!' they laughed, 'we are no more Suffering and Sorrow than you are Much-Afraid. Don't you know that everything that comes to the High Places is transformed? Since you brought us here with you, we are turned into JOY and PEACE.'

'Brought you here!' gasped Grace and Glory, 'what an extraordinary way to express it! Why, from first to last *you* dragged ME here.'

Again they shook their heads and smiled as they answered, 'No, we could never have come here alone, Grace and Glory. Suffering and Sorrow may not enter the Kingdom of Love, but each time you accepted us and put your hands in ours we began to change. Had you turned back or rejected us, we never could have come here.'

Looking at one another again, they laughed softly and said, 'When first we saw you at the foot of the mountains, we felt a little depressed and despairing. You seemed so MUCH-AFRAID of us, and shrank away and would not accept our help, and it looked so unlikely that any of us would ever get to the High Places. We told ourselves that we would have to remain Sorrow and Suffering always, but you see how graciously our Lord the King arranged for all of us, and you DID bring us here. Now we are to be your companions and friends for ever.'

With that they came up to her, put their arms around her, and all three embraced and kissed one another with a love and thankfulness and joy beyond words to express. So with a new name, and united to the King and crowned with glory, Grace and Glory, accompanied by her companions and friends, came to the High Places and was led into the Kingdom of Love.

CHAPTER XIX

THE HIGH PLACES

GRACE AND GLORY with her handmaidens Joy and Peace stayed up on the High Places for several weeks while all three explored the heights and learnt many new lessons from the King. He led them Himself to many places, and explained to them as much as they were able to understand at that time. He also encouraged them to explore on their own, for there are always new and lovely discoveries to make up there on the High Places.

Even these High Places were not the highest of all. Others towered above them into the sky, where mortal eye could no longer follow them, and where only those who have finished their pilgrim life on earth are able to go. Grace and Glory and her friends were on the lowest, the 'beginners' slopes' in the Kingdom of Love, and these were the parts which they were to explore and enjoy at this time. From these slopes, too, they were able to look down on the valleys below, and from that new view-point, gain an understanding of many things which had been puzzling and mysterious to them before. From beneath they had not been seen clearly, and even then only a small part had been visible.

The first thing, however, which they realised up there on the slopes of the Kingdom of Love was HOW MUCH MORE THERE WOULD BE TO SEE AND LEARN AND UNDERSTAND when the King took them HIGHER on future occasions. The glorious view which they now enjoyed was but small in comparison with all that lay beyond, and would be visible only from yet higher places above. It was now perfectly evident to them that there must be ranges upon ranges of which they had never dreamt while they were still down in the narrow valleys with their extraordinarily limited views. Sometimes, as she looked on the glorious panorama visible from these lowest slopes in the Kingdom of Love, she found herself blushing as she remembered some of the dogmatic statements which she and others had made in the depths of the valley about the High Places and the ranges of Truth. They had been able to see so little and were so unconscious of what lay beyond and above. If that had been the case while down in the Valley, how much more clearly, she now realised, that even up on those wonderful slopes she was only looking out on a tiny corner of the whole.

She never tired of looking from the glorious new viewpoint on the first slopes of the Kingdom of Love and seeing it all from a new perspective. What she could see and could take in almost intoxicated her with joy and thanksgiving, and sometimes even with inexpressible relief. Things which she had thought dark and terrible and which had made her tremble as she looked up from the Valley because they had seemed so alien to any part of the Realm of Love, were now seen to be but parts of a great and wonderful WHOLE. They were so altered and modified that as she saw what they extended into, she wondered at having been so blind and stupid at having had such false ideas about them. She began to understand quite clearly that TRUTH cannot be understood from books alone or by any written words, but only by personal growth and development in understanding, and that things written even in the BOOK OF BOOKS can be astonishingly misunderstood while one still lives on the low levels of spiritual experience and on the wrong side of the grave on the mountains. She perceived that no one who finds herself up on the slopes of the Kingdom of Love can possibly dogmatise about what is seen there, because it is only then that she comprehends how small a part of the glorious whole she sees. All she can do is to gasp with wonder, awe, and thanksgiving, and to long with all her heart to go higher and to see and understand more. Paradoxical as it may seem, as she gazed out on dazzling vistas, so glorious that she could not look at them steadily or grasp their magnificent sweep, she often thought that the prayer which best expressed her heart's desire was that of the blind man, 'Lord, that I might receive my sight! Help me to open myself to more light. Help me to fuller understanding.'

Another thing which gave her continual joy was their unbroken communion with the King. Wherever He went she and Peace and Joy went too, springing behind Him with a delight which at times was almost hilarious, for He was teaching and training them to use their hinds' feet. Grace and Glory quickly saw, however, that He always chose the way most carefully, and restrained His own amazing strength and power, taking only such springs and bounds as they could manage too. So graciously did He adapt Himself to what was possible to their newly-acquired capacity that they scarcely recognised in the exhilaration of leaping and skipping like hinds on the mountains, that had He really extended His powers, they would have been left behind completely. For Grace and Glory—who had been lame and limping all her life—the ecstasy of leaping about in this way and of bounding from rock to rock on the High Places as easily as the mountain roes, was so rapturous that she could hardly bear to cease from it even for rests. The King seemed to find great delight in encouraging this, and led her on and on, taking longer and longer leaps, until at last she would be quite breathless. Then as they sat side by side on some new crag to which He had led her, while she rested He would point out some of the vistas to be seen from the new viewpoint.

On one of these occasions after they had been up on the High Places for several days, she flung herself down on the lichen and moss-covered crag to which He had led her, and, laughing and breathless, said, 'Even hinds' feet seem to need a rest now and then!'

'Grace and Glory,' He answered, 'do you think you understand now how I was able to make your feet like hinds' feet and to set you on these High Places?'

She drew closer to Him and looked earnestly in His face and asked, 'How were You able to do this, my Lord and King?'

'Think back over the journey you made,' He replied, 'and tell Me what lessons you learnt on the way.'

She was silent for a while as she reviewed the whole journey, which had seemed so terribly long and in some places so cruelly difficult and even impossible. She thought of the altars which she had built along the way; of the time when she had stood with Him at the trysting-place in the Valley, when He had called her to follow Him to the Heights. She remembered the walk to the foot of the mountains; the first meeting with Suffering and Sorrow and of learning to accept their help; she recalled the shock of what had seemed such a heart-breaking detour down into the desert, and of the things which she had seen there. Then their journey along the shores of Loneliness; the empty cove which the sea had filled to the brim; and then the agony of disappointment and frustration experienced in the wilderness when the path once again had turned away from the High Places. She remembered crossing the great sea-wall, walking through the woods and valleys until the rapturous moment when the path had turned back towards the mountains. Her thoughts turned to the Precipice of Injury, the Forests of Danger and Tribulation, the great storm during which they had sheltered in the hut. And then the mist—the endless mist, and the awful moment when the path suddenly led down into the Valley of Loss, and the nightmare abyss of horror into which she had looked when she had thought of turning back. She recalled the descent down into the Valley of Loss and the peace she had found there before re-ascending to the heights in the aerial chairs, and of the days spent in that place where she had been prepared for her burial. Then that last agonising ascent, and the cave where they sheltered from the floods and where she had been tempted to cast away the promises. Then the spring called Marah, and finally the mist-shrouded grave up among the peaks where she had been bound to the altar. How little she had imagined when first she set out on that strange journey, what lay ahead of her and the things which she would be called upon to pass through. So for a long time she sat silent—remembering, wondering and thankful.

At last she put her hand in His and said softly, 'My Lord, I will tell You what I learnt.'

'Tell Me,' He answered gently.

'First,' said she, 'I learnt that I must ACCEPT WITH JOY all that You allowed to happen to me on the way and everything to which the path led me! That I was never to try to evade it but to accept it and lay down my own will on the altar and say, "Behold me, I am Thy little handmaiden Acceptance-with-Joy." '

He nodded without speaking, and she went on, 'Then I learnt that I must bear all that others were allowed to do against me and to forgive with no trace of bitterness and to say to Thee, "Behold me—I am Thy little handmaiden Bearing-with-Love;" that I may receive power to bring good out of this evil.'

Again He nodded, and she smiled still more sweetly and happily.

'The third thing that I learnt was that You, my Lord, never regarded me as I actually was, lame and weak and crooked and cowardly. You saw me as I would be when You had done what You promised and had brought me to the High Places, when it could be truly said, "There is none that walks with such a queenly ease, nor with such grace, as she." You always treated me with the same love and graciousness as though I were a queen already and not wretched little Much-Afraid.' Then she looked up into His face and for a little time could say no more, but at last she added, 'My Lord, I cannot tell You how greatly I want to regard others in the same way.'

A very lovely smile broke out on His face at that, but He still said nothing, only nodded for the third time and waited for her to continue.

'The fourth thing,' said she with a radiant face, 'was really the first I learnt up here. *Every* circumstance in life, no matter how crooked and distorted and ugly it appears to be, if it is reacted to in love and forgiveness and obedience to Your will can be transformed. Therefore I begin to think, my Lord, You purposely allow us to be brought into contact with the bad and evil things that YOU WANT CHANGED. Perhaps that is the very reason why we are here in this world, where sin and sorrow and suffering and evil abound, so that we may let You teach us so to react to them, that out of them we can create lovely qualities to live for ever. That is the only really satisfactory way of dealing with evil, not simply binding it so that it cannot work harm, but whenever possible overcoming it with good.'

At last He spoke. 'You have learned well, Grace and Glory. Now I will add one thing more. It was these lessons which you have learnt which enabled Me to change you from limping, crippled Much-Afraid into Grace and Glory with the hinds' feet. Now you are able to run, leaping on the mountains and able to follow Me wherever I go, so that we need never be parted again. So remember this; as long as you are willing to be Acceptance-with-Joy and Bearing-in-Love, you can never again become crippled, and you will be able to go wherever I lead you. You will be able to go down into the Valley of the world to work with Me there, for that is where the evil and sorrowful and ugly things are which need to be overcome. Accept and bear and obey the Law of Love, and nothing will be able to cripple your hinds' feet or to separate you from Me. This is the secret of the High Places, Grace and Glory, it is the lovely and perfect law of the whole universe. It is this that makes the radiant joy of the Heavenly Places.' Then He rose to His feet, drew her up beside Him, and said, 'Now use your hinds' feet again, for I am going to lead you to another part of the mountain.'

Off He went, 'leaping on the mountains and skipping on the hills', with Grace and Glory following close behind and the beautiful figures of Peace and Joy springing at her side. As they went she sang this song:

> Set me as a seal upon Thine heart
> Thou Love more strong than death
> That I may feel through every part

Thy burning, fiery breath.
And then like wax held in the flame,
May take the imprint of Thy Name.

Set me a seal upon Thine arm,
    Thou Love that bursts the grave,
Thy coals of fire can never harm,
    But only purge and save.
Thou jealous Love, Thou burning Flame,
Oh burn out all unlike Thy Name.

The floods can never drown Thy Love,
    Nor weaken Thy desire,
The rains may deluge from above
    But never quench Thy fire,
Make soft my heart in Thy strong flame,
To take the imprint of Thy Name.

(Cant. 8:6)

CHAPTER XX

THE RETURN TO THE VALLEY

THE place to which the King of Love now brought them was a most beautiful valley among the peaks of the High Places. The whole of this sheltered spot was laid out in quiet gardens and orchards and vineyards. Here grew flowers of rarest beauty and lilies of every description. Here, too, were trees of spices and of many kinds of fruits, and nut-trees, almonds and walnuts, and many other varieties which Grace and Glory had never seen before. Here the King's gardeners were always busy, pruning the trees, tending the plants and the vines, and preparing beds for new seedlings and tender shoots. These the King Himself transplanted from uncongenial soil and conditions in the valleys below so that they might grow to perfection and bloom in that valley high above, ready to be planted in other parts of the Kingdom of Love, to beautify and adorn it wherever the King saw fit. They spent several delightful days watching the gardeners as they worked under the gracious supervision of the King Himself and accompanying Him as He walked in the vineyards, teaching and advising those who tended the vines.

One day, however, Grace and Glory with her two attendants walked to the end of the valley and found themselves on the very edge of the High Places, from which they could look right down into the Low Places far below. As they stood there they saw a long, green valley between two chains of mountains through which a river wound like a ribbon of light. Here and there were patches of brown and red which seemed to be villages and dwelling-places, surrounded with trees and gardens.

All of a sudden, Grace and Glory gave a queer little gasp, for she recognised the place. They were looking down into the Valley of Humiliation itself, the place where she had lived in misery for so long and from which the Shepherd had called her to the High Places. Without a word she sat down on the grassy slope, and as she looked a multitude of thoughts filled her mind. Down there was the little white cottage where she had lived, and the pastures where the shepherds tended the King's flocks. There were the sheepfolds, and the stream where the flocks went to drink and where she had met the Shepherd for the first time. In that valley were all her fellow-workers and the friends amongst whom she had lived and with whom she had enjoyed such happy fellowship.

Others she had known were there, too. Away on the outskirts of the village was the cottage where her Aunt Dismal Foreboding lived and where she had spent her miserable childhood with her cousins Gloomy and Spiteful and Craven Fear. As she thought of them and their wretched existence a pang of compassion and pain shot through her heart. Poor Aunt Dismal, trying to hide the fact that her heart was broken by the unhappy marriages which her two daughters had made, and embittered by the shameful doings of her darling son. She saw the dwellings of her other relatives; the Manor House, where decrepit old Lord Fearing lived, tortured by his failing powers and his dread of approaching death. There was the house where Pride lived, and near it the homes of Bitterness and Resentment, and under those dark trees lived miserable Self-Pity. She recognised the dwelling-places of those who had so harassed her on her journey to the High Places, and round about were the homes of other inhabitants of the Valley, people who hated or despised or rejected the Shepherd.

As Grace and Glory sat looking down into the Valley the tears welled into her eyes and her heart throbbed with pain, two sensa-tions which she had completely forgotten up there on the High Places. Suddenly she discovered that her feelings towards her rela-tives and those who lived down there in the Valley had undergone a complete change, and she saw them in a new light. She had thought of them only as horrible enemies, but now she realised that they were just miserable beings such as she had been herself. They were indwelt and tormented by their different besetting sins and ugly natures, just as she had been by her fears. They were wretched slaves to the natures which gave them their names, and the more horrible the qualities which characterised them, the more misery they endured, and the more they ought to be compassionated. She could scarcely bear the thought, yet for so many years she had not only feared but also condemned them, had actually 'disdained their mis-ery', telling herself it was their own fault. Yes, she, detestable, fear-enslaved Much-Afraid HAD actually dared to disdain them for the things which made them so wretched and ugly when she herself was equally wretched and enslaved. Instead of a fellow-feeling of com-passion and passionate desire that they might be delivered and trans-formed from the pride and resentment and bitterness which made them what they were, she had just detested and despised them.

When she thought of that she turned to Joy and Peace, who were sitting beside her, and cried out desperately, 'Can nothing be done for them down there in the Valley? Must my Aunt Dismal be left unhelped, and poor Spiteful and Gloomy too, and those cousins who went so far with us on the way to the High Places, trying to turn us back! If the Shepherd could deliver me, Grace and Glory, from all my fears and sins, couldn't He deliver them also from the things which torment them?'

'Yes,' said Joy (who had been Sorrow). 'If He can turn Sorrow into Joy, Suffering into Peace, and Much-Afraid into Grace and Glory, how can we doubt that He COULD change Pride and Bitterness and Resentment and Self-Pity too, if they would but yield to Him and follow Him? And your Aunt Dismal COULD be changed into Praise and Thanksgiving, and poor Gloomy and Spiteful also. We cannot doubt that it could be done and that they could be completely delivered from all the things which torment them.'

'But,' cried Grace and Glory, 'how can they be persuaded to follow the Shepherd? At present they hate Him and won't go near Him.'

Then Peace (who before had been Suffering) said quietly, 'I have noticed that when people are brought into sorrow and suffering, or loss, or humiliation, or grief, or into some place of great need, they sometimes become ready to know the Shepherd and to seek His help. We know, for example, that your Aunt Dismal is desperately unhappy over the behaviour of poor Craven Fear, and it may be that she would be ready now to turn to the Shepherd. Then poor Gloomy and Spiteful are so wretched that though they felt no need of the Shepherd before, it is very possible that now is the time to try to persuade them to seek His help.'

'Yes!' exclaimed Grace and Glory, 'I am sure you are right. Oh, if only we could go to them! If only there were some way of helping them to find what we have found.'

At that very moment, close at hand, sounded the voice of the King. He came and sat down beside them, looked with them down into the Valley so far below, and said gently to Grace and Glory, 'Thou that dwellest in the gardens, the companions hearken to thy voice; cause Me to hear it' (Cant. 8:13).

Grace and Glory turned to Him and laid her hand upon His arm. 'My Lord,' she said, 'we were talking about the people who live down there in the Valley of Humiliation. They are my relatives, You know, all of them. They are so wretched and miserable. What can we do for them, my Lord? They don't know anything about the joy of the High Places and the Kingdom of Love. There is my poor Aunt Dismal Forebodings. I lived with her for a long time, and know that she is utterly wretched.'

'I know her,' said the King quietly, 'she is a most unhappy woman.'

'And her daughter Gloomy,' went on Grace and Glory, looking at Him entreatingly as she spoke. 'She married Coward, the son of old Lord Fearing, very rich, but much older than herself and a miserably unhappy and selfish creature. I believe she has not known a moment's peace since. There was talk in the Valley before I came away, that he was likely to desert her.'

'He has done so,' answered the King quietly, 'and she has returned to her mother in the cottage, a miserable and disillusioned woman with a broken heart.'

'And her sister Spiteful. Poor, poor soul, with her sharp tongue which makes so many enemies and deprives her of friends. She married Timid-Skulking, and they are desperately poor, and have to live in one little rented room in the house of my cousin Bitterness and his wife. I cannot bear to think of their wretched condition while I live up here in the Kingdom of Love.'

'They are wretched indeed,' said the King, even more gently and compassionately than before. 'They have just lost the little daughter whom poor Spiteful had hoped would be such a comfort to them in their dreary circumstances.'

'And then,' continued Grace and Glory with just a hint of hesitation in her voice, 'there is their brother Craven Fear.' She did not look at the King as she spoke, but paused a moment, then went on hurriedly. 'He is the most unhappy member of the whole family. He has broken his mother's heart; neither of his sisters will speak to him any more, and he goes skulking about the Valley hated by everyone.'

'I know him,' replied the King gravely, but with just a hint of a smile. 'I know him well. You do not exaggerate when you speak of his wretchedness. I have had to interfere and chastise him many times to try and correct his bullying propensities. But "though I have chastened him sore I have not given him over unto death".'

'No, no!' cried Grace and Glory imploringly, 'don't ever do that, my Lord! Oh, I beg You, find some way to rescue and deliver him from himself, as You delivered me.'

He made no answer for a little while, only looked at her very kindly and with a look of great contentment and happiness on His face. At last He spoke. 'I am more than willing to do what you suggest,' said He, 'but, Grace and Glory, these unhappy souls we are speaking about, will not allow Me into their homes, nor even permit Me to speak to them. I need a voice to speak for Me, to persuade them to let Me help them.'

'I see what You mean,' she cried joyfully. 'We will go down with You and speak to them and show what You have done for us and what You are willing and able to do for them.'

'Do you think they will listen to you?' He asked, smiling at her very gently as He spoke

'No, I don't think it's at all likely—at least, not at first,' she answered. 'I was not at all the sort of person to make them want to listen to me. I did not behave at all lovingly to them, but You will tell me what to say. You will teach me and I will say it for You. O my Lord, let us make haste and go down there. When they see what You have done for me, when they see Peace and Joy, I do think in the end they will want You to help them too. It is because they have lied to themselves about You and have persuaded themselves that You cannot do them good that they resist You and turn from Your help, but we will plead with them. Especially now, my Lord, when they are so unhappy and so despised by others. Their very misery and loneliness and sorrow will make them more willing to listen to news of Your grace and of Your desire to help them.'

'True,' He agreed, 'that is just what I think. This is indeed a specially favourable time for us to go down and try to help them.'

He rose to His feet as He spoke. She sprang up too, and all four stood joyful and radiant on the edge of the High Places, ready to go leaping down to the Valley again. Then Grace and Glory saw that the great waterfall quite close at hand was leaping down to the Valley too, with the tumultuous, joyful noise of many waters, singing as they poured themselves down over the rock lip:

> From the heights we leap and flow
> To the valleys down below.
> Sweetest urge and sweetest will,
> To go lower, lower still.

Suddenly she understood. She was beholding a wondrous and glorious truth; 'a great multitude whom no man could number' brought like herself by the King to the Kingdom of Love and to the High Places so that they could now pour out their lives in gladdest abandonment, leaping down with Him to the sorrowful, desolate places below, to share with others the life which they had received. She herself was only *one drop* amongst that glad, exultant throng of Self-givers, the followers of the King of Love, united with Him and with one another, each one equally blessed and beloved as herself. 'For He loves each one of us,' she said to herself, 'as though there were only one to love.'

The thought of being made one with the great fall of many waters filled her heart with ecstasy and with a rapturous joy beyond power to express. She, too, at last, was to go down with them, pouring herself forth in Love's abandonment of Self-giving. 'He brought me to the heights just for this,' she whispered to herself, and then looked at Him and nodded.

At that He began leaping and springing down the mountainside before them, bounding from rock to rock, always choosing, however, leaps which were within their power to follow, and sure footholds for their less experienced feet. Behind Him went Grace and Glory, with Joy and Peace beside her, leaping down, just as the waters leaped and sang beside them. They mingled their voices with the joyful music of the many waters, singing their own individual song:

> Make haste, Belovèd, be Thou like an hart
> On mountains spicy sweet;
> And I, on those High Places where Thou art,
> Will follow on hinds' feet;
> As close behind the hart, there leaps the roe,
> So where Thou goest, I will surely go.

That, as perhaps you know, is the last verse of the Song of Songs, which is Solomon's. But for Grace and Glory it was the beginning of a new song altogether.

CHRISTIAN CLASSICS FOR A NEW GENERATION

Two Timeless Books in One

Mountains of Spices

HANNAH HURNARD

KINGSWAY PUBLICATIONS
EASTBOURNE

First published by The Olive Press

Published by permission of Tyndale House Publishers Inc.
Wheaton, Illinois, USA

First British edition 1983
This 2-in-1 edition 2008

Cover design: PinnacleCreative.co.uk
Front cover photo © Perception I Dreamstime.com

ISBN 978 1 84291 388 8

Published by
KINGSWAY COMMUNICATIONS LTD
26–28 Lottbridge Drove, Eastbourne, BN23 6NT, UK
books@kingsway.co.uk

Printed in Great Britain

CONTENTS

4 CONTENTS

Make haste, my beloved, and be thou like to a roe or to a young hart upon the mountains of spices.

Song 8:14

"Thy plants are an orchard	*"The fruit of the Spirit*
of	is
POMEGRANATES . . .	LOVE,
CAMPHIRE . . .	JOY,
SPIKENARD . . .	PEACE,
SAFFRON . . .	LONGSUFFERING,
CALAMUS . . .	GENTLENESS,
CINNAMON . . .	GOODNESS,
FRANKINCENSE . . .	FAITH,
MYRRH . . .	MEEKNESS,
ALOES . . ."	TEMPERANCE. . ."
(Song 4:13, 14)	(Gal 5:22, 23)

IMPORTANT FOREWORD TO THE ALLEGORY

HERE are a few words of explanation to the reader about this book.

Years ago when I was starting out as a young missionary in Palestine I was struck one morning by a correspondence between the ninefold fruit of the Spirit in Gal. 5:22, 23, and the nine spices mentioned in the description of the "garden enclosed" and the "orchard of pomegranates" in Canticles 4:13, 14. During many happy "Quiet Times" I studied, with the help of Canon Tristram's *Flora of the Bible* and another book called *From Cedar to Hyssop*, all the details I could discover about the trees and plants listed in these verses and the lessons to be learnt by comparing them with "the fruit of the Spirit".

When, years later, therefore, I came to write this sequel to *Hinds' Feet on High Places*, the lessons of those dear earlier Quiet Times returned to my memory. As, however, the Spice Trees growing on the High Places of this book are allegorical and not literal, I have not hesitated to adapt, and in some instances to alter slightly, some of the details concerning the actual spices named. The descriptions, therefore, of the heavenly spices on the high places must not be taken as strictly accurate. I have allowed myself a little artistic licence!

The characters in this story are, of course, personifications of the unhappy and tormenting attitudes of mind, heart and temper, whose names they bear. In *Hinds' Feet on High Places* they were the enemies of Much-Afraid who sought to hinder her journey to "The High Places". In this book I have tried to show as clearly as possible that the very characteristics and weaknesses of temperament with which we were born, which often seem to us to be the greatest of all hindrances to the Christian life, are, in reality, the very things which, when surrendered to the Saviour, can be transformed into their exact opposites and can therefore produce in us the loveliest of all qualities. I have described the transformation of the deformities of character which have been the greatest problems in my own life and about which, therefore, I can speak with the most authority. I was born with a fearful nature—a real slave of the Fearing Clan! But I have since made the glorious discovery that no one has such a perfect opportunity to practise and develop faith as do those who must learn constantly to turn fear into faith. One must either succumb to the fearing nature altogether and become a "Craven Coward" for the rest of one's life; or by yielding that fearful nature wholly to the Lord and using each temptation to fear as an opportunity for practising faith, be made at last into a radiant "Fearless Witness" to His love and power. There is no middle course.

In the same way a moody temper, a sharp, spiteful tongue, or a dismally anxious and foreboding habit of mind, as well as the other temperamental characteristics personified in this book, can all be gloriously transformed into their exact opposites. Love takes our defects and deformities, and out of them, as out of "crooked Jacob", fashions princes and princesses of God.

It must not be supposed that in the conversations between the Shepherd King and Grace and Glory up on the Mountains of Spices, that I am "putting words into the Saviour's mouth", which He never spoke and claiming for them the authority of inspired truth. The conversations are simply meant to suggest the natural and sincere communion possible between any loving soul and the Lord of Love, and the way in which we can learn of Him by asking Him to give us light on all the problems which perplex us, just as surely as we can be made aware of the personal guidance each one of us is to follow. I have simply shared the way in which my own mind and understanding have been illumined as I have sought day by day to open them wide to the Saviour's love and teaching. I have no doubt whatsoever that my thoughts on these things are still so ridiculously inadequate that they fall far short of the real, unspeakably glorious, truth. But then, there are endless High Places still to ascend, and one can only describe glimpses seen on the way up. Of course all the best and loveliest things must still lie ahead!

One word about the verses and songs in this book. I often find it personally helpful to try and sum up and express in verse the new lessons which I learn and the new light which I receive, thus enabling me to fix them in my memory in a form in which I can easily recall them. Possibly others also may find these verses a help in the same way. They were all written especially for this book, but most of them have also appeared in two of my other books, *Unveiled Glory* and *The Heavenly Powers*.

CHAPTER I

MRS. DISMAL FOREBODINGS

It was a perfect spring morning down in the Valley of Humiliation, and everything seemed to be rejoicing in the warm sunshine and the soft, fragrant air. The pastures were robed in freshest green; the fruit trees were wearing festal apparel of white and pink blossoms; in the breeze the wild flowers were dancing gaily while the asphodels, with the sun shining through their transparent white blooms, stood rank on rank on the steep slopes above the blue lake like an army of wax torches. In the pastures through which the river wound, the lambs frisked about their mothers and the kids played "catch-me-if-you-can" among the rocks. Birds of every size and description worked ardently at the business of nest building, and the air echoed with the sound of innumerable notes and calls and trills, while bees and crickets kept up a constant undertone of humming. Altogether it was a perfect day down there in the valley, with everything that had breath and moved out in the open to welcome spring.

In the shadow of some old, dark, twisted trees, however, standing back from the main road which ran through the village of

Much-Trembling, was a garden, overgrown with weeds and sickly-looking cabbage plants. Moping in the middle of the garden was a most dilapidated cottage, the windows and doors of which were all tightly shut. Up from the chimney of this cottage rose a thin, furtive-looking spiral of smoke which crept up into the air as unostentatiously as possible, as though ashamed to show itself on such a perfect day as this. Inside the cottage, cowering over the smoky little fire, sat Mrs. Dismal Forebodings wearing a dreary-hued dress and wrapped in a drearier grey shawl, while her face wore an expression of deepest misery and gloom.

There came a brisk rap on the door, and almost before Mrs. Dismal's hesitating "Come in" could be heard, in marched her neighbour, Mrs. Valiant.

The contrast between the two women was as great as possible and everyone in Much-Trembling wondered at the friendship (if such a one-sided affair could be so named) which existed between them. But it dated back to their schooldays and Mrs. Valiant seemed to have a "queer notion", as the neighbours called it, of not allowing the friendship to drop.

Mrs. Valiant marched into the room, stopped short, and uttered what sounded exactly like a little snort.

"Good gracious! Dismal", she exclaimed. "What are you doing frousting in here with all the windows shut on such a perfect day as this? That horrid little smoky stove is enough to suffocate you."

"Please shut the door behind you at once, Valiant," said Mrs. Dismal fretfully. "The draught is simply cruel and this dreadful east wind always increases my rheumatism unendurably."

"East wind!" said Mrs. Valiant with another snort. "My dear Dismal, the air is as balmy as on a midsummer day, and what little breeze there is is coming directly from the south."

"My weather-cock never lies," replied Mrs. Dismal firmly, "and when I looked at it this morning the wind was in the east. Besides, I feel it all over me, in every bone and joint of my body, and do not need even the confirmation of the weather-cock."

"At least," urged Mrs. Valiant, "let me open the south window; and do, my dear Dismal, allow yourself to be persuaded to lay tier, and come out with me for a little while, for," added she in a mysterious tone, "the most delightful and unexpected thing has happened, and I have come along on purpose to take you to my cottage so that you can share in the pleasure."

Mrs. Dismal, however, refused to be either curious or interested. Instead, she poked the fire, causing a thick spiral of choking smoke to billow out into the room, and said with a shiver: "Please leave that window alone, Valiant. Even if it were the warmest of days I would not venture out of the cottage today, for my almanac tells me that it is a black day—a day of gloom and darkness and danger—and harm would most certainly befall me if I ventured outside. I have great faith in my almanac and never disregard its warnings."

"What almanac is that?" cried Mrs. Valiant, walking up to the wall on which was pinned a large and hideous monstrosity. "Why, Dismal! don't tell me you've gone in for astrology! This is printed by a well-known firm of swindling frauds, who live by exploiting the fears of other people. It's pure bunkum!"

Mrs. Dismal looked much affronted and answered tartly: "I have never known my valuable almanac to be mistaken. When it says that woe and calamity are approaching, woe and calamity of some sort always do follow, and I shall not be foolish enough to disregard its warnings today, but shall remain indoors."

"I wish you would let me tear the horrid thing off the wall and throw it on the fire," exclaimed Mrs. Valiant in exasperation, "and let me put up one of the red-letter calendars which I use myself. For today mine says, 'This is the day which the Lord hath made; we will be glad and rejoice in it.' "

"Nothing will induce me to discard my valuable almanac," said poor Mrs. Dismal. "Neither shall I venture to set foot outside the cottage today. As sure as my name is Dismal Forebodings, calamity is near."

"If I had a name like that," cried Mrs. Valiant, suddenly losing all patience, "I would certainly get rid of it and change to a better."

Mrs. Dismal was deeply offended, but whenever her warm-hearted, if rather quick-tempered, neighbour became impatient she always reacted with martyr-like resignation. So now she said in a tone of patient reproach: "It is a very ancient and honourable name, Valiant. It has been credibly demonstrated to date back to before the Flood. There have been Dismal Forebodings for longer than can be reckoned."

Mrs. Valiant laughed heartily at her friend's absurdity, though this was one of the times when she felt she would dearly like to shake a little sense into the poor silly creature before her. But she had an inner reason, known only to herself and the Chief Shepherd, for bearing long with her unhappy neighbour and learning to accept her lovingly just as she was. So now she answered cheerfully, but tactlessly: "Well, the antediluvian Dismal Forebodings must have become extinct anyhow, for there were none of them in the Ark. I wonder who was foolish enough to found the family name again!"

Mrs. Dismal was now too offended to reply. She drew her shawl closer around her shoulders, shivered, and appeared to be uncon-scious that there was anyone beside herself in the cottage.

Mrs. Valiant's conscience smote her. It was really dreadful the way she let her tongue run away with her when she had come on purpose to try to help her friend. She hurried to apologise, saying penitently: "Forgive me, Dismal dear, I know I ought not to have said that, but oh! how I wish you would let me help you out of this unhappy condition into which you have fallen, and persuade you to put off the spirit of dreariness, and to put on the garment of praise."

Mrs. Dismal burst into tears. "How can you talk like that, Valiant—you are absolutely heartless. I am sure I was always cheerful and contented enough before, but now that all this cruel trouble has come upon me what *can* you expect! A desolate widow woman all these years working myself to death to provide for my three unfortunate children" (this was a little bit of invention, Mrs. Dismal's husband having left her a small but adequate annuity), "and to bring them up respectably and prepare them for happier homes of their own than ever fell to my lot. And now what has happened? You know, Valiant—you know perfectly well—yet you are heartless enough to stand there rebuking me for being miserable. My daughter Gloomy, deserted by her graceless husband, her position lost, put to shame before all her relatives and obliged to come creeping home to her widowed mother, she the daughter-in-law of Lord Fearing himself, with no one prepared to lift a finger to help her get her rights! And then poor Spiteful—to find herself married to a drunkard who beats and abuses her shamefully, forced to live in a miserable little attic, a poor and despised relative in the house of her cousins. And Craven" (here she sobbed convulsively), "my darling Craven, my only son, wrongfully condemned on a trumped-up charge of assault and disorderly behaviour, actually put in prison! And you—you, Valiant—who did at least once have a strong husband to support you, and still have children who apparently never cause you the least sorrow, there you stand, upbraiding me and actually suggesting that I ought to put on the 'garment of praise'! Whatever sort of fantastic apparel that may be, it would obviously be utterly indecent clothing for a broken-hearted widow whose children are enduring a martyrdom of injustice and suffering."

Mrs. Valiant went up to the weeping woman and put her arms comfortingly around the shaking shoulders, saying very gently: "You misunderstand me, Dismal. I do know all about your sorrows and troubles, and it would make me so happy to be able to comfort you a little bit, and to help you find strength and courage to meet them and grace to transform them into something lovely. That is really why I am here this morning. Let me tell you the happy news, dear Dismal, and persuade you to go with me to my cottage. For do you know what has happened?—No, I am sure you will never be able to guess . . . something to gladden even your sad heart!"

She paused, hopefully looking for a gleam of interest or curiosity in the miserable face before her. But Mrs. Dismal Forebodings continued to sob and to rock herself backwards and forwards, utterly indifferent to anything else in the whole wide world except her own misfortunes.

So, after waiting a moment, Mrs. Valiant went on in a voice full of cheerfulness and pleasure: "Well, you will never guess, so I will tell you. You remember that when your crippled niece, Much-Afraid, left the Valley, people said that the Shepherd had taken her to the High Places. Well, it was true, perfectly true! And do you know what has happened, Dismal? She has just returned to the Valley on a visit, and she isn't a cripple any longer. Her lame feet are completely healed and so is her twisted mouth. She is so strong and straight you would hardly know her. Besides that she has got a new name; she is Much-Afraid no longer, but is Grace and Glory. Just fancy that! What a beautiful name to receive! She has also brought her two friends with her, lovely women named Peace and Joy; and they tell us that Grace and Glory lives now in the Kingdom of Love, and is actually a member of the Royal Household, and everywhere the King goes, she goes too. Just imagine it, Dismal. It's like the most wonderful fairy tale that you ever heard, only far lovelier because it's absolutely true. And it has all happened because she went with the Shepherd to the High Places."

If Mrs. Valiant had wanted to gain the attention of her miserable friend, she had certainly succeeded. Mrs. Dismal Forebodings sat staring at her in what appeared to be stunned silence, apparently unable to say a word. So Mrs. Valiant went on happily:

"Now here she is, back in the Valley, as I said before, and with her two friends. They are over in the cottage with my daughter Mercy and we are arranging a little party of welcome—just a few of her old friends and neighbours and you, her aunt, really must be there too. Come, dear Dismal, just for a little while. Dry your tears, for you cannot in any way help your dear ones by sitting here weeping your eyes out in this dreary room. Put on your best dress and come with me, and have a share in the rejoicing over the good things, the wonderful things, which have befallen poor, miserable, little Much-Afraid."

Mrs. Dismal Forebodings said not a word, for in truth she was almost stunned by the news, the *dreadful* news. Nothing, she felt, could be more untimely, more horrible, more humiliating, than the return of the wretched cripple they had all despised, and whose departure they had tried to thwart. Here she was, it seemed, healed, surrounded with friends, advanced to glory and honour, a member of the King's household, now returning almost as a queen to the

Valley where she had been a miserable, despised nobody. Moreover, returning just in time to find her closest relatives in the most humiliating circumstance possible—her cousin Gloomy (who had married so well) now deserted by her husband, a destitute beggar in her mother's cottage; Spiteful married to a drunkard who had nearly killed her, living a life of penurious misery in a tiny attic. And, worst of all, her cousin, Craven Fear, whom she had so insultingly refused to marry, now actually in prison. Could the return have been more untimely? Could, indeed, anything which she, Dismal Forebodings, might have imagined, be a greater calamity? "How true my almanac is!" said Mrs. Dismal to herself with a sinking of heart which even she had seldom before experienced. "A day of calamity indeed! No severer blow could have befallen me."

She said not a word however. With an immense effort she bit back the bitter lamentations which almost escaped her lips, for she suddenly remembered that an aunt would scarcely be expected to bewail the fact that a crippled niece had now returned to her old home completely cured and holding a position in the King's household. "If it had been any of our own relatives telling me the news," thought Mrs. Dismal bitterly, "they would have understood my feelings perfectly and we could have lamented together, but Mrs. Valiant is quite different; certainly she would never understand." So she sat in frozen silence.

"Come, Dismal," said Mrs. Valiant persuasively, after waiting in vain for some expression of pleasure or interest from her neighbour; "do come along with me to the cottage and see for yourself the delightful truth of what I have told you. Come and welcome Grace and Glory and enjoy the happy fellowship with other friends in my house and forget for a little while your own grief in rejoicing with another."

At that Mrs. Dismal at last found words. "Thank you, Valiant," said she, "but nothing will persuade me to leave the cottage today, or to do anything so heartless as to seek personal enjoyment at a party while my daughters eat the bread of affliction and my son languishes in prison. As for Much-Afraid," she continued, unable to conceal her bitterness any longer (she certainly was not going to call that girl by any new name the King might have chosen to bestow upon her), "as for Much-Afraid, a more undutiful and ungrateful niece cannot exist anywhere. If she chooses to return now to gloat over the misfortunes which have overtaken her relatives, it is only another example of her callous nature, and I, for one, shall certainly not present her with an opportunity to do so. Pray return at once to your party, Valiant, and leave me to the solace of solitude in my misery."

Mrs. Valiant regretfully realised that she could do no good by staying longer, that any further importunity would only increase her neighbour's resistance and resentment. So she sorrowfully took her departure, having failed in a mission which, in truth, she had feared would prove unsuccessful.

Left alone in the cottage, Mrs. Dismal Forebodings brooded on the disastrous news, and the more she brooded the worse it seemed. What a cruel blow dealt by fate to permit that girl to return just now, who, if she had married Craven as she ought to have done, would now be as disgraced and humiliated and wretched as her mother-in-law, and a convenient scapegoat on whom the family could have heaped their reproaches. But now, instead of that, here she was, gloriously free, richly provided for, and with an honourable new name. "It's scandalous!" sobbed Mrs. Dismal. "The injustice of life! The hammer blows of fate! A calamity of calamities!"

She sat there brooding bitterly, for perhaps half an hour, when she heard a light tap on the door of the cottage, and with a sickening sense of foreboding she called out sourly, "Who is there?"

"It is I, your niece, dear Aunt. May I come in?" And with that the door opened and Grace and Glory stepped into the cheerless room.

In spite of herself Mrs. Dismal Forebodings looked with eager curiosity at the girl who had once been Much-Afraid. She saw it was quite true what Mrs. Valiant had told her, there *was* a great difference in her. She was so straight, and walked with such ease and poise, that it gave one the impression that she was much taller than before. And now that the unsightly, deformed mouth was healed, and she could look unshrinkingly and without self-consciousness into the face of others, she *was* very unlike the ugly creature of former days. "Yet in another way," thought Mrs. Dismal Forebodings, "she is not at all out of the ordinary. Amongst a crowd there would be nothing to single her out, except perhaps the expression of quiet, steady happiness on her face and the light in her eyes."

Grace and Glory hesitated a moment at the door, and then, as her aunt offered not a single word of greeting, she walked quietly towards the grey, bent figure crouched in the rocking chair beside the stove, and stooping down, gently kissed her aunt's cheek.

Mrs. Dismal Forebodings recoiled almost as though a reptile had approached her, and putting out her hands, pushed her niece away.

"There is no need for insincere tokens of affection, Much-Afraid," she said coldly. "I can dispense with a kiss from you."

Her niece looked at her compassionately, but only said gently: "I can understand just how you feel, dear Aunt. I know that I was always sadly lacking in love and in attention to your wishes. But I hear that you have experienced much sorrow since last we saw one another, and my heart aches for you. I long to be able to help in some way, or at least to share your sorrow." She paused a moment and then added shyly: "I have been changed you know, since I went away, and have learned to love. I have a new name now, and, I hope, a new nature."

"So I heard from Mrs. Valiant," said her aunt icily. "But I shall certainly not call you by anything but your *real* name. It will take more than just a new name, I can assure you, to make me forget what you were before. To me you will always be Much-Afraid."

"Well, I can understand that too," said Grace and Glory, "and you may call me by the old name if you so please. But," she added smilingly, "Grace is a shorter and easier name to say, and it exactly describes the means by which all the happiness and peace and healing have come to me. Dear Aunt Dismal, if only I could persuade you, in your sorrow and grief and pain, to turn to the One who so graciously and wonderfully helped me!"

A flush of angry colour appeared in her aunt's cheeks. "Do I understand you to refer to—she stumbled over the hated name—to the Shepherd, Much-Afraid?"

"Yes," answered her niece earnestly.

"I beg, no, rather I command, that you will not ever mention that name to me again," said Mrs. Dismal Forebodings in a voice shaking with angry excitement. "You know well enough what all of us thought about your disgraceful behaviour, forsaking all your relatives in the most heartless manner! But do you know what happened afterwards? Do you know that it was that—that Shepherd of yours—who trumped up the false charge against my unhappy son, Craven, which resulted in his being put in prison?

My son, my only son, treated as a common felon and sentenced to a six months' term of imprisonment."

Grace and Glory, who had come to the cottage with her heart overflowing with love and compassionate longing to help her aunt escape from the misery which she herself had known, could think of nothing to say. She had her own personal memories of Craven Fear's bullyings, and could well understand how much some hapless victim must have rejoiced to be delivered by the Shepherd out of his clutches; also that a term in prison might well prove to be a salutary, though bitter, lesson to him. But she did not feel that it was the moment to suggest all this to his mother. So she really did not know what to say.

It was the dreadful contrast to everything which she had hoped and expected, thought Grace and Glory to herself, which made it so unspeakably difficult. Up there on the High Places in the Kingdom of Love, where every thought was love, and her companions Joy and Peace were never absent, how different things had looked! She remembered how but a short time before she had been sitting beside the King in the royal gardens, and they had looked down into this Valley, and her heart had ached and throbbed with compassion and with the longing to be able to help her relatives. Nothing had seemed too difficult for love to undertake if only they could be rescued and delivered from the tormenting things by which they were enslaved.

But now, down here, face to face with reality, how different, how almost impossibly different it seemed! Here was her aunt, absolutely shut up within her own miserable self. She could think of nothing else, be interested in nothing else, for all her thoughts were chained to the one wretched centre. She was as outside the Realm of Love as though she lived in a world of "outer darkness" where Love simply did not exist. How, oh how, thought Grace and Glory desperately, could one get into her dungeon, and how could one strike off the chains which the prisoner seemed actually to cherish and to be unwilling to be rescued from? How could one even speak to her of the only Deliverer, when she believed that He was the cause of all her unhappiness? Yes, indeed, it was one thing up there in the glory and light of the Kingdom of Love to feel a passionate longing to help and save. But when one got right down into the midst of the actual reality, *how* was it to be done? How could one reach hearts immured in impregnable prisons, and how awaken even the beginning of a desire for deliverance?

Grace and Glory remembered the whole conversation up there on the High Places, and how they had all agreed that this was the very likeliest time of all for them to be able to help Mrs. Dismal Forebodings and her family because the calamities which had overtaken them would surely make them begin to feel their need of the Shepherd's help. But now it was all so different. She remembered the voice of the King saying, "I need someone to speak for Me, for they will not come to Me themselves." And her glad, exultant cry that she would be His mouthpiece. She remembered the tone in which He had said, "Do you think they will listen to you, Grace and Glory?" What had she answered? "*You* shall tell me what to say and I will say it for You."

"Yes," thought Grace and Glory suddenly, "that is the answer. He must tell me what to say. He must teach me. I can do nothing now; but I will go to Him and will tell Him all about it, and I will ask Him to teach me what approach I am to make and how to win right through into my aunt's prison house."

However, she made one last attempt to break down the antagonism against herself. "Dearest Aunt," she said, "I do hope you will sometimes let me come to see you to do what I can to help. And perhaps next time you will let me tell you how I was delivered from all my fears and sorrows."

"Thank you, Much-Afraid," said her aunt icily, "but I am not interested. I know already just what you will say and it is the last thing that I am interested to hear."

Grace and Glory, feeling exactly as though she were holding a tiny pebble in her hand with which to try to batter down an impregnable stronghold, rose to her feet and prepared to take her departure. She put her arms around her aunt and kissed the coldly unresponsive cheek, saying softly: "Only let me love you, Aunt Dismal. Let me try to atone in some way for all my lovelessness in the past. Do let me come to see you and my cousin Gloomy and help in any way that I can."

But the only answer she received was, "You have chosen and gone your own way, Much-Afraid, and it is not my way. And I do not hesitate to tell you that even though misfortune has overtaken me, while good fortune has smiled upon you, I do not at all desire to be pitied and patronised by you. Smitten I may be, and left desolate and friendless, but patronised I will not be. You need not trouble yourself to visit here again."

Grace and Glory left the cottage and walked sadly away wondering if anything could have been more unlike her radiant, loving dreams of helping her relatives than the actual reality. For a few moments she felt almost overwhelmed.

When, however, she reached the cottage where she and Mercy had lived together, and found her friend and Mrs. Valiant bustling around full of cheerful preparations for the party, to which the Chief Shepherd Himself had been invited, and when she saw Joy and Peace (whom she had left at the cottage, telling herself that if she were accompanied by her two hand-maidens when she visited her miserable aunt, that she might appear to be showing off)— when she met their loving greeting, she did feel a balm applied to her heart. And she said to herself, "Next time I go to visit Aunt Dismal, I shall take Joy and Peace with me."

There was just time before the guests arrived for bustling Mrs. Valiant to take her aside for a moment and whisper, "Well, my dear, how did you get on and what sort of reception did you receive from that poor creature, Dismal?"

"She told me never to visit her again," answered Grace and Glory sorrowfully, "and I am afraid she really meant it."

"You would never believe how many times she has said exactly the same thing to me!" replied Mrs. Valiant cheerily, "but she would be quick enough to object if I took her at her word. Never pay any attention to anything poor Dismal says, my dear. She is starved for love and doesn't know it. Just go on loving; it always wins in the end."

Mrs. Valiant, as you may easily guess without being told, was another who had been with the Shepherd to the High Places, and wore in her heart the flowering plant of Love which made her a citizen of that Kingdom.

Then they heard the sound of footsteps outside, and of happy, laughing voices, and the next moment the Chief Shepherd Himself, surrounded by His friends, entered the cottage, and the feast began. The kettle sang on the hearth, the guests talked and laughed merrily together, the sandy cat lay purring on the Chief Shepherd's knees, and the black-and-white one curled up on the lap of Grace and Glory. The sheep dogs lay at the door, wagging their tails, and Mrs. Valiant busied herself filling and refilling the cups with tea, and all in all the cottage was the most mirthful and contented spot in the whole village—just as though a little bit of the Kingdom of Love had been transplanted down to the Valley. Which of course was the case.

"If only poor Dismal were here," sighed Mrs. Valiant just once; and then she looked across at the Shepherd and saw that His eyes were looking straight at her as though He read and understood her thoughts. Then Mrs. Valiant gave a little contented smile and said to herself, "It will be all right. He wants it even more than we do. It will take more than poor Dismal and her unhappy family to evade His love in the end."

Then she went on bustling about, filling cups and attending to the wants of everyone, and was, without in the least realising it, next to the Chief Shepherd Himself, the most cheering and heart-warming person in the room.

CHAPTER II

THE MOUNTAIN OF POMEGRANATES
(LOVE)

The Law of Love

WHEN the day was over the Shepherd called Grace and Glory and her two companions and they started back to their home on the High Places. All the way, while they were bounding and leaping up the mountain-side towards the peaks above which were already glowing with flame and rose in the sunset light, Grace and Glory was thinking about the visit she had paid to her Aunt Dismal, and telling herself over and over again that before she returned to the Valley, she *must* have a talk with the Shepherd-King and ask Him all the difficult questions which were perplexing her mind, and so learn from Him just what He wanted her to say, and how to fit the message so that it would penetrate into the dreary dungeon in which her aunt was immured.

As they all had "hinds' feet" they could leap up the mountain-side to the heights above in almost no time, and when they reached the King's Gardens, where they were lodging at that time, she made known to Him her desire. He told her to be ready very early next morning to go with Him to the Mountain of Pomegranates, and there they would talk over the whole matter together.

Grace and Glory was filled with delighted expectation. She had never been to the Mountain of Pomegranates and she loved to be taken to new parts of the High Places and to look out on the glorious mountain ranges round about from new points of view. At all times, too, the very early morning hours which she spent with the Shepherd-King before the work of the day began were the most radiant hours of her life. Often it was long before sunrise that He called her, and they would talk together for two or three hours before meeting anyone else.

The following morning, just as the first flush of an early summer dawn turned the peaks on the opposite side of the Valley rose pink, and the morning star still shone brightly in the sky, Grace and Glory heard the King's voice calling her. Leaping up she made haste to follow Him. They paused, however, for a moment to rejoice in the beauty of the snow-white peaks which seemed to be lifting themselves up towards the cloudless sky to catch the very first rays of the sun for whose rising they waited in an almost breathless hush. As the first beams appeared over the opposite mountains and the pure white slopes flushed a fiery rose, Grace and Glory looked up into the face of the King and said, "My soul waiteth for the Lord more than they that watch for the morning: I say, more than they that watch for the morning." (Psa. 130:6.)

He took her by the hand and they went leaping and bounding over the heights towards the Mountain of Pomegranates. As they went she sang a little song of:

The Mountain Peaks at Dawn.

As in the early morning
The snowy mountain peaks
Look up to greet the dawning,
So my heart longs and seeks
To see Thy face
And glow with grace.

Here like the peaks at sunrise
My mind to Thee I raise;
Clothe me with glory likewise,
Make me to burn with praise
In love's attire
Of flaming fire.

In robes of snowy whiteness
They greet their lord the sun;
I too, await Thy brightness,
On winged feet I run.
Give, now we meet,
Communion sweet.

Thus singing and leaping side by side they came to a new part
of the mountain range with which Grace and Glory was unfamil-
iar. Here in beautiful orchards grew fruit trees of every variety, but
more especially, pomegranate trees. She had often noticed how the
King seemed to rejoice in the pomegranates above all the other
fruits, and this morning she felt that she understood as never
before why He found them so delightful. They bore flowers and
fruit at the same time, both a beautiful rose colour, with shimmer-
ings of lavender in the depths of the flower petals; and the shining

green leaves, rosy fruits and flowers against a background of turquoise blue sky were so lovely that she caught her breath with delight. The trees also cast a cool shade, and when the two sat down beneath one of the largest of them it was as though they sat in a little arbour, looking out over a new range of peaks higher than any she had seen before.

"Tell me, my Lord," said she, after a little quiet pause during which she rested beside Him, delighting in His Presence and stilling her heart and mind so that she might be ready to listen to Him and to learn all that He wanted to teach her, "tell me why, as it seems, You love the pomegranates almost more than any other tree, and why this whole mountain is covered with them."

"We are now on the Mountains of Spices," said the King, "a range of nine mountains upon which grow My choicest fruits and spices. These pomegranate trees are the best picture of the first of the nine-fold fruit of the Spirit, which is Love. As you can see, it is an evergreen tree, and the peoples of the East say that it is always safe to lie down and rest beneath a pomegranate tree because no evil spirit dare approach it. Its flowers are lovely, its fruit is delicious, and from it can be made a healthful and refreshing drink. The fruit too is full of beautiful seeds and it is said that at least one seed in each fruit is from Paradise. Beautiful, fruitful, evergreen, healing and able to ward off evil spirits—do you wonder that people find it lovelier than almost any other tree?"

"No," she answered, "I can understand it very well, and I notice, too, that this mountain-side is the most beautiful of all the places that I have yet seen, and that from it we look out on an absolutely new view. And yet isn't that still the Valley of Humiliation right down there beneath us?"

"Yes," said He, "you are quite right. Tell me, Grace and Glory, what you think about this new view."

She sat beside Him quietly for quite a long time just looking at the scene spread out before her and trying to take it in. High, very high up into the sky, towered tier upon tier of gleaming white peaks, their distant summits hidden in a shimmering haze of light so dazzling that she had to cover her eyes, while in the foreground in striking contrast was a much lower mountain, beautifully shaped like a perfect pyramid, but black as coal from foot to summit as though it had been swept by fire—a great blot upon the perfection of the landscape. The contrast indeed was striking. It seemed a solitary, shattered outcast unable to hide itself from the great company of pure white onlookers; a starkly naked criminal forced to stand in the presence of his judges. As she looked at it, she actually felt tears pricking in her eyes. It was so black and spoilt, so dreadfully in contrast to everything else, but above all, so unable to hide its own shame. There it stood with every hideous mark of its ruin laid bare to the scrutiny of the undefiled peaks around.

She gazed at it for a long time until she was startled out of her reverie by the King's voice saying, "Grace and Glory, why are you weeping?"

"It's the view from this mountain of Pomegranates," she answered in a choked voice. "Why should there be such a view as this from the place where the trees of Love grow? What is that desolate, ruined mountain over there, right in the foreground? Why is it so unlike the other mountains? What happened to it? Why don't You do something about it, my Lord the King? Everything else in sight is perfect in beauty, and that—that poor ruined thing breaks all the harmony. It ought to be beautiful too. Indeed, I am sure that once on a time it was beautiful, for it is such a lovely shape. I wonder that you can bear to look at it as it is now. What has happened to it, my Lord?"

"I will tell you about the Black Mountain," said the King very gently, "and then you will understand. As you see, it stands right here in full view from my favourite mountain of Pomegranates. Love looks right out onto it and that is why long ago I determined to beautify it in a special way and to make it one of the loveliest parts of my Kingdom. With rich and fertile soil and slopes open to the sun it could be exceedingly fruitful. So I planned to make it a mountain of vineyards which should produce the wine of joy and gladness in great abundance. I commanded My gardeners and workmen to terrace the sides of the mountain from top to bottom, and we planted it with the choicest vines, as well as with many other beautiful trees to give shade and a variety of fruits. We left nothing undone for its perfecting, rejoicing in the prospect of its fruitfulness.

He paused and was silent for a long time. At last Grace and Glory asked softly, "What happened, my Lord?"

"It brought forth wild vines," said the King quietly. "An enemy sowed them, bitter, poisonous vines which bore bitter, poisonous fruits. And moreover, the wild vines ran riot, flourishing in the richly fertilised soil, growing strong and rank. They smothered and choked the vines which I had planted, and they clambered up the other trees and strangled them to death also, until there were great curtains and festoons of wild vines covering everything."

"Couldn't You have done something about it?" asked Grace and Glory sorrowfully. Couldn't You have rooted up the wild vines and got rid of them?"

"We tried doing that," said the King. "We tore them up and burned them, but the shoots ran underground, and as fast as we rooted them up, they appeared elsewhere. We tried, too, grafting the wild vines with grafts from the royal vineyards over on these mountains, but the grafts would not take. The wild vines were parasites, and they seized on the real vines as I told you, and on all the other trees, and sucked the life out of them or strangled them to death. So at last there was only one thing to be done. We set fire to the mountain and caused it to be burnt from top to bottom until all that was evil and parasitical and wild was utterly destroyed."

"And will You leave it like that, ruined and desolate and dead?" asked Grace and Glory in a trembling whisper.

"Oh no!" answered the King with a look of loveliest joy upon His face. "We will plant it again and make it of greater fruitfulness than would otherwise have been possible. For the ashes are making the soil still more fertile and are preparing it for resurrection life. One day the view from this Mountain of Pomegranates will show all the peaks round about looking down on a mountain of vineyards more fair and more fruitful than any other part of the Kingdom."

There was another long silence and then Grace and Glory spoke again. "I begin to see why You brought me here, My Lord. You understood what I wanted to speak to you about. I am so troubled and perplexed. Will You teach me? Will you let me ask all the questions which have troubled me since we went back to the Valley of Humiliation and I found my aunt in such misery and was unable to help her?"

"Ask anything you wish," said He gently. "This Mountain of Love with the view from it, is one of the best places in the world for the asking of questions and for the receiving of answers."

"Then," said Grace and Glory slowly, "I want to ask You about all the evil and the misery down there in the Valley and the cause of it. What is it, Lord, which has wrought all the havoc? Why are all the inhabitants of the Valley so wretched and miserable and dreary even though they seem hardly to realise it?"

"It is because they have broken the Royal Law of Love," answered the King. "Love is the one basic Law on which the whole Universe is founded, and by obeying that law, everything abides in harmony, perfect joy and perfect fruitfulness. But when it is broken, disharmony immediately results and then come miseries and evils of every kind. Righteousness is the condition of everything which is in harmony with the Law of the Universe and therefore RIGHT. Unrighteousness is everything which is out of harmony with the Law of Love and therefore UNRIGHT. Love which worketh no ill to her neighbour is the fulfilment of the whole Law on which the universe is founded. Holiness and happiness and health are the result of complete separation from everything which breaks the Law of Love, and a Holy People are those who are set apart to Love. Sinners are the poor miserable people who break the Law of Love and so bring evils of every kind upon themselves, such as abound down there in the Valley. When men love they fulfil the law of their being. When they break the Law of Love they disrupt and frustrate the very Law of Life. As long as they love they are healthy and happy and harmonious, but when they cease to love and begin to think envious, resentful, bitter, unforgiving and selfish thoughts, then they begin to destroy themselves, for every part of their being is then poisoned by unloving thoughts."

"My Lord and King," said Grace and Glory, "what is true Love? How can it be recognised?"

"I am Love," said the King very clearly. "If you want to see the pattern of true Love, look at Me, for I am the expression of the Law of Love on which the Universe is founded. And the very first characteristic of true Love, as I have manifested it, is WILLINGNESS to accept all other human beings, just as they are, however blemished and marred by sin they may be, and to acknowledge ONENESS with them in their sin and need. To acknowledge also that every human heart needs both to love and to be loved, and that herein lies the very root of the oneness of mankind. For unless you sons and daughters of men are loved and also love all others besides yourselves, you cannot become what you are destined to be, the sons and daughters of the God Who is Love."

He ceased speaking, and at that moment a company of the King's servants who had just approached the Mountain of Pomegranates in order to gather a store of the beautiful fruit, broke forth into singing as they began their work on a nearby slope. These are the words of their song:

> Love is ONENESS—oh, how sweet
> To obey this Law,
> The unlovely we may meet
> Need our love the more.
> Make us One, O Love, we plead,
> With men's sorrow and their need.

> We are ONE in needing Love,
> (Let us true Love show)
> Only Love's Sun from above
> Makes our spirits grow.
> "Love us!" this is our heart's need,
> "Let us love"—and live indeed!

> We are also ONE in this,
> We must love or die,

> Loving others is true bliss,
>   Self-love is a lie!
> Love of Self is inward strife,
> Love turned outward is true life.

> Let us love and fruitful be,
>   Love is God's own Breath,
> Love will kindle love and see
>   New life born from death.
> Nowhere is a heaven more sweet
> Than where loving spirits meet.

When the song had ended, the King pointed out over the wide landscape and towards the Black Mountain and said:

"See how plainly the Law of the Universe is demonstrated in all that Love has created, and how everything which the Creator's hand has formed and fashioned, when it obeys the law of its being, shares with others and acknowledges its oneness with the need of all. Behold how this Law is indeed written in everything around you."

So Grace and Glory looked.

Down in the valley far below were the green pastures where the flocks were grazing. She pictured all the myriad little blades of grass giving themselves freely to nourish the flocks and herds. She remembered the unnumbered wild flowers giving forth their sweetness and beauty and perfume even in places where there was no eye to see them, no onlooker to appreciate them, ready to be trampled down and broken, or else to bloom their whole life long without receiving praise or recompense. Then she looked at the Trees of Love growing all around them as they sat up there on the mountain, saw how laden they were with fruit which others were to pluck and enjoy, finding all the meaning of their existence in this ministry of giving. She looked up at the sun shining overhead, shedding its light and warmth so freely upon ALL, on the evil and the good, on the unjust as well as the just, on all alike! She saw that in its self-giving and self-sharing and in its willingness to enter into and become ONE with all who would open to receive its light and warmth, it was indeed the great symbol of perfect Love. She looked at the streamlets all hurrying to go lower and lower and to give themselves to refresh all thirsty things along their banks. Everywhere she looked she saw Nature exulting to give and to share with others, and, by thus doing, to become ONE with them.

Then she began to think of the many creatures who break this Law of the Universe; the beasts of prey, always seeking for themselves and giving nothing but to their own young; the parasites and the wild vines which had ruined the Black Mountain. And she realised how destructive everything is when it will not remain in harmony with the Law of Love and Oneness. She realised, too, that this same Law was indeed written in every part of her own nature. "It is happy to love," she thought, "and it is healthy too. It is utter misery to withhold love and to live only and always for oneself alone. I see that it is exactly as He says. Love must express itself in giving; must find a way to become ONE with others, just as He found a way to give His own Life to us and thereby to become ONE with us! And all the misery down there in the Valley really is because the inhabitants are breaking this Law of their existence without realising it."

While she still sat pondering upon all this, the King Himself began to sing, and these are the words of the Song which He taught her up there on the Mountain of Pomegranates:

There is one Law by which we live,
  "Love loves to give and give and give!"
And on this "Royal Law", so named,
  The universe itself is framed.
No lasting joy is anywhere
  Save in the hearts of those who share.
Life yields a thousand fold and more
To those who practise Love's great Law.

That love is far too weak and small
  Which will love some but not love ALL.
If love to one it will decline,
  'Tis human love and not Divine.
Love cannot be content to rest
  Till the beloved is fully blest.
Love leaps to succour all who fall,
And finds His joy in giving all.

When He had finished this song the King rose to His feet and
said, "Now it is time to return to the lovely work of Self-Giving
and sharing." And with that He pointed down the mountain
slopes, and then together they went leaping and bounding down
the Mountain on their "hinds' feet", down towards the little green
carpet far below which was the Valley of Humiliation where their
Ministry of Love was so much needed.

CHAPTER III

GLOOMY AND SPITEFUL

Bitterness and his wife Murmuring were the proprietors of the Village Inn at Much-Trembling. It was a picturesque, many-gabled building standing among shady trees on a corner of the village green. On one side of the inn was a bowling lawn and on the other side was a pleasant tea garden lying along the bank of the river where there were boats for hire. The bar room was clean, freshly painted and comfortable—an attractive meeting place for all the village cronies. Farmers from all over the Valley gathered at the Much-Trembling Inn on market days, and Bitterness and his wife not only had a very prosperous business, but they prided themselves on running it very respectably indeed as a comfortable, up-to-date hotel, patronised by all "the best people", including old Lord Fearing himself, who often gathered there with his friends in the private parlour.

Timid-Skulking, nicknamed Moody, a younger brother of Mrs. Murmuring, also lived at the Inn and helped in the work. He had married Mrs. Dismal Forebodings' daughter, Spiteful, but the

marriage had turned out most unhappily, for Moody had the rep-
utation of possessing the quickest and most uncertain temper in
the village, and his wife, poor girl, the sharpest tongue. Only a
short time before Grace and Glory returned to the Valley, Moody
had been sentenced to a term in prison for almost beating his
young wife to death while he was under the influence of drink,
and this just at a time when the whole village was already gossip-
ing about Sir Coward Fearing's desertion of his wife, Gloomy, who
was Spiteful's sister.

When she was first married, the Hon. Mrs. Coward Fearing had
not often condescended to visit Spiteful at the Village Inn, but
since the tragedy of her husband's desertion, a common bond of
misery and sorrow seemed to have drawn her to her sister and had
worked a great change in the haughty Gloomy. Every day since her
sister's illness she had gone furtively, and as secretly as possible, to
the attic to do what she could for her help and comfort. Outwardly, perhaps, that was not very much, for Gloomy had always
despised housework and knew very little indeed about cleaning a
room, cooking, or nursing. She had little spoken comfort to give
either. She did everything in a silent, dreary way, even gloomier
than her name. But even so her daily visits were the one bright
spot, if such it could be called, in her sister's miserable existence;
the feeling that one person at least in the world cared to be with
her was like an anchor to the soul of the poor, forlorn girl. Mrs.
Dismal Forebodings herself was so overcome by the humiliations
and disgrace which had befallen the family that she could not be
persuaded to leave her own cottage and meet the curious or pitying stares of the neighbours, though she did prepare and send
along little bits of meals—soups or broth or eggs or whatever she
could spare. Gloomy certainly had no more desire than her

mother to face the stares of the neighbours, but nevertheless, day by day, at a time when the streets were most deserted, she made her way to the attic, where she then spent most of the day. It seemed almost as though she found some slight solace for her own misery in trying to help the even deeper misery of her sister. They never spoke much together, but sometimes when poor Spiteful, overcome by weakness and exhaustion, broke into anguished tears, Gloomy would sit beside her, awkwardly holding her hand (none of the Dismal Forebodings knew how to express sympathy and affection) though speaking not a word. It was the best that she could do and more than Gloomy herself ever realised, she did lighten and ease her sister's sorrow.

On this particular morning, after washing up the two cracked plates and cups and saucers, Gloomy swept the floor, dusted the few bits of furniture, and then, taking her work-bag, she sat down by the side of her sister and began silently to help with the sewing. A huge basket of mending stood on the floor between them. Mrs. Bitterness was determined that Spiteful should help as much as possible even during her convalescence, and as she could no longer spend long hours in the scullery washing up, her work was now to do all the mending for the hotel.

For some time the two sisters worked in silence, and then there came a light tap on the door. They looked at one another, startled and puzzled. Who could it be? Spiteful had shrunk pitifully from receiving visits from the neighbours and Murmuring had also discouraged them strongly. The sooner the miserable affair was hushed up and forgotten the better, and if Spiteful kept out of sight and didn't talk, the more quickly would people forget.

The knock on the door was repeated, and then, as no one in the room answered, the caller apparently decided upon entering without permission, for the door opened, and Grace and Glory stepped into the room, followed by her two beautiful companions, Joy and Peace.

At the sight of her cousin, Spiteful sank back in her seat and covered her face with her hands as though to try to hide herself. Gloomy sat rigid and silent at her side, only making one slight, involuntary movement as though to interpose her own form between that of the newcomer and her sister.

Grace and Glory stepped forward and looked beseechingly at her cousins, and then, kneeling down beside Spiteful, put her arms around the shrinking figure and said softly, with the tears running down her cheeks: "Oh, Spiteful, please, please do not turn from me. Do let me be with you for just a little while. You don't know how often my heart has ached for you since I got back to the Valley a few days ago and heard of your sorrow. And, oh! I am so glad to find that Gloomy is here too. I have not seen either of you for such a long time. Do tell me that you are just a little pleased to see me and will let me stay."

Neither sister spoke a word, but Spiteful suddenly burst into tears and laid her head against the shoulder of her kneeling cousin as though at last all the bitter anguish of her broken heart must find an outlet.

For some time they continued like this without a word being spoken until finally the wild sobbings ceased, and Grace and Glory, taking her handkerchief, wiped the tear-stained face and kissed her cousin again and again.

Then there came a little interruption. The two tall strangers, who all this while had remained unnoticed in the background, now came forward saying sweetly: "Please come and refresh yourselves. We have made everything ready."

Gloomy and Spiteful looked up in amazement and then again shrank back as though in shame or embarrassment. The ugly, unpainted little table was now covered with a cloth. On it stood a vase in which were arranged some of the sweetest perfumed flowers that the sisters had ever seen, pure white with a golden crown at the heart of each one. Beside the vase of flowers were plates filled with wild strawberries and blueberries. Another dish held apricots, apples and pomegranates, and there was a loaf of bread, a pat of butter and a comb of fresh honey; delicacies which never before had appeared in that dreary attic or in Mrs. Dismal's almost equally dreary cottage. It was enough to tempt the weakest appetite. Peace was over by the stove pouring boiling water into the teapot, and Joy was holding a bottle of fresh milk in one hand and a little jug of cream in the other.

Spiteful looked at her sister speechlessly, and Gloomy said, in a voice which tried to be a little like the old haughty tone, "We cannot accept charity like this. Much— Much—" and then she broke off as though she couldn't finish the name, and added almost tremblingly, "as though we were beggars, Grace and Glory."

"Which is what we really are though," added Spiteful.

"This isn't charity," said Grace and Glory with a little laugh. "We picked these strawberries and blueberries up on the High Places this morning before coming down to the Valley; and the other fruits are out of the King's gardens and the honey is from His hives. My dearest cousins, nobody thinks he is accepting charity when a King gives!"

The sisters looked at one another. Then Spiteful, who through all her illness and weakness had seen nothing whatever to tempt her appetite, looked longingly at the fresh fruits on the daintily spread table, and Gloomy saw the look. She got up and taking her sister's hand said simply: "Thank you very much. Spiteful has been so weak and sick it really would be the most absurd pride on our part to refuse, and as she says, no one has less right to be proud than we have."

Then they all three sat down at the table, and Joy and Peace waited on them in the deftest and kindest manner possible. First they cut the bread into enticingly thin slices; then they served the strawberries and cream, and while those were being eaten, Joy prepared the pomegranates and apples and Peace whipped up a nourishing and delicious concoction of eggs. As they ate the meal up there in the cheerless attic Spiteful felt almost like a queen being coaxed with delicacies. A faint colour stole into her cheeks and a little light appeared in her eyes. While they were eating Grace and Glory described to them the places up on the mountains where the strawberries grew and the banks covered with blueberries, the pine woods with the lovely, spicy smell of sun-warmed cones, the humming of the bees over the fields of flowers, and even a little bit about the King's gardens and the pomegranate trees in whose shade they had eaten their breakfast that very morning. She told them of the King's love for the pomegranates and the belief of the eastern peoples on the other side of the mountains that no evil spirit can approach a pomegranate tree because it is the Tree of Love. Then little by little Gloomy and Spiteful began to speak too, hesitatingly at first, asking questions. Gloomy wanted to know what the white, golden-hearted flowers were in the centre of the table which gave forth the lovely perfume. She had never seen such flowers before. Grace and Glory blushed a little as she answered that they were the flowers of Love which grow up on the High Places, but she did not add that she had picked those particular blooms from the tree which the Shepherd had planted in her own heart.

Then they wanted to know about her journey, but Grace and Glory did not seem able to say much about that, only to speak of the Shepherd's goodness and help and over and over again to speak of the Shepherd Himself.

By the time the delicious little picnic meal was ended the three cousins were talking together with an ease and friendliness which they had never felt before. Stranger still, as Joy and Peace gathered up the remains of the repast, and insisted on doing the washing-up away in the background, something happened to Gloomy and Spiteful. They began haltingly and in low voices, often breaking off as though unable to continue, to speak about their own sorrows. Somehow even the names of Coward Fearing, Moody and Craven Fear passed their lips, poor Spiteful even murmuring excuses for her husband (it was noticeable that never once did she utter a word of blame) and Gloomy, with a dark, painful flush on her cheeks, muttered something about her own cold, haughty attitude and her unfitness for marriage, unable as she was to win and keep her husband's love. Then Grace and Glory, also hesitatingly, told them of her own experience, of the plant in her heart which she had supposed to be Love, only to find that it was selfish, possessive love and the longing to be loved, and of all the anguish it had caused her until, away up there on the mountains, it had been wrenched out of her heart altogether. She told them also of her two companions, Sorrow and Suffering, and how up on the High Places, they had actually been transformed into Joy and Peace. And the two handmaidens, hearing their names mentioned, looked round and smiled radiantly.

As she spoke it seemed that, in some miraculous way, the stuffy, miserable attic had expanded and changed, and they were sitting out on the mountain-side with the fir trees roofing them overhead, the fresh mountain air blowing around them, and the snowy peaks shining above, and the voice of the great waterfall sounding in their ears as it leaped down singing to the valleys below. Then Grace and Glory sang to them another of the songs which she had learnt on the Mountain of Pomegranates.

> O Holy Love! O Burning Flame!
>   Why should I longer roam
> Forth from the heart of God I came
>   And yearn back to my home.

> Send forth Thy Truth, O Shining Light,
>   That I may follow till
> I come at last, before the night,
>   Up to Thy Holy Hill.

> For there my soul longs to abide,
>   Within the Holy Place,
> And, when the veil is drawn aside,
>   To see my Father's Face.

> O Thou from Whom my spirit came,
>   And wanders in this wild,
> Behold I bear Thy lovely Name,
>   Lead home Thy wandering child.

As she finished singing there came another knock on the door, low but quite clear. Gloomy and Spiteful again started and looked at one another questioningly and then at Grace and Glory. A lovely colour had flooded into her cheeks and her eyes shone like stars. She knew in an instant whose Hand it was that knocked on the door of that dismal attic. As her two cousins stared at her speechlessly the knock came again, a little louder, a little more insistent.

"Oh!" entreated Grace and Glory, "Oh! Spiteful and Gloomy, it is HE whom we have been talking about. It is the Shepherd Himself. Open the door and tell Him to come in!"

Every drop of blood seemed to drain away from Spiteful's already pallid cheeks. She shrank back, casting a stricken look around the wretched room and at her own ragged clothes which scarcely covered the bruises on her body. She cringed backwards, covering her face with her hands.

For a minute there was dead silence, so complete it seemed as though the beating of every heart in the room must become audible. Then through the silence there came a third knock, and a Man's strong, gentle, patient voice was heard saying, "May I come in?"

Gloomy rose to her feet. She was trembling from head to foot but she touched her sister's arm and pointed wordlessly and entreatingly towards the door.

Then poor Spiteful, the sorrowful, destitute owner of the miserable attic, stumbled across the room and opened the door.

The Shepherd stepped inside, tall, powerful, with regal mien, and yet with a look of infinite compassion on His face. Spiteful looked at Him just once, and then cast herself full length on the ground at His feet with a bitter cry of anguish, saying, "Lord, have pity on me."

He put out His hand to lift her up, but before He could do so or speak a word, there was Gloomy, the one-time haughty daughter-in-law of old Lord Fearing, kneeling at His feet beside her sister, whispering through trembling lips, "Have mercy on me also, Lord; don't leave me outside Thy grace."

As He raised them both together with words of love and compassion, the look on the Shepherd's face was that of one who at last has achieved His heart's desire—of the Saviour who knows that now He may begin the heavenly work of saving.

Grace and Glory, with Joy and Peace standing beside her, looked on and said in her heart, "No, not even up on the High Places have we known such joy as this. This attic 'is none other than the house of God, and this is the gate of heaven'." (Gen. 28:17).

CHAPTER IV

THE MOUNTAIN OF CAMPHIRE (JOY)

The Victory of Love

A few days after the experience recorded in the last chapter, the King again called Grace and Glory and told her that He wished to take her to another part of the High Places, and He led her right across the mountain of pomegranates to the next part of the same mountain range. Up there on the High Places, above all the clouds and mist of the valley, the sky was always gloriously unclouded and the light so clear that it was possible to look out across immense distances. On this particular early morning (for the times of solitary fellowship and communion with the King were generally during the very early hours before the work of the day started), Grace and Glory saw that though all was calm and clear up there on the mountain, the valleys were filled with billowing clouds, so that they seemed to be looking out over a sea of swirling waters, and from time to time thunder came rolling up from the depths beneath.

After crossing the Mountain of Pomegranates they came to another which the King told her was called the Mountain of Camphire, for it was specially set apart for the cultivation of that spice. The camphire, or henna, bushes which grew up there, yielded a most lovely perfume, and also a costly dye.

Grace and Glory looked around with great delight. Instead of the pomegranate trees of the first mountain, these slopes were covered with fragrant little bushes from which hung clusters of small white flowers with the sweetest scent imaginable. These were the bushes which yielded the spice which in our language is called Joy.

It seemed that these fragrant groves had a peculiar attraction for the birds. Never in her life had Grace and Glory seen such multitudes of them assembled in one place. Every bush seemed to be swaying with the motion of alighting or departing birds. They flew in great flocks, weaving beautiful patterns with their feathers glittering against the sky, and the moving of their wings stirred the air, so that as they swooped or rushed past it was as though gusts of wind blew over the mountain-side. All the birds were singing together as melodiously and diversely as an orchestra of musical instruments, until the whole area seemed alive with beating wings, rushing wind and song, while everything was drenched in the sweet, tingling perfume of the camphire bushes. It was so lovely that Grace and Glory could not restrain herself but laughed aloud with joy and clapped her hands.

As they walked along the mountain slope, the King told her a little about the nature of the camphire bushes which produce the fruit of Joy. He explained to her that before the perfumed oil could be produced by the plant, the ground around the bushes needed to be manured with a bitter substance which the roots of the bushes drew in from the soil and changed into the oil of gladness.

There were certain seasons when His workmen treated the soil in this way, just before the heavy winter rains and snows began when everything on the bushes faded and fell to the ground and the branches were left completely bare. As He told her this, the King looked at His companion and said to her with one of His beautiful smiles:

"The season when the bushes are stripped bare and the bitter substance is poured into the soil and is left to be watered by the rains of heaven, is called up here 'The night of sorrow'. But this present season, when the bushes are all laden with blossom and the oil is ready to be extracted from them, is 'The morning of Joy' when all the sorrow and bitter experiences are changed into gladness. Listen to the birds singing, Grace and Glory, and see if you can understand their song."

They stood together for a few moments in silence and suddenly the singing of the birds became audible as a lovely song which she could understand quite clearly. It was this:

> Hark to Love's triumphant shout!
>   "Joy is born from pain,
> Joy is sorrow inside out,
>   Grief remade again.
> Broken hearts look up and see
> This is Love's own victory."

> Here marred things are made anew,
>   Filth is here made clean,
> Here are robes, not rags, for you,
>   Mirth where tears have been.
> Where sin's dreadful power was found,
> Grace doth now much more abound.

> Hark! such songs of jubilation!
>   Every creature sings,
>   Great the joy of every nation,
>   "LOVE is King of kings.
>   See, ye blind ones! shout, ye dumb!
>   Joy is sorrow overcome."

As she listened Grace and Glory remembered the long, bitter and difficult journey which she herself had made up to the High Places when Sorrow and Suffering had been her companions, and the "long night of sorrow" had seemed sometimes as though it would never end. As she recalled that journey she thought that never had she heard so lovely a song or understood the glorious truth that Joy is sorrow overcome and transformed. "If other nights of sorrow must come to me," she said to herself, "I can never fear nor dread them again, for I know they are only the seasons when the camphire bushes of the King are prepared and made ready to produce the oil of gladness. Oh, how lovely His thoughts and His plans are, how great is His wonderful goodness and loving-kindness. His ways of grace past finding out! Oh, that I may always react to sorrow in such a way that it will be overcome and be changed into His joy." Here and there on the slopes grew great spreading trees, and in the shade of one of these the two sat down and began to talk together.

From the Mountain of Camphire they could look out on the dazzlingly white peaks of the still Higher Places and could see the summit of the Black Mountain just appearing above the clouds and mist. And once again the contrast between the joy and the beauty of the slopes on which they were sitting and the desolation of the ruined mountain opposite struck Grace and Glory with a sensation of almost unbearable pity and pain.

As though He read her very thoughts and spoke in answer to them, she heard the voice of the King saying:

"Grace and Glory, have you ever thought of what *joy* it is to Me to be a SAVIOUR? To be able to take something which has been marred and spoilt and ruined by evil and to produce out of it something lovely and good and enduring—something which can never again be spoilt? No cost can possibly be too great in order to accomplish such a triumph as that. Whatever the price, Love will pay it exultantly and with 'JOY unspeakable and full of glory'."

As He spoke He looked across at the charred black summit of the mountain opposite as it just appeared above the clouds of swirling mist and His whole face was alight with a glory of love and joy impossible to describe. Presently He began to sing another of the Mountain songs, and in the words and the melody there was such a blending of sorrow and of joy that Grace and Glory sat as though lost in wondering awe.

The cry of all distorted things:
 "Why hast Thou made us thus?
To bear the anguish which life brings;
 Why didst Thou not love us?"
So marred that God Himself must weep—
Fit only for the rubbish heap.

The cry of every breaking heart:
 "Why were we born for this?
Evil alone is made our part
 And nothing of earth's bliss.
Why didst Thou give us human birth
If we may know no love on earth?"

The cry of each despairing mind
Ascends before Love's Throne:
"Behold us, God! or art Thou blind?
Can we be blamed alone?
If Thou be there, then answer us,
Why make us? or why make us thus?"

And Love's Voice answers from a Cross:
"I bear it all with you;
I share with you in all your loss,
I WILL MAKE ALL THINGS NEW.
None suffer in their sin alone,
I made—I bear—and I atone."

There was a long silence when the song ended and then the King said: "You know, Grace and Glory, 'it is enough for the disciple to be as his Lord', and to learn also to overcome EVIL WITH GOOD. There is absolutely no experience, however terrible, or heartbreaking, or unjust, or cruel, or evil, which you can meet in the course of your earthly life, that can harm you if you will but let Me teach you how to accept it with joy; and to react to it triumphantly as I did Myself, with love and forgiveness and with willingness to bear the results of wrong done by others. Every trial, every test, every difficulty and seemingly wrong experience through which you may have to pass, is only another opportunity granted to you of conquering an evil thing and bringing out of it something to the lasting praise and glory of God. You sons and daughters of Adam, in all your suffering and sorrow, are the most privileged of all beings, for you are to be perfected through suffering and to become the sons and daughters of God with His power to overcome evil with good. If only you realised your destiny, how you would rejoice at every experience of trial and tribulation, and even in the persecution which comes your way. You would 'COUNT IT ALL JOY'. You would take pleasure in infirmities, in reproaches, in necessities, in persecutions and distresses for Christ's sake 'for when you are weak, then you learn how to be made strong'. Ponder over the things which I have told you up here on the Mountain of Joy, and as we go down now into the valley and you meet again with the evil and cruel things which torment your relatives down there—yes and with their unloving reactions to your desire to share your joy with them—remember the lesson which you have learnt up here on this mountain and 'Count it ALL joy', for it all constitutes a glorious opportunity whereby you may learn to overcome evil with good and to share in THE VICTORY OF LOVE."

Then they went on their way again, leaping down the mountain-side towards the valley. And in the heart of Grace and Glory there was a joy such as she had never before experienced and a completely new understanding of the purpose of their work down there in the places of sorrow and evil.

CHAPTER V

BITTERNESS AND MURMURING

SOME days after the events described in the last chapters, Bitterness and his wife Murmuring were sitting together in their private room at the back of the Inn eating their midday meal. Something seemed to be troubling the thoughts of both of them, but for a little while neither mentioned it. Bitterness ate in complete silence, and his wife busied herself looking after the wants of their three children, young Grumble, the son and heir, and his twin sisters, little Sob and Drizzle, who, with bibs tied round their necks, were banging their spoons on their high-chairs and vociferously demanding attention. Murmuring dressed all her children daintily and was quite rightly proud of their appearance and good looks, but even at that early age all three were loud in their complaints if what they demanded was not instantly forthcoming.

At last Murmuring, as if unable to remain silent any longer, turned to her husband and asked angrily, "Well, Bitterness, what do you say to these constant visits of the Shepherd to Spiteful and her sister in the attic upstairs?"

Bitterness did not answer, but went on eating in gloomy silence.

"Well," snapped his wife again, "did you hear what I said? Or have you suddenly gone deaf?" (One could see at once from whom dear little Sob and Drizzle had inherited their determined manner of gaining the attention they wanted!)

Bitterness spoke at last. "I suppose there is no harm in them," he said shortly.

"Oh, you do, do you?" answered his wife stormily. "Well, let me tell you that if it gets about in the Valley that the Shepherd visits here, and there is the possibility of meeting Him, ALL our clientele will fall away and the business will be ruined. Everybody hates Him."

"There is no likelihood of people meeting Him," said Bitterness. "He does not force Himself on anyone."

"People will begin to talk about us," retorted Murmuring. "They will suggest that we are coming under His influence. I tell you I don't like it. We have had enough trouble already. Just think of the way He persuaded your cousin, Much-Afraid, to leave everything and go off to the mountains, and how disgusted all your connections were! We cannot afford to bring ourselves under suspicion."

Bitterness paused for a moment before he answered. Then he said in a low voice: "I do not see how anyone can deny that it turned out to be a most fortunate thing for my cousin that she did go with Him. I must admit that I think she is to be envied!"

"Indeed!" exclaimed his wife, her cheeks flushing hotter with anger every moment. "I seem to remember that you and others went after the said fortunate cousin in order to try to bring her back. And I believe she was charming enough to stone you, and was the cause also of her cousin Pride's being crippled for life!"

A slow flush rose on her husband's cheeks also, but there was no change in his voice as he answered quietly: "It is quite true, but we were trying to kidnap her by force, and it was her only means of self-defence. When I think of her situation now, and what it would have been if we had succeeded in turning her back and forcing her to marry Craven Fear, I cannot help feeling that she is one of the most fortunate people in the world." He paused a moment, and then, raising his voice slightly, he added, "If the Shepherd can do the same sort of thing for that poor, broken-hearted woman upstairs, I for one am not going to try to prevent it."

His wife glared at him angrily, but not exactly as though she were surprised to find him take this point of view.

"What has come over you?" she demanded after a pause. "You have never been the same since you came back from that journey to the mountains and your unsuccessful attempt to make Much-Afraid return."

Her husband went on eating with his eyes fixed on his plate, and then answered in an even lower tone: "You are right. I am not the same."

Murmuring looked startled and a little non-plussed; then she rallied and went back to the main point.

"Well, I tell you, Bitterness—and mark my words, for they will certainly come true—it you let the Shepherd continue to visit Spiteful here in this house our business will be ruined, absolutely ruined."

For the first time her husband raised his head and looked straight in her face, and his eyes were dark with bitterness and with some other emotion which she could not define. "Sometimes," said he slowly and painfully, "sometimes I think that I would not care if the business WERE ruined, if only we could get rid of the cursed thing altogether."

Mrs. Bitterness gasped with horror, and then said in a tone pregnant with wrath and accusation, "You've been talking with the Shepherd yourself, Bitterness?"

He nodded without speaking.

"Sneaking up to that attic too!" exploded his wife furiously. "You would! You would do a thing like that! Putting yourself under the influence of *that* Man!—letting Him twist you round His little finger—till you actually want to take the food out of the mouths of your own helpless little children! There you sit," she went on hysterically, "actually telling me that you wouldn't mind if the business were ruined. Our hotel! the most prosperous and well-conducted inn in the whole Valley! I wonder you don't choke on the words!"

"Listen, Murmuring," said her husband, as though suddenly deciding to speak frankly and fully. "Listen to me. What sort of business is this really? Ask yourself honestly. You say it is respectable as well as profitable. Do you really believe that? Look at the fruits of the business, Murmuring. Look at your own poor, demoralised brother Moody. If it were not for our 'respectable bar' would he be where he is now—in gaol for half killing his wife? Consider that poor girl upstairs, not only deprived of her child, but probably also of the joy of becoming a mother for the rest of her life. Look at our own children, Murmuring, and put yourself in her place."

Then he went on, without waiting for a reply, and his voice shook with emotion or pain, "And look at my cousin, Craven Fear, poor thing, also in prison for assault and disorderly behaviour whilst under the influence of drink which he likewise obtained in our 'respectable bar-room'."

"Craven Fear was always a bully," interpolated his wife hastily. "It was not just that once. He has only got what was coming to him for a long time."

"Exactly," agreed her husband in a heavy voice. "But his out-breaks of bullying were always when he was the worse for drink. Craven Fear has been drinking in this 'respectable bar-room' of ours ever since he left school, and he was sneaking drinks long before that, and you know it."

His wife was silent.

"And then think of the effect on our own children," went on Bitterness in a voice that trembled. "That is what shakes me. That comes still nearer home. What if they follow on in the same way and come under the same curse? Do you wonder, Murmuring, that I have been feeling that it would be a relief if we could get away from the business altogether?"

His words seemed only to rouse her to greater fury. "It's all the doing of the Shepherd," she exclaimed, almost choking with anger. "It's the Shepherd Who has put these thoughts into your head. What else has He been saying to you? Tell me!"

"He said," answered her husband slowly, "that we shall never know real peace and happiness, or indeed, real prosperity, until we give up this business altogether."

"I knew it!" cried his wife furiously. "It is just what HE would say! Give up everything that we have worked and toiled for! Give up the money we have honestly earned, just when at last we have succeeded in getting wealthy and now own one of the most pros-perous business concerns in the Valley! And what, pray, what does He offer you in return?"

"He will take us into His own service," answered her husband in a low tone.

"Make us shepherds—shepherds!" Mrs. Bitterness almost choked on the words. "And give us a four-roomed cottage, and a cat, and a dog, and some chickens! Bah!"

As she spoke, Murmuring looked out of the window and surveyed the domain over which she ruled so competently and with such undisputed sway. She looked at the well-filled flower garden, the clipped hedges of the bowling green, at the river and the gaily coloured boats. Down the passage, through the half-opened door, she could hear the clink of glasses in the barroom and the sound of voices and occasional laughter. She could distinguish the genial tones of the new bar-tender, a capable and experienced man named Sharp, quite different, luckily, from that weak boy, Moody. She could hear the girls in the kitchen laughing together as they ate their early meal in preparation for the busy midday hour, and she visualised the parking-place filled with cars and motor-cycles. All these things they had achieved by sheer hard work and competence (for no one could deny, thought Murmuring complacently, that they *were* a smart and competent couple), and within the few years since their marriage had transformed the shabby old "pub" which Bitterness had inherited from his father into this attractive, modern and extremely well-patronised hotel. And now here was her husband actually mad enough, under the influence of that utterly impossible Shepherd, to suggest that they would never know peace and happiness and prosperity until they gave it all up! Until they sank to the position of hired shepherds! It was madness! It was abominable folly! It was worse!

She looked at her husband, at his sad, miserable face, at the strange new pain and unrest in his eyes, and for a moment her heart quailed at the fearful possibility of losing her kingdom altogether. Then she rallied her forces and determined that she would not surrender any part of it. She reminded herself that she was the stronger of the two, and with her lay the power to prevent such a catastrophe. So she forced a laugh, as though suddenly she was amused by the whole thing and chose to treat his words as a joke.

"Your poor Shepherd!" said she. "He certainly is a crank and fanatic if ever there was one! But He will find that His weird ideas do not go down here. I fear if He tries to come forcing His way in here that He will get much the same reception that I saw Him receive at Mrs. Dismal Forebodings' cottage this morning."

Her husband said nothing, so she went on, laughing heartily as she spoke: "I was walking along the village street when I saw good Mrs. Valiant, with her Shepherd in tow, open the garden gate of Mrs. Dismal's cottage and go and knock on the door. I was a little curious to see what would happen, so I waited. And what do you think? The door was opened an inch or two and there was Mrs. Dismal wearing the most awful old brown wrapper you ever saw. Mrs. Valiant didn't seem to notice her embarrassment but just called out in her exasperatingly cheery way, 'Here He is, Dismal dear!' and tried to push inside. And poor old Mrs. Dismal gave a kind of squawk and jabbered, 'Can't you see *I'm not fit* to receive anyone like this?' and *slammed the door right in His face.* He won't go calling there again in a hurry! I thought I would make myself ill with laughing!"

The memory of it seemed to have the same dangerous effect upon her, for she nearly choked with mirth again.

While she was still laughing and mopping her eyes, suddenly a quiet voice spoke through the half-opened door behind her. "May I come in? I would like to speak with you." And there was the Shepherd Himself.

Now it was one thing to mock the Shepherd behind His back, but quite another thing to be confronted with Him face to face. There was something so regal and commanding in His manner that it had an overawing effect.

In an instant Bitterness had sprung to his feet and pushed forward the best armchair, and though his face was dark and miserable, there was a suppressed eagerness in his manner as if this visit were not really unwelcome. As for Murmuring, her laughter ceased and the contemptuous expression on her face vanished as if by magic, and she heard herself saying to the visitor she had just labelled a crank and a fanatic, and in whose face she had threatened to slam the door, "Please be seated, Sir. May we offer you some refreshment?"

He shook His head, but seated Himself in the armchair and then said quietly to Bitterness, "Friend, have you been considering what I said to you when last we met?"

"Yes," said Bitterness in the strange, low voice so unlike his usual loud, harsh tones. "Yes, my wife and I were discussing it together just now."

The heart of Mrs. Bitterness quailed within her, but she was absolutely determined to resist the Shepherd's influence over her husband and to see that He did not make her lose the kingdom on which her heart was set. For the moment she said nothing, but with all the strength of her will, rallied every power which she possessed to resist Him to the utmost. Against her will, however, she raised her eyes and looked across at the Shepherd, and saw that He was gazing straight at her as though He could read her thoughts as plainly as if she had spoken them aloud. But there was a look of compassionate pity on His face which surprised her and in some dreadful way seemed almost as though it would break through her defences. She said nothing, but rallied her powers of resistance still more desperately.

"It is hard for a rich person to enter into the Kingdom of Love," said the Shepherd, speaking directly to her.

"Why so?" asked Mrs. Bitterness, stubbornly folding her lips together as tightly as possible.

"Because one *cannot* love God and wealth too," said the Shepherd. "It simply cannot be done."

"If You will excuse me, Sir," said Mrs. Bitterness coldly, "I must tell You that I cannot justly be accused of not loving God. I attend church faithfully (whenever the business permits of it); we contribute more generously than most people do to the charities which we consider to be deserving, and all my little children have been properly baptised. As for loving my neighbour as myself (which I suppose You will quote at me next), no one, I am sure, can possibly accuse me of injustice, or meanness, or unkindness to anyone, and I do not know of anything which my Maker can justly condemn me for. Indeed, the very fact that our business has prospered makes it possible for my husband and myself to give far more generously to needy charities than we were able to do before. I repeat, I believe You to be mistaken in saying that one cannot love one's Maker and one's neighbour and wealth at the same time."

"You do not love that poor girl upstairs in the attic," said the Shepherd as quietly and as gently as possible.

A deep, angry flush rose in Murmuring's cheeks. "What has she been saying against me?" she asked through tightly compressed lips.

"Nothing at all," said the Shepherd still very quietly, but as He spoke His eyes strayed round the comfortable, airy room in which they were sitting and rested on the well-filled table. "I cannot help seeing that if you loved her as yourself she would not be lying up there in that scorching attic, weak and ill as she is, subsisting on bread and tea and any little extras which are provided for her through the kindness of others."

The flush of Murmuring's face was even deeper as she answered, "She has been lying there for months, unable to do her work, and yet I have not turned her out of my house or asked for rent. Am I expected to feed her like a princess while she lies there idle and have all the expense of hiring another person to do the work of her shameless husband who has brought disgrace on our home?"

"You know the answer to those questions yourself," said the Shepherd, and this time His voice was stern, almost terrifyingly so, but it softened again as He added, "And I repeat, it *is* hard for a rich person to know anything about real love."

"And so," cried Murmuring passionately, "and so You come here with the demand that we throw it all away—everything that we have worked for and gained through our own industry and toil!"

"Yes," said the Shepherd, rising to His feet. "Yes, Murmuring, cast it all away. It is damning you. It is hardening your heart. It is poisoning you through and through. Cast it away; for what shall it profit you if you gain the whole world and lose your own soul?"

"I won't," said Murmuring, suddenly losing control of herself and stamping her foot. "I won't. I tell You nothing on earth shall allow You to take away from us that which is rightly ours. Nothing at all!" she repeated fiercely. "All this belongs to me—and YOU shall never take it from me!"

The pity and compassion in His face, and the stubborn fury in hers, were a sight to see.

"I must tell you, Murmuring," said the Shepherd in quiet, compassionate tones, "before I leave, I must tell you that if you will not learn now the utter futility and uselessness of setting your heart on earthly riches, you will have to learn it in some other and harder way. "For how can I leave you," He added almost under His breath, "bound as a helpless, miserable slave to your money and possessions when you were made for the liberty and joy of Love?"

Then He looked straight across the room at her husband, who all this time had stood silent, with his eyes fastened fearfully and yet entreatingly on the Shepherd's face, and said, "Bitterness, come you after Me." He then turned and walked out of the room.

Bitterness took one step after Him; then his wife caught hold of him, weeping hysterically, clinging to him with all her might. "Don't go!" she shrieked. "Think of our children! Think of me! You will lose everything. He demands all."

Her husband stood still, leaned his head against the wall and groaned as though in agony. "It is *too hard*," muttered the poor rich man desperately. "It is so hard that it is impossible."

Back through the doorway came the clear, gentle and yet challenging, voice of the Shepherd saying: "With men it *is* impossible. But with God all things are possible." Then there was the sound of retreating footsteps and the closing of a door.

* * * *

Outside in the village street Mrs. Valiant caught sight of the Shepherd as He left the Inn, and she hurried toward Him eagerly. "Oh!" she exclaimed, "there You are! Please, please come with me. Ever since she slammed the door in Your face this morning poor Mrs. Dismal has been like a demented creature. She is afraid you will never go near her again—that she has lost all hope of having Your help, and that after such a rebuff You will certainly leave her to her misery. Oh, please come now—at once!"

He strode along at her side down the quiet street, and they entered the miserable, weed-filled garden round the cottage of Mrs. Dismal Forbodings. Then the Shepherd lifted His hand and knocked on the closed door. It opened slightly, and the white, miserable face of Mrs. Dismal peeped forth furtively. When she saw the Shepherd she seemed to shrink back as though expecting a blow. He waited without speaking, simply looking at her, and at last Mrs. Dismal Forbodings, trembling from head to foot, pulled open the door a little wider and the Shepherd stepped inside.

Having seen what happened, Mrs. Valiant, motherly, cheerful Mrs. Valiant, turned and literally ran back down the village street as though she had suddenly gone mad. She rushed in through the door of the Inn and up the back stairs, and, without even pausing to knock, she burst into the attic where Gloomy and Spiteful were working together on the great basket of mending. They looked up in astonishment as the door flew open and Mrs. Valiant stood before them, laughing and crying and panting for breath.

"Your mother," she gasped, and for a moment could say no more. Then in a burst of joy and tears together she brought out her glorious news. "Your mother," she said, "has just taken the Shepherd into her cottage!"

CHAPTER VI

THE MOUNTAIN OF SPIKENARD (PEACE)

THE ATONEMENT MADE BY LOVE

THE next of the nine mountains of spices to which the King led Grace and Glory was the Mountain of Spikenard, or Peace. On the slopes of this mountain grew a special variety of shrub requiring a high altitude far above the mists and clouds which so often shrouded the lower slopes of the mountains. The King's spikenard could be produced nowhere else in the world, but it grew in wonderful abundance up there on the High Places. It was from this lovely medicinal plant that He produced the famous balsam of peace, a great balm for all restlessness and pain and fever. It was extracted from the root of the shrub in the form of fragrant oil. All the inhabitants of the High Places carried a supply of this balsam with them wherever they went, but especially on their visits to the Valley below, anointing themselves with it daily. Grace and Glory was therefore delighted to see the actual shrubs from which it was produced, growing up there in such abundance that the whole of the mountain-side was clothed with a forest of these lovely shrubs of spikenard.

She discovered, too, that a great number of streams and brooks ran down the mountain-side, into which the roots of all the bushes penetrated and from which they drew in the healing property of peace and stored it up. The Mountain of Spikenard was indeed a veritable "garden of fountains, a well of living waters and streams from Lebanon". (Cant. 4:15.) The roots of the bushes thrust themselves down eagerly and thirstily into the waters along whose banks they grew, ACCEPTING and drinking up everything the streams could bring them. Nothing was rejected, but all accepted with joy, and, after being drawn within, was there transformed into beauty and fragrance and healing balm.

As they walked together amongst these bushes the King spoke to Grace and Glory and explained to her the nature of the true peace which can only be produced by acceptance with joy of all that the Will of God permits to come to His people along the pathway of life, and of the streams of pleasure which sing as they leap down from the High Places, "I delight to do Thy Will, O my God". So the streams water the soil and make them able to nourish the little trees of peace. And He taught her yet another mountain song.

In acceptance lieth peace,
        O my heart be still;
Let thy restless worries cease
        And accept His Will.
Though this test be not thy choice,
It is His—therefore rejoice.

In His plan there cannot be
　　Aught to make thee sad:
If this is His Choice for thee,
　　Take it and be glad.
Make from it some lovely thing
To the glory of thy King.

Cease from sighs and murmuring,
　　Sing His loving grace,
This thing means thy furthering
　　To a wealthy place.
From thy fears He'll give release,
In acceptance lieth peace.

Here and there amidst the groves of bushes there were ponds and lakes through which the countless streams of healing waters flowed until they emptied themselves into one great reservoir of sapphire-blue waters. In these lakes and pools swam brilliantly coloured fish like gorgeous living jewels darting about between the carpets of waterlilies. The whole scene was enchantingly beautiful but perhaps the most delightful and healing thing of all was the lovely stillness and calm which brooded over everything, for the whole mountain lay back a little from the other mountains which shut it in and protected it from wind and storm. It was so quiet there that it was only gradually the sound of murmuring streams became audible to the ears, the soft humming of the bees and an occasional low note from some bird, a species of turtle dove which nested among the bushes of Peace.

When they reached the great reservoir, the King and His companion sat down on the bank above it. There they were on the very edge of the mountain and could look straight down into the

Valley of Humiliation far below. Indeed, the King explained that the very shortest route between the Valley and the High Places was up the sides of this Mountain of Spikenard, but He added that the greatest storms and tempests, so common on the lower parts of the mountains, were generally strongest and most violent just below those very slopes on which they sat, and at such times the rolling of the thunder could be heard quite plainly and the lightning could be seen rending the clouds beneath that place, yet not a breath of any raging tempest could invade the quiet Valley of Peace up there on the High Place of the mountain.

For some time the two of them sat in perfect silence. Grace and Glory could not help comparing the deep rest and tranquillity of that place with the scenes of stress and tempest through which she had first struggled up to the High Places, and also with the storms and stresses in the lives of the inhabitants of the Valley down there beneath them. She thought of so many of her relatives down there whose inner lives were tempest-tossed and tormented by fear and bitterness, by rage and envy and covetousness, and by rivalries and evils of all sorts. Then she began to think of all the sorrows and anguish of heart endured by the multitudes in the City of Destruction which lay not far from the Valley of Humiliation, on the shores of the great sea. She had recently visited the city with the King and some of the things she had seen and heard there seemed seared upon her memory. She remembered, too, the passionate sorrow and compassion felt by the King's workers in the great city and the way in which they had seemed to feel themselves so at one with all the degraded and miserable and destitute people amongst whom they laboured, and how sometimes they said they were almost brought to despair by the suffering all around them, and especially of their pity and distress over the innocent and helpless little children born into an environment of evil and degradation from which there could be no escape for them, and in which they were doomed to be corrupted and brought into even deeper evil and misery.

As she thought of these things Grace and Glory gave a little gasp. It seemed to her that all the peace and beauty and loveliness of that spot up there on the High Places had become overshadowed and darkened; as though it were wrong for her to be sitting up there "in the heavenly places" when down in the valleys below life was so cruel and so dreadfully different. What right had she to enjoy so much when so many others never had the least opportunity to share the same joys, indeed, could not even know anything about the King of Love by Whose side she was sitting.

Then she heard His voice speaking.

"It is right and blessed, Grace and Glory, that you begin to feel something of the anguish of the world's suffering and to know your own ONENESS with all the blemished and spoilt lives everywhere. To begin to understand at last what it must mean to the Heart of Love Himself, and to realise that Love can never rest until all Evil is overcome and swallowed up in victory. Up here on this Mountain of Spikenard I would have you learn this truth, that Love can never rest until real peace, which is perfect Harmony with the Law of Love, is brought to the hearts of all men everywhere. This is the impelling incentive and motive for all witness and all the Ministry of Love in which you are being trained. For LOVE MUST SHARE WITH OTHERS OR DIE. It must give to others all that it received or it cannot remain Love. Love can only live in your heart as it propagates itself by sharing. Love is the constraining power which makes My lovers willing to go all lengths, even to death itself, in order to bring the Good News of the Love of God

to those who have never heard it. It is love to the Lamb of God
WHO BEARS the sins of the world and still must bear it and suffer
with sinners until every sin-defiled creature turns at last from their
sinning and seeks His delivering power. For as long as sin lasts and
defiles and ruins His creatures, Love cannot come down from His
cross nor cease to bear the sin of the world."

When He finished speaking intense silence brooded up there on
the Mountain of Spikenard as though all living things on the mountain knelt in trembling worship. The King Himself finally broke that
silence as He began to sing. These were the words of the song which
Grace and Glory heard, but no words can express the full meaning:

> Love is the Lord. He hears each cry,
>   His gentleness is great,
> No wounded heart will He pass by
>   Nor leave it desolate.
> For in His love He stoops to be
> AT ONE in all our misery.
>
> Love is the Lord. Love casts out fear!
>   He breaketh all sin's chains;
> The moan of sin-sick hearts He hears
>   And feeleth all their pains.
> There is no wrong that men can do
> But God's own Lamb must suffer too.
>
> Oh, understand it if you can!
>   ('Tis Love Himself Who pleads)
> Whene'r you wound a son of man
>   The Son of God still bleeds.
> And not till sin is wholly slain
> Can God's own heart be healed of pain.

CHAPTER VII

TO THE RESCUE OF SELF-PITY

MRS. VALIANT was cheerfully and energetically bustling about her cottage, busy with the morning's work. Through the open kitchen door she could look out in the garden where the brown hen was teaching her new family of yellow chicks to search for worms and tit-bits. The little ducklings were splashing about in the stream; the sandy cat was blinking in the sun and the bees were humming all over the garden. In the next cottage Mercy was singing as she went about her work.

"A really lovely day," said Mrs. Valiant to herself happily—"just the sort of day when something specially nice is likely to happen. I do hope poor Dismal's awful almanac is not foretelling calamity. I wonder whether I ought to go round to see her? I should so love to know what happened after the Shepherd went into her cottage."

Just as she reached that point in her thoughts the garden gate clicked, and, looking out, she saw a tall woman wearing a most beautiful oriental-looking shawl embroidered all over with richly glowing colours, the pattern outlined in threads of gold and silver which shone and sparkled in the bright sunshine, making it a thing of almost dazzling beauty.

Mrs. Valiant's attention was so taken by the glittering shawl, and she was so astonished that anyone so gorgeously apparelled should actually be walking up the garden path towards her kitchen door, and so occupied in wondering whoever it could be, that for a moment or two she did not recognise the face of the newcomer. When she did she gave a little gasp of bewildered amazement, and then her eyes misted over with tears of joy so that everything was blurred.

"Why, Dismal, my dear!" exclaimed she, when she could successfully get rid of a queer little choke in her voice, "Why Dismal, is that really you? I was just thinking about you and wondering whether I would go round to see you. But this is a hundred times better! Sit down here in the porch and let me look at you. It really is you, isn't it, Dismal?"

Mrs. Dismal Forebodings came forward a little hesitatingly, then went up to her old friend and did what she had never done since they were girls together at school, put her arms around her and kissed her. "Yes, it is I, myself," said she with a shy little laugh. "I expect you are wondering whatever I am doing, walking about in a shawl like this, Valiant."

"It is simply beautiful!" said Mrs. Valiant in a tone of ecstasy. "I never saw anything lovelier. And it suits you perfectly, Dismal dear. You are so tall and dignified when you are not mooning about in a drab dress and your widow's weeds. I am thankful to see that you are not wearing them any longer. But tell me, Dismal, where did you get that exquisite shawl?"

"The Shepherd gave it to me," said Mrs. Dismal simply, and told me that it was His wish that I wear it always. Otherwise, my dear Valiant, I would naturally have folded such a beautiful garment away in tissue paper as a priceless heirloom only to be worn on feast days and very special occasions, if then. But He said so firmly that it was His wish that I should wear it every day (unsuitable for a poor widow as it seems) that I do not like to disregard His request. You see, Valiant, He has done so much for me that I cannot refuse to do what He asks. He has taken me into His service, old and dreary as I am, and has spoken so comfortingly to poor Gloomy and myself that we really feel like new people beginning life all over again. He tells me that this beautiful shawl is called 'the garment of praise', and He gave one almost exactly like it to Gloomy and told us that He would give us 'beauty for ashes, the oil of joy for mourning, the garment of praise for the spirit of heaviness' (Isa. 61:3). And of course, when I had this beautiful, glittering thing over my shoulders, Valiant dear, it made my dreary old grey dress look just too awful for words. That is why, as you see, I have discarded my widow's weeds altogether, and am wearing one of the light, pretty dresses which I thought I had laid aside for ever. I am still a little self-conscious, I fear," added she with a rather shamefaced laugh, "but I shall get used to it presently, I hope, and know how to wear it more naturally and gracefully, to the glory of the One Who gave it to me."

She paused for a moment as though she could hardly go on speaking, and then she put out her hand and laid it tremblingly on her friend's arm. "It was you who brought Him to the cottage, Valiant," said she softly, and I don't know how to begin to thank you. All these years you have been so patient with me and so faithful, putting up with all my miserable selfishness and ungraciousness. If it were not for you, Valiant, none of this would have happened."

Mrs. Valiant sat there in the sun-filled porch holding Dismal's hand in both of her own, beaming like the sun itself, and quite unashamedly allowing the tears of joy to trickle down her cheeks. But speech was never her strong point; she always expressed herself much more fluently through bustling, loving activity, and when at last she could find her voice, all she said was: "Dismal, my dear, this is the happiest day of my life. I'll just slip into the kitchen and put the kettle on the fire—it's nearly boiling—and we'll have a good cup of tea together. You wait here in the porch, and while the kettle is boiling I am going across to the other cottage to call Mercy to come join us."

Away she bustled, and was over in her daughter's cottage in a moment. There, to her extreme delight, she found that Grace and Glory had just arrived and was talking to Mercy. They broke off immediately, however, and looked in astonishment at Mrs. Valiant, who stood before them, her cheeks still wet with tears and her face one radiant smile of joy. "Oh, Grace and Glory," she exclaimed, "how glad I am to find you here too! It is just right! Your aunt Dismal is over in my cottage, and you must both come and have a cup of tea with us."

"Aunt Dismal!" they both exclaimed together. "Oh, tell us what has happened! She has not been outside her cottage for months."

"Come and see!" cried Mrs. Valiant happily. "Just see what the Shepherd has done for her! You go across now, both of you, and make the tea, Mercy dear. I am just going out into the road to see whether there is anyone else about who can share our joy!"

Then out she went, and sure enough, whom should she see but Mrs. Dismal's daughter, Gloomy, hesitating at the gate. "Mrs. Valiant," said Gloomy awkwardly (in the days when she was first married to Lord Fearing's son she had not deigned to know her mother's old friend, Mrs. Valiant, the shepherdess)—"Mrs. Valiant, have you seen my mother anywhere? I think she was planning to visit you."

Mrs. Valiant took her warmly by the arm as though she were a close friend—as though she had never been snubbed and coldly ignored by the young woman now standing shamefacedly before her—and she exclaimed heartily: "Yes, indeed, she is now sitting in the porch of my cottage, and we are just going to have a cup of tea. Come and join us, my dear."

Gloomy drew back a little with a slight flush on her cheeks. After snubbing and patronising people all her life, until the tables were turned in such a disastrous fashion, she now felt miserable and ashamed in the presence of all those whom she had so treated.

Without appearing to notice this, Mrs. Valiant went on cheerfully: "Mercy and your cousin, Grace and Glory, are there already. Do come, dear Gloomy, it will make us all so happy."

"Is Grace and Glory there too?" asked Gloomy in quite another tone of voice. "Thank you, Mrs. Valiant, I shall be glad to come."

So over to the cottage they went, and what a scene it was! There in the shady, honey-suckle-covered porch was the table spread with a white cloth, and upon it the blue-and-white cups and saucers, the old brown teapot, and one of Mrs. Valiant's famous cakes, so crisp and delicious-smelling that it made one's mouth water. And there was Mrs. Dismal and her daughter, Gloomy, wearing their beautiful shawls, and Mrs. Valiant with her face as bright as the morning itself. Mercy sat on one side of Mrs. Dismal and Grace and Glory sat beside her cousin. Joy and Peace were present too. Other members of the two households joined the party also for the domestic creatures were there in full force. The white-and-black cat came walking sedately across from the cottage

next door and sat beside the sandy one, both ostentatiously washing their faces in anticipation and keeping a close watch on the
table. The brown hen, loudly clucking, hurried there with her
brood, all ready to receive the crumbs, and the ducklings left the
stream and came waddling up the path. One or two of the neighbouring dogs strolled nonchalantly into the garden as though they
had just looked in by chance. Everyone at the party was in the best
of spirits. To Mrs. Dismal and Gloomy it was as strange as though
they had suddenly been transported into a new world.

How they all talked!—sharing the news with one another and
making the two guests go over the story again and again of what
had happened when the Shepherd went into the cottage. Most of
all they talked with happy faces and happy voices about the Shepherd Himself.

When they were well on towards emptying the big teapot for the
third time, they were joined by a neighbour, Mrs. Gossip, who was
bursting with news. She said that she had just looked in to tell them
that Self-Pity ("your cousin, you know, Much-Afraid!") had been
taken dangerously ill, and his wife, Helpless, was at her wit's end,
not knowing what to do. The doctor, when he came, had said it was
a serious case of double pneumonia and that the patient must be
kept absolutely quiet, with a nurse in attendance day and night.
"And you all know how utterly unpractical and useless poor Helpless is in an emergency," Mrs. Gossip wound up, adding with dolor-
ous satisfaction: "It seems that Self-Pity himself is so terrified that he
is going to die that they can't keep him quiet. I am afraid they must
be having a dreadful time. And that youngest child of theirs, little
Doldrums, is tumbling about all over the place with no one to look
after him, getting in everybody's way and nearly falling into the fire
and likely to burn or scald himself to death—a little terror if ever

there was one! No one can do anything with him. No, thank you, Mrs. Valiant, one cup of tea is quite enough. It was most refreshing. I really must be going; thank you very much indeed."

With another curious, scrutinising stare at Mrs. Dismal and her daughter, whom she had been covertly watching all the time that she poured out her story, Mrs. Gossip departed in great excitement to impart her news at the next cottage, with the added spicy titbit that Mrs. Dismal and her daughter Gloomy, must have come into a mint of money and were all decked out in the most extravagant style. Perhaps Sir Coward had been forced at last to pay financial compensation to his deserted wife, and now she and her mother were walking about like fashion plates!

The group on the porch looked at one another, and then Mrs. Dismal groaned and said: "My poor nephew, Self-Pity! His wife, Helpless, is the most inefficient housekeeper imaginable and she knows absolutely nothing about nursing."

"Double pneumonia!" exclaimed Mercy commiseratingly, "and with no one to nurse him but that helpless little wife of his!"

And the house all upside down, and that unhappy child with no one to do a thing for him," said Mrs. Valiant. "It's dreadful!"

"And Self-Pity himself so terrified," added Grace and Glory. "I know how awful that is. And there is no one there to say a word to help him."

"And the district nurse away at the end of the valley," said Gloomy in the tone of one contributing to the pile of agony. "I met her early this morning starting off on her bicycle and she told me she would not be back until the evening."

Mrs. Valiant rose to her feet briskly with the manner of one all ready to take charge and organise a rescue party. She was in her element in any emergency.

"We must do something for them at once," said she with the utmost cheerfulness. "They need us—that is evident! Now is the opportunity for which we have been waiting so long to get into their cottage."

"As I am a trained nurse," said Mercy happily, "I will go along at once and offer to be his nurse as long as they need me. Of course, it may be that the doctor will send him to the hospital in the City of Destruction, but it is so far away that I think it unlikely they will risk moving him at this stage."

"I shall go with you," cried Mrs. Valiant, "and see what I can do to put the cottage in order and make a meal for poor Helpless and the children. I shall try to persuade her to let me bring little Doldrums home with me so that I can look after him here."

"You'll have a time of it, I warn you," said Mrs. Dismal Forebodings gloomily. "He is the most undisciplined, obstinate, brawling, destructive little brat that you could possibly have to do with, tearing to pieces whatever he can lay his hands on. You'll never have a moment's peace, Valiant."

Mrs. Dismal, you will notice, although she had begun to wear "the garment of praise", had only just entered the Shepherd's service and naturally did not yet know the language of the High Places.

"If you once offer to help Helpless," said Gloomy in a tone just like her name, "she'll roll the whole responsibility and the work onto you, and you'll find that she won't lift a finger herself, but leave you to carry the whole burden of everything."

"Oh, that won't matter," exclaimed Mrs. Valiant and her daughter, Mercy, both together, and smiling at one another without the least dismay. "That's all right. We have been wanting to get into that home for a long time, and now at last here is our chance!" Then she turned to Grace and Glory and said persuasively: "Do come with us, Grace and Glory. I can put a house to rights and cook a meal, but I'm no good at saying anything; I'm altogether too tactless." As she spoke she smiled ruefully at Mrs. Dismal, remembering her many bracing, but tactless, admonitions, and how often they had had the opposite effect to that desired. "But you'll know just how to help poor Self-Pity, Grace and Glory, and what to say to him. You were one of the Fearings yourself at one time, and will understand exactly what he needs."

"Of course I'm going with you," said Grace and Glory. "I'm not a nurse or a cook, and I don't know anything about looking after little children, but I can sit beside poor Self-Pity and try to take away his fears. For I do know from dreadful experience all about the horror of fearing death, and perhaps he will listen to me now and be comforted."

So off they went, all three of them, and the two lovely hand-maidens, Joy and Peace, went with them, each of them looking as radiant as if they were just starting for a visit to the King's Palace, so happy were they at the thought of being able at last to help the miserable family of Self-Pity.

Mrs. Dismal Forebodings and Gloomy watched them as they bustled cheerfully away, and there was a wistful envy on the faces of both mother and daughter. Then Gloomy suddenly cried out: "Oh, Mother, how I do wish that you and I could go to the High Places too and receive new names and be able to help others in the same lovely way!"

"I wish it too," said Mrs. Dismal Forebodings sadly. "But I'm afraid that I am too old, my dear, and have, most unhappily, put off turning to the Shepherd for too long. But, Gloomy, I think He might take you if we ask Him. You are still young, my love, and could go to the mountains."

"I would certainly not go without you, Mother," said Gloomy firmly. "It may be that we are both unworthy of such a wonderful privilege. I am sure I am."

"Let us go and see the Shepherd," said Mrs. Dismal after a little pause. "I do really believe that it is possible that He would take you there, Gloomy. At least we may perhaps ask Him and see what He says. It is just midday now and He and the flock will be resting somewhere in the pastures, perhaps not too far away. Let us try to find Him."

So they went together along the path which Much-Afraid had so often followed toward the open pastures. And there, to their thankful joy, they did find the Shepherd resting in the shade of some great trees. He welcomed them so graciously that both mother and daughter plucked up heart. First they told Him where they had come from and how Mrs. Valiant, Mercy and Grace and Glory had all gone off to the home of Self-Pity, who was dangerously ill, to see whether they could do anything to help.

"Ah!" said the Shepherd thoughtfully, "so they have gone to try to help Self-Pity, have they?"

"Yes, and they looked so happy," said Gloomy timidly, "just as they do when they are starting for the High Places with You, Shepherd."

"Is that so?" said He, smiling slightly. "What do *you* know about the High Places, Gloomy?"

"Nothing," she answered sorrowfully, "except that it is where You took my cousin, Much-Afraid, and gave her 'hinds' feet' and changed her name." Then she added passionately, "Oh, if only mother and I could go there too!"

"Of course you can go there," answered the Shepherd at once. "You have only to ask Me to take you!"

They stared at Him with almost incredulous joy. Then Mrs. Dismal Forebodings asked: "Do You really mean it? But we have only just entered Your service, Shepherd, and Much-Afraid worked for You for years before You took her there."

"You have waited many more years before entering My service than Much-Afraid did," said the Shepherd with His lovely, gentle smile, "but you do not have to wait as long as she did before you ask Me to take you to the High Places. If you really want to go, I will take you at once."

They went right up to Him, took His hands and said both together, "Oh, we *do* want it! We want it more than anything else in the world. Please take us there that we may receive new names and be changed completely."

"There is one condition," said He, just as He had told Much-Afraid. "I must plant the seed of Love in your hearts, or you will not be allowed to enter the Kingdom of Love of which the High Places are a part." Then He showed them the thorn-shaped seeds, one of wich He had planted in the heart of poor Much-Afraid when she tremblingly decided to follow Him to the mountains.

Then Mrs. Dismal Forebodings and Gloomy at once bared their hearts so that He could plant the seeds there too, and with His own scarred hands the Shepherd did so. He then told them to go home and make themselves ready for the journey so that when He came to call them they would be ready to leave with Him at once.

He Himself walked back with them towards the village, and when they got there whom should they see coming down the street but Mrs. Valiant, looking dreadfully hot and breathless, and holding little Doldrums Self-Pity by the hand, literally dragging him along. He was a small but sturdy infant, and at that moment was quite unbelievably ugly. He had both feet planted on the ground and was leaning backwards, pulling with all his strength, so that really the veins were swelling on his baby face and he was bawling at the top of his voice, "I won't go! Let me go, you horrid old woman! I won't go with you, I won't! I won't! Mama! Mama!"

"Oh dear! Poor, kind Mrs. Valiant," groaned Mrs. Dismal Forebodings, lapsing at once into her old desponding mood. "I tried to warn her how it would be. It looks as though the child will have a fit or burst a blood-vessel! Could anyone imagine that a little creature of that size could have such a wicked temper! Oh dear! I really think he is going to choke himself to death!"

The Shepherd strode forward. "Hullo, my little man!" said He cheerfully. "Tell Me, what is happening to make you so unhappy?"

Little Doldrums stopped bawling for a moment and opened his eyes and looked up. He appeared to hesitate as to whether he would bellow again or no. Then he put his finger in his mouth and stared in silence at the tall figure towering above him and at the kind face smiling down at him from such a height.

"What's your name?" said the cheery voice.

"Dol'dums," lisped the youngest member of the family of Self-Pity. "What Yours?"

"I'm the Shepherd," said He. "Now then! up you come on My shoulders as though you were one of My sheep being rescued from a lion. There!" said He, as He swung him up so that he sat astride both shoulders. Hold tight now, and I'll show you that not even the biggest and fiercest lion could spring as far as I can, or could catch you as long as I am carrying you." And with that He made a great, bounding leap and set off down the road towards Mrs. Valiant's cottage, with small Doldrums high up aloft, chortling and beaming and drumming with both feet on the Shepherd's chest and shouting at the top of his voice, "Faster! Faster! The nasty old lion's coming. Oh my, what a jump! Do it again, please, Shepherd, do it again!"

Mrs. Valiant laughed heartily at the picture, but Mrs. Dismal and Gloomy looked as though they could hardly believe their eyes.

They all arrived at the gate of the cottage together because the Shepherd took a roundabout way, so that by the time they got there and little Doldrums was lowered to the ground he was as cheerful as a cricket. As soon as they got inside the gate, along came the sandy cat, eager to meet her special friend, arching her back and rubbing against the Shepherd's legs and purring loudly, asking as plainly as possible where He had been all this long time. Little Doldrums immediately put out both hands to seize her by the tail, as he did to any unwary animal that chanced to fall into his clutches.

"Not that end, Doldrums," said the Shepherd cheerily. "Never the tail end. That always results in nasty scratches. But now try the head end—ever so gently, under the chin and behind the ears and on the top of the head, and see how loudly you can make her purr. Gently does it!—always. Ah—listen to that! She's purring like a baby lion."

And there was the infant, Doldrums, sitting happily in the sunny garden, while the bees hummed about the flowers and the ducklings waddled up the path towards him, with his small face positively beaming, wholly absorbed in experimenting to see whether the sandy-cat-mechanism produced the loudest purrs if tickled under the chin, or behind the ears, or scratched ever so carefully on the very top of the head, and looking, as Mrs. Dismal expressed it, as though he had never been a little Self-Pity in all his life.

Then the Shepherd left the garden and went striding off in the direction of the home of poor Self-Pity, the father. Mrs. Dismal and Gloomy watched Him until He was out of sight, and then they looked at one another and said, "He will soon be coming to call us to go with Him to the High Places. We must go home and get ready." As they spoke, the thorn-shaped seeds in their hearts suddenly throbbed, and a warm, tender sweetness seemed to flood them from head to foot, and mother and daughter kissed each other with a love and gentleness which neither of them had known before, as though already the dreary, self-centred Dismal Forebodings, and the haughty, self-willed Gloomy, were creatures of the past, and something quite new and very beautiful was appearing instead.

As for the Shepherd, He strode on down the village street and went on His way towards the lonely farm-house in which lay Self-Pity, tossing and turning on his sick bed in an agony of fear, and crying out for someone to call the Shepherd to come to help him.

CHAPTER VIII

THE MOUNTAIN OF SAFFRON
(LONGSUFFERING)

THE SUFFERING OF LOVE

THE next part of the High Places to which the King led Grace and Glory was to the Mountain of Saffron, the fourth peak in the range of the Mountains of Spices.

This Mountain, on which grew the spice flowers of Longsuffering, was far more exposed than any of the other mountains, for it jutted out some way in front of them all and was so open to the elements and to all the raging tempests, that in comparison with the other peaks its slopes were almost bare. Neither fruit trees nor flowering shrubs clothed its sides, indeed, except for a few scattered pine trees, it was bare of trees altogether. But it towered up to a peculiarly beautifully shaped peak and a great part of it was always covered with snow. All over the slopes, however, grew carpets of crocuses of the most delicate and beautiful hues. Even on the areas where the partly melted snow still lingered, they pushed themselves up through the white covering to greet the light, forming patches of delicate mauve, lavender, periwinkle blue, yellow and orange, deep purple and palest rose pink, so that no part of the mountain remained unclothed, either in the pure white of snow or the rainbow coloured robe of flowers. There were clusters of golden stamens at the heart of each crocus, and from the cross-shaped stigmas of the flowers, after they had been dried and pressed, a spicy seasoning could be obtained and also a sweet perfume. It was from these beautiful carpets of saffron crocuses, therefore, that the Mountain received its name.

The inhabitants of the High Places were accustomed to gather and dry a great quantity of this saffron of Longsuffering, which they then took down to the Valley to share with their relatives and friends and the other inhabitants of the Low Places; for the flavour of the spice was delicious, and as it could only be obtained on the High Places (except for a very inferior quality which could be cultivated on the lower slopes) it was considered a great delicacy with which even the Shepherd's enemies were glad to have their daily food flavoured, despite the fact that only His servants could provide it!

Grace and Glory had seen the saffron crocuses growing on other parts of the High Places, but never in such glorious profusion as on this mountain. It was impossible for them to walk anywhere without treading on these delicate hued flowers and using them much as a doormat! As soon as their feet were lifted from them, however, she noticed that the dauntless, gay little things bobbed up again at once, as fresh and uncrushed as though they had not been trodden upon. When she remarked on this to the King He explained with another of His happy smiles that this was the characteristic of true longsuffering. It bears quite happily everything that is done against it, resents not at all being trampled under foot, and reacts to the wrongdoing of others against itself as though no wrong had been done at all, or else as though it had forgotten all about it! For Longsuffering is really the lovely quality of forgiveness and bearing contentedly and joyfully the results of the mistakes and wrongdoing of others. When He had explained this to her, He taught her another of the mountain songs.

> Love will bear and will forgive,
> Love will suffer long,
> Die to self that she may live,
> Triumph over wrong.
> Nothing can true Love destroy,
> She will suffer all with joy.

> From resentment Love will turn,
> When men hate, will bless,
> She the Lamb-like grace will learn
> To love more—not less.
> Only BEARING can beget
> Strength to pardon and forget.

> Love must give and give and give,
> Love must die or share,
> Only so can true Love live
> Fruitful everywhere,
> She will bear the Cross of Pain
> And will rise and live and reign.

By this time the King and His companion were so far up the mountain that they had almost reached the sky-line, and now they seated themselves beneath one of the pine trees on a cushion of moss and lichen. The pungent fragrance of the sun-warmed pine needles and cones filled the air, and across from the wooded slopes of a neighbouring mountain came the clear and oft repeated call of a cuckoo. Overhead the sky was such a wonderful blue it was as though they sat beneath a roof of sapphire. In this lovely setting the King and Grace and Glory continued the conversation they had begun on the Mountain of Spikenard.

The scene was so beautiful that at first the main thought which filled the mind of Grace and Glory was that though they were surrounded with so much beauty and though every living thing around them seemed an individual cup full and brimming over with joy, they were actually sitting upon the Mountain of Suffering Love. It was this strange paradox which led Grace and Glory at last to break the thoughtful silence in which they had been sitting.

"My Lord," she said, "this is called the Mountain of Longsuffering. Has Love no power to save and help others apart from suffering? Why must Love suffer at all, and why, above all else, must Love suffer long?"

"It is because the very essence of Love is Oneness," answered the King. That is why Love must suffer. If the beloved creatures whom the Creator created for Love's sake must suffer, then the Oneness of Love makes it impossible for Him to allow them to suffer anything which He is not willing to suffer with them. It is because the whole Body of Mankind is suffering so dreadfully from the disease of sin and all its dreadful consequences, that I, Who am so ONE with Mankind, must suffer it all with them. Ever since the first sin, the Love of God has been, as it were, upon a cross of suffering. For do you not see that when I became Man I became the Head of the whole suffering Body of Mankind? You also know that it is the head which feels all the sum total of any and all suffering experienced by the individual members of the body. This is so great a Mystery of Love that men can only take it in in little fragments. But once in Time, when men were at last able to understand it, the tremendous revelation was made of 'the Son of God' made 'Son of Man', crucified by the sin of men, bearing it all, feeling it all and overcoming it all, that by so doing He might be able to overcome the disease of sin in the whole suffering Body or Race of Men. Think of what it means to be able to save and to heal. To be able to raise up out of that which has been so cruelly marred and diseased, something far more glorious than would otherwise have been possible."

For a while He said no more, and Grace and Glory, too overwhelmed by the mystery of anguish and the mystery of love could say not a word. But presently she heard the voice of Suffering Love speaking very softly, indeed, so low was the tone of His voice, she could barely discern the words, but this is what she thought she heard Him say:

> Love was "made Man." O Son of God!
> Flesh of our flesh, blood of our blood.
> We are His Body—let us kneel;
> He as our Head feels all we feel.
> This is the Love of God the Son,
> With fallen Mankind made AT ONE.
> O mystery of Adam's Race!
> This sin-sick Body with Christ's Face!
> Behold our God and Saviour thus!
> We love Him—for He first loved us.
>
> "And He was crucified." O loss!
> In us God's Son hangs on His Cross.

In Mankind's Body, there upborne,
Wounded by sin, defiled and torn.
He is our Life, our very Breath,
Yet "in the Body of our death".
All pangs of sin's disease so dread
Are suffered by Our Thorn-crowned Head.
　　Behold our God and Saviour thus!
　　Love Him—because He SO loves us.

"And He descended into Hell."
The deepest depths God's Love knows well;
So ONE with us He will not part
E'en from the hardest self-willed heart.
"Where shall we go to flee from Thee?"
Love's only answer still must be:
"Though thou dost make thy bed in hell,
Lo! I am with thee here as well."
　　Behold our God and Saviour thus!
　　Love Him—because He so loves us.

"On the third day He rose again."
Long night of sorrow and earth's pain
Gone like a dream! Death vanquished now;
The Victor's crown is on Love's brow.
The Body Sin could not destroy
Now healed and raised to life and joy.
By Adam came all sin and pain,
In Christ shall ALL men live again.
　　Behold our God and Saviour thus!
　　See what His Love will do for us.

CHAPTER IX

THE DEATH OF OLD LORD FEARING

OLD Lord Fearing, the head of the Fearing Clan, lay on a sick bed and was not expected to recover. The news spread all over the Valley of Humiliation and there was much talk and conjecture. It must be confessed at once that the news caused no very great sorrow. In his own home the old man had been a tyrant to family and servants alike; a despot over his numerous tenants, a miserly, grasping landlord, hard-hearted and without pity towards those who were in distress or unable to pay their rent. That he was very rich nobody doubted. That nobody else ever got any good or enjoyment out of his wealth was equally apparent, and there was nothing to indicate that he did either.

For a number of years he had been a widower. All his sons had quitted the parental roof and his tyrannous control as soon as possible, and his daughters, with the most eager alacrity, had also married and taken their departure. He lived, therefore, in the old family residence, half manor house and half castle, dependent for his comfort on a housekeeper and on a host of surly servants.

It was not to be supposed, after a lifetime of unbroken self-indulgence and tyranny towards others, that now, when the time at last had arrived for him to take his departure out of this world and to leave his castle and his wealth behind him, that the old man should face the inevitable either with calmness, courage or peace. From the moment that the awful realisation broke upon him that the time which he had dreaded all his life had now arrived and that here he was, actually lying upon his deathbed, never again to leave the great, gloomy bedroom until he was carried out in a coffin—from that moment he became the prey of the most harrowing and tormenting fears. And there was not one single, loving heart amongst all his hired servants to minister to him with love and compassion or to soothe and comfort his terrors.

It is true that his two elder sons and his married daughters had been informed of his illness and of the fact that recovery was not expected, and they had travelled to the castle; not in order to surround him with loving attention, but to be present dutifully at the last ceremonies and to accompany his body to the grave, and, in the case of his eldest son, to step with dignity into the father's shoes. The old man was only too well aware of these facts, and they added to his agony. One son was absent, for he had fled from the place years before to become a prodigal in some far country, afraid to return to his home, cast out and disowned by his father, who refused to allow his name to be mentioned in his presence, and had torn up, unopened, the few letters the lad had written. There had been rumours that this youngest son had repented and had sought out the people whom he had wronged and was seeking to make such restitution as lay in his power. But nobody had ever bothered to try to discover the facts of the case; and as all letters he had written had been destroyed, for his father absolutely refused to forgive him, no one knew of his address, or in what distant land he lived, so that naturally no news of his father's illness had been sent him.

So the old lord lay on his bed, surrounded day and night by nurses and attended by the most skilful doctors money could procure, anticipating death with an agony of horror impossible to describe. His fears were so great that the doctors had once suggested the advisability of calling in the help of a minister, who might be able to give him spiritual comfort, or perhaps a priest to allow the old man to ease his conscience by confessing his sins. But Lord Fearing had been an infidel for so many years that the very first suggestion of such a thing threw him into so great a rage that nobody ventured to make the suggestion again.

The tormenting days, and the still more terrible nights, dragged slowly by and the old man grew weaker. He had steadily refused to see any visitors. He knew only too well that his own cronics would despise his agonising fears and would not know what to say to him, and the sight of their health and strength and preoccupation with the things of this world, which he must so soon leave, would madden him and aggravate his own horrible fate. Ah, how they would gibe and joke about his fears among themselves afterwards!

The Shepherd's friends had made many earnest attempts to see him. Mrs. Valiant, who, before her marriage, had been a nursemaid at the castle, was one of them. So was Mercy, who would have been only too happy to share in the nursing. So was the young shepherd, Fearless Trust, who was foster-brother to Lord Fearing's youngest son. But all in vain. The old man in his fear, and in his fear of others seeing his fear, was adamant.

Then one afternoon the nurse was called out of the sickroom and returned to tell the old lord that a young woman very specially requested to be allowed to visit his lordship. It seemed that she was a relative of his own. Her name, when his lordship had known her, had been Much-Afraid. But it seemed that she had now changed her name and was no longer a Fearing. She had been absent from the Valley for some time, but had recently returned and seemed most particularly anxious to see his lordship once again.

"Much-Afraid!" muttered the old man, tossing restlessly on his bed. The name seemed to stir some kind of echo in his memory. "Much-Afraid!" Then after a moment he muttered: "Why, that was the name of the girl who refused to marry that vagabond, Craven Fear, the brother of my daughter-in-law, Gloomy. Let me see—didn't she go on some kind of fantastic journey? Yes, that was it—she went to the mountains with that mad fanatic they call the Shepherd. And that young coxcomb, Pride, went after her to try to bring her back, and it is said the Shepherd hurled him into the sea. Some of the others went too to kidnap her, but they failed. So she got to the mountains after all, did she? I wonder what happened to her?"

His curiosity was awakened, and after a moment or two of muttering to himself he said to the nurse, "So she's back again, is she?"

"Yes, my lord."

"And says she isn't a Fearing any longer! What did you say she calls herself now?"

"Grace and Glory, my lord."

"No longer a Fearing!" muttered the old man. "Grace and Glory. I wonder what happened to her? What did the Shepherd do to her?"

A last spurt of curiosity overcame him. He'd see for himself what she was like, this one-time Much-Afraid Fearing, who had eluded the whole gang who went after her, and wasn't a Fearing any longer.

"Tell the young woman she may come in," he growled out at last. And in a moment or two Grace and Glory entered the room, followed by her two handmaidens.

"Here, who are these, eh?" growled the old man testily. "I only agreed to see one. Which of you is my relative, Much-Afraid, or Grace and Glory, or whatever you call yourself now?"

"I am," said Grace and Glory smilingly, "and these are my two handmaidens, Joy and Peace. They go wherever I go."

She then stepped quietly forward and stood beside his bed. The old man and the woman who had been to the High Places looked at one another in silence.

"What's this?" he burst out fretfully after a long scrutiny. "The last time I saw you you were deformed and had a hideous squint or something. What's happened to you?"

"I bathed myself in one of the healing streams up there on the High Places," said Grace and Glory quietly, "and all my deformities were washed away."

"So that fellow took you to the High Places after all, did he?" said the old lord, half incredulously and still staring at her. "It must have been a miraculous or magical sort of stream, judging by the effect on you."

"Yes, all the streams up there have miraculous healing qualities," said she. "Those who bathe in them are perfectly healed and will never know death."

"Never know death!" repeated he, with a half sneer and a half groan. "What sort of water is that, eh?"

"The same sort of water as that which healed my deformed feet and my crooked mouth," said she, still looking at him steadily and gently. "It is the water of life."

"Mm!" said he, with what he meant to be a sneering chuckle, but which sounded exactly like a sob. "If I'd known about such streams as those, I wouldn't be lying here now on what those fools of doctors think is my death-bed!"

"No," said Grace and Glory, "you would have passed through death already and be alive for evermore."

The old man looked at her half covetously and half suspiciously. "Where did you learn that jargon, eh?" asked he. "And how do you know you will never die?"

"You see, I have been to the Kingdom of Love," said she, "and have died to the old loveless life which is death. And Love has been planted in my heart and lives there. Love is eternal. The life that is Love can never die. It is eternal life."

The old man stared at her. At last he said, still jeeringly, "How did you say this eternal life, or whatever it is, was planted in you?"

A lovely colour came into her face. "The Shepherd, Who is the Lord of Life and Love, planted it there. It is His life planted in me." As she mentioned the Shepherd's name her face shone with a beauty the old man had never before seen.

"The Shepherd," echoed he testily. "What's He got to do with it?"

"You know it was He Who took me to the High Places where everything happened to me."

"The Shepherd!" he growled again. "A mere man, just like everyone else—a madman at that! How can He give life? A crazy fairy tale!"

"He is the Lord of Love," said she softly, "the Lord and Giver of Life. That is why you are lying here now and dying, Sir Fearing," said she, looking at him with the strangest and the most compassionate look he had ever seen. "Don't you realise that you are dying because you don't know anything about Love, which is the Law of Life?"

"Love the Law of Life," he muttered. "What jargon is this? I am dying because my body is old and worn out and won't work or even exist much longer."

In spite of himself he groaned in agony as he spoke, and then started up in bed, shaking with fear.

"Oh no," said Grace and Glory, laying her hand on his, and some influence of peace seemed to quiet for a few moments his pangs of dread. "Oh no, your body is not the part which really dreads the dying. It is yourself, the tenant of the body, which is so fearful and afraid. You yourself, who must exist when your body no longer forms a temporary home for you, or a means for your self-expression and for contact with this familiar and material world."

He shivered from head to foot, then muttered, "I will not listen to any more fantastic fairy-tales about the Shepherd."

"You will have to meet Him some time, you know," said Grace and Glory gently.

"Never!" cried the old man with a sudden burst of energy. "Never! That so-called Shepherd Who I have disdained all my life!"

"I mean after death," said Grace and Glory. "You can evade Him here in the Valley all your lifetime, but not after death. He is the Judge, you know."

"Judge!" cried the old man between a shriek and a groan. "What Judge?"

"The Judge of your whole life—of how you have lived and how you have used this body which was lent you, and the things you possessed here on earth. He will judge as to whether you have obeyed the Law of Love."

"How will the Shepherd know about that?" sneered the old man. "We have never met. He knows nothing about me. Will He judge from hearsay?" and at that another look of terror spread over his face, as he thought of the things which might be said about him by so many others.

"No," said she quietly. "It is all written in you, by you, yourself, Lord Fearing—written plainly for Him to see, just as when an old tree is cut down, the whole history of its life is found written plainly in its heart, in the rings formed during each separate year of its life. One who knows how to read it can understand at a glance about the years when it was buffeted by the great storms and could scarcely make any growth, and those years when it was diseased, and those when it went forward and became strong. Or, if the heart has been eaten away little by little by worms and grubs, it all becomes plain when the tree falls and is found to be hollow and dead. You have been inscribing your whole inner life yourself as plainly as possible. And He, the One Whom you despise and reject, the Lord of Life and Love, is the Judge Who will have to read what is written in you and to pass sentence upon its worth or worthlessness."

The old man groaned. "Don't stand there telling me these horrible things," he gasped at last. "What's the good of saying all that now at the end of life?"

"Why," exclaimed she earnestly, taking a step forward, "why, Lord Fearing, if you asked Him He would plant the seed of new life and love in your heart even now, and then it would grow and come to fruition in that other world. Then it won't matter at all about your body. We are to receive new bodies which cannot die. Listen!" and she sang these words:

An empty altar is each soul
Whereon the Eternal Love
Would place a quenchless, living coal
From His own heart of Love;
> To burn and yearn back whence it came
> To union with the Parent Flame.

Yes, every soul a temple is
Wherein Love plans to dwell,
And each must make its choice for this—
To be a heaven or hell.
> If empty left, hell is its plight;
> But heaven, when God and man unite.

Christ is the Living, Purging Flame,
> And thou the altar art;
Forth from the Love of God He came,
> And seeks thine empty heart.
Receive this Lord from heaven above,
In thee to live His life of love.

"The Life of Love!" sneered the old man, and then groaned again. "Why do you keep on harping on love?"

"It is the Law of the Universe," said she, "the Law of Existence. Everything that loves, lives for ever. Everything else perishes."

"What is love?" groaned he. "I know precious little about it."

"You know nothing about it at all," said she compassionately. "To love is to give oneself, to lay down one's SELF, to share oneself with others, as the grass gives itself to the cattle, and the water to the thirsty land, and as the sun gives its light and warmth freely to good and bad alike."

"It sounds utterly detestable," said the poor, self-tormented old lord. "An existence of endless self-giving. I couldn't bear it." His whole life flashed before him as he spoke—one long process of crafty, calculated grasping and getting from others—all the time taking, and giving as little as possible.

"If that's what you eternal life means, I don't want it! Better die and cease to be."

"Then why are you so afraid to die?" asked she steadily.

"I don't know!" gasped he. "It's the horror of the thought of ceasing to be, becoming nothing, of losing everything—and for ever." The sweat broke out on his face. "Help me!" he gasped frenziedly. "Don't let me die! Hold me—hold me! Don't torment me in this way!"

She grasped his groping, trembling hand in hers and said gently: "I will tell you why you are afraid to die. For once I was Much-Afraid myself. You are afraid because deep down in your heart you know that you have broken the Law of Life, which is Love, and that you will receive no forgiveness from the Judge, because all your life long you have refused to forgive others, even your own son. And it is not extinction that you really fear (though that, too, would be a dreadful thing to contemplate), but yours is the far more terrible fear that it will not be extinction—that you will continue to exist in utterly different circumstances, lacking everything which shielded your life here and which you value. You are afraid because the Judge you must meet at last is the One you have disdained and rejected all your life. Let me bring the Shepherd to you now," she pleaded, "and everything—yes, everything—can be changed before it is too late."

"No—no—no!" shrieked the old man. "I won't see Him. Never!" He flung himself up in the bed, crying aloud in terror and hate. Doors were opened and nurses came running, just as the old man fell back unconscious on the bed.

That night Death came to old Lord Fearing as he lay in the great bed in the castle, and touching him with ice-breath whispered, "Thou fool! this night is thy soul required of thee."

CHAPTER 10

THE MOUNTAIN OF CALAMUS (GENTLENESS)

THE TERROR OF LOVE

A LIGHT breeze was blowing over the mountains in the very early morning when the King and Grace and Glory came, just before sunrise, to the Mountain of Calamus, where the spices of Gentleness were cultivated. As they approached the slopes of this mountain they heard a soft, musical sound like the murmur of water on far-off seas. This music became more audible the nearer they approached, and definite cadences became distinguishable, as though a very soft but lovely song was being played by a great multitude of sweet-toned instruments performing in exquisite harmony.

When they reached the slopes of the mountain, Grace and Glory stood still in delighted surprise, for stretching before her were fields of slender reeds, swaying in the breeze and tossing lightly in rhythmical motion like waves on a slightly rolling sea. On this sea there were lines of foamy-white crests, for at that season of the year the reeds were all flowering, and each sheath had opened out into a frothy white cobweb around the brown stamens. It was the wind blowing through this sea of gently swaying reeds which produced the low musical murmurings which so delighted her ears. But as they paused on the edge of the slope they heard also the sound of several flutelike notes, and then they saw that a group of the King's shepherds had gathered up there, and before descending to the Valley below they had cut several of the reeds and were forming them into shepherds' pipes.

Grace and Glory had often heard the curiously soft notes of these pipes, upon which some of the shepherds played as they led their flocks through the pastures in the Valley of Humiliation, but now, for the first time, she realised that these pipes through which they blew such strangely sweet little harmonies, were formed from the hollow reeds or canes of Gentleness, which grew up here on the Mountain of Calamus.

As they stood gazing out over the tranquil scene before them, some of the shepherds began to sing, while others accompanied the air of the song upon their pipes. These were the words:

> Thy gentleness hath made me great,
>   And I would gentle be.
> 'Tis Love that plans my lot, not Fate,
>   Lord, teach this grace to me.
> When gales and storms Thy love doth send
> That I with joy may meekly bend.
>
> Thy servants must not strive nor fight,
>   But as their Master be,

'Tis meekness wins, not force nor might,
Lord, teach this grace to me.
Though others should resist my love,
I may be gentle as a dove.

When presently they went on their way, the King began to tell His companion about the reeds of Gentleness. He said that the chief product from them was a lovely perfume extracted from the lower part of the canes. This perfume lingered about the persons who wore it, all day long, very fresh and fragrant and soothing. He explained also that it was the pliability of the reeds and their perpetual motion which developed the spice from which the perfume was made, and He pointed out to her the exquisite grace and lovely, unresisting meekness with which they bowed themselves before the wind, sometimes right to the ground, only to sweep upright again from that low position, without apparent effort or strain of any kind, as soon as the wind had passed over them. A lovely gracious submissiveness characterised their every movement and yet at the same time there was something grandly regal about the poise and perfect control of their motions, no weakness of any kind but the most perfect command. "They know how to be abased and how to be exalted," thought Grace and Glory with sudden understanding, and she realised that the lovely fragrance which exuded from them and which men call gentleness, sympathy and loving understanding was developed by the daily practice of bending submissively to life's hard and difficult experiences without bitterness, or resentful resistance and self-pity. She saw quite clearly that no force of storm or tempest would be able to harm or break the reeds because they had learnt to bow themselves so easily to the least breath of wind, without offering any resistance at all. It was this gentle movement of submissiveness, combined with perfect balance and graceful motion, which produced the cadences of music sounding all over the mountain-side, for the wind turned every reed into an instrument through which to play the harmonies of heaven.

In silence Grace and Glory followed the King as He walked along the narrow path between the reeds, and she noticed that the poise and grace and litheness of His movements had in them the same quality as that of the reeds, the same lovely willingness to stoop and bend, and the same buoyant and royal way of rising again, uncrippled by the stooping. As she watched Him she remembered her long journey up to the High Places, and how from start to finish it had been the gracious gentleness of His manner towards her, His perfect understanding of her weakness and fears, as though He felt with her all that she suffered, which had wooed her to follow Him, even up to the grave in the mist-filled canyon on the mountains. Then she whispered to herself most gratefully, "His gentleness hath made me great," and "Oh, how I long to be anointed with the same gentleness towards others!"

She followed Him for some way and then found that He had led her to an open space beside a broad lake, bounded at one end by a great cliff of granite rock. The King leaped up the towering cliff and Grace and Glory sprang after Him on her "hinds' feet" as agile and light as a mountain roe. They seated themselves upon the topmost pinnacle of the rock, as upon some lofty throne, and from there looked out over the lake and the fields of swaying reeds.

Everything spread out before them seemed to be swaying in the wind. There were long ripples on the waters of the lake, and long ripples on the beds of reeds, but they themselves were seated upon immovable granite rock—rock as sternly *unyielding* as the reeds below were unresisting.

This contrast became very vivid to the consciousness of Grace and Glory as she sat up there on the rocky throne beside the King of Love. On the one hand she saw the terror and the grandeur of the rocky cliffs, and on the other the grace and gentleness of the reeds which clothed the mountain slopes.

"THE TERROR AND THE BEAUTY OF LOVE."

The words suddenly came into her mind with such force and clarity that she turned and looked at the King to see whether He had spoken them.

"What is it?" He asked in answer to the wondering look she turned upon Him.

"My Lord," she said, I have another question to ask You. You have brought me here to the Mountain of Calamus where the reeds of Gentleness grow. And I know so much about the gentleness of Your Love in my own experience. But is there another side to Love? Can Love be terrible as well as gentle? Is Love really like a consuming Fire which cannot be approached without fear and trembling? Can Love even appear to be cruel and terrible?

He was silent awhile before answering, almost as though He were considering the question with her. Then He turned upon her a look which was both grave and yet singularly beautiful at the same time.

"Yes," He said, "Love *is* a consuming fire. It is a burning, unquenchable passion for the blessedness and happiness, and, above all, for the perfection of the beloved object. The greater the love, the less it can tolerate the presence of anything that can hurt the beloved, and the less it can tolerate *in* the beloved anything that is unworthy or less than the best, or injurious to the happiness of the loved one. Therefore it is perfectly true that Love, which is the most beautiful and the most gentle passion in the universe, can

and *must* be at the same time the most TERRIBLE—terrible in what
it is willing to endure itself in order to secure the blessing and happiness and perfection of the Beloved, and, also, apparently terrible
in what it will allow the beloved to endure if suffering is the *only*
means by which the perfection or restoration to health of the
beloved can be secured."

When He had said this He began to sing another of the Mountain songs.

> Can Love be terrible my Lord?
>   Can gentleness be stern?
> Ah yes!—intense is Love's desire
> To purify His loved—'tis fire,
>   A holy fire to burn.
> For He must fully perfect thee
> Till in thy likeness all may see
>   The beauty of thy Lord.
>
> Can Holy Love be jealous Lord?
>   Yes, jealous as the grave;
> Till every hurtful idol be
> Uptorn and wrested out of thee
>   Love will be stern to save;
> Will spare thee not a single pain
> Till thou be freed and pure again
>   And perfect as thy Lord.
>
> Can Love seem cruel, O my Lord?
>   Yes, like a sword the cure;
> He will not spare thee, sin-sick soul,
> Till He hath made thy sickness whole,

Until thine heart is pure.
For oh! He loves thee far too well
To leave thee in thy self-made hell,
A Saviour is thy Lord!

Grace and Glory sat by His side on the great throne of granite rock, looking down and yet further down the valley so far below. She thought of the people who lived down there so far away from the Kingdom of Love, but most especially she thought of the miserable, terrified old Lord Fearing beside whose death-bed she had so recently stood, and of the many others whom she knew who lived as though the Lord of Love did not exist; and her heart was overwhelmed within her; overwhelmed with the TERROR of Love and yet comforted by it too.

Then she looked up into the face of the King and what she saw there left her absolutely silent, but with this one thought shining in her mind like a clear lamp:

"He made us; He knew what He was doing. It is Love alone which can make all the agony and torment which men bring upon themselves and others explicable, for I see it is the means used by His inexorable will to save us and to make us so perfect that His love can be completely satisfied. Behold the beauty and the terror of the Love of God!"

CHAPTER XI

UMBRAGE AND RESENTMENT

MERCY, the daughter of Mrs. Valiant, had been talking with the Shepherd, and as a result she went to visit a friend of hers whom she had not seen for a long time, because whenever she rang the bell of her friend's house, the servants told her that their mistress was not at home. The name of this friend was Umbrage.

Umbrage had always been a bright, attractive girl, admired and liked by everybody who did not know her very intimately. Her family were all in the service of the Shepherd and Umbrage herself had entered His service also as soon as she left school. When the people of the village of Much-Trembling were all agog with excitement over the departure of Much-Afraid for the High Places, and the efforts of her relatives to force her to return, Umbrage had thought seriously of asking the Shepherd to take her to the mountains also. Mercy, who had been her school friend, and good Mrs. Valiant, had both been there, she knew, and she envied them their new names and the beauty and joy which characterised all their service; and now there was poor, ugly Much-Afraid, actually gone off on the journey to the High Places also. Umbrage really envied her and the longing in her heart had grown very strong to make the same journey herself, but one thing held her back.

Umbrage was not only extremely capable and efficient in everything which she undertook, but she had the gift of beauty also, and had been accustomed to a good deal of admiration and homage from the younger shepherds in Much-Trembling and also from some who were not in the Shepherd's service at all. She, herself, however, had given her heart to the tallest and strongest and handsomest of the Shepherds named Stedfast, one whom the Shepherd loved and trusted in a special way. He had been a close friend and neighbour of her family and the two had been to school together. Ever since she had realised her own gifts of beauty and attractiveness, Umbrage had never doubted that she would gain her heart's desire and become his wife. For a time, indeed, the close friendship between the two had been very noticeable, but for some reason Stedfast had gradually withdrawn a little, and though he remained a friend and constant visitor at the house, he showed no further desire to become her lover. Umbrage had begun to brood, first impatiently, and then fearfully, on the reasons for this unexpected change in his manner towards her, but the real reason was the last one in the world which she was willing to accept, namely, that as she grew and developed it had become very obvious that her name exactly described her nature. She was sweet and gracious and altogether delightful when she was pleased at getting what she wanted, and she expanded like a flower in the warm sunshine of admiration. But when her wishes were thwarted and she was denied her full mead of admiration, she became moody, exacting, ungracious and disagreeable so that everyone around her was made miserable and uncomfortable.

Stedfast, in a kind, brotherly fashion, had often tried to make her conscious of this unlovely fault and to tease and laugh her out of it, but even from him she had not been able to accept the truth, and whenever he made the attempt to help her in this way, she treated him to such moods of ungracious and sullen silence that at last he gave up the attempt to help her to overcome the fault, and with it all thought of making her his wife.

Umbrage, having refused to face up to the fact that her own special besetting sin was the reason why her heart's desire never came to pass, went on waiting and hoping, unwilling to leave for the High Places as long as the matter remained unsettled. Suddenly, one day, like a bolt from the blue, came the terrible shock of finding that Stedfast had passed her by completely and had become engaged to her own younger sister, Gentleness, who was much less gifted and beautiful than herself, but was blessed with a sweetness and unselfishness of temper which poor Umbrage completely lacked.

The shock had been terrible, though all her pride had risen up to hide the wound in her heart. Instead of facing the truth at last, however, that she herself was the cause of this heartbreaking anticlimax, she chose to blame Stedfast and to allow the most bitter jealousy of her sister to take possession of her.

Thus blaming them and brooding on what she chose to consider the cruel wrong they had done her, and longing for something to act as balm to her wounded pride, poor Umbrage found herself terribly open to temptation, and began to accept the attentions of an old admirer of hers, Resentment, the wealthy young manager of the Branch Bank in Much-Trembling. It was balm to her wounded pride that, though her sister's lover was one of the most outstanding of the shepherds in the valley, Resentment was, from a worldly standpoint, his superior in every way—in looks, in wealth and in social position. That he was also hot-tempered, passionate and stubborn, Umbrage, who had known him well since they were children, was also in no doubt, but she chose to tell herself that now he was a man, he knew how to discipline his temper, and that his love for her was so great that she at least would never suffer from it.

To the sorrow and distress of her family and the concern of all her friends and fellow-workers, Umbrage announced her engagement to Resentment—well known though he was to be one of the Chief Shepherd's enemies, and shortly afterwards they were married.

Since then her former friends and companions had scarcely seen her. She had assured them that her marriage would make no difference to her fellowship with them, and that she would continue as much of her former work for the Shepherd as possible, for she greatly hoped that she would be able to change her husband's attitude and be the means of bringing him, too, to desire friendship with the Shepherd.

As everyone had foreseen, however, once married, her husband's implacable resentment against the Shepherd, greatly augmented as it was by his unsuccessful attempts to thwart Much-Afraid on her journey to the High Places, had made this impossible. All too soon poor Umbrage, with her sincere devotion to the Shepherd, her stifled longings for the High Places, and her wounded heart and pride, had found herself obliged to sever all connection with her old friends and fellow workers. It is true that at first she had been almost thankful to do so, to escape what her conscience told her must be their secret condemnation of her decision to marry an enemy of the Chief Shepherd, and also to escape from the sight of the almost perfect happiness of her sister Stedfast. All these things had seemed so unbearable, and the satisfaction and pleasure in her new position as mistress of one of the biggest houses in Much-Trembling so attractive, that it had seemed a fairly simple and easy thing to acquiesce in her husband's wish that she should break all her former contacts and begin her life in a completely new circle of friends and acquaintances.

Umbrage soon discovered that this was not so easy after all. She had always lived in a home where the Shepherd's presence and love were the predominant influences, and though she herself had so often been selfish and ungracious, the others had always reacted with love and forgiveness. Now, however, she found herself in an environment where grace and true love and forgiveness were unknown. Moreover, she quickly discovered that she was not the mistress of her husband's home at all. Far from it. His widowed mother, Old Mrs. Sullen, lived with them, and her influence over her son was undiminished. She ruled the household, and very quickly the relationship between selfish, self-willed Mrs. Sullen and her strong-willed and spoilt daughter-in-law was of the unhappiest kind. For days the old lady would not speak to her daughter-in-law at all, but kept to her own room, where, however, her son visited her and spent long hours listening to her complaints against Umbrage. It must be confessed, too, that in his wife's company Resentment had to listen to almost equally bitter complaints against his mother, so that, between the two of them, there were times when he felt he had been much better off as a bachelor and that marriage was far from being an idyllic state. Umbrage was all too soon of the same opinion.

Secretly, in the depths of her heart, she had known perfectly well that she was making a mistake. Never would she forget the day when the Shepherd Himself had told her so. Looking at her with His earnest, challenging and yet compassionate eyes, He had told her just why she was doing it—because she insisted on evading the truth about herself instead of facing up to the actual facts. He had put before her the choice either of breaking the engagement with Resentment and going to the High Places with Himself, or of going through with the marriage only to find her fellowship with Himself broken and herself left completely unchanged.

Umbrage had fallen at His feet and said that she must, she simply *must* marry Resentment; that she could not live without love; that she had been so wronged and wounded that nothing else could satisfy her; that she was altogether too weak and wounded now to think of the High Places; that what she must have was love and sympathy and kindness and protection and a home of her own where she could forget the cruel treatment which she had endured; but that she would always be His follower, always.

From that day Umbrage had not seen the Shepherd personally again and had not heard His voice. She had occasionally seen Him afar off, passing along the street, leading His flock, or talking to one or another of the shepherds; but from the day she married Resentment, knowing that she could never invite the Chief Shepherd into her home—from that day she had had no personal contact with Him at all. And poor Umbrage had experienced the agony of those who have once known Him and now know Him no more.

> "For souls that once have looked upon their Lord
> Must die, or look again."

One day, when her husband was away at usual at the bank, and old Mrs. Sullen, in one of her difficult moods, was shut up in her own room, Umbrage, dreary and miserable and almost in despair, took her little three-year-old daughter into a secluded part of the garden to escape from the curious eyes of the servants, who, she well knew, spied upon her continually at the old lady's orders and repeated to her all her doings. The little girl was her only comfort, a sweet little thing whom the old grandmother was always trying to coax up to her own room and to spoil. Little Retaliation (for Resentment had insisted on giving his mother's maiden name to his daughter), though her pet name was Tit-for-Tat, had already begun to understand that if her mother forbade her anything, she had but to toddle off to grandmother to get what she wanted, along with a commiserating kiss and a sweet-meat ("for Grannie knew what little girls liked even if Mamma did not!"). And Umbrage had come to realise, with a cold sickening of her heart, that her mother-in-law was not only her implacable rival in her husband's affections but that she was using every possible means to come between her and her child too. This terrible realisation had brought her to the point of utter despair.

While she was sitting there alone in the garden weeping her heart out she heard the iron gate open. Peering anxiously through the laurels to see whether some caller had arrived, and feeling that any visitor would be an impossible agony at such a time, she caught sight of her one-time friend, Mercy, the shepherdess. She knew well that on the orders of her husband and mother-in-law the servants always turned away any of her old acquaintances who worked for the Shepherd. Now the sight of Mercy's beautiful, gentle and peaceful face brought back to mind all that she had wilfully thrown away and lost—her happiness, her lovely work, her friends and her home, and there broke over her heart an ago-nising flood of sorrow. She longed for fellowship again, for the touch of one really loving hand, for the sound of one really friendly voice, and most of all to see and to speak with someone who knew the Shepherd. The longing was irresistible. If Mercy went to the door she would be turned away with the polite assurance that the mistress was not at home. She must not be allowed to go to the door.

So Umbrage called through the sheltering hedge in a low, imploring voice: "Oh Mercy, Mercy! Is that really you? Come to me here."

Mercy heard the trembling voice and answered at once: "Dear Umbrage, are you really there? Oh, how happy I am to find you at last!" and she came round the laurel hedge and turned towards her friend such a kind and loving look that Umbrage rose, and throwing her arms around Mercy, laid her head on her shoulder and burst into heartbroken sobs.

Thus they stood for a little while, theirs arms about each other, without speaking, while little Tit-for-Tat gazed up wonderingly into the face of the newcomer.

At last, compelled by her sorrow and heartache, poor Umbrage unburdened herself, pouring out the whole tragic story of her unhappy marriage into the ears of her sympathetic friend.

"I can't bear it any longer," she sobbed passionately at the end. "I must leave this home. I can't live with Resentment and Sullen any longer. I can't, I can't! But oh, Mercy, if I leave him they will claim the child! If I am the one who chooses to leave this home, they will have the right to keep little Tit-for-Tat; and if I lose her I cannot live. God have mercy on me! What am I to do? Sometimes I feel the only solution is to end life altogether."

Mercy, her loving arms around her heartbroken friend, whispered gently: "Umbrage, you are forgetting. There *is* a solution, quite a different one, to your problem. You know what that solution is. You must tell the Shepherd what you have told me and ask Him what you are to do. And then, 'Whatsoever He saith unto you, DO IT'."

"The Shepherd!" wailed Umbrage in a desolate voice. "The Shepherd will never speak to me again. I have turned my back upon Him and have disobeyed His voice. He will not help me now, Mercy, for He warned me what would happen. And I hardened my heart and would not listen, and I 'have done despite to the Spirit of Grace', and have 'drawn back', and He will say that it is impossible to do anything for me for I have brought everything upon myself by disobedience. Oh, if only I had listened to Him! If only I could go back to the time before I sinned!"

"He will say nothing of the sort," cried Mercy earnestly. "You know, you must know, that you are saying what is not true about Him. Why, He has only waited with the utmost love and patience until the time should come when you would be ready at last to listen to Him and to seek His help."

"Then what is the meaning of that terrible passage in the Scriptures?" asked Umbrage despairingly, which says: "Of how much sorer punishment . . . shall he be thought worthy, who hath trodden under foot the Son of God . . . and hath done despite unto the Spirit of Grace . . .' 'If we sin *wilfully* after that we have received the knowledge of the truth, there remaineth no more sacrifice for sins, but a certain fearful looking for of judgment and fiery indignation.' *'It is impossible for those who were once enlightened,* and have tasted of the heavenly gift . . . If they shall fall away, *to renew them again unto repentance;* seeing they crucify to themselves the Son of God afresh, and put Him to an open shame' " (Heb. 10:29, 26, 27; 6:4–6).

"Dear Umbrage," said Mercy earnestly, "do you not see that those verses do not and cannot apply to you, for you ARE repentant? You do not need me or anyone else to try to persuade or force you to repent. The sure evidence that one has done despite to the Spirit of Grace is that he has LOST ALL POWER TO DESIRE REPENTANCE AND RESTORATION. Indeed, he WANTS to go on crucifying the Son of God afresh and to reject the Holy Spirit. But you! You are longing beyond all words to be restored and to be in communion with the Saviour again, and you can find no rest or peace until you are. That is a sure sign that His Spirit is even now working in you and beginning to restore you."

"But," said Umbrage, still in a tone of utter despair, "what about that verse which says that Esau, when he *wanted* to repent could not do so? 'Ye know how that afterward, when he would have inherited the blessing he was rejected: for he found no place of repentance, though he sought it carefully with tears' (Heb. 12:17). You see, it was too late for him to be forgiven even when he wanted to repent."

"It doesn't say anything of the sort," answered Mercy cheerfully and firmly. "You have got it all wrong, Umbrage! It DOES say that Esau sold his birthright for one morsel of meat, and then afterwards, when he was sorry that he had done so and would have liked to inherit the firstborn son's blessing after all, it belonged to Jacob. And though he repented with tears that he had despised the birthright blessing of the elder son, it WAS too late for him to get it back. But that is quite a different thing from saying that though you are now sorry you disobeyed the Shepherd He will not forgive you. Do you not see, dear Umbrage, the real meaning of the verse? Like Esau you *did* despise the Shepherd's offer to take you to the High Places because you *did* prefer and choose to marry Resentment.

And THAT you cannot alter. What is done cannot be undone even though I find you weeping your heart out here in the garden and repenting of the wrong choice which you made in bitterness and despair. You ARE married to Resentment, and you ARE the daughter-in-law of poor old Mrs. Sullen, and there is no getting away from the fact, however much you now regret it. In that sense what is done cannot be undone in spite of your repentance. But that is not to say that the Shepherd no longer loves and owns you, or that He will refuse to help you. It means that YOU NEED HIM more than ever before in these terribly difficult and tragic circumstances into which you have got yourself. Oh, my dear, dear Umbrage, will you not realise this at last and lose not a moment longer in seeking His help? For you know quite well that HE can change everything completely and bring victory out of defeat, which is the thing He loves to do most of all."

"Oh, if only it were so!" sobbed Umbrage, clasping her hands. "If only I could go to Him and tell Him how sorry I am, and implore His forgiveness and help! Nothing would be too awful to endure if only I could be back in fellowship with the Shepherd again!"

"I am here," said a strong but gentle voice close behind her, and as the two women looked up joyfully there was the Shepherd Himself. Umbrage threw herself at His feet, and Mercy, lifting her kind, loving eyes to His, smiled at Him and slipped away.

The Shepherd laid both His hands on the bowed head of poor Umbrage, and telling her that He forgave her, He blessed her. Then He lifted her up and sat talking with her for a long time. Umbrage poured out to Him in passionate relief the whole sorry story and said at the end: "It was just as You said, My Lord. I refused to be shown the truth and I have brought myself into this impossible situation. My mother-in-law hates me, my husband no longer loves me, and they are both determined to get my child away from me." She sobbed again heart-brokenly and then exclaimed: "I can't stay with him any longer. I do not love him. I never loved him. And he forbids me to have any intercourse with You and with Your friends. I am just a miserable prisoner here, and if I try to go free I must lose my child."

"*His* child and yours too," corrected the Shepherd gently.

She sobbed again and said nothing.

"Mercy was quite right," continued the Shepherd slowly and clearly. "She told you that there is no way of undoing this thing which you chose to do of your own free will. You ARE married, and though you repent of it with tears there is no way of undoing what has been done."

She cried out in anguish: "Then what am I to do? Is there no hope of escape? Must I stay here, the miserable slave of Resentment and Sullen until I die?"

"By no means," said the Shepherd strongly and cheerily. "You cannot alter the fact of your marriage or escape from it, but you CAN be 'more than conqueror' in it, and you CAN change defeat into victory."

"Be 'more than conqueror' while married to Resentment?" gasped Umbrage incredulously. "My Lord, what do you mean?"

"Yes, certainly," said He. "Do you remember, Umbrage, that when I spoke to you last I invited you to go with Me to the High Places?"

"Yes," said she, gazing at Him in bewilderment.

"Well, I ask you again now," said He, smiling upon her most beautifully. "Will you start with Me for the High Places now, Umbrage?"

"But," gasped she, "you have just told me that I may not leave my husband even though I detest him."

"Nothing can help you in this situation," answered the Shepherd gently and gravely, "until you learn to *love* your husband and your mother-in-law. And that you can only learn by going to the High Places of Love. You must learn to love them truly and to give yourself to them completely without any reserves, asking nothing from them in return."

Umbrage burst into tears again. "But I can't," she sobbed miserably. "One can't force oneself to love, my Lord. I don't feel love for them, I feel hate. Yes, actual hate. All the time I have the most dreadful feelings towards them of resentment and hate. And I can't change those feelings, they are too strong."

"We are not speaking about your forcing yourself to love your husband," answered the Shepherd gently. "I know that you do not love either him or your mother-in-law. I know that you feel hate towards them. But we are now speaking about your love to *Me*. Are you willing to be My disciple again, Umbrage?"

"Oh yes!" she exclaimed. "I long for it with all my heart."

"Then, as My disciple, there is, of course, no question of your hating anyone. You will love them as I love them. It is true that you do hate them now. But if you will let me take you to the High Places and plant the seed of Love in your heart, you will find not only that it is possible for you gladly and truly to love your husband and mother-in-law, but you will also be able to help them both in a wonderful way through your love for them."

"How can that be possible?" whispered she. "How can I go to the High Places and still stay here, a prisoner in this house?"

He smiled. "There is a short cut, Umbrage, from this house where you live with Sorrow and Pain to the High Places of Love.

I frankly confess that it is a harder way than the one by which I would have taken you if you had followed me when I first asked you to do so. But nevertheless it is a possible and a real way. Let me tell you the secret. Dear Umbrage, if you will *accept* the fact, honestly and sincerely, that it was your own fault that Stedfast did not find himself able to love you, but preferred your sister; if you will recognise the fact that he is blameless in this matter, and your sister too, and if you will begin to accept with joy and humility the right of both of them to love each other and to be completely happy together, even though you yourself are left in such utterly different circumstances, then, Umbrage, you will be half-way to the High Places. For here, in this home, and in your heart, you will find growing the heavenly flower of 'Acceptance-with-Joy' of all that is allowed to happen to you."

"This is a hard saying," said Umbrage in a low voice.

"And the second is still harder," said He gently. "Hard, but not impossible. If you will *bear* forgivingly all the antagonism of your husband and mother-in-law, bear it and use it as a means out of which to achieve victory over your own self, bearing all without allowing yourself to feel either resentment or self-pity, do you know what will happen then, Umbrage?"

"What?" she asked.

"You will find yourself up on the High Places with the Flower of Love blooming in your heart, able to love, and to rejoice in loving, those two whom you now hate, and, best of all, with power to help them too. For sooner or later, Love changes everything. Yes, you will find that you have reached the High Places without ever having left your home. For Love comes into the heart, not by trying to force it, but by accepting people as they are, and bearing all that they do against you, which is forgiveness. Are you willing for this?"

Umbrage looked up at Him through her tears and whispered again: "Yes, Lord. Please make it possible in my experience."

Just then her little daughter, who had been playing on the lawn with her ball, ran up to the seat where her mother and the Shepherd were sitting and held up her little arms for her mother to take her upon her lap. Umbrage seized her passionately, and pressing the innocent little baby face against her own, said with a sob, "Titty-Tatty, your mother is going to begin a new life."

"You know," said the Shepherd quietly, but with a little smile playing around his lips, "You know I really don't like that name for a little child. Wouldn't you like to call her (just between yourselves of course) by another name, Umbrage?"

"Yes," said Umbrage, flushing deeply. "What name, my Lord?"

"Why not call her 'Acceptance-with-Joy'? Even her father would not mind your calling her Joy as a pet name. And to you she would be a little flower of Acceptance-with-Joy growing in your home."

"Yes," said Umbrage softly, "that is a lovely name, and when I call her that I shall always remember what You have told me."

The Shepherd, with one of His lovely smiles, then said: "I don't really like your own name either. It is not a good name for a disciple of Mine to bear. Would you not like to change that also?"

The woman who had lost the man she had loved because she had been in character so like her own name, looked at the Shepherd with tears in her eyes and nodded speechlessly.

"Then," said He very gently, "we will call you 'Bearing-with-Love', or 'Forgiveness'." Then He took out one of the thorn-shaped seeds of love, and with gentle but firm hand, planted it in her heart and went His way.

When the Shepherd had left her the woman who was to go to the High Places without leaving her own home, went upstairs to her room, bathed herself and put on one of her prettiest dresses. Then she went to the apartment of old Mrs. Sullen, tapped on the door and went inside. The old lady glared at her in a surly manner and said not a word.

"Mother," said Forgiveness gently, "I have come to tell you how sorry I am that I have been such a disagreeable and unloving daughter to you and to ask your forgiveness. I hope to be very different in the future."

"Fine words, fine words!" snapped the old lady. "I am glad to see that at last you seem to have come to your senses and to be conscious of your abominable behaviour. But it will take more than words, Umbrage, I can assure you, to convince me of your sincerity. I shall see how you behave in the days to come and whether you are really willing to be a dutiful and obedient and submissive wife to my dear son. Deeds and not fine words are the sign of real penitence."

"Yes, Mother," said Forgiveness gently, and kissed the sullen old woman for the first time in many a long month. Sooner or later, the Shepherd had said, Love—the Love He had planted in her heart—would work some change in Mrs. Sullen and in her husband also. She would wait confidently with hope and peace for the change which was to come.

A few hours later, when Resentment returned to the house and went straight to his own room, avoiding his wife as his custom now was, he heard a light tap on the door, and turning, was astonished to see Forgiveness standing before him. She came up to him quietly and said in a low, trembling voice, "I have come to tell you how much I need your forgiveness, for I have been such a failure as a wife and have been so selfish and demanding and unloving."

He looked at her for a moment in silence, noted the gentle, humble, appealing look on her face, and said in a queer voice, "You have been talking with the Shepherd, Umbrage?"

She trembled all over, but answered in a low tone, "Yes."

Her husband stood for another moment in silence. She could not read his thoughts. She could not know that in memory he was once again upon the mountains where he and his friends had followed Much-Afraid in order to force her to return home. Once again he was among the precipices and the great forests and the mist, hearing again another woman's voice calling out fearfully and pleadingly as they closed in on her with their threats and jibes, "Shepherd! O Shepherd! Where are you? Come and help me!" Then came the great, leaping bound of the Deliverer Who had answered her cry and had delivered her from them all.

Resentment looked at his wife and said suddenly: "Umbrage, things have come to such a sorry pass in our life together that it is time we should do something about it. If the Shepherd can help us to begin all over again, I am willing to let Him do so."

CHAPTER XII

THE MOUNTAIN OF CINNAMON
(GOODNESS)

THE JUDGMENT OF LOVE

THE sixth Mountain of Spices to which the King led Grace and Glory was the Mountain of Cinnamon, where grew the Trees of Goodness. These trees were very beautiful and stately. They were covered with glossy dark leaves which made a beautiful background for the pure white blossoms, for it was then the season for their flowering. The inner bark of the trees was very aromatic and was of a rich, golden brown colour. This inner bark was stripped off the trees at certain seasons of the year and from it was obtained the spice of Goodness which the citizens of the High Places loved to carry about with them, concealed in their garments. Not only did this spice give forth a sweet and refreshing fragrance (which was one of the marks which distinguished the servants of the King who lived on the High Places from the

Valley dwellers), but it also possessed healing and curative properties, which were greatly valued.

The whole mountain-side was covered with a forest of these cinnamon trees, and immediately on entering these woods Grace and Glory and the King found themselves shaded from the glare and heat of a cloudless summer day. Like all the other mountains of spices, this one also was much frequented by flocks of birds of many different species, and their melodious songs echoed from end to end of the glades. Here Grace and Glory was delighted to hear again the notes of the little bird which she had heard singing among the dripping, mist-shrouded trees on the lower slopes of the mountains as she journeyed to the High Places. Up here a whole choir of them were singing together and uttering the delightful little chuckles at the end of each song:

"He's gotten the victory. Hurrah!
He's gotten the victory. Hurrah!"

She sat down beside the King in the shade of one of the trees on the edge of a little clearing, from which they could look out as through a frame onto the mountains on the other side of the valley. The sun shone on peaks of dazzlingly white snow which clothed the Higher Places as with bridal garments, and from somewhere just below them a number of voices began to sing:

Goodness is such a lovely thing!
'Tis Love's own bridal dress,
The wedding garment from our King
Is spotless righteousness;
And those who keep "The Royal Law",
Shine lily white without a flaw.

O, happy, holy ones! each day
　Their cup filled to the brim,
Love's Table spread for them, they may
　As God's guests, feast with Him.
Their happy faces shine with bliss,
With joy from Him and one with His.

Goodness is perfect harmony,
　The flawless form of Grace!
The golden mirror where we see
　Reflections of Love's face.
Goodness is Wrong changed and put Right,
'Tis darkness swallowed up in light.

When the words of the song ended all the little birds broke out again together in a burst of joyous little chuckles as of happy laughter. As she listened to them, Grace and Glory was so forcibly reminded of the time which she had spent with the King in the Place of Anointing, before she went up to the grave on the mountains and to the Altar of Sacrifice, that she turned and looked up into His face both gratefully and wonderingly, remembering the strange way in which He had led her along a path which had often seemed too bewildering and difficult to be possible.

The King turned His face to her and said, as though in answer to the look of mute wonder on her face:

"Did you think it was a very terrible path, Grace and Glory? Did you think it very strange that after dealing so GENTLY and lovingly with you all the way up to that place, I should lead you by such a strange and bitter path afterwards?"

She said nothing, only laid her hand in His and gave a little nod.

"What did you say to yourself when the path led you to the bitter Spring of Marah?"

She answered simply, "I said to myself, 'it is His love which plans this way for me and I will trust Him and follow where He leads.' "

"Yes," said the King in a glad, strong voice, "it is always safe to trust Love's plans, and every lover of Mine can sing with fullest assurance 'Surely goodness and mercy shall follow me all the days of my life and I will dwell in the house of the Lord for ever'."

It is always true, even though every single circumstance on the pathway of life may at times appear to contradict it. For Love Himself is the Judge Who knows perfectly well what is needed next in the experience of every one of His creatures in order to bring them into a fuller experience of His goodness and His love. It is true for those who are already following Him and just as true for those who are still fleeing from Him. For He is the Great Physician Who prescribes according to the need and condition of every soul who is suffering from the disease of sin as well as for those who are already recovering from it. All the "judgments" of Love are, in fact, the wise prescriptions which are intended to bring about the healing of His creatures. It is the GOODNESS of Love for "He woundeth and His hands make whole".

The woods of cinnamon trees had grown very still while the King was speaking. Not a breath of wind stirred amongst the branches, not a leaf moved. The tree beneath which they were sitting was as still as the rest. Long strips of its bark had been peeled away by some hand, disclosing a gaping wound through which the rich, blood-hued inner bark was visible, and from this wound in the side of the tree there exuded into the warm summer air a fragrant perfume so sweet and strengthening that Grace and Glory felt as though she were breathing in a life-giving tonic. In her heart

awoke a great desire that her life also might yield the true spice of
Goodness and, like the trees growing around her, she might be
"made perfect", if need be, even through suffering just as the King
of Love Who sat beside her had also "learned obedience by the
things that He suffered". As if in answer both to the prayer and the
shrinking in her heart as she thought of what it might mean to
have it answered, the King sang this song:

Love is the Judge—what comfort this
    O shrinking heart to thee,
Thou art dear workmanship of His,
    And perfect thou must be.
He knows each lesson thou must learn;
How long to let the fire burn.

He does not judge by outward sign,
    By failure, not by sin,
Each secret heart response of thine
    Each weak attempt to win;
He weighs it all, nor doth forget
The least temptation thou hast met.

He knows thy blemishes and how
    To purge away the dross,
Not overlong will He allow
    The anguish of thy cross.
Love is the Judge, and He doth see
The surest way to perfect thee.

Thou can'st not perish if thou wilt
    But turn thee to the light,

Love bleeds with thee in all thy guilt
And waits to set thee right.
Love means to save sin's outcasts lost,
And cares not at what awful cost.

Presently, as they rose to their feet and prepared to leave the mountain, a flock of the jubilantly singing birds swooped across the open glade in front of them, uttering a paean of their chortling, chuckling notes, the theme song of their tribe:

"He's gotten the victory. Hurrah!
He's gotten the victory. Hurrah!"

CHAPTER XIII

CRAVEN FEAR AND MOODY

ONE morning very early when Grace and Glory was walking near the pool and cascade where she had first kept tryst with the Shepherd, she met her aunt, Mrs. Dismal Forebodings, and her cousin, Gloomy. They were both wearing their beautiful Garments of Praise, and there was something so unusual and eager in their manner that Grace and Glory gazed at them in astonishment. That they were going to meet the Shepherd at her old trysting place she had no doubt; but the expression on their faces suddenly awakened her happy suspicions, and she could not restrain her curiosity. So after greeting them affectionately she said, "Where are you going at this early hour, for you look exactly as though you are starting on a journey?"

Mrs. Dismal Forebodings and Gloomy looked at each other, and, for a moment, said nothing, for a journey to the High Places is a secret affair and may not be paraded before others.

Grace and Glory saw the look which passed between them and gave a joyful little laugh.

"I know," she said, "but I will not ask you about it, for I know you are going with the Shepherd, and that He has told you not to speak of it. But I wish you a good journey and a safe arrival at the High Places, and oh, may you get there quicker than I did and learn all the lessons on the way with joy instead of with fear and shrinking!"

Her aunt looked at her lovingly and gratefully; but she was still Mrs. Dismal Forebodings and at the very beginning of the journey, and still without the right to a new name, so she answered: "Thank you, my dear! Yes, we are going with the Shepherd, old and dreary as I am, and of as little use to Him as I can expect to be. And though I am afraid I am too old ever to be able to develop 'hinds' feet' and to go prancing about as you do, Grace and Glory, yet the Shepherd has promised to take me to the High Places and to give me a new name, and I know that I can trust Him to do what He has promised."

The look of love and trust which shone in her eyes as she spoke the last words made her suddenly appear so beautiful that Grace and Glory was filled with wonder.

Her cousin Gloomy put both arms around her neck and kissed her twice without saying a word, then took her mother's hand and on they went to the trysting place to meet the Shepherd.

Grace and Glory hurried towards the village thinking of Spiteful left behind in the dreary attic. How would she manage now without the cheer of the daily visits of her sister and mother? What must she be feeling at being left behind?

She found Spiteful, who was still weak and not yet fully recovered, moving about the miserable attic and singing a little song with a look of wonderful peace and content upon her face. At first Grace and Glory hardly knew what to say.

"Did you meet my mother and Gloomy on your way here, dear Grace and Glory?" asked Spiteful, kissing her affectionately.

"Yes," she answered, "I met them near the trysting place."

Spiteful nodded. "Yes," she said happily, "they have gone with the Shepherd. He is going to take them to the High Places. It is too wonderful and lovely for words!"

Grace and Glory looked at her, still unable to say a word.

"I know what you are thinking," said Spiteful with a gentle and understanding little smile. "You are wondering about me and how I can bear to be left behind in this attic."

Grace and Glory nodded, still without speaking. Then Spiteful said softly: "I couldn't go with them, you know, because in a few days' time my husband will be coming out of prison, and there would be no one to welcome him or to care for him. But, Grace and Glory, the Shepherd has told me that there is a way to the High Places even from this attic, and that though I cannot make the journey with my mother and sister, yet I may go there just as surely by this other way. So, you see, I am not left behind!"

Grace and Glory looked round the miserable attic where the wife of poor Moody Timid-Skulking was awaiting his return from prison, and suddenly she understood. She remembered the little golden flower, "Acceptance-with-Joy", which she had found blooming in the wilderness, and the blood-red flower, "Bearing-with-Love", or "Forgiveness", which grew in the prison house of the rocks on the great precipice, and she realised that they were growing here too in this stifling attic, and that here indeed there was a short cut, steep and agonising beyond anything which she herself had faced, but a real short cut to the altar and the grave on the mountains on the very borders of the High Places. She also understood that her cousin Spiteful (but how could she call her by that name again?) was likely to arrive at the High Places even before her mother and sister.

She rose with a feeling of awe in her heart, and putting her arms around her cousin, said gently:

"Cousin, when the Shepherd told you about—about this short cut to the High Places, did He say anything to you about a new name?"

Her cousin blushed a little and then said hesitatingly: "He said He would give me a new name while I wait here until my husband can go to the High Places too. But the name would be just between Himself and me. It was written on a little white stone which He gave me when He planted the seed of love in my heart—a new name which no one knows save she that receives the stone."

"No one knows!" exclaimed Grace and Glory with a little tremble in her voice. "Why, that is very queer, for He has written it on your forehead for all to see! Didn't you know that?"

"No," said her cousin wonderingly. "He gave me the white stone to carry in my heart, but He said nothing about a new name written on my forehead. What name is that, Grace and Glory?"

"Why, it is one of His own names," said her cousin very softly. "He has marked you with the name, 'Compassion'."

"That is a lovely, lovely name," said the girl who had been known as Spiteful. "That exactly expresses His attitude to me. But I don't think it is my name, Grace and Glory. I think it is just the mark of His own compassion and gentleness set there to show that I now belong to Him."

"Well," said her cousin after a little pause, "I certainly cannot call you by the old name any longer, and the name on the white stone is a secret between you and Him, so I think we really must call you by

the lovely name which is written for all to see on your forehead."
Then she laughed a little and said, "Compassionate, I will sing you
a song specially meant for attic dwellers." And she sang this song:

O thou afflicted, tempest-tossed,
In sorrow's pathway led,
Behold thy suffering is not lost,
Thou shalt be comforted.
   In fairest colours thou shalt shine,
   And precious jewels shall be thine.

Foundation stones of bright sapphires
Shall garnish all thy floors,
Thy ruby windows glow like fires,
And emeralds make thy doors,
   And all thy walls and borders be
   Of precious stones and porphyry.

Fear not! thy trust ends not in loss,
I'll not put thee to shame,
There is a purpose in thy cross,
And no reproach and blame.
   One day, with glad, exultant voice
   Thou, child of sorrow, shalt rejoice.

Stretch forth the curtains of thy tent,
Lengthen the cords, spread wide,
Strengthen thy stakes with great content,
Break forth on every side.
   Thine anguish is no barren birth,
   Thou shalt have seed through all the earth.

(Isa. 54:11 and 12.)

"What a lovely song," exclaimed Compassionate, and her eyes were shining like the jewels of the song. "Where did you learn it, Grace and Glory?"

"The Shepherd taught it to me on the way up to the High Places, and I wrote it down after I got up there."

"Why is it called a song for attic dwellers?" asked Compassionate.

"Where else could it possibly be sung with greater meaning and effect?" asked her cousin with a laugh. "It has all the force and beauty of contrast, and all the glory of promise and fulfilment."

"Sing it again," begged Compassionate. "Sing it over and over again until I have learned it by heart."

So Grace and Glory taught her cousin The Attic Song just as Sorrow had taught her the song about the Hinds' Feet when she was limping on the mist-shrouded mountains. And as they sang, the dreadful little attic really did seem to undergo a transformation before their very eyes. It seemed to sparkle with glittering jewels as though it were a room in a palace, and the bare, ugly walls appeared to have melted away, leaving only a vista of royal gardens and orchards.

After they had sung it over and over again until Compassionate knew it by heart, Grace and Glory set about preparing a little midday meal for them both, and as she did so the two talked together about many things. Grace and Glory promised that she would visit her cousin every day, and Compassionate accepted the offer with overflowing joy and gratitude. As it turned out there was a special reason for this.

"Grace and Glory," she said, speaking slowly and rather hesitatingly, but with great earnestness, "if you are willing, I would like you to help me with something."

"With all my heart," answered Grace and Glory gladly, "in any way that I can. There is nothing that I should like more."

"Then," went on Compassionate, with a little flush on her cheeks, "I will tell you what I have been thinking and hoping. You know that my husband is coming out of prison in a few days' time and I am waiting to receive him. For poor and miserable as this attic is, and terribly close to temptation as, alas, it also is, it is the only refuge which he has in all the world. I shall be here to do all that I can for him," and as she spoke her face flushed with tender love and she seemed to have forgotten completely how weak she was and how utterly unfit to do anything, "but," she went on, looking at her cousin entreatingly, "but, dear Grace and Glory, my brother Craven Fear is to leave prison on the same day as my husband, and he has nowhere to go. I have no room for him in this tiny attic, neither would Mrs. Murmuring allow him to come here. They will take my poor husband back to be their drudge but not Craven. I know, dear Grace and Glory, how much you have suffered at the hands of my brother, and how—how you have never been able to bear him. But oh, I cannot bear to think of his coming out of prison with no one to meet him or to speak a gentle, loving word to him, and with nowhere to go, and made to feel that no one in the wide world will have anything to do with him. My mother and Gloomy are not here to take him home and the cottage is shut up. The Shepherd Himself chose to take them away just at this time, so it must be right. And much as I long to go to meet him, I am still unable to leave the attic. Dearest Grace and Glory, you are our nearest relative. Would you— would you feel able and willing to go to the prison to meet them both? And could you perhaps arrange with Mrs. Valiant or one of the Shepherd's other friends to let poor Craven have a room until he can find work and feels ready to face the world again?"

She broke off, trembling and sobbing, and instantly Grace and Glory was kneeling beside her with a radiant face and saying, "Oh, Compassionate, what a lovely thought that is! You don't know how I have longed to be able to do something for poor Craven—almost more than for anyone else! I have received so much, and he is so utterly destitute and miserable. Of course I will go; with all my heart I will go to welcome them both! Craven is your brother and my cousin and my closest relative. But oh, Compassionate! do you know the thought that came to me while you were speaking? It really is too lovely for words. I'm sure it came straight from the Shepherd Himself," and she laughed joyfully as she spoke.

"What was it?" asked Compassionate eagerly, and with hope dawning in her eyes.

"Why, it came to me that there is your mother's cottage standing empty and all ready to be used. You don't want your husband to come here to this attic in the inn where he will have to encounter such temptation every time he comes and goes and where he will never be out of reach of his worst enemy, drink. But see! I will take Joy and Peace and we will go and spring-clean your mother's cottage from top to bottom and make it all ready. And oh, Compassionate, you can leave this attic right away—the song is beginning to come true at once—and you and Moody and Craven can all live there together. I will come along every day, and the other friends of the Shepherd will help, I know, and I will help you with the meals and the work and you three can be together in your own home. Oh! Compassionate, you will certainly get better ever so much more quickly as soon as you get out of this oven-like attic, and your husband will be away from temptation!"

A flush of lovely colour had flooded into Compassionate's cheeks and her eyes began to shine like stars at the very mention of such a plan. But she hesitated wistfully.

"Oh, Grace and Glory, it sounds too lovely, almost like the High Places themselves. To think of being home again and out of this place of terrible temptation! But how shall we manage? We must earn something, you know, and this is the only work we can do, poor Moody and I. I do the mending for Murmuring and he will do all the rough jobs about the premises." She sighed heavily as she spoke and the colour faded again from her cheeks. "Murmuring will never let us leave as long as she can get work out of us for almost nothing!"

"No, No!" exclaimed Grace and Glory. "You can never be meant to stay here, just existing in penury and at the expense of poor Moody's safety. No, never! We will ask the Shepherd and His friends. There must be some way in which you can support yourselves, and Craven too, without being dependent on the Shepherd's enemies. I believe, too, that Bitterness will be willing to help you move, indeed, to help in any way he can in order to make some sort of atonement to you, for he is utterly wretched over the misery and suffering you have undergone since you came to live and work here. Leave it to me, Compassionate! We won't say a word to Murmuring, but I will speak to Bitterness and enlist his aid. Meanwhile I will get dear Mrs. Valiant and Mercy to help me prepare the cottage for you. Indeed, we won't waste a moment! Did your mother leave the key with you? . . . Yes! that's good; let me have it and we will set to work at once. And you, meantime, as you are able, can begin gathering together your things and packing what you need to take with you. Oh, Cousin, I am so happy. I feel as though I can't contain the joy but must burst with it! To

think of it! A home for you and your husband and for my cousin
Craven! I can help to make it ready and can go and meet them and
bring them to it! Could anything be lovelier?"

The two women kissed each other with inexpressible joy and
thanksgiving and then Grace and Glory sped on her way, first to
the home of Mrs. Valiant, then to Mercy, then to the deserted cottage of the widow, Dismal Forebodings.

Such a transformation the three women and their friends
worked in that cottage and in the garden overgrown with weeds,
as can scarcely be imagined! Fearless Trust, one of the shepherds
who was courting Mercy, and some of his friends, dug up the garden, burnt the weeds, planted the beds with vegetables and
flowers, and painted the cottage. The women scoured and cleaned
the rooms, sewed curtains, washed linen, repaired and arranged
the furnishings, and joyfully contributed from their own stores the
articles needed to restock the linen and china cupboards and to
beautify the rooms. Within a week it was the neatest, fairest,
cosiest cottage in the village, and the cupboards were stocked with
supplies—loaves and pies and jellies and fruits and vegetables and
a host of other good things. Mrs. Valiant had brought over some
fowls, and her future son-in-law had built a fine run and fowl
house. Then Compassionate was taken to the cottage and installed
there with great rejoicings, and everything was ready for the reception of her husband and brother the following day.

Her closest friends gathered round her that evening. She looked
a different woman already in her great joy at escaping from the miserable attic and having a home of her own. As she sat in the porch
with her cousin, Grace and Glory, and her friends, Mrs. Valiant,
Mercy and Fearless Trust, they talked over their plans and hopes,
yes, and still more, their fears, for the morrow. For fears there were.

They went over every point again and again and tried to comfort one another. But would it be possible, they asked one another, to persuade the two men to return to the village where their shame and disgrace were known to everybody? What would they say when they found themselves surrounded by the Shepherd's friends? How could they be weaned away from their old associates? Above all, from the tormenting slavery of drink? It was one thing to prepare and make ready for their return with all the joy of love, but how could the two men be persuaded to enter into and accept the things which love had prepared for them? Suppose they refused to come, as now seemed all too possible? Suppose they had made other plans while in prison and meant to make off and hide themselves among the teeming multitudes in the City of Destruction and so be lost beyond recovery? Compassionate and Grace and Glory shivered at the bare possibility of such a thing, Fearless Trust bit his lips and moved restlessly, and even Mrs. Valiant seemed to have nothing definite to suggest. Then there was the problem, also, as to who should go to meet them at the prison. If Grace and Glory went alone they might ignore her and just march off and leave her, whereas if too many went—and of course all of them were the Shepherd's friends whom the two men had always despised and disliked—either they might be frightened away, or else made hopelessly self-conscious and more determined than ever to go their own way. Oh, if only the Shepherd were there to tell them what to do!

In the midst of their perplexity and doubt and longing, they looked up and there He was standing beside them! With inexpressible joy and thankfulness they welcomed Him and told Him the whole situation. What were they to do? How could they win these two weak and miserable men upon whom all their hearts were now set with compassionate longing and love?

As soon as they had finished pouring out all their doubts and fears the Shepherd said quietly: "Grace and Glory is to go to the prison because she is their nearest relative. Mrs. Valiant shall go with her also, because she is motherly and understanding and unsentimental and she will neither sob nor bemoan them." Then He added, "And my friend, Bitterness, will drive you both over to the prison in his car and bring you all back here to the cottage."

There was a moment of almost stupefied silence following these last words, and then Mrs. Valiant said in a tone of quite indescribable satisfaction: "*Your friend* Bitterness? Aha! So at last You have won him!"

"Bitterness has decided to give up the Public House business altogether," said the Shepherd, "and to take service with Me. We have not yet persuaded his wife, Murmuring, to do the same thing, and at present she is going to continue to run the business as her own concern. Meanwhile, Bitterness feels that on him lies a great part of the blame for the disgrace and shame into which Moody and Craven have fallen, and he is anxious to make all amends possible and to help them. At this stage I believe he is just the man to be able to persuade them both to come home to the village." And so it was settled.

Early next morning Bitterness arrived at the cottage with Mrs. Valiant, Grace and Glory and Mercy (who was to help Compassionate with all her loving plans and contrivances for welcoming home the prodigals). After leaving her at the cottage the others drove off to the prison.

Thus it came to pass that when Craven Fear and Moody found the great prison gates at last opened to let them out, and were preparing to slink away and lose themselves in the labyrinth of city streets as soon as possible, they found the chosen three waiting to meet them—Mrs. Valiant with her beaming, motherly face, Grace and Glory, and the tall, burly figure of Bitterness, the proprietor of the inn in Much-Trembling.

Bitterness stepped forward first, and seizing Moody's hand in his, said in a voice of gruff kindness, tinged with sincere shame, "Moody, my dear fellow, I'm thankful to see you again. I blame myself almost entirely for all that has happened, and beg you to let me make any amends in my power and to help you now in every way I can."

At the same moment Grace and Glory stepped quietly up to Craven Fear, and placing her hands on his shoulders, kissed him gently on both cheeks, but found herself unable to utter a single word. Good Mrs. Valiant, however, bustled forward, and was so cheery and matter-of-fact (as though she were merely greeting and welcoming them home from a journey), that the two men found it impossible to be stubborn and resistant, and before they quite knew what was happening, Moody was seated on the front seat of the car beside Bitterness, and Craven Fear was wedged in between his cousin and Mrs. Valiant on the back seat. That remarkable lady was soon chatting away cheerfully, telling them all the news of the village, not waiting for any remarks or answers, which she knew quite well would not be forthcoming.

So they came to the cottage and to the little homely feast which Mercy had prepared for them, and to the gentle, loving welcome of Compassionate, who received her husband and brother as though they were in very truth the joy and satisfaction of her heart.

Undoubtedly it was the presence of Bitterness, the once domineering man who was now so changed and humble, which made the return possible and prevented the two men from bolting from the cottage and the village directly the meal was over. There was something so sincere and touching in his obvious remorse and desire to make amends, and in the way in which he took his place alongside them, sharing the blame and disgrace, and planning with them how all three of them could start afresh, that in the end they could not resist him, and both finally agreed to stay for some days at least, albeit with apparent sullenness and unwillingness. If any other influence had worked upon Craven Fear, he gave no sign of it, but only sat in stubborn silence, whether surly or ashamed, it was hard to say. Every now and then, however, he raised his eyes furtively and looked around the transformed room, at the gentle light shining in the eyes of his sister as she sat beside her husband, at the handsome, pleading face of the repentant Bitterness, at the kind fact of Mercy as she deftly served them, and once and again almost covertly at his cousin, who sat, nearly as silent as himself, on the other side of the table—the girl who had once been ugly and crippled, whom he had tormented again and again since she was a tiny child, and who, in the end, ran away to escape marrying him. Now here she was sitting with him in the cottage, which was so completely transformed he hardly recognised it as the same dreary place where they had all lived together, and she, too, was incredibly transformed. Only once did she say anything that evening, and that was after Bitterness had told them of his plans for starting anew in business and had pleaded with them both to stay and work with him. Craven Fear, looking covertly across the table, saw that his cousin's eyes were filled with tears and that they were turned upon him, and he heard her whisper, "Oh, Craven, you will stay, won't you?"

He made no answer, but sat with his great, oversized body slouched in the chair looking as though wild horses would not drag a word out of his lips. But he stayed.

Later that night, in the room familiar since childhood, now so lovingly rearranged and in such great contrast to the prison cell which had housed him for so many months, with none to see or hear, the great, hulking man laid himself face down on the bed and sobbed like a little child.

* * * *

A few days later the Shepherd, sitting at midday amongst His sheep in the shade of some great trees, looked up and saw the huge, slouching figure of Craven Fear coming across the fields toward Him. Never before had this man approached the Shepherd of his own free will; but now he came, hesitatingly it is true, but with a certain dogged determination toward the One from Whom many a time he had fled—the One, Who, in the end, had been the cause of His imprisonment.

The Shepherd sat quietly, looking steadily at him as he stumbled forward, his eyes downcast, his face and hands twitching nervously. Finally he stood before the One he had never dared to look in the face. Then he bent his huge form and knelt in the dust in silence. Neither spoke a word.

At last Craven lifted his eyes and blurted out, "Sir, if You will, You can make me different."

"I will indeed," said the Shepherd in a strong, clear voice. "Your name now is Craven Fear, but you shall be called Fearless Witness, and you shall be My messenger and suffer many things for My sake."

* * * *

When Craven Fear left the place under the trees where he had entered the Shepherd's service he went straight back to the cottage and sought out his brother-in-law. He found him in the little back yard drearily chopping wood.

"Moody," said Craven Fear, going up to him, "Come with me."

"Where to?" asked Moody, looking at him as though he were a ghost.

"To the Shepherd," said Craven Fear simply. "He can do everything for you that needs doing."

"The Shepherd!" gasped Moody, and cringed away backward. "What do you mean, Craven? I shan't go to *Him*. Why, the first thing that He would say is that I must give up the drink—and I can't. I can't live without the stuff. And what's more, I can't stand this life in the cottage without it any longer."

"That's just what I mean," said Craven. "You can't manage without Him any longer and neither can I. Come with me. I'll take you straight to Him. I know where He is now at this moment."

"He won't be able to do anything for me," wailed Moody miserably, cringing further away from his brother. "It's no good my listening to you, Craven. You are stronger and He may be able to help you, but I am too weak for Him to be able to do anything with."

"Well, you don't need to listen to *me*," said Craven patiently but doggedly. "Just come and see Him for yourself, and hear what He says about it." And with that he put out one of his huge hands and laid it firmly on the shoulder of his trembling brother-in-law.

It was one thing for Craven to say, "You don't need to listen to me," but quite another thing for Moody to avoid doing so. For Craven was almost a giant, head and shoulders taller than most of the men in the Valley, and possessed of great strength, which he had been accustomed to exert to the utmost during his bouts of bullying. Now, when for the first time he was engaged on a really good job, he had no idea at all of employing less strength and effort, so that the shrinking Moody found himself propelled forward quite irresistibly by the heavy and powerful arm of his brother-in-law. Off he had to go, whether he wished or no, for there was no escaping that powerful, brotherly arm.

Thus it came about that a little later the Shepherd beheld the figure of the man He had just taken into His service, who was later to become known far and wide as Fearless Witness, pushing towards Him the shrinking figure of the timid Moody. And if, at the sight, there was something very like a smile on the Shepherd's lips, there was also upon His face a look of indescribable joy and satisfaction. Moody, looking up at last and catching sight of that expression, suddenly stopped trembling and resisting and stepped forward of his own free will.

"Sir," said Craven Fear, planting the little man before the Shepherd and keeping his huge arm around the bowed shoulders, "Sir, I have brought my brother to you. He is not nearly so bad a man as I am, but he, too, needs Your help and power."

Moody again raised his eyes towards the face which was turned to him, and meeting the understanding and compassionate look of the Shepherd, blurted out in a faint, trembling voice, "Sir, I am the slave of an unclean spirit. Can You cast it out and deliver me?"

"Most certainly," said the Shepherd, and He laid His hands on him and said, "I make you free—and when the Son makes, you free, you are FREE INDEED."

CHAPTER XIV

THE MOUNTAIN OF FRANKINCENSE
(FAITH)

THE RESPONSE OF FAITH OF LOVE

THE seventh Mountain of Spices was a very lovely place indeed. Like the mountain of Cinnamon it was clothed with trees, the only difference being that here on the Mountain of Frankincense, the trees were much taller. They were gracious, stately gums and their boles were beautifully and most variously coloured, ranging from silvery grey and ivory white or cream, to palest lemon, misty blue, lavender, golden tawn, rust red and rich brown. In places there were even great streaks of crimson. But the leaves of the tree were even more beautiful. They were very long and very narrow, and they hung down in great festoons from the slender, swaying stems, so that, from a distance they looked like loosely flowing veils of silver hair. Every breeze and even the softest breath of wind stirred these lovely trees and set all the leaves whispering together and rippling like waves on the sea. As she watched them, Grace and Glory thought to herself that she had never seen anything quite so gloriously *responsive* as those countless swaying stems and leaves. It was almost startling to notice the mysterious union which seemed to exist between them and the light summer wind, as though invisible fingers were gently sweeping a keyboard of leaves and liberating whole harmonies of intricate, rhythmic motion.

As she watched and listened, she thought she heard the harmony of motion turned into sound and a song went singing through the trees.

> Faith is response to Love's dear call,
>> Of Love's dear face the sight;
> To do Love's bidding now is all
>> That gives the heart delight.
> To love Thy voice and to reply
>> "Lord, here am I."

> As blows the wind through summer trees,
>> And all the leaves are stirred,
> O Spirit move as Thou dost please,
>> My heart yields at Thy word.
> Faith hears Thee calling from beyond
>> And doth respond.

> What Thou dost will—that I desire,
>> Through me let it be done,
> Thy will and mine in Love's own fire
>> Are welded into one.
> "Lord, I believe!" Nay, rather say,
>> "Lord, I obey."

For a long time after that she sat in perfect silence, too absorbed to notice anything else. At last the King's voice broke in on her reverie:

"You are admiring the beautiful, unstudied and wholly unresisting responsiveness of My trees of Frankincense, Grace and Glory?"

"Yes," said she in a tone of great delight. "It is a perfect joy to watch them. I never before saw anything comparable to them. The slightest and gentlest breath of the wind sets them all moving as though in harmony with chords of inaudible music."

"Faith is certainly a very lovely thing," said the King with a pleased smile. "I can do anything, yes ANYTHING where there is this perfect faith or responsiveness to My Will. It is their beautiful responsiveness which wakens the music in the trees of frankincense. There is nothing in the whole wide world which gives Me more joy and appears fairer in My sight than the response of human hearts to My love. It is the WILL to obey me which makes the union complete between us and which enables Me to pour My life and power into those who love Me and respond to Me continually."

He ceased speaking and they sat in absolute silence looking out on the view spread before them. They were seated on the very edge of the Mountain of Frankincense, and in the intensely clear air they could see to a great distance. Far below them was the Valley of Humiliation which had been the home of Grace and Glory when she had been Much-Afraid, and where all her relatives lived. But from this particular mountain they got quite a different view of it, for they were looking up the whole length of the Valley instead of across it to the mountains on the other side. Grace and Glory could see that at both ends the long, green valley opened out into other valleys, and they too into yet more valleys, winding away

among the mountains. All these many, many other valleys, stretching further than her eyes could follow them, were also bounded by
other mountain ranges towering upwards to snow-covered peaks,
so that there were High Places above all the valleys. Thus it was as
though she was looking out over two worlds; a world of LOW
Places, and above them another world of High Places. But she well
knew by this time that in one sense there were three worlds, for she
knew that all the visible mountain ranges had still higher summits
beyond them, which soared up into the heavens right out of sight,
so that they were out of this world altogether. Those were the really
High Places to which the King's servants went when they had
finished their service for Him on earth.

For quite a long time she sat silently by the King's side, her
thoughts greatly occupied with the things that He had just been
saying to her. She looked long and earnestly and a little fearfully at
those far-off valleys stretching away in every direction beyond her
own little "Home Valley". How many of them there were! What
multitudes and multitudes of people must live in those Low Places
stretching over the face of the whole earth. People who knew
absolutely nothing about the High Places because they knew
nothing about the King of Love. People who never could know
and experience the joy and rapture of union with Him, unless
someone went to tell them about Him.

She moved a little uneasily in her seat on the soft mossy bank
up there on the Mountain of Frankincense, and a slight mist
seemed to cover her eyes. She wiped it away, but somehow she did
not feel like looking round at the King. The lovely, graceful trees
of frankincense whispered and murmured and rustled around her
as the wind moved gently amongst them and wooed them to
RESPONSE.

Then she looked down at the green valley below her, the "home valley", where she now worked so happily; where her own relatives were already learning to respond to the King of Love, just as she had done. After a long pause she said in a very small low voice:

"My Lord, is it not very lovely that so many of the inhabitants in the valley down there have been persuaded to become Your followers?"

"Very lovely indeed," He answered at once, in a glad, happy voice, and she could sense the smile on His face as He spoke, but for some reason she still did not want to turn and look at Him.

There was silence again for quite some time. Then, still without looking at Him, she put out her hand, took His and said in the same low, small voice:

"My Lord, why did You bring me here?"

"I wanted you to see this view," He answered very gently indeed.

"I am looking at it," she said, just a little breathlessly. "Tell me, my Lord, what do YOU see?"

He answered slowly and clearly: "I see the dark places of the earth full of the habitations of cruelty. I see multitudes of human souls fainting and scattered abroad as sheep having no shepherd, and I am moved with compassion on them, Grace and Glory."

After a long time she spoke again, but in a voice so low it was scarcely audible. "I think I understand, my Lord," she said, and then she trembled, almost as though she were not Grace and Glory away up there on the High Places, but poor little Much-Afraid down in the valley.

"Then, as you have seen what I wanted you to see," said the King gently, "we can go down to the Valley of Humiliation for the work of today."

As He spoke He rose and started leaping down the mountainside. Grace and Glory started to follow Him as usual, but for the first time since He had brought her to the High Places she found that her "hinds' feet" were inclined to wobble. So she paused one instant on a little rocky crag and whispered very softly: "Behold me! I am Thy little handmaiden, ACCEPTANCE-WITH-JOY."

Immediately her legs stopped shaking, and, sure-footed as a mountain roe, she leaped after the King down the mountainside, singing as she went:

> Entreat me not to leave Thee, Lord,
>   For Oh, I love Thee so,
> And where Thou goest Lord of Love
>   There will I also go.

> Where'er Thou lodgest I will lodge,
>   Thy people shall be mine,
> Whom Thou dost love I also love,
>   My will is one with Thine.

> As Thou didst die, so will I die,
>   And also buried be,
> For even death may never part
>   My love-bound heart from Thee.

>   (Ruth 1:16 and 17.)

CHAPTER XV

PRIDE AND SUPERIORITY

PRIDE had limped ever since that eventful day when he tried to over-power Much-Afraid on her way to the High Places and the Shepherd had come to her defence and had hurled him over the cliffs into the sea. Yes, he still limped, and his handsome face was very much scarred, and this was a very sore blow to him, for he had always been one of the handsomest and strongest men in the Valley. Doubtless it was the fact that he could no longer arrogantly flirt with all the pretty girls which had at last decided him to marry and settle down. He chose for his wife a relative of his, a wealthy young woman called Superiority, who had been waiting hopefully for several years for this event. She was by no means a beauty, but she was an heiress, and Pride had extravagant tastes far beyond the allowance which his father gave him. His wife brought him a fortune derived from invest-ments in a company which had vast mining operations somewhere in the Valley of the Shadow of Death. The mines were said to pro-duce fabulous wealth, and the parents of Pride, Sir Arrogant and Lady Haughty, both drew their income from the same source.

Strange at it may seem, the one special friend of Superiority's girlhood had been Much-Afraid, the crippled, miserable orphan brought up in the home of Mrs. Dismal Forebodings. Much-Afraid and her three cousins, Gloomy, Spiteful and Craven Fear, had all been Superiority's companions at school. She had disliked the three Forebodings very much indeed, being jealous of Gloomy's striking good looks and of Spiteful's cleverness, and she had detested the bullying Craven. Perhaps it was the fact that they all three gave her a strong feeling of inferiority, whereas championing the trembling, ill-used Much-Afraid gave her the soothing and comfortable sense of superiority her nature required, which was the real basis for this strange friendship. Much-Afraid was not only ugly and crippled, but she was also stupid at her lessons, and Superiority had no need to fear being surpassed by her in any way. The other girls and boys in general disliked Superiority, for she had far more pocket money than anyone else, and prettier clothes, and was known to be an heiress. Therefore Much-Afraid's grateful and adoring homage had been balm and incense to her self-esteem and had kept her from feeling friendless.

Even when their school-days ended and Much-Afraid entered the service of the Shepherd the friendship had not really been broken. By that time Superiority was already smarting inwardly from the constant neglect of Pride and his slowness in proposing to her, despite the fact that his parents had chosen to consider the two engaged since their school days. During his many flirtations with other girls it had soothed her wounded feelings to continue to stand up for Much-Afraid and to insist that it was her horrible relatives who had driven her into the Shepherd's service, and that no one could blame her for wanting to escape from such a home as hers as soon as possible. Then, when she went off with the

Shepherd to the High Places, the dallying Pride, still without making any proposal to Superiority, had gone off in order to try to force Much-Afraid to return, and had himself returned, not only having failed to achieve his purpose, but now so crippled and scarred of face that he was at long last ready to do what she had so long awaited—to marry her. Superiority told herself, therefore, that her friendship and gracious championship of Much-Afraid had been properly rewarded. Of course as the wife of Pride she was not tactless enough to speak of her old friendship with the one through whom Pride had experienced such a fall, and there had been no need to do so during Much-Afraid's absence from the Valley. It had been more difficult, however, when she actually returned with a new name, no longer crippled and disfigured, and attended by two regal-looking handmaidens. Undoubtedly this would have been enough to break the friendship at last were it not for the fact that Grace and Glory herself had taken such loving pains to maintain it. She had immediately sought out her friend, had given herself no airs, and had been so affectionately interested in all her friend's concerns that Superiority had been quite disarmed.

"After all," she said to herself, "she may be considerably better off than she was before, poor little soul, but my own position is unassailable. I have a husband, lovely children, a beautiful home and an ample fortune, and my husband is heir to a title. Why should I grudge my friend an improvement in her own fortune? I shall certainly not parade the friendship before my husband, and Grace and Glory shows that she is tactful enough not to do so either. It is just as well, however, to keep in with the Shepherd's friends and not to make enemies unnecessarily, as poor Pride has already found to his cost."

But Superiority had begun to find that to continue a friendship with Grace and Glory was not the simple and easy matter which she had at first supposed. Strange as it seemed, considering the great difference in their worldly positions, it was impossible not to feel a growing sense of inferiority and envy. Certainly Grace and Glory had no home of her own in the Valley, no husband, no children and no position, but in spite of that she did really seem to live like a queen—waited on hand and foot, apparently, by her two regal attendants, every possible want somehow or other supplied, and enjoying complete liberty and independence. More extraordinary still was the growing influence which she seemed to exert on others. There were her aunt and cousins, for instance, so mysteriously changed in their attitude towards her—as loving now as they had been hateful before! In addition so many of her Fearing relatives were now actually entering the service of the Shepherd! The influence and power which her relationship with Him seemed to give her and the way so many people in the Valley were now entering His service, was a bitter pill for Superiority to swallow, for it was the Shepherd Who had humbled her husband; and now He Who had been so long despised and ignored by the whole Fearing clan, was accepted by them all as a kind of King! It was not only the family of Mrs. Dismal Forebodings—they were not rich and important people, even though they were related to Lord Fearing! There was Bitterness, for instance, actually giving up his prosperous hotel in order to follow the Shepherd, and now Resentment had announced his intention of resigning as bank manager because the Shepherd had infected him with scruples about the investments in the Dead Valley Mines by which so many of the Bank clients were getting rich! There was Self-Pity, too, and his stupid little wife, Helpless, actually working for the Shepherd and apparently enjoying it! Furthermore, according to Valley gossip, a host of smaller fry were doing the same thing. Then, to top it all, Grace and Glory held a position of influence and authority amongst them which she herself, the wife of Pride, and daughter-in-law of Sir Arrogant, had never possessed!

There came a day when Superiority asked herself if it would not be better to end the friendship and to escape once for all from the growing sense of inferiority which every meeting with Grace and Glory, and with her friends, increased in her. Should she give up her friend and so sever all connection with the Shepherd and cut herself off from all news of His doings? Or should she continue the friendship and accept the fact that the one she had once patronised and championed had now surpassed her altogether?

Strangely enough, Superiority actually decided on the latter course. She could hardly tell why, except that, when it came to the point, she found she really loved Grace and Glory as she had certainly never loved Much-Afraid, and that she could not part with her friendship. As soon as she admitted that to herself, she realised also that, deep down in her heart, she not only envied Grace and Glory but also yearned passionately to find what Grace and Glory had found and to know the Shepherd Himself. She could not bring herself to confess this to anyone, but she made a secret inner choice: she would NOT give up the friendship with the one who now caused her to feel inferior and of whom she was envious.

It was shortly after this decision that Superiority noticed a change in her husband. He was increasingly moody and silent and appeared to be weighed down by some burden, whether of anxiety or annoyance she could not tell. He did not confide in her, tried to laugh off her anxious inquiries, and grew all the time more and more moody.

One morning they entered the dining-room for breakfast at an earlier hour than usual, for Pride had announced the evening before that he must visit the City of Destruction and make an early start in the morning. His cousin, Resentment, the retiring bank manager, had visited him that evening, and the two had been closeted together for some time. Superiority feared that the visit must be connected with some business trouble, for Pride had seemed so morose afterwards. She knew her husband's extravagant habits and wondered whether he had a big overdraft at the Bank. But she knew that her own fortune was ample for all their needs, and that while it was still in her hands she could curb his extravagance; so she felt no fear.

The memory of her husband's dark mood the night before, however, was swept out of her mind by the news she had to tell him—news brought by the milkman on his early round.

"Pride," said she excitedly, as soon as he entered the room for breakfast, "do you know what happened last night? The milkman brought the news this morning. Mrs. Murmuring's hotel was burnt to the ground. I understand nothing was saved at all. It seems that the new man, Sharp, whom she made her manager when Bitterness gave up his share in the business in order to follow the Shepherd—it seems this man must have been drinking in his own room on the ground floor, and somehow started the fire in that room. By the time the people upstairs were wakened, the whole ground floor was in flames and they had to escape from the windows, and when the fire-engines arrived the fire was completely out of control and the whole premises ablaze. They were fortunate to escape with their lives. Everything else is gone— everything! They say that Murmuring herself was badly burned about the face and arms while trying to rescue the children, and several other people were injured too. What a loss it will be! I am sure I hope the premises were insured!"

Her husband, who had been staring at her with a strange, stricken look on his face, now muttered: "I happen to know the place is not insured. That means Murmuring has lost everything. That man Sharp had persuaded her to use all her savings to enlarge and repair the place and to make those big alterations. The business was prospering so well that Murmuring decided this was the time to do it, and she told me that she would not insure it until all the expensive improvements were finished. What's happened to the man Sharp?"

"Nobody knows. He has completely disappeared. Whether he was burnt and lies under the ruins, or whether he escaped, can't yet be known for sure, but they think it likely he escaped, for the safe in his room was open—and of course empty. Murmuring used to let him deposit the money there each evening and she banked it the following day. It really is extraordinary the way she trusted that man, considering what a shrewd woman she was in every other way. What about Bitterness's share of the money, Pride? I suppose she couldn't use her husband's savings for those extensions and alterations?"

"I understand that he gave up all claim to the money made in the business," answered her husband in a low voice. "He said he wouldn't touch a penny of it; that it was money made by destroying men. So I imagine Murmuring had it all."

"It's complete ruin for them," said Superiority commiseratingly, but with the easy, superficial concern felt by those who have an assured fortune and cannot be faced by loss or ruin themselves.

Her husband looked at her queerly. His face was very pale and his hands were shaking. After a moment's pause all he said was: "What a good thing it is that Bitterness had already entered the Shepherd's service! They will have a roof over their heads, anyhow, and something to live on. The Shepherd appears to provide for His helpers generously when they are in need. It's a pity Murmuring didn't agree with her husband and give up the business when he did and so escape this complete loss." Giving a harsh, strange laugh he added, "In the end fate and good fortune always seem to be on the side of the Shepherd's followers, and bad luck with His enemies."

His wife looked at him in astonishment. Never had she heard him speak in such a tone of voice or mention the Shepherd in that way. Before she could say anything, the maid entered the room carrying the morning paper which had just arrived, and with an odd, scared look on her face she laid it beside her master's plate and left the room.

Pride unfolded the paper. Huge black headlines stretched right across the front page. Then Superiority saw her husband turn ashy white, the paper fell from his nerveless hands and he slumped forward over the table. She uttered a little cry of terror, rang the bell for help and hurried to her husband's side The paper had fallen to the floor but she caught sight of the headlines:

GREATEST FRAUD OF THE CENTURY

Dead Valley Mines a Gigantic Hoax

COMPLETE COLLAPSE OF ALL BANKS IN THE CITY OF DESTRUCTION. ALL INVESTMENTS A DEAD LOSS.

As her terrified eyes read these words the self-assured heiress, who had felt herself inaccessible to the blows of fate, knew that ruin as complete as that which Murmuring had met during the night had overtaken them also. Only too well she knew that every penny which she and her husband and his parents possessed came from investments in this same "gigantic hoax". Everything they possessed was gone from them like a burst bubble.

When Pride recovered consciousness he was in a fearful state of mental fear and distress. For weeks he had been dreading this calamity that had now overtaken them, hoping against hope that the rumours, of which Resentment had brought word, would prove untrue. Now the blow had fallen. Everything they possessed was gone and he knew of no way in which he could earn a living to support his wife and family, and his equally penniless parents. He had never learned to work; he knew no trade or business; he was quite unfit, from a lifetime of soft living, for hard manual labour, and the awful realisation broke over him that he was completely inadequate for this new and terrible situation—unable to face life as it now faced him. The thought of his wife and children left utterly alone and penniless withheld him from committing suicide at once, but the realisation that he himself was unable to do anything for them, even if he remained with them, was so terrible that he felt he could not bear it. He had been suddenly stripped of everything in which he had trusted, and now found himself so despicably incompetent and inadequate that it seemed a disgrace to remain alive.

His wife, Superiority, was equally terrified by the discovery of her own unfitness to face life and its demands when deprived of all the service and ease and pleasures with which wealth had supplied her. Her reactions, however, differed from those of her husband. Perhaps it was the inner decision which she had made a few days ago to continue to love Grace and Glory, because of the passionate longing in her heart—which she had at last admitted to herself—to know the Shepherd, that made her at this time, when her whole life lay in ruins about her, think, with a desperate, almost despairing hope, of appealing to the Shepherd for help. When at last her half-crazed husband could be brought to listen to her, and she made the suggestion that in their utter loss of all things they should at last turn to the One they had so long disdained and rejected, Pride's reaction was one of agonised horror and shame.

"How can we?" he almost shrieked at his wife, "how can we go crawling and grovelling to Him now? Now that we are ruined and absolutely destitute, how can we implore His help after scorning Him all these years when we were wealthy and secure? We can at least save ourselves that last, complete humiliation of grovelling before Him as beggars, pleading for a pittance flung us out of pity, and likely being despised and turned away!"

"But we are beggars!" said Superiority in a trembling voice, "and is it not better to face the fact, Pride, and to acknowledge ourselves to be what we really are? Unless the Shepherd will accept us and teach us some kind of useful work, however menial, I don't see what other hope there is for us."

Pride groaned in anguish. "There is nothing that I can do. For weeks and weeks I have thought about it and sought for some course of action to follow should this overwhelming catastrophe come upon us. But there is no solution, absolutely none. There is no way out but for me to die. Perhaps the Shepherd would help you then, but He will have nothing to do with me, for I have been His worst enemy all these years."

"Pride," said a quiet, commanding voice, "Pride, are you and Superiority willing to listen to Me at last?" Looking up in the midst of their anguish and ruin, husband and wife then saw the Shepherd Himself standing in the room beside them. His face was stern and His voice was stern, but there was a note of compassion and mercy in it also. Both trembled in His Presence and sank down at His feet, bereft of strength, yet in the depths of their hearts both felt an indescribable sense of relief and comfort.

"Pride and Superiority," went on the quiet, commanding voice, "all your lives you have been exactly what your names suggest, proud and superior toward others. But wherein did your fancied superiority consist? In the fact that you possessed wealth and possessions and privileges which others did not? Never once would you look at yourselves as you really were. Now that the wealth and possessions which gave you this superior attitude have been taken from you, wherein lies your superiority? On what can you pride yourselves now? Are you ready at last to learn of Me Who am meek and lowly in heart and to find rest to your souls? For humility is simply to see yourselves as you really are, and meekness is to admit the truth about yourselves and to act accordingly."

The two bowed their heads before Him and were at first speechless. Then Pride muttered with almost a sob, "You are right, Sir! It is all true. But how can we—how can I—come to You now asking for Your help after proudly rejecting You all these years?"

"Are you still a fool, Pride?" asked the Shepherd. "It was folly to reject Me all the years when you possessed wealth and imagined that you could manage without Me. Now that you know your utter helplessness and that in yourself you possess nothing, cannot you see that it would be sheer madness to go on rejecting Me? O foolish man! Do you not realise that this world and this earthly life are so arranged that sooner or later every single human soul *must* realise he is nothing but is absolutely dependent upon Me? If you would not learn this truth while you had temporal possessions, do you not see that there was only one thing LOVE could do to make you understand the truth—namely, take those possessions from you, leaving you naked and empty and stripped and exposed to the realisation of your own true position? It is LOVE, Pride and Superiority, LOVE Himself Who has brought this so-called ruin upon you. Is it ruin for LOVE to topple over and cast down every false screen you had erected to hide the truth from yourselves? LOVE has but arranged it so that you must face the truth at last— see yourselves as you really are, not as you have painted yourselves in your own blind imagination. Are you therefore still going to continue to reject My help and grace on the ground that you now see how unworthy you are to seek it? Will you be a madman, Pride? Or will you humble yourself so that at last I may make you what I want you to be?"

"Sir," said Pride tremblingly, "Sir, forgive me if I ask it, but can You really do anything with one so utterly helpless and despicable as I am?"

"I can make you what I planned that you should be when I created you. If you will be meek and lowly of heart and learn of Me, I will teach you, and show you how to use for My glory all the benefits and advantages and privileges which you have enjoyed. But you must be willing to begin at the very beginning with nothing at all; willing to take from My hand this loss of all on which you have counted in life, and to accept instead that which you have despised—a low position and poverty and meanness in the eyes of the world. You must learn a new standard of values, and to adapt your desires to that which I choose for you. It is a hard saying, Pride, but this is the truth which you have refused to face up to all your life."

There was silence in the room when He had finished speaking. The man who had for so long hated and resisted the Lord of Love, who had first been crippled through his own resistance and then ruined through continued resistance, and the woman, who, like her husband, had refused to see herself as she really was, sat there in silence, debating whether they would accept the truth about themselves or reject it.

Then Superiority rose, and going to her husband, took his hand and said in a trembling voice: "This is the great opportunity of our lives. We have been fools. Shall we cease to be fools from this day onwards? We have lost all but our own selves; how blessed to lose ourselves also that we may find the life we were meant to live! He says He will make us meek and lowly of heart like Himself. I am sick to death of being superior—are you not sick of being proud?"

Then her husband rose to his feet too, and they went and knelt before the Shepherd and said: "Sir, we are nothing; we are miserable beggars, unworthy to ask your aid. But we are Your slaves from henceforth and for ever."

The Shepherd said with infinite loving-kindness and love: "My slaves, Meekness and Lowliness-of-heart, 'learn of Me . . and ye shall find rest unto your souls. For My yoke is easy and My burden is light'."

CHAPTER XVI

THE MOUNTAIN OF MYRRH (MEEKNESS)

HEAVEN IS THE KINGDOM OF LOVE

THE Mountain of Myrrh was the place where the King grew the lovely trees of Meekness, which yielded in great abundance a spice which was a special favourite of His. These trees grew on the last but one of the nine peaks forming the Mountains of Spices, which together formed a lofty circle of High Places surrounding the Valley of Humiliation, although there were narrow gorges between them, leading out into countless other valleys. By the time the King and His companion reached this eighth mountain, therefore, they had almost completed the circle and only the Mountain of Aloes still lay between them and the Mountain of Pomegranates which had been their starting point.

The Mountain of Myrrh, however, differed quite startlingly from all the other mountains in the group, diverse as all of them had been. It was very similar in shape to the low black mountain in the foreground of the Mountain of Pomegranates, that is to say, it was an almost perfect pyramid, though it towered up far higher than the poor black mountain; indeed, it rose higher than any of the other eight mountains, saving only the mountain of Pomegranates on which grew the trees of Love.

The bushes from which the spice of meekness was obtained, clothed the slopes almost from top to bottom. They were unlike any of the spice trees elsewhere. They reminded Grace and Glory of the little thorn tree which had so wonderfully sweetened the bitter waters of the spring of Marah on her way up to the High Places, of which she had drunk when she knelt and accepted willingly that which was to break her heart. Indeed, the King told her, when she mentioned this, that the thorn tree growing beside that spring was a species of myrrh tree and had been transplanted from the mountain on which they stood, and planted on those far lower slopes where, although it could only live in a stunted and imperfect form, it yet contained the same precious spice which sweetened the unpalatable and bitter waters of the spring.

She noticed that all the bushes growing here in their native element were low and were covered with sharp thorns and possessed very scanty foliage. At this season of the year, however, all the bushes were in bud, preparing to break forth into blossom. The King told her that in a little while they would all be completely covered with flowers. He promised to bring her to the Mountain again at the time of blossom, and then the whole place would glow as though garbed in a royal crimson robe.

At the moment, however, just as the buds were beginning to appear at the tip of each long, sharp thorn, a group of the King's workmen were busy among the bushes, making incisions in each little tree-trunk from which would "bleed" the precious gum-resin of meekness into vessels carefully placed to receive it. Before the trees could bloom in all their glory they must offer themselves and their precious inner treasure of fragrant resin, to all who cared to gather it. They bared themselves to the sharp knife, that through the incisions thus made they might empty themselves in glad self-giving and thanksgiving.

As they worked with their knives, making incisions in all the trees, the King's servants sang this song:

> Do not fear the cutting knife,
>   Do not shrink in pain,
> Let the red drops of thy life
>   Fall like bleeding rain.
> That which thou to death dost give
> Is the seed which yet shall live.
>
> Do not fear the winter's breath,
>   Let the seed drop to the earth,
> Everything laid down to death
>   Waits a resurrection birth.
> Let the flower drop; on the thorn
> Fairer glories shall be born.
>
> Do not try to hold life's joys,
>   Or the past's years golden store,
> Love it is Who thus destroys,
>   To make room for so much more.
> Love it is, with radiant Face,
> Leading to a wealthier place.

Do not let self-pity bleed
  Bitterness, nor fierce regret.
These are worms which kill the seed,
  And sad misery beget.
With a willing heart let go,
God will richer gifts bestow.

Learn the lesson fast or slow,
  This is Heaven's Law,
We must let the old things go,
  To make room for more.
We shall reap in some glad way,
Fairer joys than lost today.

The scene was one of such special and affecting beauty that for some time Grace and Glory was quite speechless as she looked at all the little wounded thorn trees pouring themselves out through the lacerations made in their very hearts, and as she noticed that every bleeding thorn was crowned with a crimson bud just about to break forth into royal bloom. The bitter-sweet perfume of the oozing resin of myrrh (the spice specially used for anointing the dead) filled the air.

"These are My happy trees," said the King at last with one of His loveliest smiles as He seated Himself on a low bank. "These are the meek who inherit the earth—and of such is the Kingdom of Heaven."

Grace and Glory looked at Him eagerly, and waited to hear what He would say next.

They sat for a few moments in silence and then the quiet voice went on: "These little trees of Meekness, breathing out this lovely fragrance and pouring out the treasure of their hearts, have a great lesson to teach, Grace and Glory. I have brought you here that, as you sit amongst them, you may 'learn of Me, Who am *meek* and lowly in heart, and may not only find rest for your soul, but may learn the secret of HEAVEN.' When I say to you, 'Let this mind be in you which was also in your Lord . . . Who humbled or EMPTIED Himself' you have a lovely illustration all around you of what it means to empty oneself. Here you see demonstrated before you the gracious, happy spirit which yields up its very self, to be poured out for the use of others, without caring at what cost it is accomplished, nor even if it must be by means of the knife which cuts away the very deepest treasure of the heart. This meekness, this willingness to be emptied and humbled (and humility is nothing but willingness to accept humiliations sweetly and unresentfully) is the chief characteristic of the citizens of the Kingdom of Love and of all who live in heaven. It is the very nature of the Son of Man Himself! Meekness is self-giving and sharing even with those who demand all and give nothing in return; who take by force and thereby take advantage of the meekness which will not resist them. It is the very opposite of self-assertion and self-getting. Here in these little trees of meekness you have the perfect picture of the Kingdom of Heaven. For remember, the Kingdom of Heaven is everywhere where the Law of Love is practised and perfectly obeyed and where I, Who am the King of Love, reign. It is My Kingdom come in the hearts of men and then, through them, come on earth. The meek of the earth already live in heaven. That is to say, they have their roots in heaven, though for a little while longer their bodies are in the material world and subject to pain and death. The meek are like the lilies whose blossoms float on top of the water, but whose roots go down into quite another realm out of sight below the water."

For a little while they sat without speaking, watching the King's gardeners as they worked among the "happy" or blessed trees of Meekness, making incisions in them through which each tree might gladly and thankfully pour out its own self to others and in so doing be made ready to burst into a glory of bloom and fruitfulness.

At last Grace and Glory turned and looked again into the face of the King of Love, the One Who plans for all His lovers such unutterably glorious destinies in the future. As she looked into His face and put her hand into His nail-pierced hand, close to the wound in His side through which His very life had been poured forth for all mankind, she prayed Him to show her how she too might pour forth her own life to share with others.

Before they left the mountain of Meekness He sang her another of the mountain songs:

> O blessed are the patient meek
>   Who quietly suffer wrong;
> How glorious are the foolish weak
>   By God made greatly strong;
> So strong they take the conqueror's crown,
> And turn the whole world upside down.
>
> O dreaded meek! None can resist
>   The weapon which they wield,
> Force melts before them like a mist,
>   Earths "strong ones" faint and yield.
> Yea—slay them, lay them in the dust,
> But bow before them, earth's might must.

Immortal meek! who take the earth
  By flinging all away!
Who die—and death is but their birth,
  Who lose—and win the day.
Hewn down and stripped and scorned and slain,
As earth's true kings they live and reign.

O Christ-like meek! by heaven blessed,
  Before whom hell must quake,
By foolish, blinded men oppressed,
  Who yet the earth do shake.
O "seed" of Him Who won through loss,
And conquered death while on a Cross.

CHAPTER XVII

THE MOUNTAIN OF ALOES
(SELF-CONTROL)

Self-Controlled By Love

THERE came a day soon after this when Grace and Glory was led to the last of the nine Mountains of Spices, which was the Mountain of Aloes. This completed the whole circle of lovely peaks and brought her right back again to the edge of the Mountain of Pomegranates from which they had first started.

This last mountain was, she thought, in some ways the most beautiful of them all, although all the nine were so fair and wonderful it was really difficult to favour one above the rest. Indeed, they all belonged together as the range of gardens in which the King grew His own wonderful spices.

The Mountain of Aloes and the Mountain of Pomegranates possessed one feature, however, which did distinguish them in a special way from the other mountains in the chain. Between them lay a very quiet valley through which flowed a river of crystal-clear water. This valley was, as it were, the stairway up to the Very High Places above. The river flowed across the valley between the two mountains after descending in a waterfall from cliffs high up on the Mountain of Aloes. On the upper side of the quiet valley above the river was a path which led up and up and out of this world altogether, into the Upper Regions of the sky. At times some of the inhabitants of those Upper Regions came down to the further banks of the river in order to welcome across to the other side those of the King's friends for whom the time for departure from the earth had come.

On this occasion, however, it was not to the quiet valley between the mountains that the King led Grace and Glory, but to the Mountain of Aloes itself.

Here grew the lign-aloe trees of Self-Control. They were very great trees, giants of strength and loveliness. Beside them even the tallest of forest trees appeared as dwarfs. Their trunks were of immense thickness; their branches spread out gloriously, shading an area vast enough to shelter a cathedral. Also, they were magnificently proportioned and were crowned with a gracefully vaulted roof of foliage, so thick that not a drop of rain or hail could penetrate to the cool, shady depths beneath.

The trees did not grow close together but were widely spaced apart over the slopes of the mountain, each one rising like a noble and gracious temple, in the shadowy depths of which chanted a melodious choir of birds. The spice yielded by these mighty trees was obtained by stripping off the perfumed bark from the great trunks of the trees. The bark grew again so quickly that this "stripping" process could be repeated several times each year, and it always resulted in the further strengthening and growth of the trees.

To sit down in the shade of one of these great temple-like-trees was quite an awe-inspiring experience, but as soon as they were seated Grace and Glory noticed that the squirrels were frisking about on the branches as gaily as children at play, and birds were nesting and twittering above her head. Indeed, whole families of happy creatures appeared to have made their homes in the all-embracing shelter of the tree. If at first it reminded her of the solemn beauty and worship of a cathedral or temple, she soon discovered that it was a temple of joy and lively happiness. She sat admiring with almost reverential awe the graciously proportioned boughs spreading overhead, so nobly strong and so harmonious in their loveliness. It all made upon her an impression of Goodness and Beauty and Strength MADE PERFECT. As she gazed around in awed delight she found herself wondering what the aloe trees must be like which grew up in the Very High Places, if these on this side of the river grew to such magnificent and unique proportions.

Presently, from the other aloe trees on the slopes around her, she heard voices singing, as though invisible choirs were chanting together in mystic harmonies, a song of great joy and almost inexpressibly glorious melody.

> Love has made a Marriage Feast,
>   Called each wedding guest,
> Rich and poor—greatest and least,
>   All at Love's behest
> Gathered here to celebrate
> The harvest of His joy so great.
>
> See the King's Son with His Bride,
>   Wooed and now possessed,
> Here behold her at His side,

In His glory dressed.
This is what He chose her for,
To be His for evermore.

Love has triumphed, Love has won,
    Fruit from sorrow this!
All He purposed He has done,
    She is wholly His.
All her heart and all her soul
Yielded to His full control.

After the song had died away into silence the King and His companion sat quite silently, looking out from the slope of the mountain onto the view spread out before them. There were the long, long chains of mountains and the far-reaching valleys which Grace and Glory had seen from the Mountain of Frankincense, only on this Mountain of Aloes the air seemed even clearer and they could see further and more distinctly the far, far off places of the earth where LOVE was not known and where He found no response therefore to His own Love.

Grace and Glory looked out over those Low Places for a long time, then she turned in silence and looked at the King. She was wondering why He had said no more to her about those many, many valleys and the multitudes of wandering and fainting people who lived in them. Now, as she looked up into His face, with the question in her eyes which her lips did not frame, He turned on her a most radiant smile and said, "It is nearly time, Grace and Glory, but the plan is not yet quite ready for fulfilment."

She thought it sounded as though He were laughing to Himself over some happy secret. But after a moment He changed the subject and said:

"The trees on this mountain are the Trees of Self-Controlled-by-Love. They are the most fully developed and most perfectly proportioned trees up here on the High Places, and the secret of their development lies in the fact that their great roots spread out underground far beyond the spread of their branches overhead. Each of these lovely giants sends at least some of its roots down into the waters of the River of Life which you see flowing through the valley and which has come down from the Very High Places above.

"Self-Controlled-by-Love," repeated Grace and Glory thoughtfully. "My Lord, I am always asking You questions which You answer so patiently and with such loving-kindness. May I ask another? What is a SELF?"

"A self or individual will is a marvellous mystery," said the King, "for an individual will is really a part of the WILL and Consciousness of the Creator Himself, a part which He has made free so that it knows itself to be distinct in some lovely and mysterious way from all other individual wills, even from the Will of the Creator Who sent it forth. But it is so shaped and fashioned that it yearns back instinctively and with unquenchable longing for reunion with that from which it came forth. It is a capacity to love and is therefore a spark of the Eternal Fire of Holy Love, and so it can never find rest or real satisfaction until, like the leaping sparks which fall back into the fire apart from which they cannot continue to exist, it finds the way back to the Heart of God from Whom it came forth. It is a ceaseless hunger and thirst which; turn wherever it will for satisfaction, can find none till it responds to the attracting pull of the Eternal Being or SELF from which it came forth. As long as it turns away from the source of its origin it is like a wandering star or a lost meteor until it falls back into the heart of Love and yields up its own right to Self-Control. A human spirit is indeed a capacity to love and to respond to love and according to what it chooses or wills to love so will its woe or blessedness be."

Here is a Song of Love's Origin:

Love is a glory and a pain,
It is a burning fire!
A flame of life which ne'er again
Can cease to know desire.
For Love from the Eternal Flame
Came forth and bears His lovely Name.

Love kindled in a human heart
Is but a single spark
Of Love Divine—now set apart
And launched into the dark:
It no fulfilment knows nor peace,
Till from its own self-love it cease.

As every spark from Love's own fire
The selfsame nature shares,
It yearns back with intense desire
To Him Whose Name it bears.
So leaps it forth in love and greets
All other flaming souls it meets.

Yes, ONENESS is the heart of love,
To burn alone—despair,
One with its source in God above
And all men everywhere.
It burning heavenwards wears Christ's face,
And is on earth His dwelling place.

As soon as this song ended the lovely, but invisible choirs among the aloe trees again began to sing, but in a language which Grace and Glory could scarcely understand, which yet had something strangely and exquisitely familiar about it as of a language heard long, long ago in earliest childhood, then heard no more and long-since forgotten. Now, as she heard it again, it stirred in her heart sweet, haunting memories and such poignant nostalgia that the sweetness of it became almost unbearable. Presently, however, the music of the choirs became softer and sank to a low accompaniment, and then one voice, lovelier than any she had ever heard save that of the King Himself, began to sing alone. At first she thought it was an angel, then, perhaps, the first Mother of all men; but then, as she caught the words, she understood that it was the voice of the Queen herself, the Bride of the King of Love.

My bonds are very, very strong,
    I never can go free;
To Holy Love I now belong,
    And He belongs to me.
And all the power of earth and heaven
Into my Love-chained hands is given.

Controlled by Him I have no might
    To let Self plan or choose,
But this control is my delight
    And freedom I refuse.
The King of Love as Lord I own,
And sit with Him upon His throne.

CHAPTER XVIII

THE LAST SCENE ON THE
MOUNTAINS OF SPICES

SOMETIME after the events recorded in these chapters there was a Feast Day up on the High Places. A number of the inhabitants of the Valley of Humiliation had gathered with the King on the Mountain of Aloes. Among them were some whom you will recognise. Mrs. Valiant was there, with her daughter Mercy and her son-in-law Fearless Trust. Her friend Mrs. Thanksgiving was sitting beside her and with her were her two daughters, her niece Grace and Glory and her son Fearless Witness, who was head and shoulders taller than any of those present. Already he bore on his face and hands many scars received while witnessing for his Lord and King. His brother-in-law Stedfast was also there and so were Endurance and his wife Willingness, whom you would never have recognised by their old names of Self-Pity and Helpless. There was the one-time innkeeper, now named Strength, and his wife Sweet Content sitting beside him (she was the last to arrive at the High Places and was a very recent newcomer). The ex-bank manager

Generous was there and so was his lovely wife Forgiveness. Near them sat Meekness and Lowliness, who had once been Pride and Superiority. There were also a number of other guests to whom you have not been introduced in the previous pages. They were all gathered around the King and rejoicing with Him. This Feast Day was a very special occasion, for two of the company were on this day to go with the King over the River and ascend with Him up to the Very High Places in the Kingdom of Love. Dear and greatly beloved Mrs. Valiant and her friend Mrs. Thanksgiving were to leave this world and become inhabitants of the world on the other side of the River. So their friends from the Valley had come up to the High Places to wish them joy and to take leave of them for a little while.

How I wish I could adequately describe the scene as they sat there feasting and rejoicing together in the shade of one of the giant aloe trees. The lilies bloomed in the grass around them, and the sweet smell of spices perfumed the air. On one side of the King sat Mrs. Valiant and on His other side sat Mrs. Thanksgiving (the one-time Widow Dismal Forebodings). She was wearing a still more beautiful shawl than usual and all the lines of dreary discontent and foreboding had vanished from her face completely (washed away in one of the healing mountain streams).

The whole company sat listening to the King as He taught them many things concerning the life over on the other side of the River, and of the many royal mansions on the mountain ranges which were so high that no human eye could see their peaks.

Every now and then there came to their ears the sound of children's voices and their happy laughter, for in a nearby meadow were all the little children belonging to the company. Their parents had carried them up there to one of the King's Playgrounds, where they could play together under the loving care of some of the inhabitants of the Kingdom of Love. There was the child who used to be called Doldrums, and the twins Sob and Drizzle and their brother Surly, and also little Tit-for-Tat. It is lovely to be able to record that up there they all answered to new names and were already beginning to dislike their old ones. They were named after the jewels which gleam in the walls of the King's Royal City, and they themselves looked as lovely as jewels as they ran about in the sunshine.

On one side of the Mountain of Aloes near the place where the company were gathered together, there flowed a river "clear as crystal and brimming to the banks", until it reached a place where it must pour itself over the cliffs in a great waterfall to the valley below. When it reached the Low Places this river flowed through a Valley of Shadow and men called it the River of Death, because down there its waters were dark and icy cold, and those who had to pass through it came up into a part of the valley which was even colder and darker, after which their way vanished between sombre mountains where no eye could follow them.

Up on the High Places, however, this river was called "The River of Life". Those who passed through it up there came straight up out of the waters without their mortal garments, into the Kingdom of eternal Life and Love, where there is no more death, neither sorrow nor crying, and no more partings for ever.

After the company had feasted and rejoiced together for some time, and after the King had finished speaking to them they sang together one of the Mountain songs.

> Art thou fearful Love will fail?
> Foolish thought and drear,
> "God is Love" and must prevail,

Love casts out all fear!
We have seen His lovely plan
In God's Son made Son of Man.

Holy Love could not create
    Save for Love's sake sweet,
Therefore we His creatures wait
    Union made complete.
When Love's perfect work is done,
God and Man will be at one.

We may know that God is Love,
    Know His Father's heart,
He hath spoken from above
    And our doubts depart.
We have seen what hath sufficed
In the face of Jesus Christ.

After this the King rose up with a radiant smile on His face and
after blessing them all, He gave one hand to His friend Mrs.
Valiant, and the other to His friend Mrs. Thanksgiving, and led
them to the banks of the river, and all the company of their friends
went with them. The aloe trees growing along the bank cast their
shadow on the river, but their branches were full of little birds
singing most melodiously.

Here, then, for a little while they parted company. The King
Himself stepped down into the river with His two friends and led
them across to the other side. The brightness over there so dazzled
the eyes of the group on the Mountain of Aloes that they could see
nothing very clearly. But it seemed to them that the brightness
came from a host of shining figures standing on the farther bank,

as though a great company of the inhabitants of that land had come down from the Very High Places to welcome the King's friends.

They did see, however, that as soon as they entered the river, the mortal bodies of the two women slipped from them as though they were old worn-out garments, and were carried away by the brimming waters, over the great fall down to the Valley of Death far below. They thought also that they caught a glimpse of the two radiant and beautiful beings who had lived in those mortal bodies and who now stepped out free. One, an upright and golden figure, shining as though in polished armour, walked on the side of the King where their friend Mrs. Valiant had been. On His other side was a dazzling white-robed figure radiant with light. Then the brightness swallowed up everything, and their friends knew that the Valley of Humiliation would know those two no more.

As soon as they had passed from sight, the little company on the slopes of the mountain slowly dispersed and went their different ways, but the two daughters of Mrs. Thanksgiving, and her niece Grace and Glory and her son Fearless Witness stood side by side on the banks of the river a little longer, looking towards the other side where the King had led their loved ones, thinking of those who had gone with Him, and of the wonderful things which He had accomplished in their lives. Then they looked at one another, and though there were tears in their eyes, they were smiling with great joy.

"It is good to have the treasure of loved ones over on the other side of the river," said Praise.

"And we shall go there ourselves in a little while, never to part again," said Compassionate.

"And meanwhile," said Fearless Witness, "we have glorious work to do here, so that when the time comes for us to rejoin them on the other side of the river, we shall have trophies to take with us to the praise of the King's Grace and Glory."

Realising that he had unconsciously spoken aloud a name which had become very dear to him, he looked into the face of his cousin and smiled with a gentleness which one could never have associated with the bully Craven Fear. It was not Craven Fear standing beside Grace and Glory on the banks of the river, however, but one whom the King had transformed into Fearless Witness and who had already become a leader in the King's work.

Grace and Glory said no word at all, but as the four of them at last turned away from the river bank, she slipped away alone and sat down in the shade of one of the aloe trees, at a place where she could look straight out on the view of the far-reaching valleys stretching away into the dim blue distance. She sat there thinking of many things and recalling the lessons that she had learnt up there on the nine Mountains of Spices, and most of all, looking out on those far-off valleys.

Presently she saw that the King had returned and was leading Fearless Witness to the same view place, but a little distance away from the spot where she herself sat. She watched them intently as they stood side by side talking earnestly together, and could see them clearly and hear the murmur of their voices, though unable to distinguish what they were saying. She saw the King point towards those distant valleys, and she noticed how Fearless Witness threw back his shoulders and clenched his hands as if in excitement. She saw how eagerly he seemed to be listening to the King, and then noticed the King lay His arm lovingly across the shoulders of the man who had once been the bully Craven Fear and whose greatest blemish and weakness was now changed into his greatest strength. She saw the smile of affection and love which the King turned upon him, and she said to herself, almost wonderingly:

"How the King loves him! I think Fearless Witness is dear to Him in a special way. And yet that is the man who fled from Him for so long and whom I hated and feared so greatly."

As she sat quite still and stared long and earnestly at the huge scarred form of Fearless Witness across whose shoulders the King's arm still rested with such affectionate trust, suddenly it was as though the eyes of her understanding were opened and she understood a truth which she had never before perceived. "Why," she said to herself with a start of surprise, "just see what the King has done. He has made that which seemed the greatest torment and weakness and despair of my life, the thing I most dreaded and suffered from, into the best thing of all. I was always afraid that I must be Craven Fear because of the Fear which so tormented me. He, by His wonderful grace, has changed me into something I could never have hoped to be, A FEARLESS WITNESS. Oh, how wonderful the King is! Oh, what lovely plans and purposes He has, that our greatest torments and failures should become the strongest and best things in our lives. 'Out of weakness He makes us strong to wax valiant in fight and overcome'."

"No wonder the King loves him," went on Grace and Glory after a moment's pause in her thoughts, and then she gave a happy little laugh. "Why! I can see that already he is champing like a warhorse at the sound of the trumpets to be off to those far-off valleys and to be witnessing there too. All the energy and strength which he used to put into his bullying is now turned into this new service and is become his greatest asset."

Just as she reached this point in her thoughts she saw Fearless Witness turn to the King and ask a question. Then the King also gave a little laugh, raised His voice and said so clearly that she could hear the words:

"Ask and see what the answer is." Then they both turned and looked round at her as she sat alone in the shade of the great tree.

"Grace and Glory," said the King clearly, "Come here to us; we want to speak to you."

Without a moment's hesitation Grace and Glory rose and went and stood beside them, and Peace and Joy walked behind her, taller and more regal and beautiful than ever before.

"Grace and Glory," said Fearless Witness, "we have been talking about those many far-off valleys around the world, where the King needs Fearless Witnesses.

"Yes," said she simply.

"We are going to them," said the King. "Will you go with us?"

Grace and Glory then put one of her hands into His and the other into the hand of Fearless Witness and said, "Make me all that you wish to make me, my Lord, and do with me all that you wish to do."

There the three stood together, the two creatures united with the Creator. He was the Will to Love, they were the response to that will and the channels through which to express that Love.

Then the King's voice rang out clearly and strongly over the Mountain of Aloes, saying with glad assurance and command:

"Ask of Me and I will give you the heathen for an inheritance, and the uttermost parts of the earth for thy possession." (Psa. 2:8.)

Before the three turned to leave the mountain and the ranges of the Mountains of Spices, they sang together a new version of the Jewel Song. (Isa. 54:11.)

Here is the sapphire stone!
My heart a shining throne
Where Love Himself is crowned as King!
Here my obedient will
Delights to listen, till
It knows Thy choice in everything.

Here is the agate gem
(The fairest Lord of them),
My ruby stone of blood and flame;
Here is my broken heart
Made whole, and every part
Inscribed for ever with Thy Name.

Here is the emerald fair,
Life breaking everywhere
Out of the fallen, bruiséd seed.
Here will I praise the Lord,
Who hath fulfilled His word
And given the hundred-fold indeed!

With what fair colours shine
These border stones of mine!
Like royal banners bright, unfurled.
Now I go forth, my Lord,
Strong through Thy mighty word,
To stake out claims around the world.